Harlequin Rich, Rugged Ranchers Collection

Saddle up and get ready for a fantastic ride as these wealthy cowboys set out to wrangle the hearts of the women of their dreams!

Riding the range and herding cattle are only a couple talents these irresistible heroes have. Fiercely protecting their loved ones and stopping at nothing to win the adoration of a good woman are some of the reasons we can't get enough of them.

These ranchers hold honor above all else, believe in the value of a hard day's work and aren't afraid to make the tough decisions. In fact, they have everything under control... except their hearts! And once these men of the West give their love, there's no walking away.

If you enjoy these two classic stories, be sure to look for more books featuring rich, rugged ranchers in Harlequin Special Edition and Harlequin American Romance.

D1527526

The author of over seventy-five titles for Harlequin, *USA TODAY* bestseller **Stella Bagwell** writes about families, the West, strong, silent men of honor and the women who love them. She credits her loyal readers and hopes her stories have brightened their lives in some small way. A cowgirl through and through, she recently learned how to rope a steer. Her days begin and end helping her husband on their south Texas ranch. In between she works on her next tale of love. Contact her at stellabagwell@gmail.com.

Look for more books from Stella Bagwell in Harlequin Special Edition—the ultimate destination for life, love and family! There are six new Harlequin Special Edition titles available every month. Check one out today!

USA TODAY Bestselling Author

Stella Bagwell
and
Laura Marie Altom

CAPTIVATED BY THE RANCHER

HARLEQUIN® RICH, RUGGED RANCHERS

Recycling programs
for this product may
not exist in your area.

ISBN-13: 978-0-373-60120-2

Captivated by the Rancher

Copyright © 2015 by Harlequin Books S.A.

The publisher acknowledges the copyright holders
of the individual works as follows:

Cowboy to the Rescue
Copyright © 2009 by Stella Bagwell

The Rancher's Twin Troubles
Copyright © 2011 by Laura Marie Altom

Printed in U.S.A.

CONTENTS

COWBOY TO THE RESCUE
Stella Bagwell

To my late parents, who are still
guiding my footsteps.

I miss you both.

Chapter One

"Who the hell is that?"

Lex Saddler's drawled question was directed to no one in particular in the dusty cattle pen, but it was spoken loud enough for his cousin Matt to hear.

The other man followed Lex's gaze across the ranch yard to see Geraldine Saddler, the matriarch of the Sandbur ranch, approaching the corral fence. The surprise wasn't Lex's mother, an attractive woman in her mid-sixties with silver, bobbed hair, but the person by her side. The tall, young woman with long red hair, dressed in a short black skirt and delicate high heels, was definitely a stranger.

"I don't know," Matt murmured, "but if she gets any closer, she's going to get coated with dust."

Behind the two men, several cowboys were roping calves and stretching them out for the branding iron.

The indignant little bulls and heifers were bawling in loud protest as the stench of burning hair and black dust filled the hot, muggy air.

Squatting near one of the downed calves, a cowboy called out, "Hey, Matt, better come look at this one. Looks like he has a loose horn."

Grinning at Lex, Matt inclined his head toward the rapidly approaching women. "You go meet the company. I've got more important things to do."

"Yeah, right," Lex muttered dryly, not bothering to slap at the dust on his denim shirt or brown leather chaps as he walked over to the fence.

"Lex, climb out of there, please," Geraldine called to him. "I want you to meet someone."

As he mounted the fence, then dropped to the other side, he could feel the redhead eyeing him closely. Normally, the idea that a woman was giving him a second glance would have pleased him. He made no pretensions about his love for the opposite sex. Women made his world go around, and he soaked up any attention they wanted to throw his way. But something about this particular female was making him feel just a tad self-conscious. Instead of batting her eyes with appreciation, she was giving him a cool stare. Wouldn't his tough cousin have a laugh about that? he thought wryly.

Shoving a black cowboy hat to the back of his head, he sauntered over to the two women. His mother began to make introductions, but Lex was too interested in their guest to pick up more than a word here and there.

Thick auburn hair clouded around her shoulders in glistening waves. Her pale skin, with its faint dotting of freckles, reminded him of cream sprinkled with nutmeg, and her blue eyes, of a late-summer storm cloud. Beneath a faintly tip-tilted nose, her lips were plush and pink, the moist sheen on them implying she'd just touched them with the tip of her tongue.

"Lex? Did you hear me? This is Ms. Logan. Christina Logan. The private investigator that has agreed to take our case."

His mother's words cut into his meandering thoughts, adding even more shock to his addled senses. This was the P.I.? And his mother might call it *our* case, but he viewed it as hers. Even though he'd agreed to help, this was totally his mother's doing.

"Uh—yes." He jerked off his leather glove and quickly offered his hand to the beauty standing in front of him. "My pleasure, Ms. Logan."

Instead of touching her palm weakly against his, the woman totally surprised him by curling her fingers firmly around his and giving his whole hand a strong shake.

"Nice to meet you, Mr. Saddler."

"Oh, don't call him 'Mr.,'" Geraldine quickly interjected. "You'll make his head even bigger than it already is. He's Lex to everyone. Even you. Isn't that right, son?"

Lex glanced at his mother, then smiled at Christina Logan. "I'd be pleased if you'd call me Lex. After all, I'm sure we'll be getting to know each other very well in the coming days."

Not if she could help it, Christina thought as she eyed the tough cowboy standing in front of her.

When Geraldine Saddler had approached her about taking on this case of her husband's death, she'd been very excited. The Sandbur reputation was known all over the state of Texas and beyond. Besides being rich and prominent, the families had the reputation of being fair dealers. Solving this case for the Saddlers was definitely going to put a feather in her cap. However, when Geraldine had spoken of her son and the role he would be playing to help Christina with information, she'd expected Lex to be a businessman. The kind that sat behind a desk all day, giving orders over the phone. The kind that had soft hands and plenty of employees to make sure they stayed that way.

She'd never expected the rough, tough specimen of masculinity standing before her. He was tall. At least six foot three. And his body was the lean, wiry kind full of strength and stamina. Straight hair in myriad shades of blond covered his forehead and lent a boyish look to his rugged, thirty-something features. White teeth gleamed against his tanned face as his smile zeroed in directly on her.

Christina wanted to turn and run. Instead, she dropped his hand and drew in a long, much-needed breath.

"Then Lex it will be," she said as casually as she could. "And you must call me Christina."

"Will you be working here much longer?" Geraldine asked her son.

The man's dark green eyes swung away from Christina's face and over to his mother's.

"Yeah," he answered. "Probably till dark. Why?"

Geraldine rolled her eyes as though her son was growing slow-witted. "Cook is preparing a special supper in honor of Christina's arrival. I'd appreciate it if you weren't late."

"I'll try not to be," he assured her. "But I'm not going to leave everything with Matt." He smiled at Christina. "You understand, don't you?"

Christina understood that this man had probably been

charming females with that smile from the moment he'd been born.

"Perfectly," she told him, then quickly softened the word with a faint smile. After all, the man was to be admired for working at all when he clearly didn't have to. Add to that, it was obviously important to him to carry out his part of the work, instead of leaving it all to the other men. "And don't feel you have to make a special effort to hurry on my account. Your mother and I have plenty to talk over."

"Seven thirty, Lex," Geraldine warned. "After that, I'm telling Cook to throw yours out."

"Ouch!" he exclaimed, with a grimace. "All right. I'd like to eat tonight, so I'd better get back to work. See you later, Christina."

He pulled the brim of his hat down low on his forehead, then tipped it toward Christina in an outrageously gallant way before he climbed over the fence and jumped back into the dusty corral.

Sighing, Geraldine turned toward her. "I'm sorry if my son seems indifferent, Christina. But don't worry. He'll come around. I'll see to that." She closed a hand around Christina's elbow and urged her toward the big hacienda-style ranch house in the distance. "Let's get out of this dust and get you settled."

Two hours later, Christina stood in the upstairs bedroom she'd be occupying while on the ranch, peering out the window at the shadows rapidly spreading across the lawn below. From this view, she could see only portions of the massive ranch yard, with its numerous barns, sheds and corrals. The area where Lex Saddler had been working earlier was blocked from her view by the branches of a massive live oak tree.

And that was okay with her. She didn't need to be sneaking extra peeks at the man. Not when his image was still crowding her mind, refusing to leave her alone.

He had trouble written all over that sexy face, and she'd not traveled all the way from San Antonio to this South Texas ranch to let a rakish cowboy—or any man, for that matter—distract her from her job. She'd learned the hard way that men like Lex had a habit of turning a woman's life upside down, then leaving her alone to pick up the pieces. Now that she'd gotten herself glued back together after Mike's betrayal, she had no intention of letting another man turn her head.

Her lips pursed with grim determination, she walked over to a long pine dresser and gazed at her image in the mirror. Geraldine had insisted that the family didn't "dress up" for evening meals, so Christina had chosen to wear a casual skirt with a ruffled hem, topped with a sleeveless cotton sweater in the same coral color as the skirt. Her aim was not to be overly dressed up, but to still look nice enough to show respect to her hosts.

She was brushing the loose ends of her hair when a knock sounded on the bedroom door. Laying the brush back on the dresser top, she went to answer it and was faintly surprised to see Lex Saddler standing on the other side of the threshold. Obviously, he and his men had gotten all the little dogies marked with the Sandbur brand.

"Good evening, Christina."

Christina couldn't help herself. Before she could stop it, her gaze was sliding over him, noting the clean jeans and brown ostrich boots, the blue-and-white pin-striped shirt tucked inside a lean waistband, the long sleeves rolled back against corded brown forearms. At the moment his hat was absent. It appeared he'd made an effort to slick the thick blond hair back from his forehead, but a couple of strands had slipped from the restriction and were now teasing a toffee brown eyebrow. A faint stubble of whiskers said he either didn't like shaving or had lacked the time to pick up a razor.

But the faint brown shadow did nothing to detract from the man's appearance. In fact, he was even more sensual and sexual than she'd first thought, and it irked her that the mere sight of him elevated the beat of her heart.

"Good evening," she said, returned his greeting, then, with a quick glance at her watch, asked, "Am I late?"

He smiled. "Not at all. Mother's on the front porch. We thought you might like to come down and have a drink before supper."

"Sounds nice," she agreed.

She shut the bedroom door behind her, and as they started down a wide hallway leading to the staircase landing, he linked his arm through hers, smooth and easy. Christina realized he was an old hand at escorting women.

"So, do you like your room?" he asked. "If you don't, there are several more you could try."

"The room is lovely," she told him, then tossed him a glance. "And so is your ranch."

His brows arched upward, and then he chuckled. "My kind of woman," he drawled. "I think we're going to get along just fine."

Christina wasn't ready to make such a prediction. Especially when he was giving off such flirtatious vibes. She was here for work and work only. She wanted to get along with this man, which would allow her to resolve the case quickly. If she had to keep fending him off at every turn, she was in for a long row to hoe.

At the bottom of the long staircase, they crossed a wide living room with Spanish-tile floors, brown leather furniture and several sculptures and paintings depicting the history of the century-plus-old ranch. It was not the formal type of sitting room she would have expected in the home of such a wealthy family. Instead of being a showcase, it had a lived-in look, which had instantly put her at ease.

After passing through a short foyer, Lex guided her onto a long concrete porch with huge potted succulents and wicker furniture grouped at intervals along the covered portico. Somewhere in the middle, Geraldine Saddler sat in a fan-backed chair, sipping from a frosty glass.

When she spotted Christina and her son, she smiled brightly.

"I see Lex found you ready to come down," she said to Christina. "Would you like a margarita or a glass of wine?"

"A margarita would be fine," Christina replied.

"I'll get it," Lex told her. "Just sit wherever you'd like." He released his hold on her arm and headed to a small table where Cook had organized glasses, a bucket of ice and several choices of drinks.

The moment Lex left her side, it felt as though the tornado that had been traveling beside her had now moved safely away. At least for the time being.

Drawing in a slow breath, she took a seat directly across from Geraldine and smoothed the hem of her skirt across her thigh. She'd hardly gotten herself settled when Lex returned with her drink.

"Thank you," she murmured quietly.

"My pleasure," he said as he took the seat next to her. "And be careful with that thing. Cook pours in a lethal amount of tequila. You might want to drink it slowly. Not everyone can handle liquor like my mother," he added teasingly.

Geraldine scowled at her son. "Lex! You'll have Christina thinking I'm a sot! I only have one or two of these in the evenings and sometimes none at all!"

"Yeah, but one or two of those things would kick my head right off my shoulders," replied Lex.

Although he spoke in a joking tone, Christina was inclined to believe he was being more or less truthful. The sip she'd taken from her own glass was like a cold jolt of lightning. Her father would love this, she thought wryly. But then, she had to give the man credit. He'd not touched alcohol in five years and was getting his life in order again.

Christina smiled at her hostess. "It's delicious."

She could feel more than see Lex watching her.

"So tell me about being a private investigator," he prompted. "Have you always done this sort of job?"

She turned her gaze on him, then wished she hadn't. He had such a raw sex appeal that each time she gazed squarely at his tanned face and beach-blond hair, she felt her stomach clench, her breath catch.

Stop it, Christina! You're not a teenager. You're a thirty-three-year-old woman who understands firsthand how a good-looking man can wreak havoc on a woman's common sense.

"No. I was twenty-two when I first went into law enforcement for the San Antonio Police Department. I remained on the force there for four years. Then I had an offer for an office position with the Texas Rangers. I worked there five more years before I finally decided I wanted to go into business for myself."

He casually crossed his ankles out in front of him, and from beneath her lowered lashes, Christina followed the long length of his legs with her eyes, all the way down to the square toes of his boots. If there was ever a complete description of a Texas cowboy, Lex Saddler was it.

"So what made you interested in law enforcement?" he asked. "Did you follow a relative into that profession?"

Christina might have laughed if the reality of her family situation hadn't been so sad. Her father had fought his own demons while trying to work in a family business that he'd had little or no interest in. And then there was her mother, who had flitted from one man to the next in hopes of finding happiness. No, her parents had lacked the dedication it took to work in law enforcement.

"None of my relatives have been in law enforcement of any sort. I just happened to find it interesting. I decided I wanted to spend my time helping folks find lost loved ones. Most of my cases consist of missing persons."

His brows arched slightly. "Well, my father is hardly missing, Christina. He's in the Sandbur cemetery. Along with the other family members that have passed on."

Her chin lifted a fraction. "I said I work *mostly* on missing-person cases, Lex. I didn't say I worked on those types of cases exclusively."

Geraldine eased forward in her chair. "Unfortunately, my daughters Nicci and Mercedes couldn't be here this evening. But they're agreeable to what I decide, and Lex has promised to keep them informed. They, like Lex, have had doubts about their father's death. But none of them wanted to voice them out loud."

He grimaced as though the whole subject was something he didn't want to ponder. "Well, hell, Mom, we've all had our doubts. But I want to believe the police. They concluded that a heart attack contributed to his drowning. The police and county coroner made a ruling. Why can't you accept their findings? What can Christina do that they've not already done?"

Geraldine swallowed down the last of her drink and set her glass aside. "I'll tell you what. She can look into all the weird things that were going on just before your father died."

Lex drew his feet back to him and sat up in his chair. "I was living right here at home at the time, and I don't recall anything *that* weird going on. Dad was a little stressed out, but we all get like that at one time or another," he reasoned.

Geraldine sighed as she darted a glance at Christina, then her son. "Lex, when Paul's accident happened, I tried to tell you and your sisters that all had not been right with your father. Something was troubling him. I tried to get him to tell me what was going on, but he always gave me evasive replies and danced around my questions. That was totally out of character for Paul. I have no idea if his odd behavior had any connection to his death, but now with Wolfe wanting me to become a part of his life, I need to know what your father was doing and why. I don't want anything from the past to hurt Wolfe's chances for the future."

Lex was clearly disturbed by his mother's remarks, and for a moment, Christina expected him to jump to his feet and stalk off the porch. Instead, he thrust a frustrated hand through his hair.

"Surely you can't think that Dad was doing anything wrong!"

The older woman held her palms upward in a gesture that asked her son to understand. "Lex, I believe your father was an honest man until the day he died. But something was going on in his life that we didn't know about. That's why I've hired Christina. To figure it all out."

This seemed to trouble Lex even more, and he left his chair to pace back and forth in front of his mother. "Damn it, Mother, I understand that there are loose ends to Dad's life that you'd like to have explained. But I can't see the point in digging up something that is just downright painful. It won't bring Dad back. Nothing can. Now if you'll excuse me, I'm going to go see if Cook has supper ready."

Before Christina or Geraldine could say a word, he left the porch and entered the house.

With a weary sigh, Geraldine dropped her head in her hand. "I'm sorry, Christina. Before I hired you, Lex tried to dissuade me. He believes it's better to let sleeping dogs lie. But now that you're here...he'll accept my choice to find the truth. Just be patient with him."

Despite her calm demeanor, Christina could see that the woman was upset by her son's reluctant attitude.

Rising from her chair, Christina moved close enough to lay a reassuring hand on the matriarch's shoulder. "Don't worry, Geraldine. I'm sure your son is a reasonable person. He'll eventually understand that you and your whole family deserve to know the real truth of Paul's situation at the time of his death."

Smiling wanly, Geraldine nodded. "I'd better go have a talk with him. I want him to be sociable when he comes to the supper table. You might not believe it, but Lex is actually a very charming guy."

Oh, I believe it all right, Christina thought dryly. But he was clearly a strong-minded guy, too, and she wondered what it was going to take for Geraldine to draw him around to her way of thinking.

Patting Geraldine's shoulder, she said, "If you don't mind, I wish you'd let me talk to him. I think I know what he needs to hear, and it might be easier coming from an outsider instead of a relative."

With a grateful smile, Geraldine gestured toward the front door of the house, and Christina took off with a hurried stride. She wanted to find Mr. Cowboy before he had a chance to etch his mindset in stone.

Inside the house, Christina headed straight to the kitchen, and even before she pushed through the swinging doors, she could hear his voice echoing off the low-beamed ceiling.

"—she's doing! It's a hell of a thing to see the mother I've always admired so wrapped up in a man that she can't see how she's upsetting the rest of the family! I—"

Not wanting to be an eavesdropper, Christina took a deep breath and pushed on into the room. Lex immediately heard the sound of her footsteps and whirled away from the tall, black-haired woman working at a huge gas range.

Surprised, he stepped toward her. "Are you looking for something?" he asked.

Giving him her best smile, Christina walked over to him. "Yes, I'm looking for you."

For one brief moment a sheepish look crossed his face, telling Christina that in spite of his quick exit from the porch, the man apparently possessed enough innate manners to be embarrassed at the way he'd behaved.

"I'm sorry I left the porch so abruptly, Christina, but I'm—not in the mood to discuss this thing about Dad right now."

Still smiling, she shrugged. "I think we should. Otherwise, none of us will enjoy our meal." She glanced over his shoulder at the woman standing at the range. Before she'd arrived at the Sandbur, Geraldine had told her a bit about Hattie, known to most everyone as simply Cook, including the fact that she was seventy-two and had worked on the ranch for nearly fifty years. Clearly, she was a part of the family, too, so Christina didn't see any reason not to speak freely in front of her. "And from the smell of this room, I can't wait to sample Cook's dishes."

Picking up on Christina's comment, Cook said, "This young lady has some common sense, Lex. Not like those tarts you associate yourself with. You'd better listen to this one."

Tossing Cook an annoyed glare, Lex reached for Christina's arm. "All right. Come along and we'll step out back."

On the opposite wall of the kitchen, they passed through a paned glass door and onto a large patio covered with an arbor of honeysuckle vines. The scent from the blossoms was heavenly, but Christina could hardly pause to enjoy it. After several long steps, Lex turned to face her.

"Okay, say what you feel you need to, and let's get this over with."

Refusing to allow his bluntness to get to her, she put on her most composed face.

"First of all, I've known your mother for only three

weeks. But after the first conversation I had with her, it was obvious to me that she loved her late husband very much—that they had a very special relationship. If it took me only a few minutes to recognize that, I wonder why you can't see it after—" Her brows arched inquisitively. "What? Thirty-five years?"

"Good guess. But my age has nothing to do with this." Glancing away from her, he paused, then spoke again. "Listen, I'm not doubting my mother's love for my father. But now—well, I'm having a hell of a problem with these motives of hers. Especially the part about Wolfe Maddson." He planted a stare directly on her face. "The cause of my father's death should have nothing to do with their relationship, and I resent that she thinks it does."

The man wasn't annoyed, she realized; he was hurting. He believed his mother was betraying him and his father's memory. And Christina wasn't altogether sure that he was wrong. If she were in his shoes, she couldn't say she would be behaving any differently. But her job was not to judge, but to follow the wishes of her client.

"Look," she tried to reason, "it's important to your mother to have the truth—whatever that truth might be."

He moved closer and the scent of the masculine cologne clinging to his clothes mingled with the honeysuckle above their heads. She wondered if it was scientifically possible for scents to make a person drunk. What else could be making her feel so light-headed?

"Sure," he said wearily. "It's easy for you to stand there and make a pitch for Mom's plans. It's just business to you—you have no idea what it's like to lose someone as we did."

Christina kept reminding herself to keep this man's words impersonal. He couldn't possibly know that his

comments were evoking tragic memories, whirling her
back twelve long years ago, when she'd sat staring out a
dark window, wondering why her little brother had not
yet arrived home. At that time he'd been eighteen, and
she'd wanted to believe he was at a party and enjoying it
too much to leave his friends.

"So the truth of the matter isn't important to you?"
she asked in an oddly hoarse voice.

She could feel his eyes traveling over her face.

"If you're going to give me the old truth-will-set-me-
free speech, then please don't waste your time," he said,
with faint sarcasm. "I know what the truth is."

"Well, I don't," she muttered, then turned on shaky
legs and headed back toward the house.

Behind her, Lex stared at her retreating figure. Seeing her so upset had brought him up short. He'd never
meant to hurt her and he desperately needed to make
her understand that. Quickly he caught up to her as she
was about to enter the house and gently placed a hand
on her shoulder.

"Christina, what's the matter? You're the one who
wanted to talk this out."

Her face was suddenly a picture of amazement, and
Lex found himself mesmerized by the rich copper color
of her hair, the dark blaze in her eyes and the moist purse
of her lips.

"Talk, not yell," she shot back at him. "I'm your mother's guest, not your whipping boy."

Boy? With her cheeks flushed and her eyes blazing
like that, there wasn't one tiny particle about her that was
remotely boyish. In fact, he'd never seen so much sensu-
ality bundled up in one female. And he'd never felt himself reacting so strongly. Then the meaning of her words

sank in, and Lex found himself feeling faintly ashamed of his behavior. Maybe he had been out of line.

"If that's what you think I was doing, then I apologize. I was just trying to make you see that digging up the past seems fruitless to me. And even a little unhealthy. Dad is dead. Nothing will change that."

Without warning, she suddenly stepped closer. So close that he could smell her musky rose perfume, count the freckles on her upturned nose.

Her blue eyes challenged his. "You're probably thinking that I don't understand what you're feeling. But believe me, Lex, I do. Twelve years ago, my little brother disappeared without a trace. And since that time, every day I wish for the truth and someone—anyone—to help me find it."

Stunned by her revelation, his grip on her shoulder eased just enough for her to turn away from him. But before she could open the door and step inside, he caught her by the forearm.

"Wait, Christina. Please," he added softly.

Slowly, she turned back to him, and he was struck hard as he caught the watery shimmer in her blue eyes.

"I think we've both said enough," she said in a choked voice.

He grimaced ruefully. "No. I'm sorry, Christina. Really sorry."

She bent her head and instinctively he gathered her to him in a gentle hug. "If I sounded callous a bit earlier, forgive me. I didn't know you'd lost anyone. I mean, I didn't stop to think—except about my own feelings."

She pushed out a long breath, and he closed his eyes as it skittered warmly against the side of his neck.

"This—you and I—is going all wrong, Lex. Maybe

my coming here—asking you to work with me—is asking too much of you," she said. Then easing herself away from the circle of his arms, she opened the door and left him standing on the patio.

Chapter Two

By the time Lex gathered himself enough to go after her, Christina was already heading back to the front porch and his mother.

Fortunately, he caught the woman before she reached the foyer and, with a hand around her fragile wrist, led her stiff, unyielding body over to a chesterfield couch.

"No matter what you think of me at this moment," he said as he eased down beside her, "I can't allow you to go out there and tell Mom the two of us can't work together."

One copper-colored brow arched upward. "Give me one good reason not to," she requested.

"I don't want to hurt her. Not for any reason."

Approval flickered in her eyes, and Lex was surprised at how good the sight of it made him feel.

"I'm glad you're putting her feelings first," she said.

"I promise you, Christina," he said, "I always care

about my mother's feelings. I just…this whole thing about digging into Dad's death is hard for me. But I promise to help you in any way I can."

Her hand reached over and covered his, and Lex had the greatest urge to lift her fingers to his lips, to taste her smooth skin. But he didn't. He could already see that she was intelligent and strong-minded, not the sort of woman he could easily charm into a brief, pleasant beguilement.

"Thank you for that, Lex," she said quietly and started to rise.

Lex caught her by the hand, causing her gaze to lift to his. The direct connection jolted him in a way that felt totally odd. Being with Christina Logan was making him feel like a teenage virgin, which was a bit ridiculous. He'd made love to many attractive females before. There wasn't any reason for Christina to be raising his pulse rate just by looking him in the eye.

"Just a minute, Christina. I—" He passed his thumb along the back of her hand and momentarily savored the feel of her creamy skin. "I just wanted to say how sorry I am about your brother. I can't imagine what it must feel like—the not knowing about him."

She let out a heavy breath, and from the shadows that suddenly crossed her face, Lex could plainly see the emotional toll the tragedy had taken on her.

"The not knowing is the worst part," she admitted.

The need to help her, to ease her grief somehow, hit Lex in a totally unexpected way, and for a brief second, the feeling staggered him. "I'd like for you to tell me about him sometime," he invited.

"Sometime, I will." Smiling wanly, she pulled her hand away from his grasp and rose to her feet. "I think

now we'd better join your mother before she begins to
wonder where we've gotten off to."

The next morning Christina was sitting in a small office located on the west side of the house. Information
regarding Paul Saddler's case was stacked on the floor in
countless cardboard boxes and plastic storage containers.
But at the moment she wasn't digging through any of it.
Instead, she was on the phone to a friend.

Olivia Mills was a criminal lawyer, an associate of the
San Antonio firm of Mills, Wagner & Murray. Several
years ago, when Christina had stumbled onto some information that had proved a client of Olivia's innocent, the
two women had become fast friends. And when Christina
had decided to go into the private investigation business,
Olivia had encouraged her to get an office in the same
building as the firm's. As a result, Christina picked up
many of the investigative jobs the firm often required.

"So tell me about the place," Olivia urged. "Is it anything like you expected?"

Christina settled back in the leather desk chair. "Not
exactly. It's much larger than I imagined. If you drove
forty miles in any direction you'd probably still be on
Sandbur land. In fact, the ranch is organized into two
divisions. The one with the house and working ranch
yard, where I'm staying, is called the Goliad Division,
and the western half of the property is the Mission River
Division."

"Incredible. What's the house like?"

"Grandeur, but comfortable. It's a two-story hacienda
and so large that I couldn't begin to count the number
of rooms it has."

"Sounds like a lot of old money."

"It is. But these people are very unpretentious and laid-back, Ollie."

"That would be a relief for me."

Yes, it was a relief that the Saddlers weren't snobs. But maybe it would have been easier on her state of mind if Lex had been a snooty sort of person, she thought. Picking up a pencil, Christina began to doodle in a small open notebook. "So far they've treated me very nearly like family."

"Lucky dog," Olivia replied. "None of this sounds like work to me. I've always wanted to visit a big working ranch—just to see if those cowboys look as good in the rough as they do in pictures."

Christina bit back a sigh. She should be thanking God for this cushy job, which had virtually fallen into her lap, but this morning she wasn't at all convinced that she should be here. Not because she doubted her ability to find the cause of Paul's questionable death, but more because of the impact Lex Saddler was having upon her. She couldn't get the man out of her head.

"Believe me, Ollie, this case is not exactly simple. I'm going to have my work cut out for me."

"So you don't know how long you'll be staying on the ranch?"

She began to draw a horse, then a man wearing a pair of chaps. "No longer than necessary. I want to wrap this thing up as quickly as possible."

There was a long pause, and she could hear a frown in Olivia's voice when the other woman finally spoke.

"Is anything wrong? I've never heard you talk this way before. Normally, you're happily willing to invest whatever time it takes to wrap up a job."

Christina glanced at the open door to the office while

wondering if any of the maids or family members might be within earshot. To be on the safe side, she lowered her voice to nearly a whisper. "Ollie, I'm just not comfortable here. Ms. Saddler's son is not at all what I expected. In fact, he's been—quite a shock."

"Oh?" Olivia sounded intrigued. "What's wrong with the man?"

Christina pressed the fingertips of her right hand to her forehead. She'd hardly gotten four hours of sleep last night, and the lack of rest was already catching up to her. "If you don't count single, sexy and flirtatious as problems, then he's okay. I thought he was going to be a businessman, Ollie. And he is—but he's not exactly the desk sort. He's a cowboy. He wears boots and spurs and gets sweaty and dusty just like the other cowhands."

Olivia chuckled. "My, oh my, that sounds like a handful of assets to me."

Christina rolled her eyes. "You would think so. But I'm trying to keep my mind on business."

The other woman let out a disapproving groan. "You *always* have business on your mind. Maybe this—what's his name?"

Christina smiled in spite of herself. "Lex. His name is Lex Saddler."

"Maybe this Lex will remind you that you're a young, beautiful woman ready for a new man in your life."

Christina didn't know if she'd ever be ready for another man, but she wasn't going to waste time rehashing the old argument with her dear friend.

"I've got a ton of work to get started on, Ollie. I'll see you later in the week. I think I've got a handle on your missing witness, so I might be able to give you his definite whereabouts then."

"Great. We'll talk more when you get back to the city. But before you hang up just remember this—Mr. Lex Saddler isn't a police officer."

Christina grimaced. Olivia ought to know there wasn't any need for her to bring up good-time, no-commitment Mike. A woman didn't ever forget a mistake like him.

"As if that makes any difference," Christina said dryly, then quickly told her friend goodbye and folded the cell phone together.

In the back of the house, Lex was in the kitchen, dancing Cook across the tiled floor as an old country song played on the radio.

"What are you doing here in the kitchen again?" Cook, demanded. "You've already had your breakfast. You should be down at the cattle pens."

He twirled the aging but agile woman beneath his arm. "Yeah, I should be. Matt had to pull Lester off the fence building crew to take up my slack 'cause I've got other duties this morning," he said with a grimace. "I've told Mom that I don't want her fretting over Dad's case, so I'm going to be dealing with it and Ms. Logan. And this morning, she needs my assistance."

Cook's sly smile spread her ruby-red lips. "Ms. Logan, eh? Well, that ought to make you a happy man. So why aren't you smilin', and why are you wastin' time in here with me?"

He grinned. "What man wouldn't want to start out his day dancing with his sweetheart?"

She snorted. "I've known plenty."

Lex chuckled. "Then they weren't worth knowing."

Cook pinched his shoulder. "Be serious and talk to me."

Her order came just as the song ended, so he led the

woman over to a long pine table bracketed with benches made of the same wood. After she was seated, he poured two cups of coffee and carried them over to the table.

"I'm not going to beat around the bush, Hattie, I'll come right out and say that I think Mom has slipped a cog. Or that damned senator has brainwashed her!"

Clearly disgusted with his analogy, she said, "What are you talkin' about? Geraldine is as sharp as a tack."

He eased down next to her. "Hattie, when she first talked to me about hiring a private investigator, I wasn't wild about digging into Dad's death. But I could see the whole thing was important to her, so I went along with her wishes. If Dad's death wasn't an accident, then we need to know it. But last night...well, I got the impression from Mom that she's doing all of this just to prove to Wolfe Maddson that the Saddler family doesn't have any hidden skeletons that could come out and hurt his political career. I'll tell you one thing, Hattie. If that man thinks my mother has to present a clean background to him before he'll walk down the aisle with her, then he's gonna be knocked on his ass, and I'm going to be the one doing the knocking!"

Impatient with his attitude, Cook merely looked at him and shook her head. "So what if that's Geraldine's motive? You can use this opportunity to prove to Wolfe Maddson that your father was the honorable man everyone believed him to be. It'll make the man see that if he plans to keep your mother as happy as Paul did, then he's got big, big boots to fill." Her features softened as she laid a hand on his shoulder. "Besides, it won't be no skin off your hide to work with a pretty thing like Ms. Logan. She seems awfully sweet to me."

A wry grin spread slowly across Lex's face. "Yeah.

But you've always told me that too many sweets were bad for my health."

Patting his cheek, she gave him a wink. "Yes, but that's the thing about you, boy. You like being bad."

Five minutes later, as Lex walked out of the kitchen and headed to Christina's temporary office, he thought about Cook's comment. Like the rest of his friends and family, she considered him a ladies' man, a guy who worked hard but played even harder. None of them understood that most of his flirtatious behavior was just a cover, that his frequent dates were only attempts to fill the lonely holes inside him.

Both his sisters were married now. Nicci, the oldest, had a new daughter, and Mercedes, his younger sister, had announced a few weeks ago that she and her husband, Gabe, were expecting their first child. All three of his cousins also had loving spouses and growing families. Lex was the only unmarried relative left in the Saddler and Sanchez bunch, unless he counted Cook, his mother and his uncle Mingo. But who knew? By the end of the year, even the old folks would probably have lifelong partners.

What are you whining about, Lex? If you wanted to be married that badly, you wouldn't be so particular. You'd settle for a woman you liked, a woman who'd be a good wife, instead of waiting for that one precious love to come along and wham you in the heart.

Pushing those pestering notions out of his head, Lex knocked lightly on the open door, then stepped into the room.

Christina was sitting behind a large oak desk, black-rimmed reading glasses perched on the end of her nose as she studied a paper filled with typed text.

Lifting her head, she smiled at him. "Good morning."

"Good morning, yourself." Moving over to the desk, he leaned a hip against the edge. "Cook tells me you've already had breakfast."

She glanced at a small silver watch on her left wrist. "About an hour ago. What about you?"

He smiled with amusement. "About three hours ago."

Laying the paper aside, she leaned back in her chair. Lex couldn't prevent his eyes from drinking their fill. She was dressed casually this morning in an aqua-colored shirt and a pair of jeans. Her fiery hair was pulled into a ponytail, which made her look more like twenty-three than thirty-three, the age his mother had disclosed about the private investigator.

"You must be an early riser," she commented.

"It's a rancher's necessity," he told her. "If he plans to get things done."

She smiled wanly. "And I'm going to assume that you're a man who gets things done."

Was she making fun of him? It didn't matter. She was a city girl. She didn't know about his sort of life. Or him.

"When I try," he drawled. He pointed to the paper she'd been reading. "Is that something about my father's case?"

She nodded. "It is. But it's nothing from your father's personal things. I've not started going through them yet. Before I drove down from San Antonio, I gathered some general information about the company he worked for—Coastal Oil. It's a huge conglomerate now. They've expanded several times during the past few years."

The button just above her breasts had been left undone, and if he angled his head just right, Lex could see a tiny silver cross dangling in the shadowed cleavage. Strangely, the sight was both erotic and prim. Like a good girl hiding a naughty tattoo.

"I don't know of any oil company nowadays that isn't making a killing. Yet that wasn't quite true eleven years ago. Coastal Oil was close to going bankrupt."

Her expression thoughtful, she said, "The economy ebbs and flows on cyclical tides. Could be that was simply a downtime for raw crude. Or perhaps the problem was poor management."

"Yeah. Or corrupt management," Lex replied.

Her brows arched. "Why would you make a remark like that? Do you know for a fact that someone was stealing from the company?"

"Not at all. I was just speculating. Nowadays white-collar crime seems to be rampant."

The curiosity that had been marking her face swiftly disappeared. "That's true."

Feeling restless now, Lex walked over to a window that looked out upon the ranch yard. At the moment, he could see Gabe, the Sandbur's horse trainer, down at the horse pen, riding a red roan filly. The animal was trying to get her head low enough to buck, but the man was doing his best to change her mind. His brother-in-law was a genius with horses. And women, too, apparently. He'd certainly made Lex's sister Mercedes happy.

Lex glanced over his shoulder at Christina. She'd removed the glasses from her face and was eyeing him with easy anticipation. Just to look at her, Lex found it hard to imagine her working on a police force, putting herself in dangerous situations.

"What makes you do what you do?" he asked.

"My brother. When he disappeared, the police were useless—or so it seemed. I truly believed that I could do better. Later, after I finally learned how things really worked on the police force, I could see that finding a missing person wasn't as simple as I'd first imagined." She leaned forward and folded her hands together on the desk top. "Working with the Rangers was more than great—it was the chance of a lifetime to garner the experience I needed."

"Why didn't you stay there?"

One slender shoulder lifted and fell. "Because I didn't want to spend the rest of my life sitting behind a desk."

Lex gestured toward her. "Looks like you're still sitting behind one."

She appeared faintly amused as she rose to her feet and walked over to a wall lined with book-filled shelves. Lex hoped she stayed there. If she drew near him, he'd be able to smell her rose-scented perfume. He'd want to look at places he shouldn't and touch even more. He'd find it damned hard to remain a gentleman.

"But you see, I can get up whenever I want," she pointed out. "I don't have a superior telling me what to do or how to go about doing it. If I need to bend the rules a bit, I can take that risk, because I'm the only one who might get hurt."

Where was all her confidence coming from? Lex wondered. Or was it more like determination? The question lingered in his mind as his gaze wandered discreetly down her slender curves. Most of the women he'd dated were attractive, but none of them were nearly as interesting as Christina. He realized there were many things he'd like to ask her, but they were all so personal, he decided he'd better keep the questions to himself. At least, for a while.

"You obviously like being your own boss," he stated.

She glanced at him and smiled, and Lex felt a spurt of desire as he watched her pink lips spread against very white teeth. She was like a field of spring wildflowers. A man couldn't ignore all that vibrant color.

"Don't you?" she countered.

Her assumption made him chuckle. "If you think I'm the boss around here, you're mistaken. Matt Sanchez, my cousin, is the general manager, but even he doesn't consider himself the head cheese of the Sandbur. No one does. We're family, and we work as a unit—makes us stronger that way."

His words sent an odd little pain through Christina's chest. To be a part of a family, and to have that family whole and strongly webbed together with love, was all that she'd ever wanted. But her parents had never known or learned how to love themselves, much less each other or their children, as deeply as they should have. They'd split apart when she and Joel had been young teenagers. Then to add to that messy wound, Joel had gone missing, ripping away what little family she'd had left.

To hide her dark, unsettled thoughts, she quickly pretended an interest in the books in front of her. "Anything whole is always stronger than something divided." She darted a glance at him. "You're a lucky man, Lex Saddler."

He didn't say anything to that, and though her head was turned away from him, she could feel his thoughtful silence, his warm gaze traveling over her.

"So where do you plan to start this morning on Dad's case?"

Bracing herself, she turned to face him. "Right now I have copies of the police and coroner's reports, so-called witness depositions and general information about the company Paul worked for. Your mother has given me pertinent data as to where Paul grew up, how they met and a general idea of their marriage, especially around the time that he died. For the next couple of days, I'm going to delve into all that."

"So what do you need from me? I mean this morning."

No doubt he was itching to get outside, and she couldn't blame the man. From the few open spaces between the live oak limbs shading the window, sunshine was streaming through the panes of glass, slanting golden stripes across the hardwood floor. Out on the lawn, dew glistened on the thick Saint Augustine grass while mockingbirds squawked angrily at a pair of fox squirrels. It was a lovely morning. One that needed to be taken advantage of.

She looked at Lex speculatively. He was a man who needed to be doing. Sitting and talking about the past would only make him tense again.

Smiling tentatively, she walked toward him. "I'd like for you to take me on a horseback ride."

Chapter Three

Like an idiot, Lex felt his jaw drop as he stared at the lovely woman in front of him. He'd been expecting a taped question-and-answer session or, at the very least, to help her go over stacks of his father's personal papers.

"Riding? For pleasure?"

She laughed softly. "Why, yes. That's the only sort of riding I've ever done. Don't you ever ride across the hills just for the sake of riding?"

He stroked a thumb and forefinger against his chin. "Not since I was about ten years old. After that, I got on a horse to go someplace or to herd cattle. And as for hills, the only kind we have around here are fire-ant hills."

Dimples appeared in both her cheeks, and Lex felt the middle of his chest go soft and gooey. What was the matter with him? he wondered. A woman's simple smile had never affected him this way.

"Well, perhaps this morning you could pretend you're herding cattle, and we could talk a bit about your father's case along the way? It's a shame to waste the sunshine, and I'd enjoy seeing some of the ranch."

She was making spending time with her easy, Lex thought, way too easy.

"Then you've got a date." He glanced at her strapped sandals. "Do you own a pair of boots? Not the kind you wear down a fashion runway, either. The cowboy kind that will hold your feet in the stirrups?"

"I do. Give me five minutes to change. Where shall I meet you?" she asked.

"In the kitchen. Cook will give us some cookies and a thermos of coffee to take."

"I thought you didn't know how to ride for fun," she reminded him.

Feeling unexpectedly happy, he laughed. "I'm a quick learner."

Ten minutes later, the two of them were out the door and walking toward an enormous white wooden barn. At the nearest end, and along one side, wooden corrals separated groups of horses, some of which were munching alfalfa hay from portable mangers.

Inside the barn, Lex saddled a gentle mare named Hannah for Christina and, for himself, a paint gelding called Leo that he most often used as a working mount.

While he readied the horses, Christina used the time to look around the inside of the cavernous barn. Besides the outside horses, there were at least thirty stalled inside the structure, and though she was far from an expert on horse flesh, she recognized without being told that some of the animals were worth a small fortune. Their stalls were pristine, and their coats, manes and tails groomed to perfection.

A number of wranglers and stable boys were already hard at work, and she could easily see why the Sandbur was one of the largest and wealthiest ranches in the state of Texas. But whether that wealth had played into Paul Saddler's death was yet to be seen.

"We'll take them outside and mount up there," Lex told her. "Can you lead Hannah?"

"Sure. I'm not a complete greenhorn around horses." He handed Hannah's reins to her, and as they headed toward the open barn door, the gray mare fell into obedient step behind her. "One of my best childhood friends owns horses and keeps them stabled at the edge of the city. We've ridden together since we were small girls," she told him. "Only lately, I've gotten out of practice. She has to fly back and forth to California to care for her ailing mother."

He glanced over at her. "That must be stressful. What about your mother? Does she live in San Antonio?"

Christina caught herself before she grimaced. Frowning at the mention of her mother wouldn't make a good impression. Especially to someone like Lex, who obviously adored his mother. But he could hardly know the sort of life that Retha Logan had lived. He couldn't know that in her fifty-one years of life, she'd already gone through six husbands and was now working on her seventh.

"No, she lives in Dallas."

"You see her often?"

"Not too often. She stays busy, and so do I."

"What about your father?"

His questions were simple and something to be expected. Even so, they made her feel very uncomfortable. Especially when she was the one who usually did the asking, not the answering.

"He still lives in San Antonio," she conceded. "You see, my parents divorced when my brother and I were teenagers. So it's been a long time since we were all together as a family."

"Oh. Sorry."

Thankfully, they'd reached the open yard in front of the horse barn, and Christina halted her forward motion. "Can we mount up now?"

"I'm ready," he agreed, allowing Leo's reins to dangle to the ground and turning toward her. "Let me help you."

"Won't your horse run off?" she asked, with dismay.

"No. He understands what I want him to do."

"Smart horse."

He chuckled. "That's the only kind we raise here on the Sandbur."

Christina stood to one side as he slipped the bridle reins over Hannah's head.

"Put your foot in the stirrup, and I'll give you a boost," he said.

His boost turned out to be a hand on her rump, pushing her upward, but when she landed in the seat of the saddle with hardly any effort at all on her part, she couldn't be cross with him.

As he swung himself onto the back of the paint, she said, "I suppose that's a technique you use to help everyone into the saddle."

He laughed under his breath, and Christina realized she'd never heard a more sexy sound.

"Well, just the women. None of the men around here need help getting into the saddle."

Women. No doubt he had girlfriends in the plural, she thought. He had that rakish, devil-may-care attitude that drew women like bears to a beehive. She ought to know. Mike had been a charmer deluxe, the smoothest-talking man she'd ever run across. Still, that shouldn't have been any excuse for her to go on believing his gaff for four long years. Once she'd finally smartened up and left, she'd vowed to never believe anything a smooth-talking man said without some sort of action to back it up.

Lex nudged his horse forward, and Christina quickly drew the mare abreast of Leo. As they moved away from the barn, he pointed in a westerly direction.

"The river is that way, and that's where my sisters love to ride," he said. "But the trail is rough. We'll go north today and travel the road that leads to the vet's house. Maybe later, after I see how well you can ride, we'll go to the river one day."

Christina had only suggested getting out this morning because she'd believed it would be a way of getting Lex to relax and talk more freely about his father. She'd not been thinking about future days or spending any more casual time with this man. But now that they were riding along, their stirrups brushing, the wind at their back and a crooked, contagious grin on Lex's face, she could very easily imagine doing all this again. It was a dangerous thought…especially since it seemed so tempting.

"I promise not to hurt Hannah or myself," she assured him.

Forty minutes later, they reached a small stream with a low wooden bridge. On the other side of the little creek was a small house shaded by oaks, a barn and a network of cattle pens. Before they crossed the bridge, Lex suggested they stop for a break. After dismounting, he tethered their horses to a nearby willow tree and pulled the thermos of coffee and plastic-wrapped cookies from his saddle bags.

"Is that the vet's house?" Christina asked as they took seats on the side of the bridge.

"Yeah, Jubal and his family live there. He's our resident veterinarian. I don't think any of them are home at the moment, but I'm sure you'll get a chance to meet them all later. Angie has a teaching degree, but for now she's staying home to take care of their daughter, Melanie, and baby son, Daniel."

Another real family, Christina thought wistfully. The Sandbur seemed to be full of them, reminding her just how unsuccessful she'd been in finding a man to love her and give her children.

"Sounds like a nice family."

"They are," he agreed, then handed her the bag of cookies. "Here. I'd better warn you that you can't eat only one. They're too good."

After a breakfast of eggs and biscuits, she wasn't the least bit hungry, but after one bite of pecans and chocolate chips, she couldn't resist eating a whole cookie and wistfully eyeing those that remained.

He took a short drink from the thermos cup, then passed it to her. For some reason, drinking after the man felt very intimate. As Christina sipped the hot liquid, she felt her cheeks grow unaccustomedly warm.

"So your father was a rancher, too," she commented after a few moments of easy silence had passed.

He picked up a tiny piece of gravel and tossed it into the shallow water. "For most of his early life—before he went to work in the oil business. And even after that, he helped here on the ranch as much as time allowed. Even to this day, I don't know half as much about cattle as he did. He was a very intelligent man."

There was love and pride in his voice, and Christina wondered how it would feel, to know her father had lived an admirable life. She was very proud that Delbert Logan was now staying sober, holding down a good job and taking care of himself, instead of expecting someone to take care of him. Still, she couldn't help but envy the relationship Lex had clearly had with his father.

"That's what I keep hearing." She smiled at him. "It's obvious that you were very close to him. Did he spend much time with all his children?"

"As much as possible. My sisters were very close to our father, too. But whenever he was home on the ranch, he and I were practically inseparable."

"So you were living here on the ranch at the time of his death?"

He nodded grimly. "I hadn't been out of college long and had moved back home from Texas A&M. God, I'm just thankful he got to see me graduate."

No doubt, Paul Saddler would be proud of his son if he could see him now, Christina thought. Lex appeared to be a man who loved his family deeply and was dedicated to doing his part to keep their ranch successful.

"So what made your father decide to go into the oil business, anyway?"

Lex shrugged. "I'm not exactly sure. I was still in grade school when that happened. I think it was a time when cattle prices had sunk to the bottom of the barrel, and Dad decided he'd be more help to the ranch if he brought in outside money. You see, he'd graduated college with a chemical engineering degree and had always planned to work for one of the chemical plants located on the coast. But then he met my mother, and after they married, he decided that ranching would make him just as happy."

"Hmm. So he went to work at Coastal Oil out of necessity?" she asked.

Lex nodded. "But I think after he'd been with the company awhile, the money and the benefits became too good to leave. Plus, he was getting something out of his degree. And then there was always the thought of a nice retirement check, which gave him more incentive to stay."

She handed the thermos cup back to him. "Did you personally know the three friends Paul worked with? The ones who were with him the day of his accident?"

He poured more coffee into the metal cup. "Yes. They seemed to be okay guys, I suppose. Mom has always loved to throw parties for a variety of reasons, and these guys would always attend—until Dad died. After that, they never came back to the ranch. Guess they thought it might bring up bad memories for Mom or something. I thought it was a bit odd, myself." He looked thoughtfully over at her. "Have you read through their testimonies?"

She nodded. "Yes, but I'm not putting too much stock in them. Most eyewitnesses are very unreliable. They don't accurately recall what happened, even though they swear they're sure about what they saw. And the ones that seem to remember every tiny detail are usually lying."

"Oh. Do you think Dad's friends accurately described what happened that day?"

"I don't yet know enough about them or the case to form an opinion." She gave him an encouraging smile. "Can you tell me more about them?"

His expression thoughtful, he gazed out at the open range dotted with gray Brahman cattle. "They were Dad's work buddies, not necessarily friends of mine. But I recall a little about them. Red Winters was a big, burly guy. A bit obnoxious, always telling crude jokes. He thought he knew more than everybody, including my dad. Which was a joke. Red got his job because of who he knew, not what he knew. Harve Dirksen was sort of the ladies' man type. Tall, dark, good-looking, and he knew it. About a year before Dad died, he was going through a messy divorce. I guess Mrs. Dirksen had gotten tired of his cheating. But in spite of their personal problems, they were always devoted friends to Dad. If he needed their help for any reason, they'd be there for him."

"What about the third man, Lawrence Carter?"

"The epitome of a nerd. Physically weak. Smart at his job, but socially backwards. He'd always been big in playing the stock market and had a degree in business along with being a chemist. Like I said, he was smart, but Red always bullied him around. I remember Mom mentioning that Lawrence had a sickly son, but I don't know what came of that. You might ask her about it. But I'm pretty sure his wife left him, too, sometime after Dad died. But his luck turned around eventually. All three men came into a small fortune about a year after Dad died."

Christina looked at him sharply. "Oh? How did that happen?"

Lex shrugged. "Dumping a bunch of company stock right before the value crashed. Just good timing, I suppose. A lot of stockholders lost all their retirement investments. Some demanded an investigation, but nothing criminal was ever proved."

The wheels inside Christina's head were clicking at a fast rate, but she didn't voice her thoughts aloud. She needed much more time and information before she could share with Lex any of the ideas she was entertaining. Instead, she said, "Well, could be the men were just savvy traders. Sometimes it's hard to tell a good businessman from a thief."

"Yeah." He rose from his perch on the bridge and offered a hand down to her. "We'd better be getting along. If you're ready, I'll show you the family cemetery before we head back to the ranch. It's a little west of here, but not too far."

"I'd like that."

She closed her fingers around his, and with no effort at all, he tugged her to her feet. The sudden momentum tilted her forward, and she instinctively threw her hands out to prevent herself from falling straight into his arms. They landed smack in the middle of his chest, and she found her face only inches from his.

"Oh! I—I'm sorry!" she said breathlessly. "I lost my balance."

As she started to push herself away, she realized that he had a steadying hold on both her arms.

"No need to apologize," he said, with a grin. "I'm just glad you didn't teeter over into the creek. You would have probably taken me with you."

She desperately wished he would release his hold on her. Standing this close to him was creating an earthquake in the pit of her stomach. Everything about him smelled like a man, felt like a man. And everything inside of her was reacting like a woman.

"That wouldn't have been any fun," she said, trying to keep her voice light.

"Oh, I don't know. Might be pleasant to have a little morning swim together."

The suggestive drawl of his voice clanged warning

bells in the back of her head, and she quickly jerked away from the clasp of his hands. "I—uh, we better head on to the cemetery."

Christina walked off the bridge, and as she rapidly headed toward the waiting horses, she sensed him following closely behind her.

Once she reached Hannah's side, the touch of his hand on the back of her shoulder drew her head around. As she met his gaze, she felt her breath lodging in her throat.

"Christina, are you okay?"

The softly spoken question caught her off guard, and for a moment she wasn't sure how to answer. "Why, yes. Why wouldn't I be?"

His brows pulled together in a frown of confusion. "Because I saw something on your face back there. You looked at me like you were scared and wanted to run away." He gently touched his fingertips to her cheek. "You're not frightened of me, are you?"

Totally disconcerted, she looked at the leather stirrup dangling near her waist, the ground where one of Hannah's hooves was stomping at a pestering fly, at anything and everything but him. "That's silly. Of course I'm not afraid of you."

Her heartbeat hammered out of control as he moved closer and his hand slid lightly up and down the side of her arm. "You don't need to worry about me, Christina. I would never hurt you or any woman."

No. She figured this man would die before he'd ever lay an angry hand on a woman. But there were countless ways to cause another person pain, and she wondered how many women in his past had cried themselves to sleep at night, waiting for a call, waiting to hear him say, "Honey, let's spend the rest of our lives together." She'd experienced firsthand some of the ways a man could hurt a woman, and she wasn't up to getting another dose of education on the subject.

Forcing a teasing smile to her face, she lifted her head and met his gaze. "The only thing I'm worried about is convincing your mother that I don't need you hanging at my side eight hours of the day."

That obviously surprised him. "You don't?"

"No. I always work alone. It's better for my concentration that way. If I come across things I need to ask you, I'll make notes and get to you later."

The relief on his face was almost insulting.

"Well, I do have plenty of work that can't be done by anyone else but me," he admitted. "And anyway, I'm not very good at putting puzzle pieces together. Now my sister Mercedes is a different matter. She worked as an intelligence gatherer for the military."

Christina nodded. "Yes. Geraldine told me. But she's pregnant with her first child, and Geraldine doesn't want to put any undue stress on her—especially with such dark matters. And your other sister, Nicci, has her days packed full with being a doctor and caring for her family. And your mother is incredibly busy, too. So that leaves you. But I don't expect you to drop everything and alter your life just because I'm here."

His gaze was almost suspicious as it roamed her face. "Are you giving me this reprieve for other reasons?"

Forcing a light chuckle, she turned her back to him and reached to untie Hannah's reins. "Reprieve? You make it sound like spending prolonged time with me would be a prison sentence."

"That's a ridiculous notion. You must realize that

you're a very attractive woman. I'm sure you've never
had a man complain about spending time with you."

No, she thought dismally. Mike had never complained
about spending time with her. Especially while they'd
been making love. He'd just never wanted to make their
time together into something permanent.

Glancing over her shoulder at him, she said, "You'd
better get to know me before you say that."

"I plan to," he promised. Then reaching for her arm,
he helped her back into the saddle.

During the next week Christina rarely saw Geraldine
Saddler. The ranching matriarch was an extremely busy
woman, spending most of her waking hours working on
some sort of charity project or overseeing the actual running of the ranch's daily activities. It was as common to
see her dressed in jeans and chaps, driving around in her
old Ford truck, as it was to glimpse her leaving for San
Antonio in a sequin and satin cocktail dress. She was a
woman to be admired, and Christina envied her children
for having such a strong, respected mother, a mother who
viewed loving a man and raising his children as the most
ultimate blessings and responsibilities in her life.

As for Lex, she'd been meeting with him in the evenings, after supper, to go over details of the investigation. So far she couldn't have asked for him to be a more
perfect gentleman. And he'd even helped her begin to see
inside the person who'd died in the gulf waters off Corpus Christi. She had to admit that Lex wasn't the problem that she'd first expected him to be. But her reaction
to him was definitely a problem. A huge one.

She'd hoped that the more she was around the man,
the more she'd be able to control her racing heart and

quell the ridiculous heat that colored her cheeks and warmed every inch of her body whenever she was near him. Trouble was, the more she tried to fight the attraction she had for the rawhide-tough rancher, the stronger it seemed to grow.

That fact hit harder than ever later that evening, as she left her room to go to dinner. Halfway down the staircase, she met Lex coming up. He was dressed very casually in jeans and a short-sleeved polo shirt. The moss-green color set off the tawny-blond streaks in his hair and the dark tan of his arms. She drank in the sight of him like a parched flower soaking up raindrops.

"There you are," he said, with an easy smile. "I was just coming up to fetch you."

"Oh. Have you been waiting?"

"No. Mom is away for the evening, and I wanted to see if it was okay with you if we had our meal in the kitchen. I hope you're going to say yes, because I've already sent Cook home."

"Of course it's okay with me." In fact, Christina was happy about the change. Even though the dining room of the Saddler hacienda was very beautiful, she preferred a smaller, cozier setting to eat her meals, especially when there were only two people present.

"Good." He wrapped an arm through hers and began to escort her down the remaining stairs and in the general direction of the kitchen. "Would you like a drink first? Since Mom's not here, Cook didn't make margaritas, but I can shake something up."

Just the scent of him, the touch of his hand and the smile on his face were shaking her up. Much more than a splash of tequila. She wondered what he would think if he knew that. "Actually, I don't normally drink anything alcoholic."

He glanced her way. "If having it around bothers you, you should have told us."

Shaking her head, she said, "I don't expect people around me to be prudes, and I even drink spirits occasionally—you saw me drink a margarita the first evening I was here. But my father is a recovering alcoholic. Each time I take a sip, I think of what he's gone through."

"Oh, I'm sorry. How is your father doing now?"

She gave him a tentative smile. Talking honestly about Delbert Logan was something new for her. As a young girl, she'd often lied to her friends so they wouldn't know about her father's condition. Later on, as she'd grown into womanhood, she'd avoided talking about him altogether. Now, she sometimes had to remind herself that her father was becoming a different person. For the first time in her life, she could speak proudly of him. "He's not had a drink in over five years, and he's working at a good job. I never thought he'd find the determination to turn his life around, but he has. And that makes me very happy."

By now they were in a hallway that led to the kitchen, and when he paused and turned to her, she was suddenly reminded that the two of them were entirely alone in the big house.

"I'm glad for you, Christina," he said, with a gentle smile. "And I apologize if I was prying. You didn't have to tell me all that about your father. You could have told me to mind my own business."

The idea that he understood how difficult it was for her to talk about her father's problem suddenly made it all very easy, and she gave his arm a grateful squeeze.

"It's all right," she quietly assured him. "It's nice to

be able to say good things about my father. I only wish my mother could get herself on a better track."

"What does that mean?"

She urged him to keep walking toward the kitchen, and as the two of them strolled along, she said, "It means that my mother is nothing like yours. She's been married six times. Who knows? The next time I call her, it might be seven."

"Whew! And I was concerned about Mom marrying a second time."

She sighed. "Your mother is a steadfast saint compared to mine."

"What's up with your mother and all the marriages?"

Christina shrugged. "She's looking for something to make her happy," she said wearily. "Unfortunately, she believes she'll find it in a man."

"Ouch. You sound very cynical. Do I need to apologize for being male?" he teased.

She tried to laugh. "No. Just never compare me to my mother. I'm not a man hunter."

"That's not true," he countered as they reached the swinging doors of the kitchen.

Halting in her tracks, she turned an offended frown on him. "I beg your pardon?"

"You are hunting a man," he explained. "Your brother."

She visibly relaxed. "Oh. Yes. But that's different."

Taking hold of her hand, he passed his thumb softly, sensuously over the back of it. "So what you're trying to tell me is that you're not looking for a husband?"

Her head bobbed jerkily up and down as a nervous lump thickened her throat. They were walking on treacherous ground, and the fact that there was no one around to interrupt them made her even more wary. "That's right. Setting out to deliberately find a spouse is...well—"

"Unromantic?"

"Yes. Love doesn't happen by design."

The dimples in his cheeks made Christina wonder if he was finding her attitude very amusing, or if he was simply enjoying this intimate exchange with her. Either way, her heart was fluttering so madly, she wondered what was keeping her from fainting.

"And you think *love* is an important ingredient for marriage?" he asked.

Just hearing him say the word "love" was enough to steal Christina's breath. Which made her feel like even more of an idiot for reacting so strongly to this man. "It's *the* essential ingredient. Now, do you think we can go in to our supper? This conversation is ridiculous."

His smile slowly turned suggestive. "The conversation might be senseless, but this isn't."

Christina was trying to make sense of his words when she suddenly found his hands on her shoulders and his head lowering to hers. Stunned by the idea that he was about to kiss her, she mentally shouted a warning to herself to turn her head, to step back and away from him. Yet her body refused to obey the signals of her brain. Instead, she felt her chin lift and her lips part before the totally male taste of him shattered her senses.

Like a merry-go-round moving ever so slowly, Christina stood stock-still, her breath stuck somewhere in the middle of her chest as his lips made a soft, thorough foray of hers.

Heat rushed through her body, setting off tingling explosions along her skin, behind her eyes, even in the tips of her fingers. Mindlessly, she began to kiss him back, began to want and need the connection to continue.

She was drifting to some sweet, heavenly place when he finally lifted his head. The shock of the separation instantly jerked her back to the reality of the dimly lit hallway and his serious face lingering just above hers.

Licking her burning lips, she hauled in a hoarse breath. "Maybe you ought to explain what that was all about."

With a forefinger beneath her chin, he closed her mouth, then traced the curve of her upper lip. "You might not be looking for a man, Christina, but I'm looking for a woman. And I'm trying to figure out if the woman I'm looking for is you."

Chapter Four

Confusion swirled inside Christina. She couldn't deny it was flattering to have a sexy man like Lex attracted to her. Yet she realized the foolishness of taking him seriously. He could have most any woman he crooked his finger at. Besides, her work was her life now, she reminded herself. Mike had cured her of trusting another man with her happiness.

"I'm sorry, but I'm not for the taking," she said quietly.

The disappointment that flashed in his eyes was at complete odds with the teasing curve to his lips. "Who says?"

She'd already heard through the ranch's rumor mill that he was every bit as much a playboy as his flirtatious manner implied. And she supposed some women would find him an exciting challenge. But Christina had learned the hard way that changing a man's fundamental values was impossible.

"I do. I didn't come here for your entertainment."

Shaking his head with dismay, he said, "I wasn't thinking of you as my entertainment, Christina."

His kiss had been like a violent earthquake to her. But not for anything would she let him know the upheaval going on inside her. It was too embarrassing.

"Really? I got the impression you think I hand kisses out like chocolate drops," she said dully. Then, turning away from him, she pushed through the kitchen doors.

He was quick to follow, and she tried her best to ignore his giant presence as she walked over to their waiting supper, which was laid out on the long pine table.

"Christina, I suppose I should apologize to you. But I wanted that kiss. I snatched it. And it felt too damn good to feel sorry about. I do apologize if I upset you."

She was making too much of an issue out of the kiss, she told herself. The best way to deal with it and him was to keep things light. But how could she do that when the taste of his lips had woken some sort of latent hunger inside her? Now, each time she glanced at his face, all she could think about was kissing him. "At least you're honest—I appreciate that."

He eased down in the space across from her. Then, after studying her for long, tense moments, he released a heavy breath. "Do you think I'm a bad guy or something?"

Christina reached for her napkin and hated the fact that her fingers were still trembling. She didn't want to be vulnerable to any man. Especially a devil-may-care guy like Lex Saddler.

Keeping her eyes averted from his, she smoothed the

piece of white linen across her lap. "No. I've heard rumors about you, but I don't deal in rumors. I make up my own mind about people."

"Rumors? Who's been talking about me?"

"No one in particular," she said carefully. "But I've made my way around the stables, and some of the hands have tossed a few innuendos around. You have a reputation for liking the ladies."

His brows arched innocently. "Is anything wrong with that?"

There wasn't anything wrong with his fondness for women. He could have all the girlfriends he wanted. That was his business. Just as long as he didn't decide to lump her into the same herd.

"Not as far as I'm concerned. That's your business." She forced out a pent-up breath as he passed her a small wooden bowl filled with Caesar salad. "And as far as you and me and that kiss—let's just forget it and eat our supper. Okay?"

A sheepish smile slowly crept across his face. "I'm happy to hear you're not going to hold it against me for being a red-blooded man."

She rolled her eyes while trying to forget the feel of his lips moving against hers. "As long as you remember that the connection between us is only business, we'll get along just fine."

When he had kissed her a few minutes ago, her giving lips certainly hadn't felt like business only, Lex thought. But he wasn't about to point out that little issue to her now. He didn't want a mad hornet on his hands.

Digging into his own salad, he wondered what was coming over him. It wasn't his style to steal a kiss. He didn't usually *have* to steal them. Normally, his female counterparts were more than willing to share in a bit of physical pleasure.

But it was becoming plain to him that Christina Logan was totally different from the women he'd known in the past. She wasn't amused or charmed by his mere attention. No. He was going to have to show her that there was more to him than a wink and a grin and a few nights of bliss between the sheets.

"You might think that way, Christina, but I can't. I already consider you my friend."

Her attention remained on her salad, but he could see the stiff line of her shoulders visibly relax. She looked extra feminine tonight in a white peasant blouse and a tiered skirt of yellow printed calico. Her red hair was looped atop her head and clamped at the back with a tortoiseshell barrette. Silver hoops dangled from her ears, and the tiny cross she always wore dangled near the hint of cleavage exposed by the low neckline of her blouse. Just looking at her set his senses on fire.

"I can handle being your friend, Lex."

But nothing more. She might as well have spoken the words out loud, because he could feel them hanging in the air between them. And for some reason, Lex didn't understand; he felt totally deflated.

"I, um, I'm sorry if you thought...well, that I was thinking you were a man hunter like your mother," he said awkwardly. "I mean, not that being like your mother is a bad thing, but—"

She looked up at him. "You don't need to tiptoe around the truth, Lex. There's no way of saying it kindly. Being like my mother is not a compliment."

"Is that why you've never married?" he asked more

soberly than he'd intended. "Because your mother has been through so many marriages?"

"Obviously, marriage isn't a sacred union to her," she said, with a hint of sarcasm, then shook her head. "I shouldn't have said that. Mother did try—she and Father remained together for fifteen years."

He swallowed a bite of salad before he pointed out, "You didn't exactly answer my question about why you haven't married."

"How do you know I haven't been married before?" she asked.

Lex shrugged. "I don't. I just assumed. Have you?"

She glanced away from him, but not before he spotted sad shadows in her eyes, shadows that could only have been put there by a man. And for a split second, Lex wished he'd not asked her anything so personal. For some reason, he didn't want to think that she might have loved another man so much that she'd wanted to marry him.

"No," she answered. "I got close once. But it didn't work out, and now that I look back on that relationship, I realize I made an escape." Sighing, she turned her blue eyes back to him. "To answer your question, I suppose a therapist would say my mother has warped my view of marriage. But in my opinion, that's hardly the reason that I'm still a single woman. I just haven't met the right man. A man that wants the same things I want."

From what she'd said before, he knew she believed love was the essential ingredient for marriage. She was obviously a romantic, who still believed there was some man out there who'd perfectly meet all her requirements. Well, he was a romantic, too. He'd always wanted to find love. But while he understood how to do all the gentle, flowery things that impressed most women, as for love?

Other than his family, he'd never met anyone who even made him consider placing that much importance on another human being. He'd tried, but it had just never happened.

"Maybe your mother isn't looking for love, Christina," he suggested. "Could be that she's searching for financial security. Some women value that above everything."

She pushed aside her salad bowl and reached for the main course, a piping hot casserole dish full of lasagna.

"Money is something that Mother has never lacked. She has plenty to last her the rest of her life. No, her lifestyle stems from—other issues," she added glumly.

Christina's disclosure more than surprised Lex, although, he wasn't exactly sure why. Rich folks in South Texas were as common as mosquitoes after a summer rain. Still, he'd not expected to discover that Christina had come from a wealthy family. She didn't seem the pampered sort. Especially knowing that she'd worked in law enforcement for nine years. But then, he had to remember that his own sisters hardly needed to work to support themselves, yet Nicci filled her days with doctoring patients, and Mercedes had served eight years in the military. Money or not, everyone needed a purpose.

"Well, as far as Mom goes, she's not looking to Wolfe Maddson for security, either. I guess she thinks she loves the man," he added skeptically.

"Thinks? Lex, Geraldine is not the sort of woman who would marry for any other reason. Surely you can't think otherwise."

He ladled lasagna onto his plate. "No. But I—" He looked at her and wondered why he was talking to her about such things at all. Family issues were something he never discussed with girlfriends. But something about

Christina seemed to pull things from his mouth before
he even realized he was going to say them.

"Well, I'll just come out and say it," he went on. "It
irks me to think that she could possibly care for the senator in the way that she did my father. Can you understand that?"

Her features softened. "Very much. But you shouldn't
be thinking in those terms, Lex. From what I can see, no
man could take your father's place in Geraldine's heart.
She's only making room for a new love."

"I do want her to be happy," he admitted. "And for a
long time now, I could tell she was lonely."

She had to admit that Lex Saddler was a walking con-
tradiction. His actions implied that he didn't want to be a
family man, yet he was just that. He'd devoted his life to
a family job. She could see from his words and actions
that his sisters and his mother, even his cousins, were
more important to him than anything. So why wasn't he
married? Was he turned off by the idea of a wife?

Forget those questions, Christina. Toss them out the
window with the rest of your foolish dreams.

"I guess having your kids around doesn't fill all the
gaps," he added wryly.

"No," she sadly agreed. "If it did, Retha wouldn't be
working on husband number seven."

Nearly a week later, just before sundown, Lex and
Matt were riding home from a far west pasture, where
they'd been searching most of the afternoon for a bull
that had failed to appear with his usual herd. It was past
supper time, and Lex figured Christina and his mother
had already eaten without him.

That was more than okay with him, Lex thought a

bit crossly. Sitting across from Christina, mooning after her like some sick little bull calf who'd lost his mother, was not his style. He needed to snap out of this mental fog he'd been in since the P.I. had arrived. So what if she wasn't interested in falling into his arms? She would soon be gone from the ranch, anyway, and then she'd just become a dim memory.

As the horses picked their way through prickly pear and green briars, Matt said, "I don't know about you, but I'm dog tired. When we get back to the ranch, I'm going to try to talk Juliet into giving me a back rub."

"Humph," Lex snorted. "I doubt you'd end up getting any rest after a back rub from your gorgeous wife."

A tired grin spread across Matt's face, and Lex felt a spurt of envy. What would it feel like to know that he was going home to a loving wife? That she'd be at the door waiting, with a kiss and a smile?

Hell, what was he pining about, anyway? Cook was always there to pinch him on the cheek and serve him a good meal. And she didn't give him any wifely orders with it, either.

"You could be right about that," Matt agreed, with a chuckle, then glanced thoughtfully over at him. "You've been awfully quiet on the ride back. I thought you were happy about finding the bull. You ought to be. We hadn't seen him in over a week, and you gave twenty-five thousand for him. I thought he was too damned skinny for a price like that, but I'll grant you, he's spreading out really nicely now."

Lex sighed. No one had ever accused him of looking unhappy before. Is that what Christina had done to him? If so, that was added proof that it didn't pay to concentrate on just one woman.

"Yeah," Lex replied. "I realize I took a chance on him, but I think he'll pay off in the long run."

They rode in silence for a few moments while behind them, the last fiery rays of sun slid below the flat horizon, leaving the whole countryside bathed in golden twilight. The day had been hot, and both men were covered in dust. Lex didn't know what he wanted most, food or a long, cold shower.

"So how is the investigation going into Uncle Paul's death?" Matt asked.

Up until now, Matt had hardly mentioned Christina or the reason she'd come to the Sandbur. His cousin had always been astute about not butting into private matters unless he was invited. Lex was glad he'd brought it up. He had been wondering what the other man was thinking about the whole situation.

"Christina has begun going through Dad's papers and things, but she's not said much about what she's found so far," Lex told him. "Hell, after nearly twelve years, how can anyone figure out how something happened?"

"Clue by clue, I suppose. How long do you expect this private investigator to hang around the ranch?"

Lex shrugged. That was something he'd been wondering, too. He'd just been getting used to Christina being in the house and around the ranch yard when she'd announced she had to return to San Antonio for a few days to do some follow-up work on another case. Supposedly, she would be back this evening, and he was amazed at just how much he wanted to see her again. While she'd been gone, the place hadn't been the same. He hadn't been the same. And that was an unsettling thought. Lex didn't want his happiness to depend solely on a woman.

"I have no idea. Christina hasn't mentioned any sort

of timetable to me. And Mom is gone so much, I haven't had a chance to ask her. Maybe that's a good thing. I don't like talking to her about any of this."

Matt quietly studied him. "Why is that?"

Lex bit back a curse. "Because I think Mom should leave things alone. Let Dad rest in peace."

"But what if things didn't happen as the police think?" Matt asked. "Wouldn't you like to know?"

Dead or alive, I want, need to know! Christina's emotional statement about her missing brother drifted through Lex's mind like a whispered plea.

"I suppose. But digging up the past is painful to me. Dad is gone. Whether he was killed or died from a heart attack, the truth won't bring him back."

"No. But it might bring justice to his memory."

Lex stared, with surprise, at his cousin. "Justice? You say that like you think he might have been murdered! Is that what you really believe?"

"I remember back before it happened, Lex. Uncle Paul seemed very distracted, and he'd lost so much weight that I was beginning to worry about him having some sort of disease."

All had not been right with your father.

His mother's remarks only reinforced what Matt was saying, and Lex felt shaken right down to the heels of his boots. He didn't want to think that anyone could have intentionally harmed his father. Paul had been such a gentle, caring human being. He'd loved everyone. Why would anyone have wanted to hurt him?

"He must have had a disease," Lex mumbled. "Coronary disease."

"But he'd just gone through a complete physical with

his family doctor," Matt pointed out. "They would have discovered if anything was physically wrong with him."

Lex tugged on the brim of his dusty straw hat. "You're only thinking in sinister terms because of what happened to Uncle Mingo. You think because someone nearly killed your own father that it must have happened to mine, too."

"I'm not thinking anything of the sort!" Matt retorted. "The thugs who attacked Dad didn't have murder on their mind, obviously. Otherwise, they wouldn't have left him breathing."

Releasing another long breath, Lex lifted his gaze toward the pink and gold sky. "There must be something about the Sandbur, Matt, that draws misfortune," he said pensively. "Our grandfather was murdered. Your first wife was killed in a horse accident. Your father was mugged, beaten and left for dead. Then my father died in a suspicious accident. Little Marti was kidnapped. What next?"

"Lex, it's not the Sandbur that causes these things," Matt said sagely. "It's life. Pure and simple."

Lex grimaced. "Then you ought to tell Mom that," he said sourly. "Then maybe she'd send Christina Logan back to San Antonio—for good."

Matt's black brows pulled together with confusion. "What's the matter? Don't you like the woman?"

Hell, why had he said such a thing? Lex wondered. He didn't want Christina to go anywhere. The past few days without her had been awful. He'd gotten attached to her company and for the first time in his life, he missed being with a woman. And that reluctance of hers was getting to him more than anything. He didn't want to have to seduce her. He wanted it to be her own idea to want him. But there was no need to let his cousin know how soppy he was beginning to feel for the private investigator. After all, nothing would likely come of it. Especially when she seemed dead set against having any sort of relationship with him.

"I like her well enough," Lex said shortly. "Now do you think we can kick up these horses? I'm damn nigh starving."

It was after eight o'clock that evening before Lex finally showered and then headed down to the kitchen to find himself something to eat. Cook was already gone for the evening, but she'd left him a covered plate on the stove, with a note containing instructions on how long to leave it in the microwave.

He'd bring her a rose in the morning, at breakfast, Lex decided as he waited for the fried chicken and accompanying vegetables to heat. Hattie would like that. And he liked letting the woman know how much he loved her.

And what about Christina? he asked himself. Why didn't he try offering her a rose? Because she wouldn't want it, he thought dourly. She wanted things between them to be proper and platonic. Damn it. He had to change her mind. Somehow. Someway.

Once the plate of food was heated, he decided he didn't want to eat alone in the kitchen. Memories of the last meal he'd shared with Christina were still too fresh in his mind, so he stepped out a back door, with intentions of eating on the patio.

To his surprise, he found Christina and his mother sitting in the semidarkness, exchanging words in a low tone, which became even lower when they spotted his approach.

Lex watched his mother exchange an odd look with Christina, then straighten upright in her chair.

"I see you finally made it back to the house," Geraldine said to him. "Did you find the bull?"

Lex greeted both women, then carried his plate over to a nearby table. As he pulled up a redwood chair, he answered his mother's question. "We found the bull. He was down in the river bottoms, minding his own business. Didn't appear to be a thing wrong with him. I guess he just needed to be away from the womenfolks for a while."

"Maybe they needed to be away from him," Christina suggested dryly.

He rested his eyes on her and felt his heart thump with pleasure at seeing her again. "Believe me, they'll want his company sooner or later."

He picked up a chicken leg and chomped into it, while a few feet away from him, Geraldine cleared her throat, then abruptly rose to her feet.

"If you two will excuse me," she said, "I have things in the house to do."

Lex stared after his mother as she quickly walked away, then turned his attention back to Christina. "It's nice to have you back on the ranch. Did you make any headway on the other case you're working?"

She nodded. "Thanks for asking. I found the man I was looking for, and thankfully, he'll be able to testify for a person my friend is defending."

His brows peaked with interest. "You have a friend that's a criminal lawyer?"

"Yes. Olivia Mills. You'd like her."

Lex grinned. "Is she pretty?"

"She's beautiful and intelligent."

"Like you, then."

She glanced away from him, and Lex could see that his simple comment troubled her. But why? He thought women were supposed to like compliments, but he was learning more and more that Christina wasn't the norm.

When she failed to make any sort of reply, Lex turned his attention to eating, but after a few bites, he couldn't remain silent. "What's the matter with Mom? She practically ran back into the house."

"She has a lot on her mind."

Grimacing, he reached for the beer he'd carried out with him. "You two were discussing something when I walked up. What was it? Me?"

She groaned. "You must think *everything* revolves around you."

Odd that she should say that. If anything, Lex had always thought exactly the opposite. He was the middle child and the only male, at that. Lex had always felt that his mother focused more on his two sisters. In spite of all her good qualities, Geraldine could be a hard woman. Sometimes she could make Lex feel as if he was little more than a glorified ranch hand, rather than her son.

"Not hardly. I got the impression that she was talking about something she wasn't keen on me hearing. What was it? Dad's case?"

She let out a heavy breath. "Yes. But she was too upset to go into it with you tonight."

He took several bites of food as he waited for her to elaborate. When she didn't, he finally prompted, "So? What about Dad's case? You've uncovered something that upset her?"

Rising from the rattan chair, he watched her move aimlessly across the brick patio. Tonight she was a slim picture in white slacks and a black-and-white tropical-print blouse. Her bright copper hair was fixed in a curly mass on the crown of her head. She not only looked beautiful, he realized, but she also moved with a lithe grace, which only intensified the sexual aura surrounding her. He took a minute to just admire her, enjoying the chance to watch her again after the too-long days she'd spent away from him.

She said, "I told Geraldine that the more I study the police reports and couple them with what you've told me about Paul's friends, the more suspicious I get about his death."

Mixed feelings swirled through Lex as he considered Christina's suggestion. Since he'd talked with Matt on the ride home, he'd been telling himself he needed to keep an open mind about this whole matter. Yet to think the three men that he remembered as friends of the family might have done his father harm was almost too farfetched to imagine. He hated the uneasy feeling in his stomach, and it made him lash out.

"So why was she upset about this news? For the sake of Dad's memory? Or because it might ruin her marriage plans to Wolfe?"

Christina stopped in her tracks long enough to glare at him. "What a horrible, cruel thing to say!"

Disgusted with himself and with her, he reached up and swiped a heavy hand through his hair. "Maybe it was," he admitted, "but I'm only trying to be honest with you and myself. If she's going to dig up this painful time in our lives, I wish she'd do it for herself and her family. Not for Wolfe Maddson."

Even in the dim lighting he could see disappointment on her face. It was not the sort of expression he wanted to garner from this woman.

"It's obvious you don't understand anything about being in love."

"And you do?"

She stared at him for a few long, awkward moments and then turned her back to him. "Look, Lex, right now you need to put Wolfe Maddson out of the equation. Yes, Geraldine loves him, but she also loved your father. It's very upsetting to her to think that people Paul trusted might have harmed him."

Ignoring the last bites of food on his plate, Lex rose to his feet and went to stand behind her. "We'll talk about Dad's case in a minute. Right now, I'd like you to answer my question," he said quietly.

As he waited for her to reply, he could hear a nearby choir of frogs warming up for their nightly performance. Down by the bunkhouse, faint sounds of laughter mingled with accordion-laden Tejano music. A warm, heavy breeze rustled the honeysuckle vines above their heads and swirled the sweet aroma around them like a soft cloud.

It was a hot, humid night. Just perfect for making love. His thoughts drifted to the woman standing next to him and he felt his libido begin to stir.

"My love life doesn't pertain to any of this," she finally said.

"It does when you start lecturing me on the subject."

She glanced over her shoulder at him. "It's obvious that you resent the idea of your mother loving a man other than your father."

In spite of her jarring words, Lex found his senses distracted by her nearness. Even as he told himself not to touch her, his hands itched to settle on her shoulders.

"I didn't realize you were a psychologist along with a private investigator. When did you acquire that degree?"

Slowly, she turned to face him. "Cutting me down won't change the facts, Lex."

"All right, I'm a selfish bastard. Is that what you want to hear me say? That I have no compassion or understanding for my mother's feelings?"

"Do you?"

He muttered a curse in frustration. How could he explain that it felt better to let himself believe his father had died accidentally? How could he make her see that he couldn't bear to image his father dying violently, at the hands of someone else? "Of course I do. I want her to be happy. But I also have to wonder if she's stopped to think what this digging into the past is doing to the rest of the family. Does she care?"

"Perhaps you should ask her that."

He shook his head. "When my mother gets her head set on something, there's no changing it. No matter the consequences. And you being here isn't helping matters. Especially when you throw out little tidbits to make her believe you're onto something."

"I didn't throw her any tidbits! I only expressed my thoughts to her, which she asked for! What am I supposed to do? Lie and try to dissuade her from searching for the truth? Tell her that it's an impossible task and to forget it?" She shook her head. "I can't do that. And I don't know why you would want me to. Unless you're scared."

Lex stiffened. Of all the things he'd been accused of, especially by a woman, being cowardly wasn't one of them. Was she right? Was he scared? Scared of learning his father had been murdered. And scared of being around her every day and feeling himself falling deeper and deeper under her spell.

But he wasn't about to admit any such thing to her. He didn't even want to admit it to himself. "You're wrong," he insisted. "If you think I'm worried that you're going to dig up something criminal about my dad, you couldn't be more off base. He was a good man through and through. Deep down, I'm more certain of that than I am of my own name."

She tilted her chin a fraction upward. "If that's the case, then you must be making all of this fuss because you want me gone from here. Why?"

Desire wrapped around his frustration and finally pushed him to reach for her. As he folded his arms across her back and lowered his lips to hers, he whispered, "Maybe because I'm tired of not being able to do this."

Chapter Five

For the past week, Christina had been telling herself over and over that she was never going to kiss the man again. That she wasn't even going to give Lex Saddler the chance to kiss her a second time.

Yet the moment his arms had come around her and his lips had fastened over hers, she'd been as lost as a raindrop in a downpour.

Without stopping to think at all, she angled her head to match his and latched her fingers over the tops of his shoulders. Her response was countered with his hands on her back, drawing her tight against the front of his body.

The intimate contact swamped her body with heat, and she was certain her blood had turned to liquid fire as it swam through her veins at lightning speed. The taste of him was dark, wild and exciting, and too good to resist. With a tiny moan deep in her throat, she opened her mouth and accepted the insistent prod of his tongue against her teeth.

Sweat began to dampen her skin, then roll in tiny rivers between her breasts and into the waistband of her slacks, while the air in her lungs was slowly but surely disappearing. At the same time she could feel his hands kneading her back, then slipping lower and lower, until his palms were cupping the curve of her rear.

It wasn't until he hauled her hips tightly against his that reality hit her. Their kiss had gone beyond a meeting of lips. It was a sexual embrace that was rapidly leading her to a total meltdown.

Mustering all the strength she could find, she finally managed to drag her lips away from his and twist out of the heady circle of his arms.

Long moments passed before Christina was composed enough to speak, yet even then her voice was raw and husky.

"You like going against my wishes, don't you?"

He chuckled softly, and she felt his fingers tangling in the loose tendrils of hair sticking to the sweat on the back of her neck.

"Who are you trying to kid?" he asked in a low voice. "You wanted that kiss as much as I did."

The fact that he was so right only made her feel more frustrated with herself. Yet even as she told herself she should step away from him, the touch of his fingers was luring her, seducing her. "Okay. Earlier you were trying to be honest with me," she said huskily. "So I'll admit that I—" She forced herself to turn back to him. The dark shadows slanting across his face gave his rough-hewed features an even more rakish look, and she was forced to swallow hard before she managed to finish speaking.

"I find you very attractive. And there must be some sort of—chemistry between us."

"Must be? Oh, baby, we're like two matches striking off each other."

Yes, she felt like a match that had just exploded into flames. Heat was still tingling in her hands and cheeks, her breasts and loins. It was scandalous how her body had reacted to his.

"Setting a fire isn't always a good thing," she tried to reason. "It could get out of control."

"Yeah. But I'd rather be singed by a wildfire than frozen by a blizzard."

Turning away from him, she walked over to the edge of the patio and wiped a hand across her damp brow. Never in her life, not even with Mike, had she ever had one kiss fill her with such longing. When she'd had her hands on Lex's shoulders, when his hard, warm body had been pressed against hers, it had felt right and good. As though he'd been made for her and she for him.

But that thinking was crazy, she mentally warned herself, and she had to stop it before her heart got all mixed up with physical desire. She was here on the Sandbur to do a job and nothing else.

Once again she felt him walking up behind her, and this time when his hand touched her shoulder, a thick lump filled her throat.

"I wish you wouldn't run away from me, Christina."

She was probably a fool, but there was something in his voice that sounded almost vulnerable, that drew her to him in a way that frightened her. But she was determined to resist it—and him.

"I'm not running from you." Bracing herself with a deep breath, she turned to meet his gaze. "In fact, I was about to ask you if you might take off work one day this week and take a little trip with me."

Her suggestion floored him so much that for a moment or two he didn't speak.

"A trip with you? Are you kidding me?"

Suddenly feeling as though a tight band had been lifted from her heart, she laughed softly. "No. I'm serious. I'd like for the two of us to drive down to Corpus Christi."

He placed his palm against her forehead. "I think I should call Nicci and have her come over here and examine you. A bug or something must have bitten you."

She'd been bitten all right, but it wasn't by any bug. "I feel very well at the moment. And I need you."

Impish grooves appeared near the corners of his mouth. "Now you're talking, honey. That's exactly what I wanted to hear."

How could a woman resist a man who was so playful and sweet? It was impossible, she thought. It was even more impossible to keep a smile from curving her lips.

"I was talking about your mind," she told him. "And your mental support."

He must have sensed the change that had come over her in the past few moments, because he seemed to know that she wouldn't pull away when his hands rested gently on top of her shoulders.

"I've never had a woman want me for my mind," he said, with a chuckle, then his expression sobered as he brushed the back of his forefinger beneath her chin. "I think I kinda like the idea. And who knows, you might just get to needing the rest of me."

Everything inside her was turning to a melting, quivering mass, and she had to fight to prevent her arms from sliding around his neck, her mouth from seeking his.

Clearing her throat, she said, "And you might decide I'm not worth the effort." Before he could make a reply to that, she eased a step back from him and quickly added, "The trip is about Paul. Not you and me."

Lex was hardly about to let that squash his optimism. No matter what she said, he'd felt things in her kiss that she couldn't deny. Longing and hunger and a plea for him to appease those needs. But was making love to this woman all he really wanted? No, he wouldn't think about that now. He didn't want to think anymore tonight; he simply wanted to enjoy having her home again.

"I'd already concluded that."

"Then you agree to go?"

As if he could deny her anything, Lex thought wryly. One long, hot embrace with the woman had left him feeling like her puppet. It was downright scary, but in a very irresistible way.

"I do. But I am curious as to what you think this trip will accomplish. Besides a pleasant visit to the beach."

She gave him a short smile. "I've discovered that the same bait house where your father and his friends regularly bought bait is still in existence. I'd like to question anyone that might have remembered seeing the quartet that day or even on any of their other fishing trips."

"The police didn't do this originally?"

"There's one brief interview on record with a man working at the bait house, but it was hardly enough to satisfy my curiosity."

"You can't do this over the telephone?"

This time her smile was patient. "I'd rather do my

questioning face-to-face. You can pick up on things that you'd miss over the telephone."

"I see. But don't you think it's doubtful that anyone would still be working at that same bait house after nearly twelve years?"

She shrugged. "You have to start somewhere. If not, we'll hopefully find someone from the shop still living in the city. Besides, that's not all I want to do. I also want to charter a boat to take us out to the coordinates where Red, Harve and Lawrence said your father went overboard. At least, the coordinates they gave to the police."

Lex's mind was suddenly jerked away from the lingering pleasure of her kiss. "Why in the world is that important? There's nothing out there but water!"

"You've been there?" she questioned.

"Well, no. Seeing where my father died isn't particularly something I've ever wanted to do."

She reached out and curled her hand over his forearm. The feel of her fingers against his skin was oddly comforting and provocative at the same time.

"You don't have to go on the boat with me. But I need to get a sense of where Paul and his friends were fishing at the time of the incident. How far they were away from land or a shipping lane where boats might have been passing."

Lex grimaced. "The police report stated that no one else witnessed the accident."

"According to Paul's friends," she replied. "They also state that they radioed the Coast Guard for help, but if you look at the time that call was made and the time they arrived on shore, they're only a few minutes apart. That doesn't jive with me."

"I don't find that overly suspicious. Could be the men

were too caught up in trying to pull Dad from the water to think about calling anyone."

"Could be. But I want to take a look down there just the same. When do you think you might be free to go?"

"Tomorrow, I have a buyer coming to look at bulls. And Thursday, we're starting a roundup for a herd of cattle I've sold to a ranch in Florida. Then on Saturday, Matt wants me to go with him to an auction."

"So that means you won't be free until Sunday?" she asked.

"I'm sorry, Christina. This is a particularly busy week for me."

Her expression turned thoughtful. "Don't worry about it. I've got a busy schedule, too. Something has come up on another case that requires me to go back to San Antonio. While I'm there, I'm going to use any extra time I have to try to interview Red, Harve and Lawrence."

She had to leave again. The news disappointed him. And the idea of her going alone to see his dad's old boating buddies left him a little uneasy.

His fingers curled around her upper arm, then slid slowly to her elbow. "Are you sure you have to go back so soon?" he asked. "You just got back here."

Her gaze flickered shyly away from his, and Lex wondered if she was thinking about their kiss. The idea stirred him almost as much as touching her. Yet he realized that now wasn't the time to press her for another. Hopefully, if he gave her time to think about the two of them together, she'd begin to come to terms with wanting him as much as he wanted her.

Her gaze traveled back to his, and this time he could see a soft light flickering in the blue orbs, tenderness bending the corners of her lips. He didn't know what he'd done to find a bit of favor in her sight, but whatever it had been, he hoped to hell he could repeat it.

"I'm afraid so," she answered. "Work calls. But if all goes well, I'll be back here Thursday evening."

To Lex, that sounded like an eternity. Especially when all he wanted to do was pull her into his arms and make slow, sweet love to her. "The roundup is going to be an overnighter, so I'll probably be out on the range when you return. But I'll catch up with you before our trip to Corpus."

She nodded, then cast him an awkward smile. "I'm glad you're going with me, Lex. And I'm glad you're not making a fuss about this."

He chuckled softly. "Why would any man make a fuss about taking a trip with a beautiful woman?" he asked teasingly, and then suddenly his smile faded and his voice turned sober. "These past few days I've decided I want to prove to anyone and everyone that no matter how Dad died, he was always a good, honest man."

Her fingers reached up and squeezed his forearm. "Whatever your motives, it's good that you want to know the truth."

That bit of praise caused his gaze to drop awkwardly to the toes of his boots, which only made Lex feel more like an idiot. Compliments from other women rolled off his back like rain on an oiled duster. At thirty-five, he'd been to town more than once, and he was wise enough to know that it was easy for the opposite sex to say pretty words when it suited their cause. So why did he believe Christina's were sincere? Why did they leave him feeling sheepish and susceptible?

Because she was that sort of woman. The honest, open

kind. The kind that made good daughters, wives, mothers and sisters. The family kind.

Lifting his gaze back to hers, he said, "I've been thinking about your brother, Christina. Do you believe you'll ever find him? Or do you think that he's…not alive anymore?"

A pensive shadow fell over her lovely features. "In my darkest moments, I fear that he's gone. But then I hear of other cases where missing people have been found alive after many years and my hope bubbles up all over again."

His heart suddenly ached for her. "Hope is a good thing, Christina."

"Yes, and I'm doing my best to hang on to mine." She carefully eased her arm away from his grasp. "I need to go in now, so I'll say good night, Lex."

"Good night."

She turned and walked back to the house. As Lex watched her go, he realized he wanted her to be happy. He cared about her feelings, her life. So what did that make him? A sap? Or was he finally beginning to see what an emotional relationship with a woman could be?

Either way, the answers shook him. And what bothered him the most…was that he kind of liked it.

Two days later, just as the sun was dipping and the broiling temperature beginning to ease, Christina parked her car at the west end of the ranch house. She was tired. The past two days had been filled with frustration and roadblocks of every imaginable sort. The tip she'd had on the missing person's case had turned out to be fruitless, just wishful thinking by a desperate relative.

As for Paul Saddler's so-called friends, she'd not been able to catch up with any of the three. Red Winters had been away on a trip to Vegas with his second wife. Harve Dirksen had been out of town on a business trip. The maid who'd answered his door had told Christina that her boss was a land developer and had his hand in building strip malls.

As for Lawrence Carter, she'd only been able to talk to his wife. Second wife, that is. A large, blustery woman with a poodle dog under each arm. From what Christina could gather from her, Lawrence now worked as an investment advisor for a local bank in San Antonio. Only he'd been sent to Dallas, to a sister bank, and wouldn't be home for another week.

Usually, Christina expected her job to include such delays and obstacles. She made it a point to never let them get under her skin. But these past two days, her work had only been a part of the reason for the weariness settling over her. The whole time she'd been in San Antonio, her mind had been on Lex. She'd missed him and imagined him in every possible scenario, including being in her arms, kissing her the way he'd kissed her beneath the arbor of honeysuckle.

Trying to shake away that tempting thought, she fetched a small leather duffel from the trunk of the car and entered the house by way of the kitchen.

She found the usually busy room empty, with everything cleaned and in perfect order. A note from Cook was attached to the refrigerator, telling her that Geraldine was out of town, Lex was on roundup and that there was a shepherd's pie in the fridge if she wanted to heat it.

Sighing, Christina left the kitchen and headed upstairs to her room. The house felt so empty without Lex. And even though she'd known that he'd be away on roundup this evening, a tiny part of her had hoped he would remember she'd be arriving and take the time to be here to greet her. But that was foolish thinking. The ranch was huge, and he was probably miles and miles from the house. He had lots of work to do, and she wasn't that important to him.

Do you want to be that important to him?

As Christina stepped out of her linen dress and tossed it on the bed, she was trying to answer that question, trying to convince herself she wasn't falling for Lex Saddler when a knock suddenly sounded on her bedroom door.

"Christina? Are you in there?"

Lex's unexpected voice jolted her, and she hastily reached for a silk robe and headed to the door.

"Yes! Uh...just a moment." She fumbled with the tie at her waist, then made sure she was modestly covered before she partially opened the door and stuck her head out. "Lex, what are you doing here? I thought you'd be out with the other wranglers."

His gaze slipped to the spot between her breasts, where her hand was gripping the edges of the robe together, then back to her face. "I was out with the men. I'm sorry if I caught you at a bad moment. Have you been here long?"

"All of ten minutes, maybe. Why?"

He suddenly smiled, and Christina felt the weight of the past couple of days melting away.

"Then you haven't eaten?"

"No. But I'm not that hungry."

He laughed, and she realized it was a sound that she'd missed, a sound that filled her with good feelings.

"You will be. Pull on a pair of jeans and boots, and meet me out on the patio in five minutes. I'm going to take you to a bona fide cowboy cookout." As he turned away from the door, he tossed over his shoulder, "And bring a bag with whatever you can't do without for one night."

"A bag? What for?" Christina called after him.

As he headed down the hallway to the staircase, he called back to her. "Tonight we're going to sleep out under the stars."

Sleep under the stars? Was he crazy? Or was she crazier for following his orders? she wondered as she hurried to the closet to find a pair of jeans.

Minutes later, the two of them were in one of the ranch's work trucks, barreling across rough pastureland. As they jostled their way toward the spot near the river where the men had camped, it dawned on Christina that Lex hadn't once asked her about what, if any, information she'd found in San Antonio. And to her surprise, she realized that she was glad he wanted to be with her for no other reason than her company.

"It would have been nicer to have ridden out here on horseback," he said as he steered the truck around a patch of blooming prickly pear. "But since we didn't have time for that, we'll have to do it another time."

Another time. Did he think there would be other times they'd be together? she wondered. Did he think that once her job was finished, she'd ever return to the Sandbur? No. She didn't want to think about that now. Tonight she was on an adventure, and she was going to enjoy it.

"Do you have roundups often?" she asked, her gaze sliding over to where he sat behind the steering wheel. His jeans and gray chambray shirt were dusty, and his hat was so coated, it looked more brown than black. Spurs were strapped to his boots, and between them on the seat lay a pair of worn bat-wing chaps. He was in his element, she realized, and doing something he was born and bred to do.

"Three or four times a year. Depending on how many cattle we decide to sell." He pointed to a spot in the distance. "There's the camp. And if the men have already eaten, they'd damned sure better have left us some cobbler."

As they grew nearer, Christina could see an actual chuck wagon with a canvas cover and a campfire with several men milling around it. Nearby, a dozen or more horses were tethered to a picket line. Christina recognized one of them as Leo, the paint that Lex usually rode. Saddles and horse blankets dotted the ground, and the smell of burning mesquite and strong coffee filled the air. It was a scene right out of the western movies Christina often watched.

Since she'd spent some time exploring around the ranch yard, she'd met most of the hands that were working the roundup. The ones she'd not met, Lex quickly introduced to her, then wasted no time in leading her over to the chuck wagon, where they filled red granite plates with the traditional cowboy fare of steak, potatoes and barbecued beans.

"Let's take our meal down by the river," he suggested. "It might be a bit cooler there."

"Lead the way," she told him.

The riverbank was steep, but once they reached the bottom, the ground leveled out to a sandy wash shaded by willows and salt cedars. Lex found a short piece of fallen log to use for a seat, forcing them to sit close together as they ate the hearty food.

"It's so nice and quiet out here," Christina said, with a sigh. "No traffic or technical gadgets ringing or beeping."

"That's what I like about it the most. When I have to travel and jump from one plane to the next or answer a dozen messages left on my phone, I long to get back on the ranch and in the solitude like this. 'Course, I suppose it would get boring for a woman like you."

Not if I'm with the right person. Keeping that thought to herself, she said, "I'm not easily bored, Lex. I love the outdoors."

He glanced at her. "Do you live on acreage in San Antonio?"

She smiled wanly. "No. I live in an apartment, not far from the office where I work."

"You like living in the city?"

"I've never thought about it. I've always lived there."

"Your parents were city folks?"

Nodding, she said, "Dad's parents owned a chain of successful nightclubs across Texas, and he was involved in that business for years. Mom came from an oil family. Besides the oil, her parents also owned a construction company, so both my parents never lacked for money. They could have purchased all sorts of country property, but that wasn't their style."

"So you weren't interested in following in those family businesses?"

Shaking her head, she said, "By the time I became old enough to think about a career, my grandparents were dying off. My parents didn't bother trying to pass their legacies on to their children. I suppose it was because neither was very interested in what they did or where their money came from. They weren't like your parents, Lex. You've had a family legacy passed on to you from generation to generation. You have a solid foundation beneath your feet, and you appreciate that. It's something for you to be proud of."

His smile was gentle as he reached up and squeezed her shoulder, and for a moment, Christina feared her eyes were going to fill with tears.

"Well, someday you'll have children of your own, and you can do things better for them."

Would she have children? After her breakup with Mike, she'd practically given up on having a family. She'd been trying to convince herself that a career as an investigator was enough to keep her life full. Yet since she'd met Lex, thoughts of children, a home and a husband kept creeping into her dreams. Now, each time she walked into her apartment, it felt totally empty. Darn it. Why was she letting this man toy with her heart and all the plans she'd tried to make for herself?

"Uh, Christina? You've gone quiet. Have I said something wrong? You don't want children?"

A bit embarrassed for letting him catch her daydreaming, she busied herself with slicing into a hunk of rare rib eye. "I'd love to have children. Someday. When I meet the right man." She dared to glance up at him. "What about you? Do you ever plan to have children? You have so much to pass on to them."

He looked out across the river, and for the first time since she'd met him, Christina spotted a crack of uncertainty in his armor. "I think about it sometimes. But I'm not sure I'd be good at being a parent."

"I expect no one is sure—before they take on the job. But I can't see why you'd question yourself. You've had great examples to follow."

He grimaced. "Yeah, that's just it. Dad was a great parent. I can't think of a time he ever disappointed me. I'm not sure I could ever live up to his standard." He released a heavy breath, then turned a faint smile on her. "Besides, you have to meet the right woman to want children."

"And that's never happened? You've never met a woman who's made you think of having a family?"

A coy smile suddenly curved one side of his lips. "What would you say if I said I might be looking at her now?"

Christina's heart was thumping so hard and fast, she was certain he could probably see the front of her shirt shaking. "I'd say a mosquito has probably bitten you and given you a fever," she purposely teased.

The smile on his lips remained, but there was a soberness in his eyes that shook her right to the core of her being.

"I'll take an aspirin and look at you again in the morning," he murmured.

She was wondering how she could respond to that when the sound of a guitar being strummed drifted over them.

Glad for the distraction, she glanced over her shoulder and said, "It sounds like we're going to have entertainment tonight."

"That's Eduardo. He's the only one of the bunch brave enough to play and sing." He rose from the log and reached down for her hand. "Come on. If you're ready, we'll go back and find a good seat for the concert."

Back at the campground, the two of them topped their meal off with apple cobbler and cups of strong coffee, then took seats on the ground and used a wagon wheel for a backrest.

As night fell and the stars became visible in the wide Texas sky, Christina forgot about everything but Lex and sharing this part of his life, even if it was only for one night.

After a while, Lex's lips bent near to her ear. "Do you know what Eduardo is singing now?" he asked.

The song was in Spanish, but since Christina knew the language fluently, she had no trouble following the lyrics. "He's singing about a woman who ran away and left all her riches behind just to be with her lover—the gypsy Davey."

It was an erotic tune, especially for a trail song, and hearing it only made Christina more aware of Lex's strong arm next to hers, his long legs stretched out in front of him. And before she could stop herself, her head listed sideways and nestled comfortably on his strong shoulder.

Next to her ear, she heard him sigh, and the sound tumbled right through her heart.

By the time Sunday morning rolled around, Christina was still thinking about her night spent on the roundup. Lex had taken great pains to make her a comfortable bed an arm's length away from his. She'd lain there in the dying firelight, gazing at his profile and thinking how exciting and full a life with him would be.

But morning had brought reality back with a jerk. After a hasty breakfast, Lex had saddled up Leo for a day's work, and she'd driven the truck back to the ranch to begin her diligent sifting through Paul Saddler's papers. Since that time, she'd only spoken with Lex briefly. At that time he'd assured her he'd be ready for the trip to Corpus.

This morning, as Christina waited for him to join her on the front porch, the temperature hovered near eighty degrees. Cool shorts and a halter top would have felt good, but she'd decided a simple cotton sheath splashed with flowers in pale yellow and lime green would be more appropriate.

Since they'd be spending most of the day on the coast, she'd wondered if Lex would forgo his boots and jeans and hat, but when he finally appeared, she saw that the only concession he'd made was a white polo shirt. Even so, he looked rakishly handsome as he took his place behind the wheel of his personal truck.

Christina wasn't sure if the accelerated beat of her heart was due to his close presence or the fact that the two of them were headed out on an unpredictable journey.

"You haven't forgotten anything, have you?" he asked as they passed under the huge entrance of the ranch yard.

She patted a small briefcase lying on the console between them. "Addresses and photos are all here. And I've already called ahead and scheduled the boat charter. They'll take us out at eleven. Or me out, if you prefer to stay ashore."

He glanced knowingly over at her. "I'm not about to let you go out alone on a boat with a group of strange men. Who knows what could happen."

His remark surprised her. She'd never expected him to want to protect her. Her parents certainly had never sheltered her. And even Mike, a veteran police officer, had never been particularly protective of her. He'd always believed she was capable of taking care of herself. And she liked to believe she was. Still, it was sweetly old-fashioned to have Lex wanting to be her defender.

"If I understood it right," she told him, "there'll only be one man accompanying me on the boat."

"Then I'm sure as hell going," he said sharply. "You can't trust anyone nowadays."

"I'm glad you're going," she admitted, then gave him a playful smile. "But who's going to be my bodyguard when I go back to work in San Antonio?"

Even though she'd been teasing, he didn't look as though he was when he said, "Maybe you should just stay, instead."

Chapter Six

An hour and a half later, the truck was climbing up the huge causeway spanning the ship channel on the north side of the city. To the left of them, the sun sparkled on Corpus Christi Bay and the docked World War II aircraft carrier, the USS Lexington, which now served as a museum. To their right, shipping barges chugged to and from loading docks, while directly in front of them, the skyline of the city carved niches from the green-blue ocean.

Lex exited onto Ocean Drive, and in a few short minutes, they were parked in front of a small, weathered building. The lapped siding looked like it had once been painted coral, but sand, wind and salt had since buffed it to a puny pink. Above the wooden screen door, a creaky sign read Ray's Bait.

As they walked across the small parking lot graveled with crushed oyster shells, Lex glanced doubtfully over at her. "I hate to be a pessimist, Christina, but this seems like a long shot."

"In my profession, long shots are things I often have to take. And when I sometimes win, the payoff is usually more than I ever expected."

He grunted. "I've never been much of a gambler."

"You put your fortune in livestock, which could fall over dead without warning or lose their value according to the whims of the market. I'd call that big-time gambling."

"You might think so," he said, with a vague smile. "It's just a way of life for me."

By now they'd reached the entrance to the building. Lex opened the screen door and allowed Christina to step through before he followed. Inside, the small interior was dim and smelled of fish, beer and burned coffee. To the immediate right, a long counter was equipped with a cash register and lined with jars of fishing lures and jigs. To the left, a separate room was outfitted with concrete tanks filled with bubbling water.

At the moment, a plump blond woman in her early twenties was dipping out tiny shad and placing the bait in a customer's foam bucket.

Christina and Lex waited to one side until she'd finished the task and taken the other man's money. Once he'd ambled out the door, Christina stepped up to the counter, while Lex hung back just behind her shoulder.

"Can I help y'all?" the young woman asked.

The young woman was chewing gum, and her long bangs were battling with her eyelashes for hanging space.

Clearing her throat, Christina said, "Uh, yes. We're looking for Ray Pena. Is he around?"

The young woman's brown eyes darted suspiciously

from Christina to Lex and back again. "The owner? He's not here today. He had to go down to Falfurrias. Somethin' to do with his sister." She chewed on her bottom lip. "Is he in trouble?"

"Does trouble commonly follow Mr. Pena around?" Lex asked dryly.

The blonde shook her head. "No. But you two smell like cops to me. Sorta look like it, too."

Christina quickly interjected, "We're nothing of the sort. We're simply looking for some information. Will Mr. Pena be back tomorrow?"

"Said he would. Guess you could try again in the mornin'."

"We'll do that," Christina told her. "And thank you, Miss—"

"Sally. Sally Donner."

Christina smiled and reached to shake the woman's hand. "Thank you, Sally. It was nice meeting you."

"Yeah. Sure."

Christina and Lex walked outside, pausing several steps away from the open entrance to the bait house.

"What are we going to do now?" Lex asked. "I don't have time to drive down here tomorrow morning. Matt is expecting me to go with him to auction tomorrow afternoon."

She fished her sunglasses out of her purse and jammed them on her face. "If we stay here tonight and talk to Mr. Pena in the morning, you'll still have time to make the trip with your cousin."

Lex stared at her. "Stay here in Corpus tonight?"

"Do you have a better idea? Or would you rather drive down here again next week?"

He considered her questions for a moment, and then

suddenly a grin spread across his face. "What the hell. I haven't stayed on the beach in a long time. We can have red snapper for supper tonight or shrimp or whatever your heart desires."

Relieved that he was being so compliant about it all, she felt her spirits lift. "What about shell searching? I love doing that."

He curled his arm around her waist and urged her toward the truck. "Then we'll find a whole load of them for you to take back to the ranch," he promised.

On down the bay-side street, they found a little coffee shack with outside tables, where they drank coffee and shared a danish before driving to the charter-boat place. Business there was hopping, but the personnel quickly waited on them, and in a few minutes' time, they were on board a twenty-foot cruiser with inboard motors and a covered deck.

The captain was Eric, a young man in his late twenties with jet-black hair and bronze skin. He was good-looking in a beachcomber sort of way, and in Lex's opinion, he paid entirely too much attention to Christina. But then, Lex could hardly blame the man. She was like a wild rose with her red hair flying in the wind and her blue eyes sparkling brighter than the sea itself.

Since the night of the roundup, he'd hardly been able to think of anything but her. And though he knew he was getting far too attached to her, he couldn't seem to do a damned thing to stop it. The more time he spent with her, the more he wanted.

"Can you tell us how far you think it is to the coordinates I gave you?" Christina asked Eric once they'd pulled away from the dock and headed out in the bay.

Eric answered with a pleasant smile. "Not exactly. Maybe ten, fifteen miles."

"That far?" Lex asked from a spot beneath the canopy, where he was sitting next to Christina.

"I can't be sure," Eric answered. "But I'm guessing it will be that distance."

The young captain turned his attention back to maneuvering the boat. Lex looked skeptically over at Christina. "I used to come here with Dad to fish, and I'm a bit familiar with the area. If we go that far, we'll be close to the islands."

"You're talking about Mustang and Padre?"

He nodded. "But that wouldn't make sense. If Dad fell off the boat while closer to the islands than to Corpus, then why would they bring him all the way back here for medical attention?"

For the first time since she'd met Lex, she saw suspicion flicker in his eyes, and she understood the next hour was going to be hard on him. Laying a hand over his, she said, "Let's wait and see where we are when we get there."

For the first half of the trip, the waters were full of all sorts of sailing vessels. Everything from small catamarans to commercial-sized shrimp boats to massive freighter ships could be seen bobbing atop the choppy water. But as they headed farther out to sea, only the larger vessels were visible, and they were few and far between.

Lex raised his voice to speak to the captain. "Eric, is this area normally fished?"

The young man glanced around at the open waters before looking over his shoulder at his passengers. "It depends on the time of the year and how the fish are running. Today is a slow day, but that's probably because it's Sunday morning."

Lex's attention turned to Christina, who'd been listening intently. "I suppose on a Saturday it wouldn't have been odd for my dad and his friends to be fishing this area."

Frowning, Christina nodded. "I'm still anxious to see where we'll be when we reach the right coordinates."

"So am I," Lex grimly agreed.

As the boat plowed forward into gulf waters, the wind grew stiffer, making their ride extremely rough. With his arm around Christina's shoulders, Lex kept her firmly by his side on the padded bench seat.

It was a relief when the captain finally eased off the throttle. "We're almost on top of the spot. I'll let down an anchor so you can have a better look around."

Lex was expecting to see nothing more than water. Instead, it was a shock to see land lying in front of them and less than a minute or two away.

As he and Christina rose to their feet, she asked the captain, "What's that island to the south of us?"

"That's Mustang Island. Port Aransas is about five miles to the east of us."

Lex felt as though someone had whacked the air from his lungs, and he found himself gripping Christina's hand. "Five miles, Christina! Five miles from land. Why didn't they go there instead of turning around and heading back to Corpus? It doesn't make sense! Why didn't the police question them about this?"

"They did. It's in the report. But apparently, the police decided the men had been too shaken to make clear-headed choices."

Lex couldn't stop a frustrated groan from rumbling up from his chest. "That's damned idiotic!"

"People do strange things when they're in shock, Lex." She turned her attention back to the captain. "Do you know if there are any medical services on the island? Or law officers?"

"Yeah, sure," Eric answered. "It's a state park. They have people around to take care of medical emergencies and other problems."

Lex could see the questions running through Christina's mind were the same as the ones running through his.

"Twelve years is a long time. Maybe the islands didn't have any of those services back then," he suggested. Yet even as he said the words, Lex knew it was a far-fetched notion. It was clear that Port Aransas and medical help would have been much closer for his father than the long trip back to Corpus.

"That's something I definitely intend to research," she told him.

After a couple more minutes, Christina informed Eric that they'd seen enough, and the young captain headed the cruiser back toward the mainland. If anything, the waters had gotten rougher during their excursion, forcing her to hold on tightly to Lex's arm to keep her body from being tossed to the deck.

By the time they reached Corpus, a gray line of squall clouds had spread across the city. The two of them quickly climbed into Lex's truck and were on the verge of leaving the charter-boat service when a deluge, complete with ragged streaks of lightning bolting all the way to the ground, hit the parking lot.

"I don't see any point in getting out on the street in this stuff," Lex said. He started the engine and turned the wipers on high, but the swipes didn't come close to clearing the windshield of the tropical downpour. "The rain will probably let up in a few minutes."

"Okay by me," she said. "Looks like we got back just in time. Otherwise, we could have been toasted by lightning."

"Yeah, I don't know which is worse, being caught out on the water during a storm or caught on a horse. They both draw electricity." He turned on the air conditioner to stir the stifling air inside the vehicle. "A few years ago, we were out on spring roundup when lightning knocked one of the wranglers and his horse to the ground. He wasn't breathing when we reached him. Thankfully, Nicci happened to be riding with us that time, and she performed CPR to revive him. Later, she explained that the jolt had stopped his heart."

"Did the man have any lasting effects?"

"No. But the horse did. It frazzled his nerves. The slightest bit of sound would make him go crazy. Matt wanted to sell him after that. He feared the animal would end up injuring someone, but Cordero, Matt's brother, refused to let that happen. He said all of us, even animals, need time to heal. He took the horse to Louisiana with him, and now he's right as rain."

"We all need time to heal," Christina repeated softly.

"Yeah. I think your cousin is right about that." She turned an empathetic expression on him. "I know the trip we just took was hard on you, Lex."

He reached across the seat and clasped her hand in his. "It wasn't something I'd want to repeat. But I'm glad we went. Seeing that place opened my eyes to a lot of things, Christina. The accident happened closer to landmass than we'd first thought. Still, the men admitted to the police that they were frazzled. And who knows, under that sort of shock I might have used bad judgment, too."

"Geraldine knew your father inside out, and she had an innate feeling that something was wrong. We just don't know what that something was."

Christina had hardly gotten the words out when a bolt of lightning struck close behind them. She jerked with fright, and he tightened his fingers around hers. As Lex held on to her hand, he felt something inside him softening, and he ached to simply put his arm around her and nestle her head on his shoulder the way she had when Eduardo had sung about the gypsy Davey. The gentle urge was like nothing he'd felt before and it filled him with an achingly sweet wonder.

Thankfully, before he could allow himself to get too sentimental, the rain let up as abruptly as it had started. He used this as an excuse to drop her hand and reach for the gearshift.

"Let's go get a hotel room," he said in a strained, husky voice.

As he steered the truck onto the street, Christina reached over and touched his arm. "Uh, Lex—I'd better say something right now."

He darted a glance at her. "What?"

"We need to get two rooms," she said awkwardly. "One for me. One for you."

Lex pressed down on the accelerator while telling himself he wasn't disappointed. "I wasn't expecting anything else, Christina."

Five minutes later, they entered a beachside hotel and took adjoining rooms overlooking the bay.

As they rode the elevator up to the fifth floor, Lex edged closer to Christina's shoulder. "We look ridiculous getting two rooms and not carrying one bag or piece of luggage between us. I'm sure the staff behind the counter thinks we've rented two rooms just for appearances' sake."

Lifting her chin, she glanced away from him. She couldn't let him see just how easy it would be for him to seduce her into sharing one room. One bed. "I don't care what the staff thinks, or anyone else for that matter," she said stiffly.

They stepped off the elevator without exchanging any more words and found their rooms at the end of the hallway. With her entry card already in hand, Christina quickly opened the door that matched her number.

"Christina?"

His hand came down on her shoulder, and with her heart hammering, she paused to look up at him.

"Are you angry with me?" he asked.

The innocent, almost puzzled expression on his face was so endearing that she felt everything inside her melting.

"No. Why do you ask?"

"I'm not sure. A minute ago in the elevator, you sounded a little sharp."

Dropping her head, she stared at the carpet. "I didn't mean to, Lex. I knew you were only teasing."

"Look, Christina, this trip," he said lowly, then shook his head. "The reason for this trip today is not easy for me to deal with. If I seem to be making a joke at the wrong time, it's only because I—need to lighten things up. Can you understand?"

How could it be, she wondered, that he could so easily touch her heart with just a handful of words? It was scary what this man could do to her.

"Yes," she said, her throat tight. "And if I seem stiff, maybe it's because the reason for this trip is difficult for me, too. These past days, I feel as though I've gotten to know Paul personally. It bothered me to see the place where he died." Lifting her head, she looked at him and smiled. "Let's forget all this and enjoy the rest of the evening."

A smile spread across his face, and like an idiot, she felt her heart dancing at the sight. She didn't want to ask herself why this man's happiness was so important to her. For right now, it was enough that they were together.

"I'm all for that," he agreed. "After we check out our rooms, let's go down to the beach. I think the rain is all gone now."

"Give me five minutes and I'll be ready," she told him.

A short time later, Christina emerged from her room to find Lex standing in the hallway, with a cell phone to his ear. The moment he spotted her, he ended the call and slipped the small instrument back into his jeans pocket.

"I was letting Cook know that we won't be returning to the ranch tonight," he told her. "She says we're not missing a thing. It's raining cats and dogs up there now."

"I'm glad you called her. She would have been worried when we didn't show up this evening." Christina glanced wryly down at her flower-printed white dress. "Well, I'm not exactly clothed for beachcombing, but this will have to do."

Curling his arm around the back of her waist, Lex urged her down the hallway, toward the elevator doors. "Don't worry. If you get your dress dirty, I'll buy you another one."

None of her boyfriends had told Christina such a thing before, but then she'd never known a man like Lex before. She could only wonder how she would ever be able to forget him once she left the Sandbur for good.

When they reached the beach, the sun was beginning to dip low behind the skyline of the city. The wind was whipping the rolling waves, tossing Christina's red curls wildly about her face. The brown sand was damp and packed from the earlier rainstorm. She pulled off her sandals and Lex carried them for her as they strolled leisurely along the surf's edge.

"It's beautiful here," Christina said, with a wistful sigh. "Makes me realize just how long it's been since I've taken a walk on the beach. Far too long."

"It's been a long time for me, too," he replied. "I get so caught up in the ranch, the auctions, buying and selling cattle. I forget that there are other things out in the world. What about you? What reason do you have for not visiting the coastline?"

"The same reasons, I suppose. My work." She bent down and brushed the sand away from the edge of a shell. A sand dollar emerged, and though one side of the fragile sea urchin had crumbled away, she picked it up, anyway.

Lex gestured toward the shell resting in the middle of her palm. "No need for you to keep a broken shell, Christina. You'll probably find a whole one farther on down the beach."

A faint smile touched her lips. "Sometimes a person can miss out on a lot while he's searching for perfection. I think I'll keep this one."

Lex watched her fingers close around the sand dollar and wondered if he was one of those misguided persons she was talking about. From the time he'd been old enough to think about girls and the role they would play in his life, he'd decided that he'd find the perfect woman to fall in love with. His parents' marriage had been one of those rare relationships that seemed complete and happy in every way. He wanted that same sort of union for himself. But he'd never fallen in love or found that perfect woman. Maybe Christina was right. Perfection was hard to find. Or maybe he was just beginning to recognize what was perfect for him?

For a moment, an uncharacteristic stab of melancholy struck him, but he thrust it away as he curled his arm around the back of Christina's waist and smiled down at her.

"I see a restaurant on down the beach. Are you ready for some snapper?"

"Sure. Maybe you'll find that perfect shell before we get there," she impishly suggested.

"For you?"

She shook her head. "For yourself. I've already found mine."

They ate their meal of seafood on a screened-in deck overlooking the beach. Throughout the dinner, Christina was vaguely aware of the seagulls and pelicans diving and swooping over the rolling surf, of the soft music drifting from the main section of the restaurant and the delicious food melting in her mouth. Yet none of those distractions could compete with Lex.

His presence across the small wooden table was consuming her senses, and she found it almost impossible to keep her eyes off him. The moment she'd first met him, his image had practically paralyzed her with its raw sexuality. But now that she was beginning to know the hardworking, family-loving man, he was even more attractive, more of a pull on her heartstrings. And that was beginning to worry her very much. She wasn't supposed to be liking the man or his company this much.

"Looks like we're going to have a long walk in the dark," Christina remarked as she forced her eyes away from him and out toward the bay.

"So there's no reason for us not to stay and have dessert," he replied. "Thirty minutes from now, it won't be any darker."

Placing her fork on the table, she looked at him with disbelief. "Dessert! I'm too full of fish and shrimp to eat a bite of dessert!"

He grinned. "Okay. You can watch me."

He motioned to a nearby waitress, and after the young woman had given him a verbal rundown of the desserts the restaurant had to offer, he ordered some sort of chocolate concoction and coffee for both of them.

"Cook has you totally spoiled," she teased.

"She does," he admitted. "She's spoiled all of us down through the years."

"What are you going to do when she's gone?"

He looked at her sharply. "I refuse to think about that day."

"But one day she'll be too old to work for hours in the kitchen," Christina pointed out.

His gaze dropped to his plate, as though he didn't want her to see she'd discovered a soft spot in him. "I don't want to think about that, either. She's stalwart. She was on the Sandbur before I was even born, and I grew up thinking of her as a second mama. Some of my earliest memories are of standing next to her skirt, waiting for her to hand me a cookie or bandage a cut finger. When she gets…too old to work, someone else will take over." His gaze was full of conviction when he lifted it back to hers. "But Hattie will remain in the house with us. I'll make sure of that."

Impulsively, Christina reached across the table and covered his hand with hers. "I didn't mean to upset you," she said gently. "Cook is as strong as an ox. I'm sure she'll be with you for many, many more years. And I—what I'm really thinking is that I'm very jealous of you."

His brows inched upward as he glanced around them; then he leaned toward her and grinned slyly. "I don't see any other females in here giving me the eye. How could you be jealous?"

"I didn't mean in that way, Lex." Although, she had to admit to herself that the idea of any other woman clinging to his side, pressing her lips to his was too unpleasant to consider. "I'm talking about your family. You have lots of relatives living close by, plus people like Cook who are part of the Sandbur, too, and you all love and support each other. I—well, I can't imagine how nice that must be."

His thumb slipped from beneath her fingers and curled over the top of her hand. "It's not always a perfect situation, Christina. Sometimes there are arguments between us. And we often have opposing ideas on how to run the ranch. But you are right. It is nice to have family all around me. To know they'll be there if I truly need them. That's something that money can't buy."

A chill brushed across her, and she shivered slightly. "You're so right. If money could bring Joel back, I would have found him years ago."

His expression turned to one of interest. "I'm curious about your parents, Christina. What did they do when Joel went missing? Did they search for him? Were they torn up, or did they think he'd come back after a few days of partying?"

Just as she started to answer, the waitress returned with Lex's dessert, a gooey-looking brownie topped with ice cream. After she'd served them each a cup of coffee and left the table, Christina replied, "Actually, Dad had to sober up to even realize that Joel was gone. And Mom, well, she kept saying her son had just gone off on some jaunt with a friend and would be back when he got good and ready."

Lex dug his spoon into the rich sweet. "But you weren't thinking that way."

Christina thoughtfully stirred cream into her coffee. "No. Joel was very responsible. At least, he was with me. We lived together at the time. I was only twenty-one. He was eighteen. We were both in college and had moved out of the family home. Joel and I wanted to be independent. And we tried to take care of each other. God knows, we couldn't depend on our parents. They supplied us with money, but little more. By the time Joel disappeared, they'd already been divorced for eight years."

His gaze studied her face for long moments. "So when your brother went missing, your parents weren't too worried about their son?"

"No. It wasn't until a week passed that Dad decided something was wrong and launched an investigation of his own. He and Mom both hired private investigators to search for Joel, but nothing ever came from it. The few leads that came into the police department never led anywhere. It was like Joel was home one day, and the next he'd completely vanished."

Shaking his head with dismay, he said, "What was your brother like? Were you two close?"

Cradling her coffee cup in one hand, Christina used the other hand to push her tumbled hair away from her face. Other than her friend Olivia, no one ever mentioned Joel to her. Even her own parents had pushed him to the distant past. And as for Mike, she didn't think he'd ever really cared that her brother couldn't be accounted for. To have Lex express real interest about Joel touched her in a way that was impossible to describe.

"Quiet, but humorous at times. He was planning on becoming a doctor. He was brilliant with math and science, and learning came easy for him. He didn't have a steady girlfriend, but he dated frequently. He was particular about his friends and he—"

"What?" Lex prompted.

She frowned. "He literally hated our parents' behavior. Hated the way they'd hacked up their marriage—the way they'd ignored the two of us. His relationship with them was worse than strained. But he loved me. That much I never doubted."

Christina watched a thoughtful crease build in the middle of his forehead. "Do you think he might have simply walked away? That he wanted to cut himself completely away from your family?"

"I've asked myself that question a thousand times over. And I suppose he could have left without wanting to be found. But why would he want to hurt me in that way? Why would he have let me suffer all these years?" She shook her head. "I can't bear to think he'd be that cruel to me."

"Well, I have a feeling you'll find him someday. Probably where you least expect him to be."

There was such tenderness in his words that tears stung the back of her eyes. She looked away from him and swallowed. "Thank you for the optimism, Lex. I know it's a long shot, but I won't give up. I can't."

Several seconds slipped by in silence, and then he said, "Here. Try some of this. It's delicious."

She looked around to see that he was holding a spoon-ful of the chocolate dessert toward her as though it was a cure-all. Christina couldn't help but laugh.

"Lex, I'm stuffed. You eat it."

"No. I won't eat another bite until you do," he insisted.

Rolling her eyes in a good-natured way, she caved in. "All right. One bite. Just to make you happy."

"That's my girl." His eyes gleamed as she opened her mouth and leaned toward the spoon.

As Christina slipped the bite of dessert into her mouth, it felt almost decadent to have him feeding her, especially with the same spoon his lips had touched.

"Mmm. It melts right on your tongue," she told him. "You're right. It's delicious."

Sensing that things between them were changing to something far too intimate, Christina leaned back in her chair and turned her attention to her coffee. Lex contin-ued to eat his dessert, but all the while his eyes were on her, arousing her in ways that left her feeling slightly drunk and even more reckless.

Finally, to her relief, he put down his spoon and an-nounced, "I'm done. If you are, I'll pay us out."

There was no point in staying longer. Her coffee cup was empty, and they had to return to the hotel sooner or later.

"Yes. I'm ready whenever you are."

Lex motioned for the waitress, and in only a few min-utes, they were out the door and once again walking across the beach. Lights from nearby businesses were enough to faintly illuminate the sandy pathway. Even so, Lex insisted on keeping his arm around the back of her waist.

"I don't want you to fall," he said as he urged her close to his side.

The connection to his body left her heart thumping fast and hard, making her voice sound a bit breathless. "We're walking on sand, Lex. If I fell, I'd hardly hurt myself."

"Hmm. Don't be so practical. I have to have a reason to keep my arm around you."

"Do you? Have to have a reason?"

She didn't know why those teasing words had come out of her mouth. Something about being alone with this man, away from his family and home, was doing strange things to her thinking. Or was it her body that was doing all the thinking? Either way, she couldn't resist his touch.

With a grunt of pleasure, he tugged the front of her body up against his and settled his hands at the small of her back. "It doesn't feel that way to me. Not tonight."

She started to tell him he was taking a lot for granted. But the words didn't have a chance to form on her tongue before he was lowering his head and fastening his lips over hers.

He tasted like chocolate and coffee and Lex. An utterly sinful combination and one that quickly squashed what little resistance she'd been trying to hold on to. Her mouth opened and slanted against the hard curve of his lips; her hands slipped up and linked at the back of his neck.

The strong trade winds crashed against their bodies, but they weren't nearly enough to cool the heat rushing from the soles of Christina's bare feet all the way to the roots of her hair. Unconsciously, she pressed herself closer. His eager kiss left her feeling as though he was lifting her completely off the ground.

His hands swept across her back and down the length of her spine until they reached the curved swell of her buttocks. Once there, they urged her hips forward until she was clamped tightly against his swelling manhood.

The fact that he was reacting so strongly to her and letting her know it somehow fueled her desire even more. For the next few minutes, she forgot that they were on a public beach, forgot that she was supposed to be guarding herself against this man's charms.

It wasn't until her dazed senses noted nearby voices that she was finally able to gather enough strength to pull her lips away from his and step out of his arms.

He tugged on her hand and murmured huskily, "Christina, come back here."

Unable to meet his gaze, she whispered, "Here comes a group of people. We have an audience."

Muttering an impatient curse under his breath, he started down the beach, tugging her along with him. "Don't they know this is our little strip of beach?"

"Guess they didn't see the Private—Keep Out signs," she tried to joke, but even to her own ears, her voice sounded strained and odd. Their embrace had gone far beyond just a kiss, and they both knew it. Her next question probably sounded inane, but she asked it, anyway. "Where are we going now?"

He glanced down at her, and she was surprised to see there was no sexy, teasing grin on his face. Instead, his expression was quietly serious as his gaze intently probed hers.

"To the hotel. To my room. Are you…agreeable to that?"

All she had to do was say one little word and everything would stay the same. She'd wake up in the morning with her world safely on its axis. But the night ahead would be cold and empty. Just like the nights of the past three years, since she'd walked away from Mike, had been.

"Lex, I—"

With a hand on her shoulder, he stopped her forward progress long enough to plant a kiss on her cheek. "Don't spoil this night by thinking too much, Christina. I want you and you want me. That's enough for now, isn't it?"

It had to be, Christina thought. Because she couldn't seem to stop him from leading her wherever he wanted to go.

She silently nodded, and they walked the rest of the way to the hotel without exchanging another word.

Chapter Seven

Inside the hotel, they went straight to the elevator, and once the doors cocooned them inside the small, private space, Lex used the opportunity to pull her back into his arms and kiss her.

The contact, though brief, was enough to overwhelm her all over again, and she was barely aware of her surroundings when they left the elevator and walked down the quiet hallway to his room.

The nicely furnished space was a replica of hers, but unlike her, he'd left the drapes pulled back on the glass doors leading out to the balcony. Beyond, stars were hanging over the gulf waters, sparkling the beach with diamonds.

With the door shut behind them, Lex took her by the hand and led her over to the sliding glass doors. "Let's step out on the balcony," he said softly, "where I can look at you in the starlight."

They stepped outside on the small balcony enclosed by black wrought iron. From this height, the wind seemed even stronger, and it whipped Christina's hair across her face as she gazed out at the rolling surf.

"It's beautiful," she said wistfully. He was standing directly behind her, and the bare skin on her shoulders was sizzling where his fingers rested. "And I'm glad we're here. Even though the reason for the trip isn't a pleasant one."

Turning her toward him, he cradled her face with his palms and lowered his lips toward hers. The idea that they were well and truly alone and about to make love made her whole body ache with anticipation.

"This trip was meant to happen, my sweet. Just like a lot of other things."

She didn't know exactly what he meant by that. But the moment his mouth touched hers, it stopped mattering. Nothing mattered but his touch.

They kissed for long moments, until the connection was no longer enough to satisfy their needs, and Lex led her gently back inside and over to the king-size bed.

With nothing but the starlight filtering through the glass doors, he found the zipper at the back of her dress and slowly pulled it downward. Christina closed her eyes and bit down on her bottom lip as his hands followed the garment down her curves, then onto the floor.

Shivering, she carefully stepped out of the pool of fabric, and he tossed it toward the armchair sitting in the corner of the room.

"Are you cold?" he whispered, with concern.

Daring to meet his gaze, she felt her heart squeeze with inexplicable pain. "No. I—I'm just not sure I—

we—should be doing this. That I should be…wanting you this much."

Smiling, he rested his forehead against hers. "Hang on, baby. If this is a mistake, we'll be making it together."

This couldn't be a mistake, Christina thought moments later, as Lex gently peeled away her undergarments and lifted her onto the massive bed. Even without the touch of his hands, she was on fire for him, mindlessly needing to feel his skin, his body against her.

She waited patiently for him to shed his boots and clothing, but once he lay down next to her, she reached for him eagerly and sighed with contentment when his mouth once again came down over hers. The stroke of his hands, the hungry plunder of his lips were enough to push her senses over the edge, and soon she was writhing against him, urging him to connect their bodies.

If anything, she'd thought that Lex would be a smooth, practiced lover, that his moves would be controlled and predictable. But nothing about his ragged kisses or the shaky, erratic movements of his hands showed a man on automatic pilot. He kissed her, touched her as though each time was a new experience and he could hardly wait for the next one.

His eagerness left her breathless, her body coiled with a hunger that ached deep within her. Like a warm rain shower, he kissed her cheeks, nose, chin and eyelids. Then on a slower track, he moved his attention behind her ear and down the sensitive side of her neck.

She felt like the bud of a flower, and each time he touched her, one more petal opened to expose the very center of her being. When his lips found a nipple and pulled it deep within his mouth, she was certain she was going to break apart. A broken cry gurgled in her throat, and she wrapped her legs around his hips.

"Make love to me, Lex." She whispered the plea. "Now. Please!"

He lifted his head. "Are you—"

Guessing his question, she finished for him. "I'm protected."

Whispering her name, he touched her face with the tips of his fingers, then slid them into her thick hair. At the same time, he lowered the bottom half of his body down to hers and entered her as slowly and gently as his raging desire would allow. But once the sweet, damp folds of her womanhood enveloped him, his control crumbled.

A hot ache gripped his loins, forcing him to thrust deeply and rapidly as he searched for relief, for something inside her that would quench the flames threatening to consume him.

At some point, he became aware of her hips driving up to meet his, her open mouth exploring his chest, her tongue teasing his nipples. She felt small and fragile beneath him, yet her abandoned movements told him that she wanted everything he was giving her and more. The idea aroused him even more than the feel of her body, and before he could stop himself, he was blindly pounding into her.

Time seemed suspended as sweat slicked his body and dripped onto hers. His hands raced over her smooth ivory skin, cupped around her breasts, then finally anchored themselves at the sides of her waist.

From somewhere far away, he could hear her soft cries, the whisper of his name, but the sounds faded as his heartbeat roared louder and louder in his ears. The ragged breaths he sucked into his lungs did little to ease their fiery pain, until suddenly breathing didn't seem to matter at all. He'd been flung to paradise, and Christina had taken the journey with him.

Long, long moments passed before Christina drifted back to the quiet room, and even then her awareness returned only in increments. Everything was still spinning, but she could feel Lex's cheek resting on hers, his heart pounding against her breast, his legs tangled with hers. Sweat was stinging her eyes, while her lungs were straining to draw in another breath.

Her eyes fluttered open just as he rolled his weight off her. Groaning softly, she shifted to face him, then sighed as he reached to tuck the front of her body up against his. Her lips curved into a satisfied smile as he pressed tiny kisses across her forehead.

"It has to be a hundred degrees in here," he said.

The unexpectedness of his words deepened the smile on her face. "The air-conditioning must have gone off."

He chuckled lowly. "Or maybe all this heat is coming from the firebrand in my arms."

Feeling like more of a woman than she'd ever felt in her life, she trailed her fingers along his damp cheek. "I didn't think it would be this way with us," she said lowly.

In the dim light of the room, she could see the corners of his mouth tilt upward.

"How did you think it would be?"

In spite of the wild ride they'd just taken together, Christina could feel a blush creeping over her face. "I— I'm not sure. More reserved, I suppose."

That brought another rumbling chuckle up from the

depths of his chest, and Christina realized it was a happy, soothing sound. One that made her glad to be alive.

"Honey, nothing between us will ever be lukewarm."

His hand slid slowly from her shoulder to the curve of her hip. Desire stirred deep within her, shocking her with its quick reappearance.

"And that scares me, Lex."

Groaning, he cupped his palms around the sides of her face. "Oh, Christina, nothing about this—about you and me—should scare you."

He would think that way, she thought dully. This wasn't a life-changing event for him. And she'd be naive and childish to think it could be.

Doing her best to push away the raw ache in her heart, she said, "You're right, Lex. Nothing should worry me tonight."

With a groan of pleasure, he crushed her body even closer and brought his lips to hers. Christina thought she was too exhausted to make love a second time, but Lex proved her wrong, and as the moon rose over the bay, she clung to him and wondered where this night was going to take her. And how soon it would be before her heart was broken all over again.

The next morning Christina woke at the sound of a door opening and closing. When she cracked her eyes open, sunlight smacked her in the face.

"Good morning, beautiful. Ready for some coffee?"

Rolling to her back, she saw Lex holding a paper carrier with four cups nestled safely inside it. He was already dressed in the clothes he'd worn yesterday, and when he pulled off his hat, she could see his blond hair was brushed smoothly back from his forehead. He couldn't have looked more sexy or handsome, and she felt her heart flutter like a lost leaf in the wind.

Clutching the sheet to her breasts, she quickly scooted up in the bed. "Four cups of coffee! Were you planning on jolting me awake with caffeine?"

Laughing, he sat down on the edge of the bed and placed the cups of coffee on the nightstand. "No, I wanted us to have plenty. Besides, I was going to kiss you awake before too long. I have a surprise for you."

After taking the lid off one of the foam cups, he poured in cream, then handed it to her. She thanked him, then took a careful sip of the steaming liquid. "A surprise?" she repeated groggily. "What sort of surprise?"

He left the bed and moved across the room, to where a small desk was positioned a short distance away from the balcony door. She watched with complete dismay as he lifted a shiny silver gift bag from the desktop and carry it back to the bed.

"Where on earth did that come from? A shop in the lobby? I didn't see anything last night," she said.

"The coffee came from the hotel lobby. But not this. While you've been sleeping, I've been out shopping."

"Why didn't you wake me? It's late, and we need to be getting to the bait house. You need to get back to the Sandbur and—"

He held up a hand. "Quit worrying. We'll be back to the Sandbur soon enough."

He was certainly right about that, she thought. Soon this time they'd had together would end, and she didn't have a clue what the future would bring for the two of them. Last night his pillow talk had been light and playful, and she'd taken his cue and kept hers the same. Yet deep down she was scared to death that she was falling head over heels for the man, and she didn't have the courage to even give him a hint as to how she was feeling.

Gently, he took the coffee from her hand and pushed the gift bag toward her. "See if you like it. I picked it out myself."

Christina peeked inside the bag and saw some sort of garment neatly folded at the bottom. With a cry of pleasure, she forgot about holding the sheet to her naked body and concentrated on pulling the item out in the open.

Ice-blue fabric spilled across her lap, and she quickly discovered it was a dress fashioned from polished cotton. The waist was nipped in with a belt edged with white piping, the top was V-necked and sleeveless, while the skirt flared out in deep gores, which would swish against her calves as she walked. It was very pretty and even more sexy, and she couldn't wait to try it on.

"Oh! Oh, how sweet of you, Lex! It's beautiful! I love it!"

"I thought you'd like something fresh to put on this morning."

She couldn't believe he'd done such a thoughtful, romantic thing for her. She wanted to believe that she was the *only* woman who'd ever received this sort of treatment from him, but that was highly unlikely. From what she'd heard, the man had made a career out of women since he'd been old enough to flirt.

You knew that beforehand, Christina. So don't think about it now. Just enjoy this moment with him.

"I do," she murmured, then leaned forward and placed a soft kiss on his lips. "Thank you."

He didn't say anything. Instead, he simply touched

her cheek and gazed at her as though he were watching the sun rise. Every word, every intimate touch that had passed between them last night replayed in her mind, and after a few moments, Christina was so overwhelmed with emotions that she had to clear her throat and ease back from him. Otherwise, everything she was feeling was going to be there on her face for him to read.

"I'd better shower and get dressed," she said huskily.

Wrapping the sheet around her, she scooted off the bed and headed toward the bathroom. She was about to step through the door when Lex called out to her. Glancing over her shoulder, she arched her brows at him.

"Christina, I just wanted to say—in case you're wondering—the dress wasn't meant to be any sort of…payment."

She stiffened. "I never thought it was."

Suddenly he was across the room, reaching for her hand and drawing the back of it to his lips. "Forgive me, Christina, if that sounded coarse. I—I know you think I do this sort of thing often. That I go through women the way I buy and sell cattle. But that's far from the truth. And if I'm not doing any of this right, well—" One corner of his mouth turned upward in a hapless grin. "I've just ruined the hell out of my reputation."

Softly, she touched her fingers to his cheek. "Lex, you bought me the dress because you wanted me to have it. You were being sweet and thoughtful and nothing more."

Relief flooded his expression. "You're a special woman," he murmured.

Was being special the same as being loved? she wondered dismally. No. She didn't think so. But being special to a man like Lex was probably the most she could ever hope for.

Tears suddenly stung the back of her eyes.

"I'll be ready in a few minutes," she told him, then hurriedly shut the bathroom door between them.

A half hour later, after checking out of the hotel and grabbing a bite of breakfast at a seaside grill, Lex drove the two of them back to Ray's Bait.

Unlike yesterday, the bait shop was busy with several customers. Christina and Lex waited to one side until the store emptied and the stocky man behind the counter was alone. Then they stepped up to introduce themselves.

Ray Pena had salt-and-pepper hair, a broad face, a thick neck and shoulders and enormous hands to match. A faded tropical shirt was stretched tightly across his belly. He smiled affably at the two of them before settling his appreciative gaze back on Christina.

"You two don't look like you're goin' fishin' today. What can I do for you?"

At least the man was observant, Christina thought, with a measure of hope. "You're right. We're not here to buy bait. I don't know if your assistant told you or not, but we stopped by yesterday, when you were out."

Ray Pena grimaced. "No. Sally don't tell me much. 'Cept she don't make enough money." He snorted. "Young people nowadays think they deserve a raise just for showin' up." His squinted gaze vacillated between Christina and Lex. "You folks work for the Texas Rangers or somethin'?"

Christina could see how the man might take Lex for a Ranger. Lex had that solid, authoritative look about him. As for her, there was no way this man could know that she'd put in five years with that organization. "No. I'm a private investigator and—" she glanced over to Lex "—he's my client. If you have a minute, we'd like to show you some photos and ask you a few questions."

Ray shrugged. "Sure. Ain't got no customers now, anyway."

Christina stepped closer to the counter, while Lex moved up behind her left shoulder. Instantly, she was aware of his body heat, the faint scent of masculine cologne lingering on his clothing. His nearness was more than a distraction, but she forced her mind to focus on one of the few witnesses that had seen Paul Saddler the day he died.

"This is about a drowning that happened close to twelve years ago," she explained to Ray Pena. "Some businessmen bought bait in your shop, then went out in the gulf for a day of fishing. One of them didn't return to Corpus alive."

Ray's broad face wrinkled into a thoughtful grimace. "Ma'am, people drown in the gulf all the time. Never think the water is a danger until it's too late."

Christina glanced up to Lex, and he flashed her a hopeless look. Determined, she pulled a packet of photos from a manila envelope in her handbag and spread them across the glass counter. "Well, you might remember this event because the police came around to question you about that day. You see, there was an inquiry about the way this man died. His name was Paul Saddler. He was a prominent rancher from the Sandbur and a businessman for Coastal Oil."

"Hmm, sounds familiar. Let me see."

He fetched a pair of reading glasses from his shirt pocket and, after jamming them on his face, leaned over the photos. The snapshots had been taken at a Coastal Oil Christmas party and saved along with many of Paul's papers. Christina had considered it lucky to find photos for which all four men had posed together, with their faces in full view of the camera.

"Yeah, yeah," Ray said after a quick study of the photos. He tapped a finger on Paul's image. "I remember this was the man who drowned. The story was all over the papers and on the TV news."

"So you remember that day?" Christina eagerly prompted.

"Sure." He turned around and poured himself a cup full of burned coffee. As he added a hefty measure of sugar, he went on, "Before the drowning, those guys had come in here pretty regular. I was always happy to see 'em 'cause they usually spent a lot of money."

Christina left the photos where they lay. "Do you recall the day of the drowning?"

"Damn right. I heard the emergency call come over the police scanner. I used to listen to one of those all the time, but the damn thing got struck by lightning and I never got another one. The old lady was afraid if it happened again, it might burn the whole place down."

Christina waited patiently while he took a long swig of the coffee. "So when you heard the police call, you recognized Paul Saddler's name?" she asked.

Ray shook his head. "Nope. Before that, I didn't know any of their names. They were just customers, you know. Guys that would shoot the bull while waiting for me to sack up their bait. I didn't know it was him that had drowned until I saw his picture in the paper the next day.

Hit me hard. Knowin' that I'd been talking to him that mornin' and a few hours later he was dead."

Christina looked up at Lex again. This time his expression was grim. She thrust her hand behind her until she found his fingers and latched hers tightly around them.

"Yes, I know exactly what you mean," Christina told Ray. "So, can you tell me anything about that particular visit from the men that day? Did anything seem unusual with any of them?"

Ray pointed to Red Winters. "The big redhead was loud. But he was always like that—tellin' crude jokes and ordering the other guys around—kinda teasin' like, you know, but obnoxious. That day, the thin man with the glasses barked at him in a testy way. Surprised the hell out of me. He never showed much spunk."

"What about Paul? Was anything different about him?"

Ray thought for long moments, and as they waited for him to answer, she could feel Lex's fingers tightening around hers even more. At that moment, Christina realized how very much she wanted to solve this case for Lex's sake. He'd loved his father deeply, and he deserved to know the truth about his death.

"Come to think of it, I seem to recall I told the cops that he was real quiet that mornin'. Didn't talk much at all and stood off by himself most of the time. I thought he might be sick. He sorta looked it."

"What made you think that?" Christina questioned. Being sick and being nervous could produce the same outward symptoms. "Was he coughing? Running to the restroom? Anything like that?"

Ray shook his head. "Not as I remember. He just

looked pale and like he wasn't havin' a good time. But who could have enjoyed a fishin' trip with that redheaded bastard? He's the one who needed to go overboard. The guy that drowned—now, he was a class act. Always nice and friendly. I hated hearin' that he was dead. Really hated it. He treated me like an equal, you know? The others—they were different."

Christina knew all too well what Ray Pena meant, and she was beginning to get a whole new picture of Paul Saddler's coworkers.

"So after Paul's death, did the other three men ever show up here at the bait house again?"

"Once. Not the skinny man with the glasses. But the other two stopped by not long after the drowning. The redhead was real surly, and I was about to order him to leave when the other guy—the pretty boy—got him and took him out to the parking lot. I think the both of them might have been a little drunk, but since they left without causing any trouble, I didn't call the cops."

"And they never came back after that?" Lex asked.

"No," Ray replied. "Guess their friend's death must have taken the enjoyment out of fishin'."

Christina returned the photos to the manila envelope. After she stuffed it back into her handbag, she reached across the counter to shake the shop owner's hand. "Thank you very much, Mr. Pena. You've been more helpful than you can imagine."

After Lex also shook the man's hand and offered his appreciation for the information, they turned to leave the bait house, but Ray had a question of his own that caused the two of them to pause at the door.

"What's this all about, anyway? Y'all think Paul Saddler was murdered or somethin'?"

"We're looking into every possibility," Christina told him.

"Seems like a long time ago to be worryin' about it now," Ray muttered, more to himself than to them.

They left the bait house and climbed back into the truck. As Christina fastened her seat belt and Lex started the engine, he said, "I could tell by the way Ray Pena talked about Red that he remembered the group of men and the day Dad died. That surprised me."

"When a tragedy occurs, it usually sparks a person's memory." Crossing her legs, she turned toward him. "His recollection of Lawrence Carter barking at Red was the thing that caught my attention. Would you say that behavior was out of character for Lawrence?"

Lex nodded as he steered the car onto a major boulevard. "It surprised the hell out of me, too. I never knew Lawrence to say a sharp word to anyone. But everybody can reach a breaking point, and that morning, Red might have been getting on Lawrence's nerves."

Ideas about how the tragedy happened were slowly beginning to form in Christina's mind. Still, there were pieces of the puzzle that still needed to be found. That meant gathering more information and more time spent on the Sandbur.

The idea left her torn. Every fiber of her being wanted to be near Lex, to make love to him any and every chance she got. But the sensible part of her brain knew that would be a dangerous gamble and the stakes would be her heart.

"You look extra beautiful this morning," Lex commented, breaking the short silence. "Must be that pretty dress."

Glancing down, she smoothed a hand across her lap. "You have very good taste."

"I know."

The suggestive lilt to his words had her glancing up to see his wicked gaze traveling up and down the length of her. The look caused desire to simmer in the pit of her stomach, yet at the same time, she was chilled with fear, terrified each hour, each day in his company would only make her fall in love with the man just that much more.

"Lex...about last night. I think—"

Her words halted as he reached across the console and folded his hand around hers.

"Last night was something I'll never forget," he said gently.

She drew in a shaky breath. "Neither will I."

From the corner of her eye, she could see him glance at her, and for a split second, she thought she saw genuine affection on his face. Would she be crazy to think he might want more from her than just sex?

"Is something wrong? You look a little sad."

Shrugging, she prayed he couldn't see the turmoil inside of her. "I wish...we could have stayed here at the beach a bit longer."

A smug smile spread across his face. "Don't worry, honey. I'll come up with a reason for us to make another trip down here. And soon."

That was exactly what Christina was afraid of. One more repeat of last night and she'd be totally lost to the man.

Chapter Eight

As soon as Lex and Christina returned to the ranch, he was caught up in business. A cattle buyer from New Mexico was already there, waiting for him to arrive. Later that day, he had to drive out to the Mission River Division of the ranch, where the hands were cutting more cattle to be sent to market. Tuesday was taken up entirely with a trip with Matt to a cattle breeders convention in Austin. By the time he'd returned home, Christina had already retired for the night, and Lex had gone to bed frustrated. Since their time in Corpus, he'd not had a chance to spend five minutes with her, and they'd only spoken briefly a few times on the phone.

But that didn't mean Lex had forgotten one moment of their time together. Just the memory of having her in his arms left him aroused and desperate to make love to her again.

Make love. Make love. Why are you thinking in those terms, Lex? Have you fallen in love with Christina?

The question jolted him. He'd never been in love before. Infatuated maybe, but not the deep sort of love that burrowed into a person's heart and stayed there. If he was in love with Christina, he wasn't sure what or how he was supposed to feel. He only knew that being with Christina, in any capacity, had become very important to him. He knew he didn't want this time with her to end.

So what was he going to do about it? The questions continued to gnaw at him as he made his way to the small room where Christina had set up her office, yet he did his best to push them aside as he knocked on the open door and stepped over the threshold.

"Good morning, stranger," he greeted, with a grin. "Cook told me you already had breakfast and were here working. You've started early."

Snapping her cell phone together, she laid the instrument aside and gave him a halfhearted smile. "Your father must have kept everything he ever worked on. I still haven't made it through all these folders."

Even though she looked as gorgeous as ever in a pale pink blouse and a dove-gray miniskirt, he could sense a change in her, and he wondered what could have happened with her these past days he'd been away from the ranch house.

"If my memory is right, I believe there are even more of Dad's things in the attic." He gestured toward the boxes stacked near her desk. "Have you found anything helpful here?"

"I've come across a few interesting notes about the company shares and an e-mail from Red to Paul, urging

him to buy more shares, saying that he had a solid tip the
value was going to go up."

Lex stepped closer to where she sat. "When was the
message dated?"

Christina glanced at a legal pad lying on the corner of
the desk. "About a year before Paul died."

Shrugging, Lex said, "Well, that's nothing suspicious.
It was a well-known fact that Coastal was hatching an
enormous venture at the time. A trans-state pipeline that
would supply several states with natural gas. If everything had gone as planned, the project would have made
Coastal billions of dollars. But state legislation began
to bog things down, and then a big backer got cold feet.
When the idea was shelved, Coastal's stock plummeted,
and it took nearly a decade for it to climb back to its former worth."

Christina's brows arched with interest. "What about
your father's shares? I've not come across any sort of
documents showing that he sold them."

Lex shook his head. "He kept them. And then Mom
hung on to the stock through all those thin years. Dad
had always voiced his confidence in the company, so
Mom figured she should trust his judgment. Turned out
he was correct. She still has the stock, and it's now worth
a small fortune."

"Hmm." Christina thoughtfully tapped a pencil
against the legal pad, then she rose from the chair and
walked around the desk to stand near him. Lex felt like
a weak fool as his heart began to thump at a high rate of
speed. What was it about this woman that affected him
so? he wondered. The exotic scent she wore? Her smooth,
luscious skin, the curves hidden beneath her clothing?
Or was it her eyes and the way she looked at him? The

way they darkened and lightened to her moods, the way her lips tilted when she smiled at him? God, he wished he knew, because he felt as though he was losing control of his own life.

"I'm not yet ready to say. I still need to do a lot more digging." Her blue eyes connected with his. "And I'm glad you came by this morning. I needed to let you know that I'm planning another trip."

An eager grin flashed across his face. "For us?"

Her gaze darted uncomfortably away from his, underscoring his earlier suspicion that something had changed with her. Now he could only wait, like a horse thief waiting for the trapdoor to fall from beneath his feet. What made her put up this invisible wall between them? He'd thought making love would move their relationship forward, not back.

She drew in a deep breath and blew it out. "No. I'm driving up to San Antonio tomorrow. Alone. I have several things to do."

It was crazy how disappointed he felt. He'd never dreamed that any woman could make him feel *this* much. And he couldn't stop himself from reaching for her. As soon as his hands came down on her shoulders, her eyes turned misty, and the sight tore a hole right in the middle of his chest.

"I thought…I was hoping you'd want me to go along," he murmured.

She closed her eyes, as though his question pained her. "I've been thinking about that, Lex. About Corpus—"

Hearing the misgivings in her voice, he interrupted her with a loud groan. "Oh hell, Christina, don't tell me you've been having second thoughts about our night together."

He crossed the room and carefully shut the door, co-cooning them in the private office. His mother was away on a business trip, but he didn't want any of the maids coming by and disturbing them.

With a helpless shake of her head, she pressed the heel of her palm against her forehead. "Oh, Lex. I don't regret it. Or—well, maybe I do, a bit. Because—" Her gaze dropped from his. "I think I've sent you the wrong signals."

"Signals?" he repeated as he walked back over to her. "What are you talking about?"

Her head lifted, and the misery he saw in her eyes tore at him. He didn't want to hurt this woman. More than anything, he wanted to make her happy.

"I made it look as though I was willing to have an affair with you. And I shouldn't have done that. Because I'm—I can't have that sort of relationship in my life again. It would be wrong for me, and you."

His nostrils flared as unexpected pain plowed through him. She wanted to write him off. Without even giving him a chance. Giving the two of them a chance.

"Christina, why did you go to bed with me?"

She swallowed hard as her eyes turned watery.

"I'm only human, Lex. I wanted you. And I told myself that I could deal with having casual sex with you."

In his past, Lex would probably have been relieved to hear a woman describing their time together as casual. But he wasn't now. He felt offended and even a bit crushed. And the fact only pointed out to him just how much he'd changed since he'd met Christina.

"Christina, nothing about that night—our night together—was casual. And you know it!"

She looked anguished. "Oh please, Lex. You've never

talked about looking for a permanent woman in your life. So don't pretend with me now. That would—that would make everything worse."

Stepping forward, he reached for her hand and pressed it between his palms. "I haven't been looking for a permanent woman, because I gave up on that idea. This love thing just never happened for me! Still, that doesn't mean I don't care about you. About us being together."

Like heavy stones, disappointment fell to the bottom of her heart. Caring was nothing like loving. He wanted their bodies to be connected, but not their hearts. "Is that supposed to be enough for me?"

"I'm not going to pretend with you, Christina. That's not my style. We have a good thing going between us. I don't know where it's going, but I'd like to find out."

The smoldering look in his eyes warned her that he was about to kiss her, and Christina knew she was in far too vulnerable a state to let that happen. One taste of his lips and she'd be promising him anything.

Sighing, she pulled her hand from his and walked over to a window that overlooked the lawn. He followed, and as he came to a stop behind her, his hands lapped over her shoulders, branding her with tempting heat.

"Christina, the only way we can get to know each other is to *be* together."

The ache of frustration caused her to close her eyes and pinch the bridge of her nose. "Oh, Lex, Mother admitted that the only thing that had drawn her to Dad in the first place was sex. I've never wanted to follow in her footsteps. But now I'm beginning to wonder if something in me is just as weak as her."

"Listen, honey," he said gently, "making love to me hardly makes you a duplicate of your mother."

Turning, she looked up at him, and as she did, she realized his face had become a dear image in her heart. It was something she wanted, needed to look upon every day of her life.

"Lex, I think you need to know that I spent four years in a relationship with a fellow law officer. His name was Mike, and I thought—well, I believed—he loved me. He certainly told me that often enough. But they were just empty words. Just like his promises of marriage. It took me a long time to realize that I was wasting my time with the man and a whole lot of willpower to finally pack up and leave."

He was clearly surprised, and she wondered what he was thinking of her now. That maybe she was a woman who couldn't hold on to a lasting relationship?

"Four years," he repeated. "That's a long time. You must have loved the man."

Glancing away from him, she swallowed as emotion filled her throat. Now that she'd met Lex, it was plain that she'd never loved Mike. Not the eternal kind that outlives good times, bad times, old age and even death. With Mike, she'd simply loved the idea of being a wife, having children and a family of her own. There was a wealth of difference.

"I'm not sure I knew what love was back then. But at the time I believed that I loved him. Otherwise, I wouldn't have lived with him."

His eyes widened, and she realized she'd surprised him even more. But she couldn't worry about how he was viewing her now. He needed to understand where she was coming from and where she intended to go. She wasn't going to make the same mistake with him that she'd made with Mike. Living on hope was no longer enough for her.

"You lived with him?"

Christina nodded. "Does that shock you?"

His head wagged back and forth. "Well—uh, it shakes me more than anything. When you told me that you'd come close to marriage, I thought you'd probably just worn some guy's engagement ring for a few months. Living together is—that's commitment."

"Not to him," she said dully.

Before he could reply, she walked over to her desk and sank into the leather chair. The small space she'd put between them wasn't enough to ease the trembling inside of her, the ache to rush back to him and fling her arms around his neck.

Looping his thumbs over his belt, Lex moved in front of the desk and stared directly into her blue eyes. It amazed her that she didn't see revulsion or disappointment in his eyes. Especially knowing how he admired his parents' relationship and wanted that same sort of relationship for himself. She was far, far from being a flawless human being.

"All right, Christina. I've listened to what you've had to say. Now listen to me. And I'm going to put this in simple terms. I'm not the playboy some people think I am. And I'm not like this Mike you once—knew."

Fighting back tears, she said, "It's wrong of you to ask me to jump into a heated physical relationship with you, Lex! We need to get to know each other better before we make such a serious connection."

For long moments, his gaze searched her face, and Christina suspected he was searching for a gentlemanly way to end things between them. But he surprised her when he finally spoke.

"All right, Christina. For now, we'll do this thing your way. We'll go slow and get to know each other better. But just remember that all the while, I'll be wanting to make love to you. And you'll be wanting to make love to me. We'll be wasting time when we could be making each other happy."

Maybe he was right, she thought dismally. But her feelings for him had become too important. She needed to know whether the caring he felt for her had a chance at turning into love, or if his desire for her would quickly burn itself out.

Rising from the chair, she walked around to where he stood and placed a whisper-soft kiss on his cheek. The tiny expression of affection couldn't begin to describe the gratitude swelling in her heart. "I know you're not happy with me about this, Lex. But I'm glad you're willing—for now—to go along with my wishes."

She eased back from him before her arms could turn traitorous and fling themselves around his neck.

With a reluctant grin, he rubbed the spot she'd just kissed. "One of these days—and soon—you'll be planting a kiss on my lips instead of my cheek. But only when you're ready. I promise you that," he murmured huskily. Then, before she could guess his intentions, he lifted the back of her hand to his lips and took his time pressing a kiss against the soft skin. "So, why are you going to San Antone this time? Another case, or Dad's?"

Relieved that he'd changed the subject, she said, "Your father's. I'm going to try again to catch up to Paul's old friends. I want to hear with my own ears how they recount the day your father died."

Worry chased everything else from his face, and he quickly clasped both her hands between his. "Christina, we're not entirely sure these guys were being truthful about Dad's accident! That puts them all under suspicion! I don't like the idea of you seeing them. Not one bit."

"I have to interview them in person, Lex. That way, I can see if they're hiding something. And more than anything, I need to catch them off guard."

"I can understand that. But if these guys actually did have anything to do with Dad's death, they might be dangerous. Especially to you, since you're digging open the case."

Did his show of concern mean anything? she wondered. Only minutes ago he'd admitted that he cared for her, but did that sort of caring warrant this much worry?

Don't let yourself start believing the man actually loves you, Christina. He's already said that heartfelt emotion wasn't for him. Remember that.

Emotions knotted her throat, making her voice husky when she spoke. "You're forgetting, Lex, that I worked as a law officer for several years. I know the danger signs to look for, and I know how to be careful. Besides, this is what your mother hired me to do."

The scowl on his face said her words hadn't assured him all that much. She had to remind herself that if he was the one putting himself in danger, she wouldn't like it. In fact, she wanted to make sure, before this was all over with, that he didn't get anywhere near Paul's old friends.

Tossing his hands up in a helpless gesture, he said, "Well, I can't tell you how to do your job. Just like you couldn't tell me how to go out and rope a wild bull that might gore me or my horse to death."

The image of his words sent a shiver down Christina's spine. City folks like her never stopped to appreciate the constant dangers of a cowboy's life. Everything about Lex was opening her eyes. And her heart. But what good was that going to do her if his own heart was closed to love?

"I'll be very careful, Lex. I promise." Then before she could stop herself, she gave in to the overwhelming need to touch him. She stepped closer and lifted her mouth to his. He instantly took the initiative, and for long moments, his lips searched and coaxed until she was moaning deep in her throat and wrapping her arms around his waist.

By the time he finally lifted his head, Christina's cheeks were on fire. One more minute and her vow to resist him would have crumbled. The worst part was the smug grin on his face that said he knew she'd been on the verge of melting.

"When I said you'd soon be kissing me on the lips, I didn't realize it was going to be in a matter of minutes."

"That was a goodbye kiss," she said, with as much dignity as she could muster.

His chuckle matched the sexy glint in his eyes. "I can't wait to see what your hello is going to be like when you return."

Turning her back to him, she bit down on her lip and blinked at the mist in her eyes. She wasn't like Retha Logan. She wasn't even that same young woman who fell victim to Mike's charming lies, she told herself. But, oh, it was going to be very lonely while proving that to Lex. And herself.

Three days later, on her way from San Antonio back to the Sandbur, Christina drove to the riverside area where

Olivia's law firm and Christina's own working office were located.

As suspected, Olivia was still at her desk, even though it was far past time for the doors to close. The black-haired woman, who was only two years older than Christina's thirty-three years, looked up in surprise, then smiled with pleasure when she spotted Christina standing in the open doorway of her office.

"Chrissy! You're back!" Jumping to her feet, she rushed around the wide desk and hurried over to give Christina a hug.

Unexpected tears burned the back of Christina's eyes as she held her friend tightly. "How are you, Ollie?"

"The same as usual. Going crazy with a stack of work in front of me and not enough time to do it all in."

Slipping an arm around the back of Christina's waist, Olivia urged her over to a long leather couch positioned in front of a plate-glass wall overlooking the River Walk. This building was located in a beautiful area of town. Part of the office was furnished to the hilt with expensive antiques from the estate of Olivia's parents, who'd passed away ten years before in a plane crash. Losing her parents wasn't the only misfortune Olivia had faced. Olivia had become a partner of the reputable firm at an absurdly early age, but not without a price. She'd lost a husband along the way. But whether that was from Olivia's long hours at work or his roaming eye for the women would be hard to say. Their shared problems with love was just one of the many things Christina and Olivia had in common.

"Sit down, honey," she said to Christina. "Want some coffee? I'll call Mimi and have her make us a pot."

Christina rolled her eyes. "You mean you're making

your poor assistant stay after hours? Really, Ollie, when are you going to slack up on this pace?"

Olivia's arms lifted, then fell uselessly to her sides. "I can't ever find a stopping place. But Mimi is being paid well, and she doesn't mind the extra hours, thank God. I really don't know what I'd do without the woman. It's a good thing she decided to come out of retirement." She sat down next to Christina and affectionately patted her knee. "Now tell me what you're doing here in the city. I thought you were making hay down on the farm."

"It's a ranch, Ollie. Remember? Just one of the biggest in the state of Texas. And I've been working on a case, not making hay."

Olivia laughed. "That's too bad. The way you described Mrs. Saddler's son, I thought things might be—" She broke off as she saw a pained look skitter across Christina's face. "Oh, don't tell me that I've actually hit a nerve."

Sighing, Christina said, "I don't want to talk about Lex Saddler right now. I came by to take a short breather before I make the trip back to the Sandbur. I've finished interviewing two of the three men that were with Paul Saddler the day he drowned."

Olivia's expression turned serious. "Oh. Did you glean anything from them?"

Wearily, Christina leaned her head against the back of the couch. She didn't know why she was so exhausted. Normally, she thrived on this part of investigating, but for some reason, leaving Lex and the Sandbur behind had been even harder this last time.

"I believe the men I spoke to are telling the truth about what they saw that day of the accident."

"So you couldn't trip them up—get them to change their testimony?"

"No. Oh, they both wavered a little from the initial facts they'd given twelve years ago. But I'm mainly going on their behavior as a whole. They both seemed genuinely sorry that Paul was gone."

"Hmm. Well, you ought to know. You've always had a canny knack for reading people."

Christina grimaced. She hadn't read Mike's true colors. And she wasn't sure she was seeing the real side of Lex, either.

"What about the third one?" Olivia asked.

"Lawrence Carter," Christina said. "Unfortunately, he's still out of town on business. And he's actually the one I wanted to talk to the most. So the meeting with him is on hold for right now."

Olivia's eyes narrowed. "Does he have a wife?"

Christina nodded. "He's got one now, but the one he was married to at the time of Paul's death divorced him not long afterwards. Whether there was some sort of connection there, it's impossible to say. I'd like to talk to that particular woman, but from what I can gather, she's moved to California. Anyway, he's currently married to a loud woman, who's beginning to get suspicious about me coming around asking to see her husband."

Olivia suggested, "Perhaps you should fly out to California and find the first wife. I'm betting she could tell you plenty."

Squaring around to face her friend, Christina sighed. "I still have a bit of work to do on Paul's things before I take that step. Besides, the only thing Lawrence Carter might be guilty of is taking a fishing trip with his friends."

Olivia nodded, then reached over and briefly squeezed her hand. "I've never seen you looking this tired, Chrissy. Haven't you been feeling well?"

"I'm fine. It's been—hectic this past week, and the weather has been so darn hot. What about you? Has the Miers case gone to trial yet? I know you've been worried about it."

Olivia said, "It starts tomorrow morning. That's why I'm here and probably will be here until twelve or one tonight. I'm not ready by any means. I can't find one witness to corroborate my client's alibi. Hell, I can't even find one person willing to be a character witness. On the outside, he appears to be a scumbag, but on the inside, I think he's just a scared little boy that got caught up in the wrong crowd. But that's another story." She smiled brightly as she ran her gaze up and down Christina. "Tell me where you found that sexy dress. I love it!"

Christina glanced down at the blue dress that Lex had given her. The garment was special to her, and she intended to enjoy it, even if she didn't know if their relationship would end as soon as Paul Saddler's case was finalized.

"Oh, I—picked it up down in Corpus this past week," she said as casually as she could.

Olivia continued to study her as though she were on the witness stand. "So you've been to Corpus, too. You're a lady on the move."

Christina shrugged. "Unfortunately, this case covers a lot of area."

"Well, I'm sure Mrs. Saddler is taking care of all your expenses. How do you like her?"

Christina's smile was genuine. "I like her very much.

She makes no bones about speaking her mind, and that suits me. But I hardly ever see the woman."

"And her son?"

Groaning loudly, Christina rolled her eyes toward the ceiling. "I told you that I didn't want to talk about him."

"That's exactly why I do want to talk about him."

"Why do you have to be such a—lawyer?" Christina countered. "You think you have to cross-examine everyone that gets near you."

A wan smile touched Olivia's pretty face. "Only the ones I care about."

Olivia did care, Christina realized. She was one of the few people who would always be there for her through thick and thin, no matter what.

Restless now, Christina left the couch and walked over to the plate glass. The scene below was beautiful, with the narrow river lined with tropical trees and plants. Currently, people were gathered around park benches, cooling themselves in the shade. This city had always been her home, and she loved it, yet she was already yearning to head south to the Sandbur. To Lex. How could she have changed so much in such a short time?

"Okay, I'll just come straight out and tell you that I—I think I've fallen in love with the man."

Olivia's loud gasp had Christina turning to face the other woman.

"In love!" Olivia sputtered. "Are you serious? I was just hoping you'd been having a little fun with the man. And you hit me with something like this!"

Christina groaned again. "I realize it sounds crazy—"

"No, not crazy. Just unexpected," Olivia interrupted. "I mean, since you left Mike, you've been so determined to remain single and independent."

A chilly hand touched her heart, and she quickly looked back toward the river so that her friend couldn't see the pain on her face. "I figure I'm still going to remain single and independent."

"Why?"

She swallowed. "I don't think Lex Saddler is the marrying sort. And I'm stupid to let myself feel anything for him in the first place."

"Oh, honey, we don't *let* ourselves feel anything. That just happens whether we want it to or not."

Frustrated tears burned the back of her eyes as she looked over her shoulder at Olivia. "If that's true, then why do I have to feel things for the wrong kind of man? You would've thought Mike had taught me a lesson," she said, with a great deal of self-directed sarcasm.

Leaving the couch, Olivia walked up behind her. "Let's forget about your past for a minute. What about Lex? Why are you so sure he's not the marrying kind? Has he already been burned by one marriage?"

Christina shook her head. "No. As far as I know, he's never so much as had a fiancée. Just a string of girlfriends a mile long." Shoving a hand through her tousled red hair, she looked at Olivia. "He cares very much for his family and the ranch, but he says he's never been in love, and frankly, I don't think he ever will be."

Olivia frowned. "Honey, you could be wrong about him. I can't see you falling for a man that is incapable of loving."

"Oh, he's capable. He loves his family dearly."

"Family is different. That sort of love is something that starts as a baby and grows as you grow. Loving a spouse is an emotional tie—an investment that some men have trouble making. But you've not known this man for that long, Chrissy. He might decide he doesn't want to live without you."

Pinching the bridge of her nose, Christina sighed. "I don't know what to do. Lex says he cares about me, but he says that love isn't for him. And I'm scared. Scared that I'm getting myself into another hopeless situation. I groveled at Mike's feet for four long years. I did everything to make him see how much I cared—how much I wanted the two of us to be a real family—but in the end he didn't care one whit. I'm not about to humiliate myself like that again. Not for any man."

Olivia's fingers squeezed her shoulder. "Maybe this Lex Saddler isn't just *any* man."

Chapter Nine

Throughout the long drive back to the Sandbur, Christina thought plenty about Olivia's words. Lex Saddler really wasn't just any man. From what she could see, he wasn't the sort who lied and manipulated. He was decent and honest and hardworking. So what was the matter with her? Why wasn't she breaking her neck to jump into his arms and enslave him with her feminine charms?

Because she didn't want him to love just her body. She wanted him to love *her*. Totally. Completely. She wanted a man who would give her children, remain at her side even after she was wrinkled and gray. If Lex couldn't be that man, then she'd have to move on and forget him.

In spite of her miserable thoughts, though, her heart began to sing the moment she parked near the ranch house and spotted Lex walking across the lawn to greet her.

"I see you kept your promise and made it back safely,"

he said with a smile, then lowered his head and placed a swift kiss on her cheek. "Do you have bags?"

"One. In the backseat."

He fetched the bag, and Christina walked beside him as they headed to the house.

"So how did things go?" he asked. "No trouble?"

"No trouble," she said while her hungry eyes kept creeping over to his profile. Tonight he was dressed in a pair of old jeans and a faded red T-shirt. The sight of his bare arms reminded her even more of his wiry strength and how it had felt to have those arms wrapped tightly around her.

"I'm glad," he said. "I've missed you."

By now they'd reached the back entrance to the house. The porch light hanging to the left of the door shed a faint pool of light on his grinning face.

God help her, but just looking at him left her breathless and longing to kiss him and never stop. "And I've missed you, too," she said softly, then inclined her head toward the door. "Let's go in, and I'll catch you up on what I've learned."

When they entered the kitchen, she spotted Cook sitting at the long pine table, sipping from a tall iced glass.

"Good to see you back, young lady," Cook greeted her, with a smile. "Want to join me and Lex with something to drink?"

"Give me a minute to freshen up, and I'll be right back," Christina told her.

Grabbing her bag from Lex, she raced upstairs to her bedroom. After a quick visit to the bathroom and a hasty brush of her windblown hair, she hurried back down to the kitchen.

Cook patted the bench space next to her. "Sit here, Christina. Lex will get you whatever you'd like."

Glancing around the room, Christina eased down next to Cook. "Is Geraldine out for the evening?"

"She'll be gone for the next few days," Lex said from a spot at the cabinet counter. "Nicci had to go to a medical convention in Houston, and she wanted Mother to accompany her. They hardly get to spend any time together, so Mother agreed to go."

"I think that's very nice," Christina said, while wishing she could have had such a caring, responsible mother. As it was, Retha contacted her daughter in unpredictable spurts. There were times she'd go out of the country for weeks without letting Christina know of her whereabouts. But Lex's family was different. They were knit together with love. Oh God, why did she have to keep thinking of that word, *that* emotion?

Lex held up a coffee mug. "Would you like coffee or lemonade or soda?" he asked, then added, with a sly grin, "Whatever my lady desires."

My lady. Just hearing him say the words, even teasingly, made her heart beat faster. "Coffee would be great."

While Lex poured the coffee and added cream, Cook said, "We've been wondering if you got Paul's old buddies to tell you anything helpful."

Before she could make a reply, Lex arrived at the table with the coffee and took a seat next to Christina. His closeness was both sweet and tempting, making it difficult to focus on Cook's comment.

"I should have called," Christina said. "But since I didn't have anything concrete to report, I didn't want to get your hopes up."

Besides that, she didn't want Lex to think she couldn't

go for two days without hearing his voice. She already felt as though she were wearing her feelings for him on her sleeve. Especially after giving him that melting kiss right before she'd left.

"Did you get to interview the men?" Lex asked.

"Two of them," Christina answered. "After Red's very young wife told me where to find him, I caught up to him on the golf course. I'm not sure he appreciated me showing up and interrupting his game. But he was polite enough. And I found Harve at his downtown office and didn't have any problem getting in to see him."

"What did you think about them?"

Shrugging, Christina took a careful sip from the steaming mug. "I'm not certain, but my hunch tells me that Red and Harve did nothing to harm your father."

Lex looked utterly surprised by her announcement. "Why would you think that?" he asked, with dismay. "Both Red and Harve lost almost everything they had in divorce battles. They both needed money and more than likely committed insider trading."

Christina shook her head. "That doesn't make them killers. And remember—I said this is just my hunch," she reminded him. "I've got to find proof before I can come to any sort of conclusion about this case."

"Forget about the stock thing," Lex countered. "There's the pertinent fact that the men could have taken Dad to Mustang Island or even Aransas Pass for medical help. Instead, they wasted precious time taking him back to Corpus! They waited about calling the Coast Guard! Shall I go on?"

"I'm aware of all of that, Lex. And, yes, it does look suspicious. But when people are in shock, they don't always do the right thing. It's my job to keep an open mind to anything and everything. And I'm not ruling Harve and Red out yet. Are they thieves? It smells like they are. Murderers? I'm not sure."

"Wait a minute," Cook interjected. "You haven't mentioned anything about that dried-up, scrawny Lawrence. What about him?"

Sighing, Christina said, "The maid said he still hadn't returned from his business trip. But I'm pretty sure he's having the house help lie for him. I think he is home and is doing everything he can to avoid talking with me."

"The little bastard," Cook muttered.

Lex clucked his tongue in an admonishing way at the older woman, and Christina could hardly keep from smiling at the two. If Lex could only love her a fraction as much as he loved Hattie, then she'd be a cherished woman for the rest of her life.

Cook scowled at him. "Well," she reasoned, "he was a cold little man, but Paul went out of his way to include him in parties and outings. I never could cozy up to him myself. He'd come back here to the kitchen, wanting a certain type of cup or glass. Or he'd want hot tea when everyone else was drinking iced—as though he was special or something. I remember Paul saying the man was a hypochondriac. Ran to the doctor for every little ache. I think he felt sorry for him."

"So you're thinking Lawrence is hiding from you because he might know more than what he told the police?" Lex asked Christina.

"We'll see. I've got someone staking out his house. If he's seen, I'll know about it. And when he does show his face he'll have to answer a few questions," she told him.

Lex was about to ask her another question when his cell phone rang. He answered it immediately, uttered a few short words, then snapped it shut. As he rose to his feet, he said, "I'm sorry, Christina. That was Matt. A buyer that was supposed to be here this morning has arrived tonight. He's over at the Sanchez guesthouse, and I've got to go welcome him. I'll be back as soon as I can."

Christina nodded that she understood. "I have plenty of work to keep me busy."

He tossed her an apologetic smile, then strode quickly out of the room.

As Christina watched him disappear, Cook said, "Lex has been worried about you."

Surprised, Christina turned her gaze on the older woman. "Did he tell you that?"

"Not in those exact words. But I could tell."

The idea that Lex had expressed any sort of concern about her to Cook plucked at Christina's heartstrings. "Lex cares about people."

Cook grunted with amusement. "Some more than others."

Afraid to analyze what Cook meant by that, Christina sipped her coffee and let a few moments slip by before she said, "Cook, you probably know Lex better than anyone here outside of his family. Why do you think he's never married?"

Cook's dark eyes softened as she looked at Christina. "That's hard to say. When he was younger, he used to tell me that he never knew if the girls liked him just for him or for his money. It ain't no secret that many a woman in these parts would have liked to set up camp here in the Saddler house. Can't blame any of 'em for trying, though. A wife of his wouldn't have to want for anything."

"No. I expect not," Christina thoughtfully agreed. She'd had her own problems with guys viewing her as a money machine. But she'd learned to spot the users, and no doubt Lex had, too. "But Lex is a smart guy. At his age, I'm sure he can spot a woman like that a mile away."

"Sure he can. That ain't the reason now."

"What is?" Christina persisted.

"I ain't sure. I expect his daddy dyin' had something to do with it. After Paul left us, Lex wasn't the same. Oh, don't get me wrong. He still liked the ladies, and they all seemed to fall in love with him, but he never looked at them in a serious way. Instead, he threw himself into runnin' the ranch. That's all that seemed to matter to him." A wan smile touched her red lips as she reached over and patted the top of Christina's hand. "A farmer has to invest a lot of time and work into makin' a crop grow. It's the same way with love. Lex just never took the time to plant the seed."

And if he planted the seed with her, would it grow? Christina wondered. Or would it wither and die, the way her parents' love had died?

Sighing, Christina rose from the table and carried her coffee cup over to the sink. "Thank you for the coffee, Cook. And the conversation. Now I'd better get to work."

"Work! Tonight? You just got here."

Nodding, Christina started out of the room. "I feel as though I'm getting closer to finding some sort of clue to pull this case together. I've got to keep searching."

She was about to push through the doors, when Cook said, "Christina, I guess you know that Lex is like a son to me."

Pausing, she looked back at the table, where Cook was still sitting. "Yes. That's always been obvious to me."

"I want him to be happy," she said. "And I believe you could make him happy, if you were so minded to."

Cook's words were so unexpected, so touching, that Christina's eyes stung with tears and her voice turned husky. "Thank you for saying that, Hattie."

Cook winked. "Don't thank me. Just remember what I said."

Almost two hours later, Christina was sitting on the floor in her makeshift office, sifting through the last of the manila files, when Lex knocked lightly on the open door.

"I saw the light from the hallway and figured you were still working. Don't you think you should put that stuff away and rest? All of this will still be waiting here for you tomorrow," he reasoned.

Instead of agreeing to quit for the night, Christina held up a sheet of paper and motioned for him to join her. "Come here. I want to show you something."

He grinned. "Forget the paper. I'm still waiting on my hello kiss."

"You'll have to wait a little longer. I think I've found something."

Curious now, he walked over to where she sat and peered over her shoulder at the paper she was holding.

"What is this?" he asked.

"That's what I'm trying to figure out. Your father scribbled some sort of list on this company stationery. Do you recognize the woman's name listed at the top?"

"Edie Milton," Lex voiced out loud. "Hmm. That sounds familiar."

"Apparently, your father had some sort of connection to this woman," Christina said.

He snapped his fingers. "I remember. She was secretary to Coastal Oil's CEO at the time Dad worked there."

She looked at him hopefully. "What about now? Is she still there?"

"No. About a year after Dad died, she was killed in a car accident. Her brakes failed, and she crashed into the back of a semitruck."

Christina's interest was piqued even more. "Do you have any idea why Paul would have put her name on a list?"

Shaking his head, Lex began to read the list out loud. "Edie Milton, Red's office, Lawrence's broker, Harve's wife, bank statements, photocopies, tape recorder with a question mark. I wonder what this means at the bottom of the page? See disk."

Christina glanced over her shoulder, and as her eyes met his, she could see that only a part of his mind was focused on the paper in her hand. The hungry, smoldering lights that flickered in the brown depths fed her need to be closer, to feel the warmth and the comfort of his arms around her.

Clearing her throat, she said, "That's what I was about to ask you. If he meant a computer disk, I've not found any of them in these boxes. Is this absolutely all your father's things?"

His thumb and forefinger cradled his chin as he glanced at the mounds of papers and other articles that Christina had already sifted through. "Well, Mom gave Dad a desk and computer for a wedding anniversary gift one year. After he died, I guess the sentimental attachment made it difficult for her to keep using them. But she didn't want to get rid of them, either, so she had us store the desk away in the attic and the computer in a downstairs closet. She'd planned one day to go through the computer, just to see if there were any photos or things on there that the family might want. But that day has never come. Nicci mentioned the computer to her not long ago, and she promised to check it out. But you see how it is with Mom. Her plate is always full."

"Yes, I do see. But I wonder why Geraldine didn't mention those things to me," Christina mused aloud.

Lex shrugged. "She probably figured the stuff was personal, family-type things instead of work matters. Or she might have forgotten. Either way, it doesn't matter. If you're game for a little dust and heat, we'll go up to the attic and see if we can find anything."

"That would be great. If your father put information on a disk regarding this list, it might shed some light on what was taking place at the company. Especially with the stocks."

He frowned. "You keep coming back to those damned stocks. Why?"

"Because oftentimes one crime leads to another."

"That's what I was trying to tell you in the kitchen. We only have a suspicion that Harve and Red are guilty of insider trading. But if they are, they could be guilty of murder, too."

"It's possible. Even though I'm not getting those sorts of vibes from them. We need more information to prove that anything criminal took place. Let's hope something will turn up in the attic."

His heavy sigh whispered past her ear, and then his hand wrapped around her arm and tugged her around to face him.

"I'll take you to the attic in a minute," he said lowly. "But before we go, I want to talk to you. Not about Dad's case. About us."

Her heart shifted into high gear as she forced her eyes to meet his. "Lex, I'm not sure this is the right time."

"Why? You're not ready to hear that I've been thinking of you night and day?"

The soft huskiness of his voice sprinkled goose bumps across her skin. "Every woman likes to be remembered," she told him.

"And does every woman also like to be kissed?"

Her gaze landed on the hard curve of his lips, and suddenly her heart was pounding out of control as her body begged to get close to his.

"If the right man is doing the kissing," she murmured.

"Then maybe you'd better decide for yourself if I'm the right man," he whispered.

His head bent, and then his lips fastened over hers in a totally dominating kiss. In a matter of seconds, Christina was mindlessly winding her arms around his neck, fitting her body next to his. This connection to Lex was the very thing her heart was longing for, begging for, and she could resist him no more than a rose could resist the hot June sun.

In a matter of seconds, the kiss turned bold and hungry. Christina could feel her body heat skyrocketing, her lungs burning for breath. Sometime during the embrace, his arms had moved around her, crushing her against him in a way that plainly said how much he wanted her.

Her senses were about to dissolve into smoke when he finally tore his lips from hers and began to nuzzle the soft spot behind her ear.

"I've never had a woman get in my head the way you have, Christina. You've become an important part of my life. Does that mean anything to you?"

Torn by his question, Christina dropped her head and

fought to keep her tears at bay. "Of course, it means something to me," she whispered. "But I—oh, Lex, I don't want us to start an argument about this tonight. I just got back here."

And she was too vulnerable and weary to resist him, she thought. If he continued to kiss her, she'd soon be willing to let herself believe that an affair with him was better than pining for a love she'd never have.

Sighing heavily, he curled his hand around her upper arm and turned her toward the door. "All right. Let's go up to the attic and get this over with."

A few minutes later, in the upstairs hallway that led to several bedrooms, Lex pulled down a trapdoor and unfolded a built-in ladder.

"Better let me climb up first," he told her. "I know where the light switch is located."

"I'll be right behind you," she assured him.

Other than the kitchen, most of the ceilings in the ranch house were very tall. The height forced them to climb several rungs of the ladder. After Lex crawled inside the attic and switched on a light, he reached down and gave Christina a careful hand up.

"Whew! This place is stifling!" she exclaimed as she stood on her feet and looked around at the piles of furniture and stacks of cardboard boxes.

"There's an air conditioner in the window. I'll turn it on."

In a matter of seconds, cool air was blowing across the attic, though it would still be a while before it truly cooled the stuffy space. He walked back over to where Christina stood waiting. When he stopped in front of her, with only an inch or two separating their bodies, she could see his mind was still focused on her instead of on finding his father's things. And she didn't know whether to feel flattered or frightened.

"Is the heat up here doing something to your brain?" she asked. "We're not finding Paul's things like this."

"Downstairs, you wouldn't let me finish. And when I told you we'd come up here and get this over with, I didn't exactly mean finding Dad's things. I realize you don't want to talk about us. But I do."

His hands closed over her shoulders, and she groaned out loud. "Lex, for God's sake, now is not the time! I don't—"

He interrupted her words with a muttered curse. Then, sliding his hands to the back of her waist, he asked lowly, "What do you want from me, Christina? A declaration of love? Would that make you feel better?"

Anger sparked in her blue eyes. "I don't want or need empty words, Lex. I've had those before."

His mouth tightened. "I'm not *him,* Christina. So don't try to make a comparison."

She swallowed, then cleared her throat. His touch, his nearness, was messing with her mind, mixing up every thought, every word she tried to form on her tongue. "I'm sorry, Lex. I'm not saying you're the same sort of man as Mike was." She drew in a painful breath, then slowly released it. "He was a liar, and you've been nothing but honest with me. You've not promised me rainbows and I'd much rather have that honesty from you than hollow platitudes."

As Lex's gaze swept over Christina's troubled face, he wondered why everything inside him was pushing and pulling, making him feel as though he were going to split apart. He cared about Christina. More than he ever thought he could care for any woman. But was it love?

The only thing his heart was sure about was that he didn't want to lose her. He wanted their time together to go on and on. He wanted to be close to her and have her want to be close to him. If that was love, then he was a goner.

A heavy breath rushed past his lips. "If you don't want promises from me, then what do you want, Christina?"

Lex could see anguish swimming in the depths of her eyes, and then her lips parted as though she was about to speak. But long, tense moments passed before any words finally passed her lips.

"I don't know, Lex. I only know that I lost so much when I hung my hopes on Mike. When those hopes were crushed, my self-esteem crumbled along with them. So did my ability to trust—not just men, but everyone. I guess I need time. I need to see for myself that you're capable of having a serious relationship."

It infuriated Lex to hear her compare him to the sleaze that had dished out so many worthless promises to her. He'd seduced a few women in his time, but he'd never lied or led them to believe he was in love with them just to get them into his bed. And he wasn't about to start with Christina.

His hands splayed against her back as he inched closer to the front of her body. "I want you to assure me that you'll give us a chance, Christina. I'll court you. I'll show you—"

She interrupted his words by placing a gentle finger against his lips. "You're not the marrying kind, Lex. To even pretend that you are would only make you miserable, and that would make me miserable."

Wrapping his hand around hers, he pulled her finger away from his lips. "You couldn't know that. I don't even know myself whether I'm marriage material," he countered. Then, with a weary sigh, he moved away from her and stared, without seeing, at the stack of boxes in front of him. "You may not believe this, Christina, but by the time I became a teenager, I knew I eventually wanted to have a wife and family of my own. I wanted to be just like my father. He was always hugging and kissing my mother, making her laugh and making her happy. He was always there for us kids, guiding us, loving us and punishing us whenever we needed it. He and my mother together made an incredible team, and I wanted that very same thing for myself."

"That's what I meant, Lex, when I told you how blessed you were to have parents like yours."

Turning, he looked at her and, for a split second, felt his heart fall and crack, like a dove's egg spilling from its nest and hitting the ground. Pain splattered through his chest, the sort of pain he'd not felt since the moment he'd heard that he'd lost his father. His parents had been blessed to have shared so much love while they'd been together. The idea that he might be losing his chance at that kind of happiness with Christina pierced him deeply.

"I was blessed with great parents. But not with love," he said huskily.

Clearly perplexed, she walked over to where he stood. "What does that mean?"

Grimacing, he thrust a hand through his tousled hair. "My mother and father had a special love. And I wanted the same for myself."

"Wanted? You no longer want what they had?"

Groaning, he slid his hands up her back and curled his fingers over her shoulders. "It's not a matter of wanting, Christina. God knows I've tried to find love. Maybe that's the problem. Maybe I've tried too hard."

Her beautiful blue eyes were full of shadows as they studied his face.

"Are you trying to tell me that a man like you can't find anyone to love? That's ridiculous, Lex. You're a man with everything. Looks, wealth, intelligence. I'm sure women have been throwing themselves at you since your high school days."

"Oh, I've had more than one woman fall in love with me. And each time it happened, I tried like hell to love her back, to fall in love with her. But trying couldn't make it happen. I'd end up asking myself if I had the same deep feelings that my father had for my mother. Would I want her by my side for years to come? Would I give up my very life for her? The answers were always no. And then I'd feel even worse about the relationship and about myself. I'd wonder if I was completely heartless, and now—well, I'm not sure I know how to love. Or if I ever will feel that overwhelming emotion Dad felt for Mom."

Slowly, tentatively, her palms came to rest against the middle of his chest, and Lex wondered if she could feel his heart throbbing against her fingers. If she realized, even for one second, how much he wanted her.

"Lex, you can't *make* yourself feel something for another human being. Love comes to your heart on its own, without an invitation. Whether you want it or not. Maybe you ought to think about that."

Bending his head, he brushed his lips back and forth against her cheek. "I could think about it a lot better if you'd make love to me," he whispered huskily. "But I'm not going to push the issue with you anymore. A man has honor, too, you know. If we make love again, you're going to have to do the asking."

He released his hold on her shoulders and stepped back. Surprise flickered across her face.

"Do you really mean that?" she asked

"I'm not a wolf, Christina." Forcing a lightness he was hardly feeling into his demeanor, he gestured toward a narrow walking space between a pile of boxes and shrouded furniture. "And we've got work to do."

Lex turned to start down the walkway, only to have her grab him by the arm. Pausing, he looked at her expectantly, while secretly hoping and praying that she'd changed her mind about making love to him.

Clearing her throat, she said, "I just wanted to thank you, Lex. For sharing your feelings with me."

Sharing? No. He'd never been good at sharing his feelings. Not the deep ones, the ones that made him feel uncomfortable and vulnerable and even afraid. Was that what loving a woman was all about?

If it was, then Lex had just taken a mighty big fall.

Chapter Ten

Trying his best to push away the deflated feeling that had suddenly settled upon him, he said, "C'mon. It's getting late."

He nudged her shoulder, and the two of them began to wind their way through a maze of items, which had seemingly been forgotten. Layers of gray dust covered everything.

"It doesn't look as though anyone has been up here for a while," Christina commented.

"Mom sends the maid up here every now and then to get rid of some of the dust, but that doesn't happen very often," he told her. "They're always too busy with the regular household chores to deal with this."

At the far end of the attic, next to the outer wall of the house, Lex spotted his father's old work desk, which was covered with a pair of old tacked denim quilts.

"This was his desk," Lex told her as he removed the quilts and tossed them to one side. "There's still stuff in the drawers. And a few things in the boxes beneath it."

"I'll go through the drawers in the desk while you pull out the boxes," Christina suggested.

"That's fine with me."

After a few moments, it was clear to Christina that there was a substantial number of notebooks and folders filled with all sorts of work projects pertaining to the Sandbur stored inside the desk drawers.

"This is going to take a while," she said. "Do you think we could carry all of this down to my office? It would be much more comfortable going through it there. I have to go through each paper to be sure I didn't miss anything."

"Sure. Let's put everything in boxes and carry them over to the ladder," he agreed.

It took several minutes to get all the boxes safely down the ladder and into her office. Before Lex set the last one down in the corner of the small room, Christina was already sitting cross-legged on the floor, rifling through the paper material. And from the intense look on her face, Lex knew she wasn't planning on breaking for the night anytime soon.

"I'll go make coffee," he told her.

Looking up, she gave him a grateful smile. "That would be great, Lex. But you don't have to stay up and help. This is my job, remember?"

He slanted her a wry glance. "I assured Mom that it was mine, too. And Paul was *my* father. I want to help."

During the next half hour, Christina and Lex dug for anything that could possibly be connected to the list she'd found earlier this evening. But so far they'd found nothing but Sandbur papers.

"Here's a receipt," Christina said as she ran her gaze over the yellow square of paper. "For seventeen hundred dollars. Looks like it's from a jewelers in Victoria. In one corner Paul's written 'Keep hidden from Geraldine.'"

"What's the date?"

When she read the date, Lex chuckled. "That's two days before my parents' wedding anniversary. Dad probably bought her something in silver and turquoise. She loves the stuff, so he gave her a lot of it."

"Hmm," she said thoughtfully. "Everything I've discovered about Paul tells me he was a man who liked to make people happy."

Funny that she could see his father so clearly from just a piece of paper and yet she couldn't see how much Lex wanted, needed her. Or maybe she did see and had decided that wanting and needing just weren't enough to make her happy, he thought miserably.

"You're right. Everything he did, he did for others. He was a very unselfish man," Lex told her. "That's one of the reasons I never really suspected anyone of killing him. He was good to everyone. He didn't have any enemies."

"Yeah," she quietly agreed. "Just like I find it difficult to believe that Joel simply walked away from me—his only sibling."

The husky note in her voice had Lex glancing over to see her head was bent, and as he studied the crown of her shiny red head, he realized the mystery of her brother was still affecting her, the same way the puzzle of his father's death was now tearing at him. Christina had been right those few weeks ago when she'd first arrived on the Sandbur. Finding the truth was always important.

Forcing his attention back on the plastic container

jammed between his knees, he continued to rifle through the contents, most of which seemed inconsequential. Until he reached the bottom, where he discovered a flat cardboard tin box.

"Here's a box with something rattling inside," he announced, with a bit of excitement.

Jumping to her feet, she hurriedly crossed the small room to where he was sitting. "Open it! It's probably the disk!"

Lex quickly opened the box, and Christina drew in a sharp gasp at the sight of several computer disks nestled inside the container. "Oh my! Let's pray that one of these disks will hold some clues, Lex!"

Lex began to sift through the disks. All of them had paper labels attached to the front, but most of them had either one or two words that meant little or nothing to Lex and Christina.

"Right," he said. "Let's see if we can find anything important on them."

She pulled out the desk chair and slipped into it. While she brought the computer to life, Lex shoved the plastic disk into the slot on the tower. The task forced him to bend close to her shoulder, and it was all he could do to keep from turning his head sideways and kissing her cheek, burying his nose in her fragrant hair. He'd told her he was no longer going to press her to go to bed with him. But he knew the bold promise was going to be hell to keep. Especially whenever he was near her like this.

Clearing his throat, he said, "These disks are nearly twelve years old. There's no telling what sort of program they were written on."

"True," Christina agreed. "But we might get lucky."

Fifteen minutes later, Christina didn't feel lucky at all. Instead, she wanted to throw up her hands and scream. None of the five disks they'd discovered in the box would open.

"The frustrating part of this is that we don't even know if one of these disks is connected to the list your father made," she grumbled.

"That's true," Lex said from his perch on the corner of the desk. "That's why we've got to find a way to open and read them."

Christina sighed. "It shouldn't be this difficult to convert the text on a floppy disk," she said. "Do you have any more suggestions?"

He chuckled. "Me? Are you kidding? I keep track of my cattle sales on the computer, but that's the extent of my ability. What we need is a computer whiz."

A thoughtful frown crossed Christina's face. "I know a good one, but he moved away from San Antonio, and I have no idea how to contact him," she said glumly, then turned a hopeful look on him. "Do you know anyone? Some of your family?"

He searched his brain for a moment. "Mercedes. She's a whiz with computers."

"She's also pregnant," Christina added, "and suffering from horrible bouts of nausea and fatigue. It's already so late in the evening. She's probably in bed. Let's not bother her. Anyone else?"

Lex raked a hand through his hair as he tried to think. "Lucita. She uses them at school and at home." He glanced at his watch. "It's getting a little late, but she won't mind if I call her. She and Ripp are probably up with their new baby girl, anyway."

Pulling a cell phone from his shirt pocket, he searched until he found his cousin's number, then punched it in. After a couple of rings, Lucita answered it herself, and Lex quickly explained the problem to her.

"Do you have any suggestions for us?" he asked.

"The easiest way to make sure you can open the thing without destroying the contents is to use the same computer it was created on. Do you still happen to have Uncle Paul's old computer stored away somewhere?"

Lex glanced at Christina, who was watching him expectantly. "Yes. Mom put it away in a closet. Thanks for the suggestion, Lucita. And before I hang up, how's little Elizabeth?"

Lucita's soft chuckle was full of loving pride. It made Lex feel good to hear his cousin's happiness. She'd been through so much tragedy, it was time her life had changed for the better.

"Right now Ripp has rocked his daughter and himself to sleep. So all is quiet."

"You'd better get off the phone and enjoy it," Lex told his cousin. "I'll let you know tomorrow how we got along with the disks."

The two cousins quickly exchanged goodbyes, and as Lex slipped the phone back into his pocket, Christina asked, "How is Elizabeth?"

Surprised that her first question would be about the baby rather than a solution to the disk, Lex said, "She's fine."

A wistful smile touched her lips. "I'd very much like to see her and Nicci's daughter before I leave the ranch. Geraldine tells me they're both perfect little beauties."

"Humph. She looks like Ripp. And I don't see him as a beauty. But I guess Mom knows about babies and how they'll look when they grow to a more human size. I sure don't." He eased up from the desk and walked over to a window where lights from the bunkhouse flickered through the branches of a live oak.

Behind him, he could hear Christina pushing back her chair, and he glanced over his shoulder in time to see her standing behind the desk, stretching her arms above her head. The sight of her curvy silhouette struck Lex with desire, and he was amazed at how much he wanted to take her upstairs to his bedroom, to take her into his arms and forget everything else.

"This probably sounds crazy coming from someone with a mother who is unorthodox, to say the least," she said quietly, "but I happen to think I'd make a good parent. I've already learned all the things *not* to do while raising a child."

The dim lighting of the room left soft lights and shadows flickering across her face. As Lex looked at her, he could easily picture her with a baby in her arms, cuddling, loving, nursing.

"That night of the roundup, when we talked a bit about children, you seemed eager to be a mother. But you also seem like a career woman to me. Which one are you?"

Clearly unnerved by his question, she glanced down at the disks scattered across the desk. "I am a career woman. Because that's—that's all I have, for now."

The hollowness in her voice touched some place in him that was much too deep for comfort. He shoved his hands in his pockets and walked over to where she stood. "This Mike...did you want to have his children?"

Turning her back to him, she answered in a low, strained voice. "At one time. But I had no intentions of ever having a child out of wedlock." Sighing, she glanced over her shoulder at him. "If I'm ever lucky enough to have children, I want their lives to be totally different from mine. I want them to have two loving parents, who will always be around."

It was on the tip of Lex's tongue to tell her that he didn't want her having any man's child, unless it was his. Did that mean he wanted a deeper connection between them? One that would last forever? Did that mean he was falling in love with her? He'd never even imagined having children with any of the other women he'd dated.

The idea addled him, shook him right to the soles of his feet, and he was struggling to come up with some sort of reply to her comment when she thankfully changed the subject.

"What did Lucita suggest about opening the disks?"

He walked back over to where she stood. "I've got to fetch Dad's old computer from the closet. It should be compatible with the disks."

Ten minutes later, Lex carted the computer to Christina's office. Thankfully, it fired to life, and Christina didn't waste a moment thrusting one of the disks into the proper slot and punching in the cues.

They both held their breaths as the machine made a few ratcheting clicks, then continued to rattle and whir.

"This is taking forever," Lex complained after several moments passed without anything appearing on the screen. "Apparently, it's not working right."

"Be patient. This is an archaic machine. It takes time for it to work."

Nearly forty minutes later, after reading through three of the disks, they declared them totally unimportant and started on the fourth. By now, Lex was losing hope, but Christina was determined to keep searching.

"We have this disk and one more to examine," Christina told him. "If we don't find anything here, there may be more information in the rest of the things we brought from the attic."

Lex eased his hip off the edge of the desk and moved across the small room to the mound of things they'd carried down from the attic. "I suppose I could start looking for more while you read through that."

She tossed an apologetic glance at him. "It's getting late, Lex, and I know you have to be up early for work. You don't have to stay and help. Unless you want to."

He met her glance. "I want to," he said simply.

Christina's heart winced with emotion. No matter what happened in the future, it was sweet to have him working by her side, as though they were a real couple with mutual goals.

Sighing, she turned her attention back to the monitor and was immediately caught by the words that had just flickered onto it.

Leaning closer, she studied the typed information on the monitor. "Oh my," she breathed with hushed excitement, "Come here, Lex! I think we've found some sort of personal journal!"

Hurrying to the back of her chair, Lex hunkered down low enough to be able to read over her shoulder. After a few paragraphs, he felt himself going cold, and the words from the page rasped hoarsely against his lips as he spoke them aloud.

Tuesday. July 14th. I can't let my beloved Geraldine know what's going on. It would worry her sick. And if she did know, it might put her in danger. Her and

*our children. No, I must keep this to myself until I
get more evidence.*

Emotions suddenly strangled him and Christina continued on.

*Wednesday. July 15th. Slipped into Lawrence's of-
fice while he was at lunch. Worse than I expected.
He's getting info that only the president or CEO
should know. Suspect the latter's secretary—Edie.
Rumors she'll do anything for money. Met Lawrence in the hall. Not sure if he saw me come out
of his office, but I believe he did.*

Christina looked up to see that Lex was now leaning
his hip against the edge of the desk. His fingers were
kneading his closed eyes as though he was trying to rub
away what he'd just seen.

The sight of his anguish tore Christina, but she realized he couldn't avoid the truth. No more than she could.

"Maybe I'd better read the rest of this to myself," she
gently suggested.

"No," he said, his voice choked. "Go on. I want to
know."

Forcing her attention back to the screen, Christina
began to read aloud.

*Thursday. July 16th. Pushed my luck and searched
Red's office. Found nothing. Maybe the guy is more
honest than I thought. He showed up before I could
leave. I played it cool. Came up with the excuse that
I was hunting for a lost folder on pipeline corro-*

*sion tests. He didn't appear suspicious, and I felt
like a heel for spying on a friend.*

When Christina ended the longer passage, Lex
straightened to his full height and looked down at her.
"Is that all he entered on that day?"

"That's all. Here's Friday."

*July 17th. An hour before I left work, Lawrence
stopped by my office and invited me on a fishing
trip to Corpus tomorrow with him, Red and Harve.
He threw this trip together quick. Why now? Harve
was supposed to take his son to Dallas to visit relatives. And Lawrence didn't look me in the eye the
whole time he was inviting me. Dear God, the little bastard knows I've figured out he's brewing up
some sort of stock scheme. But whether Harve and
Red know about his plot is unclear. I'm thinking
about asking them point-blank. But what if they're
in on it with him? What might they do? Insider trading is hard to prove without concrete evidence. I
need time. But we're leaving the ranch at six in
the morning.*

With his fists gripped at his sides, Lex closed his eyes
and groaned. "Christina, you can't imagine how it feels to
hear the last thoughts that were going through my father's
mind just before he was killed. It's almost as though he
understood that he might be in danger, but he was more
concerned about exposing a crime than he was about
keeping himself safe."

"Obviously," Christina said sadly. "Here's the last entry.
It was made early on Saturday, before he left the ranch.

*Saturday. July 18th. Geraldine has suspected some-
thing is wrong for a couple of months now. She
seems to think it's my health or, even more ridiculous, an affair with another woman. Oh God, I'm
eventually going to have to tell her what this is
all about in order to ease her fears. She's the only
woman I will ever love.*

*Maybe it's a good thing she's away now, that she
took our daughters on a summer trip to Europe.
But I wish she was here. At least to warn her that
this fishing trip might turn out to be dangerous.
Lex and all the guys are over at Mission River on
roundup. I need to let him know about this before
I leave the ranch. But how?*

The last time Lex had cried was the day they'd buried
his father, but he was damned close to it now.

Christina's shocked gaze lifted up to his face. "Apparently, he didn't get a chance to send any sort of message to you."

He wiped a hand over his face. "Twelve years ago
most people didn't carry cell phones around with them,
especially when they were out in the middle of nowhere,
working cattle. And if he left a note here at the house,
no one found it."

"Oh, Lex, I—I'm so sorry. So sorry." Rising to her
feet, she gathered his hands in hers and held them tightly.

He swallowed hard, then sucked in a long, bracing
breath. "Somewhere in the deepest part of me, I feared
that my father had been intentionally killed. But the idea
was so horrible, so heinous, that I wouldn't allow the suspicion to bloom. I wanted to shove it all away, to pretend
that I'd lost him simply because the Lord wanted to take

him. But now—now I have to accept that it was nothing like that. He was murdered."

She nodded with grim certainty. "Circumstantially, this proves that there was a motive for his death and that it probably was plotted and planned ahead of time. But I'm afraid that none of this would prove the case in a court of law. Paul suspected that Lawrence knew he'd been snooping, but there's no hard evidence of insider trading, much less murder."

The misery in his eyes was suddenly swept away by outrage. "Lawrence—the wimpy little bastard—he was always scared of his own shadow. Apparently, he was afraid of my father, too. Afraid he would sic the law on him and expose his white-collar thievery." He jabbed his forefinger at the monitor screen. "Why wouldn't this journal work in a court of law? It was obviously written by my father!"

"But it doesn't offer proof, Lex, just theories. A good defense attorney would probably get it thrown out altogether. No, we've got to think of some other way to prove this murder happened."

Lex inclined his head toward the boxes of papers they'd carried down from the attic. "We still have a few more things to go through. Maybe we'll find something concrete."

"Perhaps," she mumbled. Then, stepping past him, she began to pace thoughtfully around the room. "But I'm doubting we'll find the smoking gun we need. In his last entry, Paul spoke of needing more time. Clearly, he didn't have enough evidence to go to the police, so it's unlikely there would be anything here."

Frowning with frustration, Lex glanced her way. "Then what do you propose we do next?"

She paused in her pacing as a plan began to form in her head. "From what I can gather from the autopsy report, the coroner believed Paul had some sort of incident with his heart before he went overboard, but he indicated the cause of death was drowning."

"Where is this leading?"

"I've been thinking about this for a good while now, Lex. Your father had no outward injuries. No blows to the head, no suspicious bruises or cuts. I think Lawrence gave Paul some sort of drug that disabled him. Maybe he stabbed him with a syringe or put it in his beer. I don't know. But I believed he drugged him."

Lex stared at her, confusion furrowing his brow. "No! That couldn't be right. The drug would have shown up in the autopsy. Wouldn't it?"

"Yes, if it had been something very obvious. But some drugs slip under the radar, and a corpse has to have extensive testing for each individual drug before it can be detected. In Paul's case, that testing wasn't done. Probably for county expense reasons—particularly when there wasn't a reason to think that a murder had occurred."

"If you believe he was given some sort of drug," he said, "where does that leave us now?"

Christina walked back over to where he was standing. "On the offensive," she stated flatly.

"What does that mean?" he asked warily.

"It means that I plan to draw Lawrence out. Force him to expose his crime."

His eyes widened. "I—don't think I like the sound of this."

She held up her palms in an innocent gesture. "Look, Lex, I'm not going to do anything foolish."

"That's right. We're going to contact the police. Now. Tonight!"

"Forget that, Lex! I know what a police department does with mere suspicions—they put them on the back burner. Especially when a case was pronounced closed a long time ago. No, I've got to draw Lawrence out and then call the police in on this. Otherwise, they'll have no reason for an arrest."

He reached out and snared a desperate hold on her upper arm. Christina's head jerked up, and her gaze clashed with his.

"And just how do you plan to get Lawrence to incriminate himself? The man is obviously smart. Like a fox. Smart enough to hide his crimes all this time. If anyone would have asked me before, I would have told them that Red would've been the most capable of harming Dad out of the three. God, that shows you how wrong appearances can be! Lawrence used his mousy demeanor to mask all his guilty tracks!"

The touch of his hand on her arm was sending electric impulses straight to her heart, causing it to thump even faster. "I'm going to visit Lawrence and let him know that I've discovered how Paul really died. I'm going to step out on another limb and tell him that I know he gave Paul the drug that caused his death—that we have iron-clad evidence against him."

"But we don't!" Lex countered.

"He won't know that I'm bluffing. I'm going to tell him that I'll take the evidence to the police—unless he agrees to pay Geraldine twelve million dollars. One million for each year that your father has been dead."

"Twelve million dollars! That's blackmail! What good is that going to do?" Shaking his head, he led her over to the desk chair and eased her down on the seat. "Have you gone crazy, Christina? None of this makes sense! We don't want money. We want the man arrested!"

She smiled patiently up at him. "That's right. I only want Lawrence to believe the blackmail scheme. He's not going to want to shell out the millions—he might not even have that sort of money now, anyway—so when he tries to make a deal, I'll be wired, with the police listening in."

Frowning, he framed his chin with a thumb and forefinger. "I don't like it. He might get wise, and then where would you be?"

"I'm a trained police officer, Lex, and I'll have the help of the San Antonio police to help me with the wiring. I can do this."

Groaning, he pulled her to her feet while his gaze desperately searched her face. "You won't be going to see Lawrence unless I go with you!"

Amazed by this protective attitude, Christina stared at him. "Absolutely not! Your presence would ruin everything. I want him to believe that Geraldine and I are the only ones who know about his crime. That she has the evidence locked away in a safe. He'll figure he can handle two vulnerable women. In the meantime, your mother is away for the next few days, so she won't be put into any sort of danger."

His eyes widened as though he couldn't believe her audacity. "But what about you? You're setting yourself up to be either harmed or killed! I won't allow it! I'll take this—" he jabbed a finger at his father's old computer "—to the police first!"

Christina frowned. "They didn't do a very good job on this case the first time. Are you willing to chance that happening again? To risk letting your father's killer remain free? I'm sure as hell not!"

He suddenly wrapped his hands over her shoulders, and Christina did her best not to shiver as his green eyes bored into hers.

"What I'm not willing to risk is your life, Christina!"

Something about his voice, the passionate blaze in his eyes made her almost believe that he cared about her, that he wasn't just trying to play macho man. But to let herself think in those terms would only be setting herself up for a far bigger hurt than anything Lawrence might try. Only a few hours ago, Lex had admitted that he'd never fallen in love before.

But there could be a first time, Christina.

Not about to let herself dwell on the tempting little voice in her head, she tried to reassure him. "I promise not to meet Lawrence in a secluded place with no one else present. Will that make you feel better?"

His jaw remained hard and unyielding, yet she could see the light in his eyes turning tender, and it was that gentleness that nearly had her breaking down and promising to let the authorities take over the investigation. But twelve years ago the authorities had missed their chance to find the truth. For Lex's sake, and for his late father, she had to bring it out in the open.

"Not really. I'd like to forbid you to get anywhere near Lawrence! But I'm smart enough to know those old-fashioned manly tactics won't work on you."

Her expression wry, she rose to her tiptoes and pressed a kiss on his cheek. "Thank you for understanding that much." With her feet back on the floor, she allowed her hand to slide up and down his forearm in a reassuring way. "This will all be over with soon, Lex. And your life will get back to normal."

Tonight the discovery of his father's journal had taken her a giant leap closer to finishing this case, Lex thought. And once that happened, she'd be leaving the Sandbur for good. How could his life be normal then? She'd changed his life. She'd changed him. So what was he going to do about it?

Chapter Eleven

"Hattie, I think this is the wrong thing to do!"

The next morning, long before daylight, the old cook stared in dismay at Lex as he angrily paced up and down the long kitchen.

"You need to remember that Christina is in charge of this investigation," she pointed out. "You ain't in no position to be telling her how to do her job. Think about it, son."

Lex skidded to a halt in front of Cook, who was standing at the kitchen counter, pouring a cup of coffee.

Grimacing, he jabbed the air with his forefinger. "Policemen have partners for a reason. No law officer in his right mind tries to handle a job alone. And that's just what she's doing."

Cook picked up a plate of bacon and eggs and carried it over to the kitchen table. "Quit preaching," Cook scolded.

Annoyed that the woman wasn't taking his side in things, he stalked over to the table and threw a leg over the bench that served as seating. "I'm only trying to save her neck."

"Humph," Cook snorted sarcastically. "That's not the way I see it."

"Hattie, you know I love you, but you'd better hush, or I'm going to lock you in the pantry."

"You'd have a hell of a time doin' that, sonny," Cook warned as she headed back to the gas range. "I may be gettin' a little age on me, but I can still put up a good fight. What you need to do is leave Christina alone and let her do her job."

Leave her alone. Maybe that was his whole problem right there, Lex thought grimly. He didn't want to leave the woman alone. He couldn't. When he tried to imagine himself moving on to other women, other interests, all he could see was a blank hole. Last night, when she'd returned from her trip to San Antonio, something had happened to him. He couldn't explain it or understand it. He'd wanted to find her ready to fall into his arms. That hadn't happened. She'd seemed even more resolute about not making love to him. And then, when she'd talked about her parents and children, about all the things she'd missed and longed for, he'd felt scales peeling from his eyes. Suddenly, he was viewing all his past relationships in a new light, and all the things he'd thought he would never want or care about had taken on new significance.

"Hattie," he said quietly, "last night we showed you Dad's journal. You read it. You know what happened. Lawrence is a killer."

Returning to the table, the old woman patted his back. "Lex, your daddy died a hero, and Christina will soon make sure that everyone knows it. I love her for that. And so should you."

Love Christina? Is that what this anguish inside him was? Is that why he was frightened out of his mind to let her get near Lawrence? Is that why he couldn't bear to think of this ranch without her on it? If all of this meant he was in love, then love was making him more miserable than he'd ever been in his life.

An hour later, as gray light was straining to get through the limbs of the live oaks shading the front yard, Lex followed Christina onto the front porch. The only thing she was carrying was a small beige handbag. Inside it was a pocketbook with identification, credit cards and a small amount of cash. The handbag also held a single tube of lipstick, a compact, a cell phone and a loaded snub-nosed .38 revolver.

"When do you expect to be back?" he asked as she paused on the top step.

"This evening. Hopefully before dark. If I can find Lawrence at home, this little tête-à-tête shouldn't take long." She looked at him, and the stark longing on his face made her want to fling her arms around his neck, to assure him that she would return safely. But what good would that do? she asked herself. It would only send him mixed signals, and every time she touched the man she lost a little more of her heart. If she didn't wind this case up and leave the ranch soon, there would be little of her heart to drag back to San Antonio.

"Christina, last night—I'm sorry I questioned your plans to nab Lawrence. You're the professional. And I was letting my personal feelings get in the way of everything else."

Even though the early morning temperature was past seventy, she felt the urge to shiver. She'd never expected him to utter such words to her, especially right now, and it shook the ground beneath her.

Swallowing, she glanced across the lawn to where one of the yellow curs was stretched out beneath the shade of a live oak. The dog appeared to be dead tired from rounding up cattle the day before, but if Matt or Lex was to whistle at him, he'd be up in a flash and ready to go. In many ways, Christina felt just like the cur. A word, a touch, a look from Lex made her long to please him, to give him anything and everything. Yes, she loved him. But she was determined not to fall in the hopeless trap she'd found herself in with Mike. She wasn't going to live on half-baked promises.

Glancing back at him, she tried to keep all emotion from her face. "And just what are your feelings, Lex?"

He moved forward, and her heart quivered as his fingertips came to rest beneath her cheek. "I think we need to talk about that, Christina. Tonight, when you come home."

Come home. If only he knew how much those two words meant to her. If only he meant them in the true sense of the word, she thought longingly. Her heart would sing loud enough to be heard in heaven.

"Yes," she said lowly, "we'll talk." Before she'd left Olivia's office, the other woman had pressed Christina to tell Lex that she'd fallen in love with him. Maybe her friend was right. Maybe it was time to let him see exactly what he was doing to her, and then she could see for herself if he really cared.

Her eyes closed against the emotions bombarding her,

and she felt his lips pressing first against her forehead and finally against her lips.

"Be very careful," he whispered.

The lump in her throat made it impossible to speak, so she simply nodded and hurried off the steps before he could see the tears welling in her eyes.

By mid-morning, after checking at Lawrence Carter's office and being told the man wasn't there, Christina was pulling into the elaborate drive circling the front of his house. To most regular folks, the place would be considered a mansion. Even so, the estate wasn't nearly as elaborate or stately as Red's or Harve's, and she wondered if the nervous little guy had deliberately kept his lifestyle modest so as not to draw attention to himself.

The front entrance was flanked by two tall Norwegian firs. As Christina punched the doorbell, she turned her back to the double doors and peered carefully around her. The neighborhood was extremely quiet, without so much as a bark of a dog to interrupt the twitter of birds perched on an ornate birdbath adorning the front lawn. Lawrence Carter lived in a very upscale area of the city, she thought grimly, and all at the expense of Paul Saddler's life.

"Yes? May I help you?"

Christina turned toward the young maid. "I'm here to see Mr. Carter. And before you tell me he isn't home, I know better. So you go tell your boss that I have some interesting information for him."

With a startled look, the maid said, "Yes, ma'am. Just a moment, please."

Leaving Christina standing on the porch, the maid hurried away, and then less than a minute later, a soft voice sounded behind her.

"Good morning. You were asking for me?"

Christina turned to see Lawrence had partially opened the glass door to stand on the threshold. His sparse hair was a drab ash-brown and plastered carefully to one side of his head. He was dressed all in polyester, as though his wardrobe was still stuck in the eighties. The brown slacks and yellow printed shirt looked hot enough to roast a pig.

"Good morning, Mr. Carter. I'm Christina Logan. I've been hired by Geraldine Saddler to look into her late husband's death. I'd appreciate it if you could answer a few questions I have. I promise not to keep you long." She glanced at her wristwatch as though she were in a great hurry. "I have a meeting across town, so I can't dally, anyway."

Faint annoyance registered on his thin face. "I…really don't have time." He glanced nervously over his shoulder. "My wife and I are getting ready for a little vacation."

"Oooh," Christina drawled pleadingly. "Couldn't you give me just five minutes? Red and Harve have already been so helpful in this matter. I'm certain your memory will be even better than theirs." Plastering a smile on her face, she stepped closer. "You don't have to invite me in. If you prefer, we can talk right here."

Clearing his throat, he quickly shut the door behind him and hurried her off the concrete porch. "Uh—let's go around to the side of the house," he suggested. "I really don't want my wife to hear this."

"I'm sure," Christina said under her breath.

She followed Lawrence along a cobblestone path until they reached a grouping of wrought-iron furniture sitting in the shade of a Cyprus tree. She'd promised Lex not to meet the man in private, but here on the lawn could hardly be called that. Especially when the wife was most likely watching from a nearby window and would clearly burst out of the house if she saw her husband physically attacking a woman.

Christina casually took a seat on one of the chairs, but the older man didn't appear to be interested in sitting. Instead, he stood a few steps away from her, his arms folded protectively against his scrawny chest.

"I'll be honest, Ms. Logan. My wife told me you'd asked to speak to me, and Harve already told me that you'd been around asking questions. Frankly, I don't get it. Everyone, even the police, knows that Paul's death was a terrible accident."

"Well, I'll be frank with you, Mr. Carter. Geraldine has never been satisfied with the police's theory. And some information has come to light that proves her suspicions right." She crossed her legs and smoothed her fingers down her calf. Lawrence Carter might be a nerd, but he was still a man, and she wanted him distracted. She wanted him to be totally off guard when she gave him the news. "And I thought you'd be interested in hearing it."

His eyes narrowed shrewdly, yet the sight of his Adam's apple bobbing up and down his skinny neck said she'd rattled his nerves.

"Information," he repeated slowly. "You mean—about Paul's death?"

"I'm not calling it a simple death, Mr. Carter. I'm calling it murder."

If she'd slapped the man on both sides of the face, she couldn't have shocked him more. The blood drained from his skin, leaving his face the color of a sick mushroom. His jaws flopped as though they'd suddenly become unhinged.

"Murder?" he finally echoed. A nervous titter rushed

past his colorless lips. "You must be mistaken, Ms. Logan. Paul wasn't murdered. The autopsy proved that."

With a catlike smile, Christina shook her head. "No, the autopsy proved that Paul drowned. But I've discovered why he drowned and I have the evidence to prove it."

She'd say one thing for him: the skittish little man did a quick job of gathering his composure. He smiled faintly and pleated his hands in front of him, as though he had all the time in the world to discuss the matter.

"If you have all that, why come to me?"

She tapped the air with the toe of her high heel. "Well actually, I'm not here to get your recollection of that day Paul was killed. I already know how it all happened. Paul drowned because he was unable to swim and save himself. You made certain of that when you gave him succinylcholine to make his muscles useless. In that condition, it was easy to nudge him overboard while the other two men weren't looking. And with just enough of the muscle relaxant in Paul's system, he'd never be able to swim. Never be able to take the facts of your insider trading to the police."

The man's sharp features hardened. "You're bluffing. I didn't leave any—"

She didn't hide her loathing as she stared at him, waiting for him to hang himself. "Go on, Carter. You were about to say you didn't leave evidence? If you want to take the chance that I'm bluffing, then by all means go ahead. But Geraldine has it safely tucked away, just waiting to hand it over to the DA. Unless…you're interested in making a deal."

To her surprise, the man marched toward her, his eyes filled with a menacing light. She discreetly opened the latch on her handbag and prayed he would decide to play it cool with her.

"What sort of deal?" he asked gruffly.

The question was a complete admission of guilt, but Christina wasn't surprised by it. She was just thankful her plan was working.

"Geraldine actually wanted you to rot away in prison, but I convinced her that was too easy. A man like you values his money far more than his freedom. So she's decided she'll sell you the evidence for the neat little sum of twelve million. One million for each year she's had to live without her husband."

The scrawny man's eyes began to bulge, and Christina realized he was struggling to keep from gagging.

"That's blackmail! And there's nothing you could have on paper that could incriminate me!"

Christina enjoyed giving him a sickeningly sweet smile. "Who said anything about it being on paper?"

His narrow eyes cut across her face, and then his gaze turned to the house behind them. Whether he was thinking about the luxurious digs or the loud wife inside was impossible for Christina to guess.

"I don't have twelve million dollars," he muttered.

"You work for a bank. You can get it."

Spluttering, he jerked his gaze back to her. "That sort of money is difficult to get. It might take weeks, even months!"

"Geraldine doesn't have that long to wait. We're giving you two days."

Pure venom was etched upon the man's face. "The woman doesn't need money! I've never had a fraction of what she's got!"

Rising to her feet, Christina said, "It's not the money

she wants. It's retribution. And this is her way of getting it." She pulled a card from her handbag and handed it to him. "Here's the time and place we'll make the exchange. Red Road Inn—it's just off I-10. Make sure you're there no later than three-thirty, or we're going straight to the police."

He read the information on the card, then jerked his attention back to her. "This is a busy truck stop! Are you crazy?"

"What sort of meeting place would you prefer? A quiet, dark alley? We're not the crazy ones here, Mr. Carter."

With that, she swished past him and began to walk toward the front of the house, where she'd left her car. Before she'd taken five steps, he caught up to her.

"Does anyone else know about this?" he asked in a hushed voice. "Has Geraldine told her family?"

Christina summoned all the acting ability she possessed. "Your questions are getting stupid—especially for a supposedly smart man like you. Do you think she'd want her family to know she's committing blackmail? No. Only she and I know, and that's the way things will stay. Once we turn the evidence over to you, that will be the end of this. You'll be out of Geraldine's hair, and we'll be out of yours. Deal?"

He hesitated, but only for a moment. "Yeah. It's a deal."

Later that night at the Sandbur, Cook served Christina and Lex a special dinner of shrimp jambalaya, along with an assortment of fresh seafood. The mini feast was meant to be a small celebration for uncovering the truth about Paul's death. But Lex hardly appeared to be in a celebratory mood.

Throughout the meal, he remained quiet and only picked at the food on his plate. God knew, he had plenty on his mind, Christina thought. He'd already expressed his concern over the plan she'd hatched to allow the police to catch Lawrence red-handed. But a part of her wondered if his sober demeanor might have something to do with the talk he'd requested that morning. He'd seemed so serious when he'd said they needed to talk. Was he going to tell her he'd lost interest?

He could have sex with most any woman he wanted. He doesn't need to wait around on you.

That little voice inside her head had pestered her throughout the drive back from San Antonio and was still gnawing at the back of her mind, making it impossible to think about little else.

Maybe she'd been wrong all along by putting a halt to their physical relationship. Their night together in Corpus had rocked her, transported her to the closest thing she'd ever experienced to heaven on earth. But even more than that, she'd felt a connection to Lex that superseded anything she'd ever imagined. She didn't want to lose that. Lose him. Yet she didn't want to let herself slip into a relationship that might never go further than the bedroom.

The two of them had just finished dinner and were retiring to the living room when Lex's sister Mercedes stopped by to discuss the progress they'd made on Paul's case. While she and her brother talked, Christina excused herself, stepped out on the front porch, and made a phone call to Geraldine to let her in on the plans she'd made with the authorities in San Antonio to attempt to catch Lawrence. Geraldine was eager to have the man convicted and put behind bars, but she was also concerned about Christina's welfare.

She reassured Lex's mother as best she could and ended the call just as brother and sister emerged from the house.

The pretty blonde walked over to where Christina was sitting on a wicker love seat.

"I wanted to thank you," she said, "for what you've done for our family. It was very hard for me to hear that my father was murdered. Especially by that creepy Lawrence. But at least we know the truth now."

Christina smiled gently at Lex's sister. "It's not completely over yet, Mercedes. But I promise I'll do everything I can to help convict the man."

"I wish I could be more help," Mercedes said as her hand slid protectively to her belly, "but I've not exactly been feeling up to par here lately."

Rising from her seat, Christina gave the woman's shoulders an affectionate hug. "You shouldn't worry about that for one minute. The important thing is to take care of yourself and your baby. Besides," she added impishly, "Lex has made a great Dr. Watson."

Mercedes turned an affectionate grin on her brother. "Lex is a man of many talents—when he wants to be. You should get him to tell you about riding broncs on the college rodeo team. He was a wild man in those days."

"Mercedes!" he scolded lightly. "Christina doesn't want to hear about that."

Laughing now, the woman stepped off the porch. "I'm heading home. Gabe will be worried if I don't show up soon."

She waved goodbye, then climbed in a black pickup truck and drove away.

Once she was gone, Christina sank back onto the love seat. "I like your sister very much. I wish I could've gotten to know her under better circumstances," she said.

Lex strolled across the porch and took a seat beside her. When he reached for her hand, Christina felt the gentle touch all the way to her heart, forcing her to bend her head to hide the emotion on her face.

"I like my sister, too, but I've been counting the minutes until we could be alone," he said quietly. "I was so relieved when I saw you return to the house this afternoon. I kept having this awful vision of Lawrence trying to harm you."

She looked up at him, and it suddenly struck her that he had been well and truly frightened for her safety. The idea made her heart want to hope that he might actually care for her, that his caring might one day turn to love.

"Whenever I told Lawrence that your mother wanted money, I honestly believed he could have put his hands around my neck and choked the life out of me. But I knew he wouldn't. The man is the epitome of a wimp. Still, he's dangerous. I have no doubt about that."

His fingertips began to slide gently against the back of her hand. "I kept imagining him following you, maybe trying to run you off the highway. Sometime back, that happened to my cousin, Luci. And she could have easily been killed."

"Well, thankfully, neither he nor anyone else followed me. Now we've got to hope that Lawrence will be desperate enough to show up at that restaurant with a satchel full of money."

With a slight shake of his head, he tightened his fingers around her hand and leaned his face toward hers. "I don't want to talk about that anymore tonight, Christina. I want to talk about you—us. You said you wished that you'd met Mercedes under different circumstances. Well I can't help but wonder how things would've been if we'd met some other way."

"I'm not sure we would have met. I live in San Antonio. You live here. Our paths would have probably never crossed."

"No. You're wrong about that. We were meant to meet." His eyes softly roamed her face. "I've been thinking a lot, Christina, about that night we spent out on roundup. You seemed like you really enjoyed being outdoors with the cowboys and the horses—and me."

She looked away from him while wondering why her heart was hammering, why she suddenly felt so scared. Funny how she'd faced plenty of dangerous situations during her years as a law officer, yet none of them shook her like the thought of never having this man's love. In some strange way, the night they'd spent sleeping in bedrolls under the stars had affected her even more than the night they'd actually made love. Something about sharing that part of his life had given her an even deeper glimpse of the man than being physically connected to him had.

"I did really enjoy it," she told him, then tried to laugh to ease the turmoil in her heart. "I thought sleeping on the ground would kill me, but it didn't."

His fingers continued to massage the back of her hand. "Not very many women like the ranch. Not after they're on it for any length of time," he admitted. "It's very isolated."

"I don't think of it as being isolated. The ranch is always full of activity—a little settlement unto itself."

His eyes grew warm and tender, but then he quickly looked away, as though he was embarrassed that he'd let his emotions show. "You're different, Christina. From the moment I met you, I realized that, but I didn't want to admit it to myself."

His gaze turned back to her, and this time there was a hint of regret on his face. "I've been looking at everything—at you—in the wrong way."

Christina couldn't stop her groan. "Oh please, Lex, don't expect me to believe that you've had this sudden emotional lightning bolt hit you and you think it's love. I—"

"I wasn't going to tell you that I love you. I wouldn't do that unless I was sure. I'd never lie to you like that. Besides, you wouldn't believe me if I said such a thing to you."

Feeling as if she was being torn to shreds, Christina rose to her feet and walked to the edge of the porch. With her back to him, she said, "I'm glad you realize that."

Long, pregnant moments passed before he moved behind her and slipped his arms around her waist. "I guess I want you to understand how important you've become to me."

Christina was suddenly trembling all over, as though she was standing on a dangerous precipice and the slightest breeze might topple her over. Everything inside of her was urging her to turn to him, to tell him that she loved him. Loved him utterly and completely.

I've had more than one woman fall in love with me.

The words Lex had spoken to her in the attic were suddenly spinning through her head, blocking the vow of love from spilling from her lips. He'd been told by more than one woman before that he was loved, but that obviously hadn't brought out any sort of commitment from him. And like he'd said, it certainly hadn't made him love the women in return. It would be stupid of her to think that telling him she loved him would somehow fix anything.

Bending her head, she pushed the next words past the lump in her throat. "I believe that, Lex."

Instantly, he turned her toward him and fastened his lips over hers. As soon as the soft, moist curves yielded beneath his own mouth, hunger struck him hard while, at the same time, joyous bells clanged in his head. She was the very thing his heart, his soul, had been searching for. He didn't just want this woman; he *needed* her.

Once the kiss threatened to completely steal his breath, he broke the contact between their lips and mouthed against her neck, "You can believe me, darling."

Suddenly her hands were in the middle of his chest, levering a small, cold gap between them. The forced separation had him looking questioningly down at her.

Her beautiful features were full of pain, and the sight totally confused Lex. The only time he'd ever made women miserable was when he'd given them a final goodbye. Yet Christina seemed to be just the opposite. The closer he tried to get, the more miserable she appeared to be.

And it suddenly struck him that making love to Christina, hearing her say their relationship would keep going, was only a tiny portion of what he wanted. He wanted her to be happy, deep-down happy. He wanted to love her. Really love her.

Oh God, what was happening to him? he wondered. And what could he do about it now? She'd never believe he was falling in love with her. He wasn't even sure he could believe it himself.

"I—um, I'm sure you're very tired," he said gently.

"And I've got a long day ahead of me tomorrow. Maybe we'd better say good night."

The relief on her face actually stung him, but then she gave him a wobbly smile, and his heart felt like a piece of iron that had just been thrown into a smelting pot.

"I think you're right," she said, then carefully eased out of his arms. "I've got a busy day tomorrow, too, getting things coordinated with the Bexar County Sheriff's Department."

To his surprise, her eyes suddenly turned watery, and for one split second, he started to jerk her back into his arms, to beg her to listen to what had just dawned in his heart. But she needed time, he realized. And he did, too. Time to figure out how to prove his sincerity, his newfound devotion to her.

When you love a person the way I loved your father, you just know.

A few days ago, Lex couldn't comprehend what his mother had once told him about falling in love. But now the meaning of her words was crystal clear to him. He loved Christina, and because he did, he saw more, felt more, understood things that had only been mysteries to him before. It was like stepping into a new world, and even though the path was scary, he realized he had to keep walking ahead.

With a wry smile, he stepped forward and ran a gentle hand over her red hair. "Don't worry, my sweet. Everything is going to be all right."

Chapter Twelve

The next day, in spite of spending most of her time on the telephone with one law official after another, Christina couldn't shake Lex's parting words of the night before.

Everything is going to be all right.

What had he meant by that? Had he been talking about the sting to catch Lawrence or their fragile relationship? God, she wished she'd questioned him before he'd left the porch and retired to his room.

She'd thought she'd have a chance to speak with him this morning, before the day became hectic, but her sleep had been erratic, and by the time she'd finally pushed herself out of bed and stumbled down to the kitchen for breakfast, Lex had already left the house.

Now it was growing late in the evening, and he was quite late in returning to the house. Cook had prepared supper, but Christina had told the woman to put the whole meal in the warming drawer. Sharing supper with Lex had become her favorite part of the day, and she wanted to enjoy it for the few evenings that were left before her time here on the ranch was over.

She was in the den, going over a folder of information she planned to hand over to the DA while watching the evening news on the television, when she heard a vehicle drive up at the west end of the house.

Since Lex always parked his truck in that area and entered the house through the kitchen, she jumped from the couch and hurried through the house to greet him. Just knowing he was home filled her with relief. For some unexplainable reason, she'd been anxious about his safety.

By the time she reached the kitchen, she expected to find Lex already there. But the room was empty, and an odd feeling of alarm sent a chill through her.

Something wasn't right.

She stepped onto the back patio and glanced toward the west end of the house. When she did, her breath caught in her throat as a sinking feeling hit the pit of her stomach.

Lawrence Carter was walking rapidly toward her. And from the cold look on his face, he wasn't on the ranch to make a deal. Why hadn't she guessed something like this could happen?

Of all the days for Lex to be delayed, this wasn't the one he would have chosen. He'd planned on being home early this evening to eat supper with Christina, and then he'd planned on taking her on a leisurely drive over a few parts of the ranch she'd not yet seen. She'd been working herself to the point of exhaustion over his father's case, and he wanted her to relax, to forget about Lawrence Carter and insider trading and paralyzing drugs. But mostly he simply wanted to be alone with her, with no outside distractions.

But one problem after another had occurred today, and he'd spent the past four hours helping the hands move a herd of cows from a pasture with a broken windmill to an area of the ranch where water was plentiful.

After unsaddling Leo and leaving him in the capable hands of a stable groom, Lex left the horse barn and started across the ranch yard on foot. Since most of the cowboys had already retired to the bunkhouse, the work area was quiet, and the long shadows of evening were beginning to cool the hard, packed earth.

Halfway to the house and lost in thought, he was faintly surprised when he suddenly spotted his teenage niece, Gracia, riding one of her cutting horses toward him. Normally, she rode those particular horses only in the practice arena.

When she reached him, she pulled her mount to a rapid stop. "You're out late this evening," she observed.

"So are you, young lady. Why aren't you riding in the arena?"

She shrugged. "Cloud Walker needed a bit more exercise, so I rode him down the road for a couple of miles." She wrinkled her nose and glanced back in the direction she'd just traveled. "Who is that creepy man at Aunt Geraldine's house? I saw him on the back lawn with Christina. They were walking together toward the house. Christina was smiling like he was a friend, or it looked like she was smiling. Is he a guest of hers?"

Icy fear rushed through Lex as his gaze shot past Gracia and on toward the house. "A man? What did he look like?"

She made a face of disgust. "Like a weirdo. Skinny and sorta old, with plastered hair. What is he doing here?"

Jerking his cell phone from the pocket of his jeans, he tossed it to the teenager, then took off in a run toward the house. "Call your father, and tell him what's going on!" he shouted over his shoulder. "Now!"

As Christina reentered the house, her mind was frantically searching for a way to deal with the maniac pointing an automatic pistol at her back.

Clearly, he had evil on his mind, and she had to think fast to come up with some diversionary tactic and snatch the weapon from him before he decided to use it.

As they walked into the kitchen, he asked gruffly, "Who else is in the house?"

"I don't know," she lied. "The maids could be upstairs."

Christina wasn't about to tell him that Cook and the maids had left hours ago. With Lex still out working, there was no one here but her.

"What about that old crow that calls herself a cook?"

Christina silently promised herself she was going to make this man pay for every evil thing he'd said and done to the Saddler family.

Looking over her shoulder at him, she said, "If you mean Hattie, she's retired for the night."

He grunted. "What about Geraldine and Lex?"

"I—I don't know. This is a big house."

After mouthing a few curse words, he waved the gun toward the swinging door that led from the kitchen to the rest of the house. "I'll take care of them if I have to. Where's the safe in this dump, anyway? In Paul's office?"

"Why would Paul still have an office? He's been dead

for twelve years. Thanks to you," she said coldly. "The safe where Geraldine locked the evidence is in the den."

Actually, the only safe in the house that Christina was aware of was located in the den. And she only knew about that one because Lex had opened it one night to show her a set of antique jewelry that had belonged to his great-grandmother.

"Take me to it! And be quick about it!"

He shoved the gun against the back of her rib cage in an effort to hurry her along. Christina shouldered through the swinging doors, then made a sharp right down the dimly lit hallway leading to the den. Normally, the room was the least used in the house. Mostly, Geraldine stuck to her office in the parlor, and Lex used the kitchen for his hangout. As for Christina, she spent most of her time in her little office, but this evening she'd taken her work with her to the den so she could relax on the couch while she waited for Lex to return. Now she took hope in the fact that the den was located at the rear of the house.

If she could throw something through the picture window that faced the back lawn, there was a slight chance one of the men at the bunkhouse would hear the crash and come to investigate.

"You're making a mistake, Lawrence," she said in a deliberately calm tone. "This isn't the way to handle things."

"You said I was stupid, but you and that bitch Geraldine are the stupid ones for thinking I'd give you a cent," he gritted between clenched teeth.

She'd been stupid, all right, Christina thought, for not anticipating this deranged man making a counter move of some sort. But not in a million years would she have thought he would be crazy enough to show up here at the ranch. Damn it! If only she had her revolver. But it was stashed away in the bureau in her bedroom.

When they reached the den, she could see the room appeared the same as when she'd left it. A table lamp shed a small oval of light near the end of the couch where she'd been working. Nearby, on a small table, a fat scented candle flickered in the semidarkness. Next to it, she'd dropped the folder jammed with notes concerning Paul's case when she'd hurried out to meet Lex. Across the room on the television screen, a female news anchor was continuing to read the evening news and the wild thought that her homicide might be the next story flashed through Christina's mind. But just as quickly, she flung the thought aside.

She had to fight in every way she could against this man. She had to stay alive—to stay with Lex as long as she could, in any way she could.

Deliberately drifting toward the table where the papers were lying, she pointed to the farthest wall of the room. "The safe is over there. Behind that shelving with the horse sculptures."

Following close on her heels, he said, "Get over there and open it! And don't try anything funny!"

"I wouldn't dream of it," Christina said sarcastically. "I'm not a funny kind of girl."

"Shut up and do as I say!"

Intensely aware of the gun pointed at her back, she walked ever so slowly across the room. All the while, her mind was racing, calculating. The only things she recalled being inside the safe were the jewels and a few old maps of the ranch from when Lex's great-grandparents had first purchased the property. There was nothing that she could use to fake Lawrence out, even for a few seconds.

Stall, Christina! Stall! Lex will surely be home soon!

The moment she reached the table, she paused and glanced back at her captor. His gaze was roaming wildly about the room, as though he expected someone to jump out of the shadows. For a second, while his eyes darted away from her, she considered leaping straight at him, but before she could make a move, his eyes were back on her, demonic and threatening.

"Did I tell you to stop, bitch?"

"No. But I don't have the combination to the safe. Besides, all the evidence isn't here. Geraldine has some of it with her."

"Then you'd better get it here. Fast!"

Christina stared at him. If he was brazen enough to walk into the house without knowing how many people might be inside, then he'd obviously come here prepared to shoot whoever got in his way.

"She isn't here. She's away—on a trip with her daughter."

"You're lying! She was supposed to meet me tomorrow at the Red Road Inn. She couldn't be away on a trip."

Seeing she'd obviously confused him, she pressed her luck even further in hopes that she'd get him so distracted, he'd lose his focus. "I don't know where you got the idea that I would allow Geraldine to join our meeting," she told him. "The only guests at that little party were going to be you and me, buster."

His face turned beet-red; then he sucked in a deep breath and shook like a wet dog. Christina braced herself, half expecting him to lift the pistol and fire at her.

Instead, he surprised her by suddenly taking on an eerily calm appearance.

"I'm beginning to see right through you," he said, with smug certainty. "You and Geraldine don't have any evidence at all. You're running a bluff. You can't prove anything."

Even as he spoke, Christina's mind was racing ahead, planning her next move. "That's where you're wrong. Geraldine has a tape recording that Paul made a week before you killed him. We discovered it among his things only a few days ago. He was having a very enlightening discussion with Edie Milton."

His beady eyes widened, telling her that she'd momentarily stunned him.

"Edie? She didn't know anything about Paul's little accident."

"Maybe not, but she knew you were a major thief. That's why you disabled the brakes on her car so that she'd be killed on the interstate."

He sneered. "She was greedy—like you. That's why I killed her. She wanted more hush money. But I know she wouldn't have talked about the stock thing. She didn't want to go to the penitentiary any more than I did."

"She did talk," Christina flung back at him. "And so did the person who got the succinylcholine for you. Geraldine has a signed confession."

His mouth fell wide open. "Gloria Westmore? How— she moved out of the state! You couldn't have known about her!"

Suddenly, from somewhere inside the house, the sound of a door opening and closing caught Lawrence's attention, and his gaze swung toward the open doorway.

Christina realized it was her one opportunity to make

a move. All at once, she snatched up the burning candle and leaped to one side, out of the path of the gun barrel.

From the corner of her eye, she could see him turning, aiming and preparing to shoot. At the same time, she ducked and flung the candle straight at the picture window. The heavy metal holder crashed through the glass, while the burning wax stuck to the lace curtains, sending small flames crawling up the fabric.

"Christina!"

Lex's yell sounded somewhere in the hallway and she tried to shout a warning back at him, but the sound of her voice was blocked out as Lawrence fired the pistol at her.

Wildly, she dove behind an armchair while across the room the flames were growing, filling the room with smoke. She could hear bullets sinking into the padded upholstery as Lawrence began firing the gun into the chair. At that moment, Christina wondered if she'd ever see Lex again.

When Lex shot into the room, he hardly noticed the fire consuming the curtains and spreading across the outside wall. Through the smoke, he could see Lawrence, the gun raised in his hand as he moved straight at Christina.

Fear and rage poured through Lex, blinding him to everything except saving the woman he loved. Like a rampaging bull, he charged across the room and, with a flying leap, tackled the man from behind.

When both men hit the floor, the impact was so great that Lawrence lost his grip on the pistol and the weapon went sliding across the tile. Lex immediately rolled Lawrence on his back, with plans to smash his fist into the other man's face, but he was already knocked unconscious and was as limp as a rag.

Seeing the man was no longer a threat, Lex rose to his feet and shouted, "Christina! Where are you?"

Sobbing with relief, she emerged from behind the chair and stumbled straight into his arms.

"Oh, Lex, thank God you finally got here!"

"Christina! Oh, Christina!" His hands raced wildly over her face and down her arms as he tried to reassure himself that she was alive and safe. "Are you okay? The bullets didn't hit you?"

"I'm fine—you came just in time!" She glanced down at Lawrence. "We'd better get him and get out of here. This room is about to go up in flames!"

Nodding, Lex quickly leaned down and grabbed Lawrence by the front of his shirt, while nearby Christina scooped up the pistol to use as evidence later.

"Some folks would find it easy to leave him here to burn," Lex muttered as he began to lug the man toward the door. "But, damn it, I can't!"

Christina reached to help him drag the man's dead-weight, and as her gaze met his, love flooded her heart. There was no point in denying it anymore.

For more than a century, the Saddler house had endured storms, lightning strikes and grass fires. With the ranch miles away from any sort of fire department, barns and sheds had often burned to the ground, but the house—the ranch's very heart—had always remained like a proud, invincible fort.

Lex, Matt and several cowboys from the bunkhouse desperately fought the flames with garden hoses and saddle blankets. Miraculously, they managed to contain the fire until a fire truck arrived and doused it completely.

But not before the flames had eaten through the outer wall of the den and onto the vine-covered patio.

Later, after the sheriff had carted Lawrence away in handcuffs and the commotion around the house began to settle down, Christina and Lex stood staring at the charred ruins. The sight of his beloved home so scorched and scarred filled her with regret, and she dropped her head onto his shoulder and began to sob.

"I'm so sorry about the house, Lex! I caused the fire with the candle. But I had to do something—he was going to kill me."

Groaning, he let his arms circle around her, and as he held her tightly against him, he buried his face in her thick curls. "It doesn't matter, darling. Even if the whole thing had burned, it wouldn't have mattered. As long as you're safe."

Lifting her face up to his, she tried to smile through her tears. "Thank you for saving my life," she whispered.

"No thanks necessary," he murmured.

He was bringing his lips down on hers when Matt rounded the corner of the house and cleared his throat loudly.

"Uh—Lex? Sorry to interrupt. But Ripp is waiting out front to take you and Christina to the sheriff's department. Sheriff Travers is waiting to speak with you."

Lex glanced regretfully at Christina. "We'll take this matter up later," he whispered in her ear.

Hours later, just before the sun was beginning to break through the branches of the crepe myrtles surrounding the sheriff's office in Goliad, Christina and Lex finally left the building and headed back to the Sandbur.

The night had been long and weary, but neither one

of them had really noticed or complained. Lawrence had been booked on several charges and was finally behind bars, where he belonged. Christina and Lex had spent the past couple of hours giving information to law officials. However, this was only the beginning of the testimonies they'd need to give. Due to the multicounty crimes involved in the case, the Texas Rangers had been called in to deal with the investigation. This afternoon, after Christina and Lex had a chance to rest, they'd be supplying depositions, along with Paul's journal, to the Rangers.

"I just don't get it," Lex said to Christina as he turned the truck onto the main highway that would take them to the Sandbur. "Why did Lawrence show up at the ranch instead of waiting to meet you at the restaurant? He was taking a hell of a chance at being caught."

Christina crossed her legs to get more comfortable, and as she did, she noticed that soot stains from the fire smeared down the front of her jeans. When she'd thrown the candle at the window, some of the hot wax had fallen onto the back of her hand. Blisters had now risen on her skin, but the minor injury couldn't begin to dim the satisfaction she'd felt when they'd watched a deputy escort Lawrence to a jail cell. She'd not captured him exactly the way she'd planned, but he was now where he belonged, and he'd live the rest of his life behind bars. She had no doubt about that.

"Because he didn't have the money to obtain the evidence from us. So he figured he was going to have to get it the only way he knew how—by force. I should have suspected as much, but I was expecting him to show up at the Red Road Inn with a stalling story, which would have been enough on its own to incriminate him."

"Don't feel badly. None of us were thinking Lawrence had enough guts to show his face on the Sandbur. But we should have been considering his sanity rather than his guts," he said, then glanced thoughtfully over at her. "There is something else you can explain to me, though. How did you guess that Lawrence had administered succinylcholine to Dad? That's not an everyday, common compound that normal folks are familiar with."

"After I read the autopsy report on your father, the fact that he had no cuts or contusions kept haunting me. From photos and the information Geraldine had given me, it was obvious that your father was a strong, strapping guy. Over six feet tall and well muscled. Lawrence wouldn't have physically been able to toss him over the side of the boat, and even if he'd tried, the scuffle would have caused some minor injuries, not to mention alerted the other two men that something was happening. Without any outward signs of struggle on Paul's body, it stood to reason that he'd been disabled in some other way."

Lex nodded. "I see the deduction. But the succinylcholine—how did you come up with that particular drug?"

"Lawrence worked as a chemist for Coastal Oil. True, that's different than working in medicine, but he still had a good idea of how chemicals and compounds worked. When he decided to kill your father, I calculated that he'd probably looked for a drug that would be hard to trace, but possible to get his hands on without throwing up too many red flags. Yet in the end, Lex, I guess you could say that I simply made a lucky guess."

His profile grim, Lex shook his head. "Now that Lawrence is talking his head off to try and save his hide, we know that he had a nursing friend that worked in surgery. Apparently, he'd given her a pretty penny to steal a bottle of the stuff from the hospital pharmacy. He'd given her some cock-and-bull story about his wife needing it to relax a bad back, and she'd bought the excuse."

"Her name was Gloria Westmore. I tricked him into letting her name slip while he was holding me at gunpoint in the den," Christina said.

He cast her a wan smile. "You're smart. You know that?"

"I try to be," she said, smiling back at him. But was she really? Christina asked herself. Maybe she was clever about solving crimes and finding people that didn't want to be found. But had she been smart to fall in love with Lex? Her heart kept singing yes, but her mind continued to worry and wonder.

Just before they'd entered the jail, they'd had a couple of minutes alone together, and Lex had used the time to hold her close and kiss her briefly on the lips. He'd told her how terrified he'd been when Gracia had told him about seeing Lawrence and how relieved he'd been when she'd stumbled out from behind the armchair. Yet he'd not said anything about loving her or about what the future might hold for their relationship. But then, maybe expecting that the trauma of the night might have made him open his heart to love was taking hope a bit too far.

She was lost in her thoughts when he said, "There's still one more thing that I'm curious about, Christina. Red and Harve, how did you know they were innocent in all of this? All the evidence made it appear that they were probably just as guilty as Lawrence in the stock scheme and Dad's death. I believed they were."

Realizing it was important for him to understand what had happened all those years ago when his father died, she answered, "Red and Harve couldn't fake the emotion they showed when they spoke to me about Paul's death.

Even after all this time, it shook them to recount the story about their late friend. Both of them said they were so frightened when your dad went overboard that they panicked and ended up making stupid decisions about where to take him for medical help. As for the stock scheme, they simply believed that Lawrence had given them a smart tip, and they'd always been grateful to him for giving them the chance to make a pot of money. Neither man had any clue that Lawrence had stolen private company information and used it to his own advantage."

With a disbelieving shake of his head, Lex said, "What's so incredible to me, Christina, is that Dad went out of his way to be a friend to Lawrence. How could he have turned on him?"

She reached across the console between them and touched her hand to his. "Greed overtakes a lot of people, Lex. But Lawrence is going to pay for his greed now. And in the end, that's what matters the most."

"Yeah," he said softly. "You were so right that first evening you came to the Sandbur, when you spoke to me about finding the truth. It is more important than I could have ever imagined."

By now they had reached the ranch house and Lex parked the truck at the side of the structure, next to Christina's vehicle. Gray daylight was spreading across the yard, and behind them she could hear the guys from the bunkhouse heading down to the barns. The realization suddenly hit Christina that this place had truly become her home. She couldn't picture herself going back to the city and not waking up to Cook's breakfasts, to Lex sitting across the table from her, or to riding across the range with him at her side, eating off a chuck wagon and listening to music around a campfire. Yet now that

Paul's case was wrapped up, she had no right or reason to stay here, and that fact was settling in the bottom of her heart like a heavy chunk of ice.

"Finally. We're home and alone," Lex said. Then, with a weary but happy grin, he reached over and pulled her toward him. "And I have about a thousand things I want to say to you."

Home. Could he possibly know how wonderful that sounded to her? The soft look in his eyes sparked a bit of hope in Christina, and she studied his face closely as he drew his head down to hers.

"A thousand?" she whispered. "That's…quite a bit of talking."

"I thought talk was what you wanted."

Hearing him say that he loved her had once seemed so important. But after last night, after going through moments when she'd not known whether she'd remain alive to say anything to Lex, she realized that words weren't always the solution. And right now Christina felt it was more important to show him that she trusted him and how very much she wanted him in her life.

"I've had time to think about that, Lex," she murmured, then reached beneath his arm and pulled the latch on the door. "And we—uh—need to go inside. I want to—show you something important."

His brows peaked with interest, but he didn't ask questions as he climbed to the ground, then helped her out of the cab.

As they walked to the house, she wrapped her hand around his and didn't let go even after they were inside.

The kitchen smelled like fresh coffee, telling her that Cook was already in, but not anywhere to be seen in the room. As much as Christina loved the other woman, she was glad she wasn't around. Christina didn't want anything or anyone to interfere with her plans.

"Where are we going?" he asked as she led him out of the room, down the hall and on toward the staircase. "Don't you want breakfast?"

"We can eat later. This is too important," she told him in a hushed voice.

"There's no reason for being so quiet," he reminded her as they reached the second floor. "Mom is still with Nicci, and they won't be home until later this evening. We're not going to disturb anyone."

"That's right," she told him with a wicked smile, then opened the door to her bedroom and tugged him inside.

After she carefully shut the door behind her, she turned to him and saw a puzzled, almost comical look on his face.

"Christina, what are you doing?"

Smiling seductively, she said, "I thought you were an experienced man, Lex Saddler. Do I have to spell this out to you? I want us to make love. And you told me if that ever happened again, I'd have to do the asking."

The confused look in his eyes suddenly turned somber, and she began to tremble as he cupped his hands around the sides of her face.

"Why now, Christina?"

Regret filled her eyes. "Last night, when Lawrence started firing his gun, I was terrified he might kill you or me and that I—I'd never have the chance to tell you how much I love you."

His eyes full of wonder, he cupped his hands against the sides of her face. "You love me? Oh, Christina! Why didn't you tell me before?"

Why hadn't she? Now that both of them had been in

serious danger of losing their lives, her reasons seemed ridiculous. "I didn't think it would matter to you. You'd said that other women had fallen in love with you and they'd not gotten any love from you in return—I thought I'd be just one more."

The soft glimmer she saw in his eyes looked incredibly like love, and the idea set her heart pounding loudly in her ears.

"Oh, darling, you're not just any woman. You're my life!" Bending his head, he brought his lips next to hers. "The night we found the disk with Dad's journal, I realized I loved you, but I couldn't tell you. I knew the words would be just that—words to you and nothing more. And then last night—when I saw Lawrence about to shoot you, I was seeing my world ending right before my eyes. Christina, weeks, months, years wouldn't make me love you any more than I do now. I want you to be my wife. You've got to believe me."

Incredible joy swept through her, and she stared at him in amazement. "Your wife? I never thought I'd hear you say those words."

"Well, I'm waiting to hear your answer. I'm waiting to hear you say you can be happy living here on the Sandbur, with me."

She blinked rapidly as happy tears filled her eyes. "I love the ranch, Lex. I was just wondering how I was ever going to be able to leave it—and you. Now I won't have to. I've been a career woman for over ten years, and it's been good. I want to be a wife and mother now—more than anything."

Laughing now, he lifted her off her feet, then allowed the front of her body to slide against his until the tips of her toes were back on the floor and her lips were hovering beneath his.

"Dad has been gone for nearly twelve years," he said gently. "When you first came to the ranch, I never believed that you—that the two of us together—would ever discover what really happened to him."

"But we did," she whispered happily.

"Yeah, we did. But more than that, Christina, you walked into my heart and showed me what it's like to love. Really love. And, honey, I may not be the ideal husband or the greatest dad, but I'm damn well going to try."

"That's all I'll ever ask, my love," she whispered, then with a happy sigh, closed the last breath of space between their lips.

Epilogue

Six weeks later, on a hot September evening, the wedding guests finally vacated the backyard at the Saddler house. The band had carried away the last of their instruments, and now all that was left behind of Lex and Christina's reception was a few family members, the mess and plenty of fond memories.

Weary, but very contented, Geraldine wandered through the empty tables piled high with leftover food, dirty plates and champagne glasses. She'd just seen her last child married, and though she expected some mothers would be feeling a bit melancholy, she wasn't. Her prayers had finally been answered. Lex had found and married the love of his life.

Pausing at the end of one of the tables, she looked toward the arbor, where Nicci and Mercedes were sitting in lawn chairs, visiting with their cousins. It hadn't taken long for carpenters to repair the fire damage to the house, but it would take the honeysuckle much longer to grow back, and she hated that.

"Looks as bare as a newborn's butt, don't it?"

Geraldine looked toward the voice to see Cook sitting alone beneath the branch of a live oak. The older woman was all dressed up in red silk and black high heels, and her long hair was wound in an elaborate chignon at the back of her head. In spite of her age, she still looked beautiful, and earlier this evening Geraldine had had to fight back sentimental tears as she'd watched her son dance Cook around the dance floor.

"Yes, it's bare," Geraldine replied. "But it will grow back."

She walked over to where Cook sat on a wrought-iron bench and sank down next to her.

"Why are you sitting here alone? Are you feeling okay?"

Cook snorted. "Course, I am."

"You're not fretting about all this mess, are you? I've hired extra workers to take care of all this, and remember, you have Caroline to help you now."

Gabe's childhood friend had finally managed to make the move down here to the ranch from Oklahoma City. So far, she was working out well, and Cook had already grown fond of the woman and her young son.

Cook waved a hand through the air. "I'm not worried."

Geraldine sighed. "It was a lovely wedding. Christina looked gorgeous. They should have a nice honeymoon on Padre Island. The Morgans are letting them stay at their private beach house. They'll have the place to themselves for a whole week."

"Mmm. It was a beautiful wedding," Cook agreed. "And I was glad Christina's parents managed to attend. Her mother came off as a bit of a floozy, but she seemed happy for Christina. Guess that's the important thing. I liked her dad. He was quiet, but in a nice way."

Geraldine smiled wistfully. "I'm glad Retha and Delbert were able to attend this special event in their daughter's life. I only wish Christina could find her brother. I got the feeling that she was thinking especially about him today."

"Well, sure," Cook agreed. "She'd like to have her brother back."

"Oh. Speaking of finding people," Geraldine said. "Did you hear that Ripp and Mac have started searching for their missing mother? They've gotten a clue as to her whereabouts, and they've decided they need to find out what really happened with her. The same way I needed to know about Paul."

"Everybody needs family," Cook murmured sagely.

Both women went quiet after that; then suddenly Cook bent her head and pressed a handkerchief to her eyes. Rattled by the sight, Geraldine laid a comforting hand on the woman's shoulder.

"Why, Hattie, are you crying?"

She sniffed. "I can't help it. Lex has always been my little boy, too."

Smiling now, Geraldine patted her back. "He's not going anywhere, Hattie. He'll be living right here like he always has. And think of it this way. We'll have babies in the house again."

Lifting her head, Cook dabbed away her tears and chuckled. "That's right. And knowing Lex, it won't take him long to get them here."

* * * * *

Laura Marie Altom of Tulsa, Oklahoma, is a bestselling, award-winning author of over forty books. Her works have made several appearances on bestseller lists, and she has over a million books in print worldwide. This former teacher and mother of twins has spoken on numerous occasions at both regional and national conferences, and has been married to her college sweetheart for twenty-six years. Visit her online at lauramariealtom.com.

Look for more books by Laura Marie Altom in Harlequin American Romance—the ultimate destination for romance the all-American way! There are four new Harlequin American Romance titles available every month. Check one out today!

THE RANCHER'S
TWIN TROUBLES
Laura Marie Altom

This story is dedicated to all of the friends
who've helped raise our kids.
We couldn't have done it without you!

Special thanks to Tom and Karen Gilbert,
Lynne and Tony Beeson, Susie Thornbrugh,
Kim Blackketter, Jennifer Crutchfield,
Jackie and John Butts, Karen and Jack Lairmore,
and Melinda and Scott Taylor. This list is
woefully incomplete, but to fill it, I'd need a
dedication book, rather than page!

Chapter One

"Are we talking about the same kids?" Dallas Buckhorn shifted on the pint-size chair in his twin daughters' kindergarten classroom. Across a sea of tiny tables, his angels made dinner in a play kitchen. "Because my Betsy and Bonnie wouldn't pull a stunt like that."

Uptight Miss Griffin folded her hands atop her desk, full lips pressed into a frown. Her mess of red curls had escaped the clip at the back of her neck, making her look more like a pretty teen ditching school than a full-grown woman teaching it. "While the girls are lucky to have such wonderful support in their corner, the fact remains that our classroom fish tank had an entire package of Kool-Aid spilled in."

"Yes, well—" the tank's purple-tinged water forced Dallas to hide a chuckle "—the goldfish don't seem to mind."

"Since you seem to find this amusing, Mr. Buckhorn, you should know that at the time of the incident, your girls were the only children near the tank."

"Yeah, but did you see them do it?"

After a moment's hesitation, she said, "No, but—"

Dallas stood. "Ever heard the phrase 'innocent until proven guilty'?"

"Sir, with all due respect, this isn't the first time I've had trouble with the girls. They've put popcorn in the plants to see if it would grow. Sneaked cafeteria food into our play kitchen and served it to other students. The last time it rained, they—"

"Whoa." Slapping on his Stetson, Dallas said, "I don't know what you're trying to prove, but *if* Bonnie and Betsy did all of that, sounds to me like my babies aren't getting adequate supervision. Maybe you're the one who needs looking after?"

On her feet, hand on her hips, she said, "I've been teaching for ten years, and trust me, I understand it must be hard hearing your children are, well…out of control, but—"

Dallas whistled for his girls and they came running. "Did you two do that to the fish tank?" He pointed at the purple mess.

"No, Daddy," they said in unison, big blue eyes wholly innocent.

"There you have it." Hands on their backs, he ushered them to the classroom's door. The smell of crayons and paste was bringing on a headache. Clearly, the teacher must've been sniffing too much of that white school glue. "My girls said they're not guilty. End of story. Before we go, want help switching out the water?"

* * *

"He didn't?"

"Oh, he did." Josie put a carrot stick to her mouth and chomped. The teachers' lounge was blessedly quiet. Josie had a free period while her kiddos were in music class, and she was enjoying every minute with her best friend, Natalie Stump. "Then he and the girls cleaned out the tank. Does that sound like something the father of innocent children would do?"

"No…" Natalie struggled opening a chocolate milk carton. "But it was decent of him. Maybe he has issues with admitting his daughters are anything less than perfect." As Weed Gulch Elementary School's counselor, Natalie was always on the hunt for the best in people. Usually it was a trait Josie found endearing, but in this case, already dreading the twins' next stunt, she wished Dallas Buckhorn would wake up and see the delinquents he was raising.

Josie sighed. "Bonnie and Betsy are adorable and funny and smart, but both have an ornery streak I can't control."

Without thinking, Josie took Natalie's milk carton and had it open in a flash.

"You're good at that."

"I'm pretty sure I had a college course on stubborn milk."

"Nothing on tough-to-handle kids though, huh?"

"More than I can count, but these two beat anything I've ever seen. If they continue this trend, by third grade they'll be robbing ice cream trucks."

Natalie chuckled. "They're not *that* bad."

"Mark my words. This isn't the last time I'll have to confront their father."

"At least he's hot." Natalie poked Josie in the ribs with an elbow. "Makes for interesting parent/teacher conferences."

Heat crept up Josie's neck. *Hot* was hardly the word. The man was more in the realm of drop-dead gorgeous, but that was beside the point. "He's all right. If you go for that sort." Tall, spiky dirty-blond hair, faded jeans that hugged his—

"Don't even try lying to me. That porcelain skin of yours gives everything away. You're blushing."

"Am not." Josie had always hated her pale complexion, and this was just one more reason why.

The late September day was warm and she dumped her last two baby carrots in the trash, preferring to stand in front of the window air-conditioning unit, letting the cool wash away her crabby mood.

"Let's hope," Natalie said, thankfully off the subject of the all-too-handsome cowboy, "this conference will serve as a wake-up call for the girls. I bet you don't have a lick of trouble from now to the end of the year."

"Betsy! Bonnie! Get down from there before you break every bone in your little bodies!" Beneath the mammoth arms of an oak that'd no doubt been on the playground since before Oklahoma had even been a state, Josie stared up at the Buckhorn twins. How had they scrambled so high? Especially so fast? The first branch was a good five feet from the ground. She'd cautioned the three teachers on playground duty to keep a close watch on the twins, but they reported that the girls had been too quick for anyone to stop them.

"Look at me!" Bonnie shouted, hanging upside down monkey-style at least fifteen feet in the sweltering air.

"I can do it, too!" Betsy shouted, much to Josie's horror, mimicking her sister's stunt. It'd only been a week since Josie's meeting with their dad and already they were finding mischief.

Winded, Natalie approached. "I called their father and he's on his way. Luckily, I caught him on his cell and he's already in town."

"Thanks," Josie said. "Obviously, the girls aren't listening to any of us. Maybe he can talk them down."

"I'm flying!" Bonnie shouted, holding out her arms Wonder Woman-style.

"I wanna try," said pigtailed Megan Brown who gazed at her classmate with wide-eyed awe.

"Me, too!" All of a sudden at least twenty of the thirty-eight kindergarteners outside stormed the tree base. Jumping up and down, they looked more like a riotous mosh pit than normally well-behaved children at recess.

"Bonnie, please," Josie reasoned, hand to her forehead shading her eyes from the sun. "Halloween's almost here and you wouldn't want to ruin your costume with a big cast, would you?"

"Casts are cool!" Jimmy Heath declared. "I broke my leg sledding and Dad painted it camo."

"Ooh…" was the crowd consensus.

Josie prayed for calm.

What she got was a black truck hopping the parking lot curb to drive right up onto the playground. At the wheel? Dallas Buckhorn. Lord, how she was well on her way to despising the man. If only he'd taken her seriously during their conference, maybe this wouldn't be happening.

"Come on, kids," Natalie and the other teachers on duty called, gathering the children a safe distance away.

Dallas positioned the truck bed beneath the girls before killing the engine.

Exhaust stung Josie's nose, causing her to sneeze.

"Bless you," he said with a grin and a tip of his hat.

"Daddy!" Betsy cried, waving and swinging. "Look what I can do!"

"I see you, squirrel." He didn't look the least bit disturbed. "Now, before you give your teacher a heart attack, how about you two scramble down from there and into the truck bed."

"Do we have to?" Bonnie asked. "I thought you said it was good for us to climb trees?"

"It is, but that's at home. My guess is that around here, shimmying up things taller than you breaks more than a few rules." Wearing faded jeans, weathered boots, a red plaid Western shirt and his trademark hat, the man looked nothing like a father. More like a cowboy straight off the range.

Natalie leaned over and whispered, "He's so handsome it hurts to look at him."

"Hush," Josie snapped. "This is a serious situa—"

Before she could finish, the girls had scurried down the tree and into the truck bed. Legs rubbery with relief, Josie finally dared to breathe.

"See?" Hat in hand, Dallas sauntered over. His walk was slow and sexy. "My girls are expert climbers. I don't even know why you called."

Stunned by his cavalier attitude, she wasn't sure what to say. "Do you realize that if either of your girls had fallen from that height, they could've been seriously injured?" Focusing on maintaining a professional demeanor, Josie folded her arms and adopted her best stern-teacher expression.

"Do you realize my angels have been climbing trees practically since they could walk? I've taught them to look out for weak branches and to always plan a safe path down." Checking his truck to find the girls surrounded by their friends, he added, "I've done some of my best thinking in an old oak—at least back when I was a teen."

Shaking her head, she struggled for the right words. "You have to understand that at school, there has to be a certain order to our days. There are procedures and rules to follow—not just for safety, but for learning. By condoning your daughters' actions, you've essentially told every student out here that disobeying my rules and those of the other teachers is not only perfectly okay, but heroic."

"Aren't you exaggerating just a tad?" When he held his thumb and forefingers together, he winked. Despite the fact that he was handsome enough to make her swoon, she held her ground. The man was impossible and he brought out the worst in her. She was never this much of a shrew. But she'd also never encountered someone quite so blind. As young as the twins were, now was the time to temper them. Not in their teens when they were already lost.

"No, sir," she said, standing her ground. "I don't believe I am."

"Then where does that leave us?"

Us? She rationally knew he meant their parent/teacher relationship, but the way he'd slapped his hat back on his head, hooking his thumbs into his back pockets had her distracted. What was wrong with her? Why was it that whenever she came within five feet of him her mind turned to mush and her body fairly hummed? She was finished with men, so why wouldn't her body obey?

"Um…" Josie cleared her throat. "Perhaps you might want to spend time in the classroom with the girls. You'd be able to see what's expected of them, and then pass along the message."

Blanching, he said, "Me? Back in school? No, thanks. Tell you what I will do, though. The girls and I will have a nice, long talk about no more recess tree climbing."

"I'd appreciate it," Josie said, unsure what to do with her hands.

Thankfully, seeing how most of her class had joined the twins in the bed of Dallas's truck, she had more pressing matters than the study of how his hat brim's shadow darkened his eyes.

"Mom," Dallas said that night, chopping an onion for her famous spaghetti sauce, "I swear that woman's going to drive me off the deep end."

Georgina Buckhorn sighed. "How can you be intimidated by a scrap of a kindergarten teacher?"

"Who said I was intimidated?" Dallas brought the knife down especially hard on the onion. The clap of metal hitting the wooden cutting board echoed in the big country kitchen. "She annoys me, that's all."

"Because she speaks the truth and you don't want to hear it?" Her back to him, she took pasta from an upper shelf. She was a tall woman made all the more imposing by the top knot she'd formed with her long silver hair. Once upon a time, before Dallas lost Bobbie Jo, his mother's words had been gold. Now, Dallas resented her for getting into his parenting business. It wasn't that they didn't get along, but where the girls were concerned, they no longer shared the same values.

She always nagged him about the twins needing more

discipline, but to his way of thinking, wasn't losing their mother enough? Bobbie Jo had died giving them life. Her last whispered words had been for him to put his love for her into their babies. By God, every day since, that was exactly what he'd done.

Bonnie and Betsy were his world and no one—not his mom and certainly not their teacher—was going to tell him he was a bad parent when his life was dedicated to their happiness.

"Dallas," his mother said, dropping pasta into a pot of already boiling water on the industrial-size stove, "this house is big enough that we can generally keep to our own business, but this is one matter on which I refuse to bend. Sunday night, I caught Betsy drawing all over her bathroom mirror with lipstick. *My* brand-new Chanel lipstick I bought last time we were in Tulsa. When I asked her to help clean the mess, she crossed her arms, raised her chin and flat out told me, 'no.' Now, does that sound reasonable to you?"

After dumping diced onions into a pan filled with Italian sausage, he took the cutting board and knife to the sink, running them both under water.

"Ignore me all you want, but deep down, you know I'm right." Behind him, her hand on his shoulder, she added, "A large part of being a good parent is sometimes being the bad guy. You have to set boundaries. Just like your father and I did with you and your brothers."

"That's different. We were all hell on horseback."

She snorted. "Like your girls are any different because they're only riding the ponies you gave them for Christmas?"

"They love those cuties." He bristled. "Ponies topped the twins' Santa lists."

"Doesn't make it right." She stirred the meat and onions that'd started to sizzle above a gas flame. "Clint Eastwood topped my wish list, but you don't see me out gallivanting, do you?"

"You're impossible." His back turned, he took his work coat from the peg mounted alongside the back door. "I'm going to check the cattle."

"Mark my words, Dallas Buckhorn, you might temporarily hide from this situation, but sooner or later you have to deal with your rambunctious girls."

"Got it! And it only took ten strokes." Friday evening, on hole seven of Potter's Putt-Putt, Natalie performed a little dance that revealed she may have had one too many beers. It was the monthly ladies' night and judging by the slew of high scores, none of the foursome would give the LPGA a run for their money any time soon.

First grade teacher, Shelby Foster, pushed the counselor aside. "Let me show you how a professional does it..."

"Professional what?" Cami Vettle, the school secretary teased in a raunchy tone.

For the first time in what felt like weeks, Josie truly laughed and it felt not only good, but long overdue. Until just now, she hadn't realized how much stress she'd been under. She'd always loved her job. As a general rule, kindergarteners were a lovable, trouble-free bunch. Oh, sure, she'd dealt with plenty of mischief, but nothing as regular and confounding as the stunts of Betsy and Bonnie Buckhorn.

"You all right?" Natalie asked while waiting for the other women to take their turns.

"Sure," Josie said, swirling her plastic cup of beer.

"Why wouldn't I be?" White lights decorated the course's trees. With temperatures in the seventies, it felt as if fall had finally arrived. Shrieks of laughter mingled with top-forty music blaring from loudspeakers. The mouthwatering scent of the snack bar's trademark barbecue normally would have her stomach growling. Lately, though, she'd been so consumed with dreaming up a delicate way to manage the twins that she forgot to eat.

"You seem awfully quiet. Man trouble?" Tipsy, Natalie leaned on Josie's shoulder. Beer mingled with her pretty floral perfume, again causing Josie's lips to curve into a smile.

"Oh, sure. As you full well know, I haven't been with a man since Lyle, and he was a disaster."

"Only because you didn't put an ounce of effort into the relationship. It's been four years since Hugh died. He wouldn't want you to be lonely."

Then why had he left her?

"Who said I am?" Josie swigged her beer. "And who are you to talk? When's the last time you went on a date?"

"Two weeks ago, thank you very much."

"Your turn," Cami said to Josie, writing down her score. "What are you two gossiping about?"

"Nat, here, says she had a date." Josie centered the ball on the putting mat before giving it a swat. It landed between a giant plaster frog and a rubber lily pad. "You believe her?"

"Absolutely. It was with the UPS man. I witnessed him asking her in the front office."

"Impressive…" Josie's shot landed her ball ten feet from the moat's dragon. Sighing, she stepped over a second lily pad to set up for stroke three.

"Kind of like Betsy and Bonnie's dad. Whew." Cheeks

flushed, Cami fanned herself with the scorecard. "He's gorgeous."

"Don't look now, but he's also headed this way..." Natalie downed the rest of her beer.

Upon meeting Dallas's penetrating stare, Josie hit her ball all the way to Hansel and Gretel's cottage on hole fourteen!

Chapter Two

"Ladies…" Dallas tipped his hat to Bonnie and Betsy's teacher and three other women he'd seen around the girls' school. "Nice night to be on the links."

The tall brunette laughed at his joke.

"Miss Griffin?" He was intrigued by the notion that she found it necessary to hide behind a pine.

"Please," she mumbled, ducking out from behind a particularly full bough to extend her hand, "outside of school you can call me Josie."

When their fingers touched, he was unprepared for the breeze of awareness whispering through him. It'd been so long since he'd noticed any woman beyond casual conversation that he abruptly released her. Just as hastily broke their stare. Had she felt that shift from the ordinary, too?

"Hi, Miss Griffin!" The twins and three of their more giggly friends danced around him.

"H-hi, girls," their teacher said. Had she always been so hot? Maybe it was the course's dim lighting, but her complexion glowed as pretty as his mama's Sunday pearls. Her hair hung long and wild, and she wore the hell out of a pair of faded jeans and a University of Oklahoma sweatshirt. Red cowboy boots peeked out from beneath her hems. "You all having a party?"

Bonnie nodded. "Daddy's letting us have a sleepover for doing good on our chores all week."

"Congratulations," their teacher said, patting Bonnie's back. "I'm proud of you."

His daughter beamed.

Feeling damned proud for having raised such a conscientious sweetheart, Dallas couldn't help but grin.

"Come on, Daddy." Betsy yanked his arm. "Let's play."

"Well..." Oddly reluctant to end the conversation, Dallas said, "Guess I'd better get going. My bosses are calling."

The look Josie Griffin shot him was painful. As if she disapproved of his play on words. The notion annoyed him and brought him back to the reality of who she was in the grand scheme of things. A teacher he'd never see again after his girls' kindergarten graduation. As for his musings on her good looks? A waste of time he wouldn't be repeating.

"I know, Kitty, the man's infuriating, isn't he?" While Josie's calico performed figure eights between her legs, she spooned gourmet cat food onto a china saucer. Her friends thought she was nutty for lavishing so much attention on her pet, but Kitty had been a wedding gift from Hugh. When she one day lost her furry friend, she didn't know what she'd do. In some ways, it would be like losing her husband all over again.

Another thing her friends nagged her about was worrying over events that hadn't happened. But surviving the kinds of things Josie had taught her to never underestimate any signs—no matter how seemingly insignificant.

"Kitty," she said, setting the saucer on the wide-planked walnut floor, "do you think when it comes to the Trouble Twins I'm looking for problems where there are none?"

Chowing down on his Albacore Tuna Delight, Kitty couldn't have cared less.

Josie took a banana from the bowl she kept filled with seasonal fruit. Usually in her honey-gold kitchen with its granite counters, colorful rag rugs and green floral curtains, she felt warm and cozy. Content with her lot in life. Yes, she'd faced unspeakable tragedy early on, but as years passed, she'd grown accustomed to living on her own. She shopped Saturday morning yard sales for quilting fabric and took ballet every Thursday night. Even after three years, she was the worst in her class, but the motions and music were soothing—unlike her impromptu meeting with Dallas Buckhorn.

Her hand meeting his had produced the queerest sensation. Lightning in a bottle. Had it been her imagination? A by-product of beer mixed with moonlight? Or just Nat's gushing praise of the man's sinfully good looks catching like a virus?

On Monday morning, as calmly as possible, Josie fished for the green snake one of her darlings had thoughtfully placed in her desk drawer. Finally grabbing hold of him—or her—she held it up for her class's squealing perusal. "Don't suppose any of you lost this?"

Bonnie Buckhorn raised her hand. "Sorry. He got out of my lunch bag."

"Yes, well, come and get him and—" Josie dumped yarn from a nearby plastic tub, and then set the writhing snake inside. "Everyone line up. We're taking a field trip."

"Where? Where?" sang a chorus of hyper five-year-olds.

Bonnie took the tub.

"We're going to take Bonnie's friend outside—where he belongs."

"You're not letting him go!" Bonnie hugged the yellow tub, vigorously shaking her head.

"Yes, that's exactly what we're going to do. Now, I need this week's light buddies to do their job, please."

Sarah Boyden and Thomas Quinn scampered out of line to switch off the front and back fluorescent lights.

"Please, ma'am," Betsy said while her twin stood beneath the American and Oklahoman flags crying, "Bonnie didn't mean to put Green Bean in your desk."

"Then how did he get there?" Josie asked as Sarah and Thomas rejoined the line.

"Um…" She gnawed her bottom lip. "He wanted to go for a walk, but then he got lost."

"Uh-huh." Hands on her hips, miles behind on the morning's lesson, Josie said, "Get in line. Bonnie, you, too."

Bonnie tilted her head back and screamed.

Not just your garden-variety kindergarten outrage, but a full-blown tantrum generally reserved for toy store

emergencies. A whole minute later she was still screaming so loud that her classmates put their hands over their
ears.

Josie tried reasoning with her, but Bonnie wouldn't
hush longer than the few seconds it took to drag in a fresh
batch of air. Not sure what else to do, Josie resorted to
pressing the intercom's call button.

"Office."

"Cami!" Josie shouted over Bonnie, "I need Nat down
here right away."

The door burst open and Shelby ran in. "What's
wrong? Sounds like someone's dying."

Nat followed, out of breath and barely able to speak.
"C-Cami said it sounds like someone's dying."

Both women eyed the squirming student lineup and
then Bonnie. Betsy stood alongside her, whispering
something only her twin could hear—that is, if she'd
quieted enough to listen.

"Sweetie," Josie tried reasoning with the girl, "if
Green Bean is your pet, I won't let him go, but we'll
have to call your father to come get him. You know it's
against our rules to bring pets to school when it's not for
show-and-tell."

For Josie's ears only, Natalie said, "Hang tight, I'll get
hold of her dad."

"Look," Dallas said an hour later. When he'd gotten
the counselor's call, he'd been out on the back forty, vac-
cinating late summer calves. It was a wonder he'd even
heard his cell ring. "If my girl said the snake got in her
teacher's desk by accident, then that's what happened.
Nobody saw her do it. Even if it did purposely end up
there, how many boys are in her class? Could one of them

have done it?" In the principal's office, Bonnie sat on one of his knees, Betsy on the other. Stroking their hair, he added, "I'm a busy man. I don't appreciate having to come all the way down here for something so minor."

Principal Moody sighed. With gray hair, gray suit and black pearls, she looked more like a prison guard than someone who dealt with children. "Mr. Buckhorn, in many ways schools are communities. Much like the town of Weed Gulch, our elementary maintains easy to understand *laws* by which all of our citizens must abide. I've been at this job for over thirty-five years and not once have I seen a snake *accidentally* find its way into a teacher's desk. I have, however, encountered fourteen cases of students placing their reptiles in various inappropriate locations."

Hardening his jaw, Dallas asked, "You calling my girl a liar? Look how upset she still is…"

Bonnie hiccupped and sniffled.

The woman rambled on. "All I'm suggesting is that Bonnie may need additional lessons on appropriate classroom behavior. Perhaps you and your girls should schedule a conference with Miss Griffin?"

Imagining the girls' scowling teacher, Dallas wondered what kind of crazy dust he'd snorted to have found her the least bit attractive. "As I'm sure you know, I went to this school, as did all of my brothers. My parents never had to deal with this kind of accusatory attitude."

"You're right," the principal said. "When y'all attended Weed Gulch Elementary, a simple paddling resolved most issues."

After ten more minutes of way-too-polite conversation that got him nowhere, Dallas hefted himself and his girls to their feet and said, "These two will be leaving now with me. Is there something I need to sign?"

The principal rose from her regal leather chair. "Miss Cami in the front office will be happy to show you the appropriate forms."

With everyone back at their tables, chubby fingers struggling with the letter *F,* Josie sat at her desk multi-tasking. On a good day, she managed putting happy stickers on papers, entering completion grades on her computer and eating a tuna sandwich. On this day, she had accomplished only one out of three.

What sort of excuse would the twins' father make this time? He and the girls had been in the principal's office for nearly an hour.

"Missus *Gwiffin?*" She glanced up to find Charlie Elton sporting a broken crayon. He also had several missing teeth. "I *bwoke* it. *Sworry.*"

"It's okay, sweetie." Taking the red oversize crayon, she peeled off the paper from the two halves. "See? Now it works again."

"Thwanks!" All smiles, he dashed back to his table. Toothless grins were what led her to teaching. Feeling that every day she made a positive difference in her students' lives was what kept her in the career. Which was why the tension mounting between herself and the Buckhorn twins was so troubling. Not only was her job usually satisfying, but school was her haven.

This weekend, she'd head into Tulsa. There were some school specialty stores that might have classroom management books to help with this sort of thing.

The door opened and in shuffled the sources of her seemingly constant consternation.

"Hi," Josie said, wiping damp palms on her navy corduroy skirt. "Everything all right?"

"Daddy brought Green Bean's jar," Bonnie said with enough venom to take down a pit viper.

"He's got Green Bean and said we need to get our stuff and go home." Betsy looked less certain about their mission.

"Sure that's what you want to do?" Josie asked, kneeling in front of the pair. "We're learning about the letter *F*."

"Let's stay," Betsy said in a loud whisper. "I *love* to color new letters."

Bonnie shook her head.

At the door, their father poked his head in. "Get a move on, ladies. I've still got work to do."

"Okay, Daddy." Hand in hand, the girls dashed to their cubbies.

"Mr. Buckhorn…" Josie rose, approaching him slowly in hope of attracting as few little onlookers as possible. Today, the stern set of his features made him imposing. Miles taller than he usually seemed. Yet something about the way he cradled Bonnie's pet in the crook of his arm gave him away as a closet teddy bear when it came to his girls. Trouble was, as a parent—or even a teacher—you couldn't be nice all the time. "While the twins gather their things, could we talk?"

He gestured for her to lead the way to the hall.

With the classroom door open, allowing her a full view of her diligently working students, Josie said, "I'm sorry this incident inconvenienced you. Pets are only allowed on certain days of the year."

"So I've heard." *Cold* didn't come close to describing the chill of his demeanor.

"Yes, you see, the snake itself is the least of our problems."

"*Our* problems?" He cocked his right eyebrow.

"Bonnie and Betsy—well, in this case mainly Bonnie, but—"

"Hold it right there." In her face, he whispered, "I'm sick and tired of accusations being made against my kids when their class is no doubt full of hooligans."

"Hooligans?" Maybe it was the old-fashioned word itself, or the sight of harmless Thomas Quinn wiping his perpetually runny nose on his sleeve—whatever had brought on a grin, she couldn't seem to stop.

"Think this is funny? We're talking about my daughters' education."

"I know," she said, sobering, trying not to notice how his warm breath smelled strangely inviting. Like oatmeal and cinnamon. "Mr. Buckhorn, I'm sorry. Really I am. I'm not sure how we've launched such a contentious relationship, but you have to know I only have the twins' best interests in mind. Kindergarten is the time for social adjustments. Nipping problem behaviors before they interfere with the real nuts and bolts of crucial reading and math skills."

"Why do you keep doing that? Implying my girls are difficult? Look at them," he said, glancing into the room where Bonnie and Betsy had gravitated to their assigned seats and sat quietly coloring with the rest of the class. "Tell me, have you ever seen a more heartwarming sight?"

Nope. Nor a more uncharacteristic one!

Typically by this time of day, Bonnie had carried out her second or third dastardly plan. Whether *freeing* the inhabitants of their ant farm or counting how many pencils fit in the water fountain's drain, the girl was always up to something. Betsy either provided cover or assisted in a speedy getaway.

"They're even self-starters," he boasted. "Their mother opened her own horse grooming shop. Looks to me like I have a couple of entrepreneurs on my hands."

"I agree," Josie was honestly able to say. The girls were already experts when it came to launching funny business. "But with all due respect, the twins are currently on their best behavior. With you here, I doubt they'll find trouble."

"Right. Because it's not them causing it in the first place."

Josie might as well have been talking to a rock wall. "My job is to make sure Bonnie and Betsy are prepared to do their best in first grade, right?"

He snorted. "Only correct thing you've said since I've been standing here."

"All right, then—" she propped her hands on her hips and glared "—what do I have to gain by making up outrageous stories about your girls?"

The question stumped him.

"That's right," she continued. "A big, fat nothing. No one wants the twins to be perfect more than me. Their future behavior is a reflection of not only your parenting, but my teaching."

"Why are you bringing me into this?" He switched Green Bean to the crook of his other arm.

Just when she thought she'd broken through the wall....

"I mentioned this to you before, but I really think it would help the situation," she said, recalling a child development class she'd had where parents sat behind two-way mirrors, watching the differences in their children's

behavior once they'd left the room. "How about if starting tomorrow, you attend class with Bonnie and Betsy?
Just for a few days."

It wouldn't be as idyllic as a blind study, but at least it
would give her a stress-free week, plus maybe in some
small way show the girls their father cared about their
actions at school.

"Seriously?" He scratched his head. "What good is
that going to do?"

*In a perfect world, open your eyes to the scam your
angels have been pulling.*

After dinner, Dallas made a beeline for the barn to
muck stalls. He told himself it was because the horses
deserved a perfectly clean environment, but the truth of
the matter was that he needed time alone to think. As
if listening to his mother lecture had been the price for
heaping portions of her famous tuna casserole and peas,
she'd yammered on and on about what pistols he and his
brothers had been at school. And how she wasn't surprised to now find his proverbial apples not falling far
from the tree.

Usually the scent of straw mingled with saddle leather
and horseflesh soothed his darkest moods, but this one
he found hard to shake. The principal's accusatory glare
hadn't sat well. Yes, education was important, but it
wasn't everything. After high school, some of Dallas's
friends had gone on to college, but all he and Bobbie Jo
had wanted was to get married and start their family.
It didn't take a degree to learn ranching, but plenty of
days spent working in brutal sun, cold and every sort of
weather in between.

Lord, he missed his wife. She'd know what to do.

"Gonna be out here brooding all night?" His brother Wyatt broke the barn's peace. Wasn't there anywhere a man could go to be alone?

"I'm not brooding."

"Uh-huh." Tugging on leather gloves, Wyatt split a fresh hay bale in Thunder's stall.

The black quarter horse snorted his thanks.

"Just saw Mom. She told me to tell you the girls are waiting on you to read them a story and tuck them in."

"I know…" Wind whistled through the rafters, making the old building shudder.

"Then why aren't you with them?"

Dallas stabbed his pitchfork in the meager pile of dung he'd collected in the wheelbarrow. "Beats me."

"You gonna do it? Take the girls' teacher up on her offer?"

Glancing at his younger brother over his shoulder, Dallas asked, "Think I should?"

Wyatt hefted another bale, carrying it to the next stall. "I asked around and Josie Griffin is an excellent educator, not prone to spinning yarns. She's tough, yet compassionate. From what I've heard, always acting with her students' best interests at heart."

"Okay…so Miss Griffin's a saint. That doesn't mean she's justified in calling my girls trouble." Nor did it make him feel better about his wicked thoughts at the minigolf course.

"If that's truly the way you feel, then take her up on her offer. Henry and I will handle things around here." Henry was the ranch foreman and had been practically family since Dallas had been born.

"Not that simple," Dallas said, putting extra effort into cleaning Buttercup's stall. The palomino had been Bobbie Jo's. His wife had spent hours prepping to show the horse. Brushing her coat until Dallas could've sworn the mare purred. "What would you say if I told you there's a reason I don't want to be at that school?"

"What's more important than taking an active part in the twins' education?"

Dallas winced. Wyatt had always had a knack for zeroing in on the heart of any matter. "That's just it. The other night, when Bonnie and Betsy had that gaggle of girls over for a sleepover, we ran into Miss Griffin." Sighing, he admitted, "The sight of her rear end in faded jeans just about fried my brain. Not good, seeing how the last thing I need is to be hot for teacher."

Chapter Three

Why wasn't Josie surprised Dallas had chosen to make a mockery of her suggestion?

Tuesday morning, on Weed Gulch Elementary's sun-drenched front lawn stood not one pony, but two. The docile pets put up with dozens of stroking little hands. For the students who weren't enraptured by cute creatures, there were cupcakes—dozens! Box after box of whimsically frosted treats, each sporting either plastic cowboy or cowgirl rings. In the center of the mayhem stood Dallas Buckhorn wearing jeans and a blue plaid Western shirt, accompanied by leather chaps, a Stetson hat and boots. Oh—the mere sight of him made her heart flutter, she'd give him that, but from a teaching standpoint, he'd ruined her whole day.

How was making construction paper analog clocks and then learning to read them going to top this?

"Miss Griffin!" Bonnie and Betsy ran up to her, hugging so hard around her waist that Josie nearly toppled over.

"Did you see what our daddy brought?"

"I sure did…" *And we're going to have a nice, long talk about it.* "Are those your ponies?"

"Uh-huh," Betsy said with a vigorous nod. "Mine is named Cookie because she has chocolate chip spots."

"Mine's Cinderella," Bonnie noted. "Just like the princess because she has long, blond hairs."

"Those are wonderful names." Josie was glad she'd worn capris and sneakers as the lawn she marched across was still dew-soaked. "You two were clever to match them so well to each pony."

"Thanks!" both girls said, skipping alongside her.

Before dashing ahead, Betsy shouted to her sister, "Come on, Cinderella pooped!"

Giggles abounded.

Thank goodness the older kids were already in class or off-color bathroom jokes would already be spreading. When it came to potty humor, fifth and sixth graders were experts.

"I've got a man here to clean all of this." Josie had been so focused on what she'd say to Dallas that she hadn't noticed he'd come up beside her.

Hand to her chest, she said, "You startled me."

"Sorry." Nodding toward the shrieking kids, he added, "I knew the ponies would be a hit, but I didn't expect a riot."

"When it comes to kindergarteners, it doesn't take much."

"I'm seeing." His smile rocketed through her. Despite his many faults, he was undeniably handsome. Never more so than now. It was clear he belonged outside. The sun lightening his Buckhorn-blue eyes. Glancing over his shoulder, he signaled to an older man who knelt alongside Bonnie, helping her with her pet.

"Yeah, boss?" The man's easy smile, laugh lines at the corners of brown eyes and weathered skin had Josie guessing him to be in his mid-fifties. His playful spirit around the kids made him seem much younger. Like Dallas, he wore Western wear complete with a cowboy hat.

"Josie Griffin, meet Henry Pohl. He's worked our ranch longer than I've been alive."

Shaking Josie's hand, the man winked. "I wouldn't say it was *that* long. You are getting a tad long in the tooth."

In under twenty minutes, Dallas was true to his word and had begun loading the ponies into a custom, miniaturized horse trailer attached to a shiny black pick-up. The Buckhorn Ranch emblem of two battling rams had been stenciled on both doors.

While settling the children into their daily routine of standing for the Pledge of Allegiance, stilling for a moment of silence and then getting out their printing paper to practice writing their new letter and number, she watched Dallas through the wall of windows overlooking the school's front lawn.

Firmly, yet gently, he corralled the suddenly stubborn animals into their temporary home. With Henry's help, Dallas soon had all of the cupcake liners and white bakery boxes in the trash, leaving the area looking untouched save for sneaker tracks trailing through silvery dew.

Josie's students fidgeted and fussed. Too hyper from cupcakes and fun to want to settle into their routine. The childlike part of her she didn't often let escape sympathized with them. Outside, it was shaping up to be a beautiful fall day. She had dreaded Dallas's visit, but was now surprised to be anticipating his return to the room.

"You do know your circus broke about sixteen school rules?"

Dallas took another bite of his ham and swiss sandwich and shrugged. "Way I see it, my girls need to know I'm not here to punish them. I want them and their friends to be happy I'm in for a visit."

Josie Griffin pressed her full lips together like there was a whole lot she wanted to say, but was holding back.

"Out with it," he coaxed, biting into a pear. It was the first one he'd had in a while. Firm, yet juicy and sweet. Kind of like he'd imagine kissing Josie would be—that is, if she'd ever erase her pucker. Not that he'd done a whole lot of thinking about kissing the teacher, but cute as she was, he wouldn't have been normal if the notion hadn't at least crossed his mind.

For the twenty minutes while the kids were at recess, Josie had suggested they hang out in the teachers' lounge. The room was unremarkable save for a pleasantly efficient window air-conditioning unit and grown-up chairs. Dallas hadn't realized how many muscles in his back could possibly ache until he'd spent his morning pretzelled into munchkin chairs.

"Since you asked…" Her eyes narrowed. Was she fixing to yell at him again? "I didn't invite you here to throw a party, but observe your daughters in their daily setting. My hope is that they'll soon grow comfortable enough with you being in their surroundings to revert back to their usual naughty behavior."

"Whoa. What you're essentially saying is that you've set a trap you hope they spring?"

She at least had the good graces to flush. "I would hardly call a long acknowledged child psychiatry technique a trap. More like a tool. I can sit here telling you about the girls' sins until I run out of breath, but that still won't make you a believer. I want you to catch them in action. Only then will you understand how disruptive their pranks are to my class."

"And if they turn out to be the good kids I expect them to be?"

She damn near choked on a carrot stick. "Not that I'm a betting woman, but if I were, I'd put down a hundred on Bonnie and Betsy finding some form of trouble by the end of the day."

"You say that with such glee," he noted, wadding up his trash. "Like you want my daughters in hot water."

"Far from it. They need to understand that school is for learning, not horseplay. But wait—with this morning's stunt, you've pretty much blown that lesson out of the water."

"For the record—" he eased his legs out in front of him to cross at the ankles "—Cookie and Cinderella aren't horses, but ponies."

Josie was beyond mortified when Thursday morning had come and gone and still the twins hadn't so much as dropped a pencil shaving. Had she been wrong about them? Overexaggerated their penchant for mischief?

"Hungry?" Dallas asked as twenty-one squirming bodies raced for the door.

"I am," she said, motioning for the line leaders to guide them to the hand-washing station. "It's fried chicken day. Want to brave the cafeteria?"

"Is it safe?"

She laughed. "On turkey tetrazzini day," she wrinkled

her nose, "not so much, but you're actually in for a treat. Mashed potatoes and white gravy with big yeast rolls. If we're really lucky, chocolate cake for dessert."

"I'm in." His white-toothed grin was made brighter by faint golden stubble. Not enough time to shave before beating the first bell?

After getting everyone through the line, Josie turned to Paula the lunch lady and said, "Please give Mr. Buckhorn a double serving and put it on my tab."

"Yes, ma'am." Heaping on gravy, the bosom-heavy brunette asked, "How's your cat? Heard he had a sick spell."

"Better, thanks." Josie loved how everyone in the school was an extended family. What she lacked for company at home, she more than made up for at work. "How's Teddy's job hunt?"

"Great." Her sixteen-year-old had been saving for a car. "He starts at the drive-in on Friday."

"Wonder—"

"I hate you, Thomas! Take your stupid cake!"

Josie peered through the serving-line door just in time to see Bonnie fling a chocolate square at poor little Thomas Quinn. As if that wasn't bad enough, she then smashed it into his hair.

"I hate you, too!" Betsy hollered. "Bonnie's a princess and you should've just given her the stupid cake."

"Girls, knock it off!" Dallas said, surging into the melee.

Thomas started to wail and showed no signs of letting up. "Sh-she g-got cake on my new g-glasses!"

"Let me clean those for you, bud." Dallas set his lunch tray on the table and then took the boy's gold-rimmed frames. To Josie, he said, "Be right back."

"Th-there's c-cake on my shirt, t-too. Mommy's gonna yell."

"No she won't, sweetie," Josie assured the boy. To the twins, she demanded, "What were you thinking?"

Hands on her hips, Bonnie said, "He should've just gave me that cake."

"Yeah," Betsy said, adopting the same pose.

"I'm Bonnie Buckhorn." Wearing a satisfied grin, Bonnie added, "Daddy says I'm one half of a perfect bunch and that I can do whatever I want."

After handing Thomas his freshly cleaned glasses, Dallas grabbed the collars of his daughters' matching pink T-shirts. "Ladies, we need to talk."

If Dallas hadn't seen the whole incident with his own eyes, he never would've believed it. Steering the girls into their quiet, dark classroom, he said, "Put your behinds in your chairs."

"But, Daddy," Bonnie whined, "why are we in trouble when Thomas was the one being mean?"

"We gave him cupcakes," Betsy thoughtfully pointed out.

Dallas rubbed his throbbing forehead. "You can't just take your friend's dessert. It's wrong. And—"

"You tell us we can do whatever we want." His eldest by a minute held his stare.

"Yes, but, hon, that doesn't give you the right to do bad things." Was everything else his girls had been accused of true?

"We aren't bad, Daddy." Betsy left her chair to crawl onto his lap. Bonnie soon followed.

"I'm sorry, Daddy." Bonnie wrapped her chubby arms around his neck.

"Both of you need to get it through your pretty heads that just because you're Daddy's princesses, that doesn't give you the right to do whatever you want. At school, you have to follow the rules."

Bonnie chimed in with, "Miss Griffin never said we couldn't put cake in Thomas's hair."

The statement was so ridiculous, Dallas had to chuckle. "Honey, I can think of very few situations where you *should* put cake in anyone's hair."

"Do you still love us?" Betsy asked.

Hunching over, he made growling, tickle monster noises, attacking their rib cages to the accompaniment of shrieking laughs.

Now that both girls had been scolded, it felt good to return to their usual Buckhorn family fun.

"Who wants coffee and donuts?" Friday morning, Josie halted her walk around the classroom to see Dallas and his girls wielding *snacks*.

"Me, me!" The majority of the class didn't even bother raising their hands before running over to claim their share.

Betsy and Bonnie beamed.

Thomas sank down in his chair.

"Stop!" Josie hated always being the bad guy, but this was ridiculous. "The school has a healthy snack policy and last I checked, coffee and donuts aren't on the list."

"But it's Friday," Dallas complained, sounding suspiciously like his daughters. "Plus," he nodded across the room, "as an apology, my girls wanted to give a special offering to that little fella."

If Thomas scooted much lower, he'd have dissolved into a puddle on the floor.

"I don't care if it's Christmas," Josie argued, "you're not caffeinating my kindergarteners."

"You're impossible." Turning his back on her, he said to his crew, "Come on, girls."

"Where are you going?" Josie asked, following them into the hall.

"Teachers' lounge. Or will you deny your coworkers a happy start to their weekend, too?"

Beyond furious with the man, she folded her arms and watched them go. Unfortunately, back in the classroom, she was met with much whining and pouty stares.

Nipping that behavior, she refocused her students on their daily writing practice. When Bonnie and Betsy returned with their father, she already had their tablets and pencils ready to go.

"You're a killjoy," Dallas noted once she sat at her desk to finish writing next week's lesson plans.

"And you're a child disguised in a grown-up's body."

"A *man's* body," he said with the slow grin she'd grown to alternately hate and adore. Every time he pulled this stunt, he was usually trying to get himself out of hot water. No wonder his children were such a mess. Look who they had for an example! Worse yet, Dallas wielded that grin like a weapon. Same as his daughters, he knew how to pour on the charm.

"You're impossible."

"Thanks." He had the gall to combine his grin with a wink.

How, she didn't know, but Josie managed to survive the morning and lunch hour and even afternoon recess without suffering a meltdown. Everywhere she went there was Dallas, being generally helpful and offering to pass out papers. Which only put her that much more on edge.

Friday afternoons, she always introduced an art project that was fun, but also worked on building a sense of community. For this week's lesson, she'd had the children draw names of a friend. Once paired up, they would then create each other's portraits with finger paint.

After letting each student pick a cover-up from the pile of men's and women's oxford shirts she'd collected at yard sales, she passed out the oversize paper and spent a few minutes going over ground rules.

"Now," she asked once she'd finished, "raise your hand if you can tell me where the paint goes."

Megan Brown was first. "On the paper!"

"Right. Excellent." Over the years, Josie had learned to never underestimate the importance of explaining this point. "Does anyone have questions?"

Thomas raised his hand. "I forgot how to get the lids off the jar thingees."

"Like this," Josie said, holding up a plastic container from the nearest table. "Just twist, and then carefully set your lid on the table. Stick your hand in one finger at a time to get your paint. Kind of like your finger is the brush. Make sense?"

He pushed up his glasses and nodded.

"Any other questions? Okay, let's take the lids off our containers and begin."

Since the twins were on opposite sides of the room, Dallas spent a few minutes with one before moving on to the other. When he was with Betsy, Josie happened to be alongside him. "My girl's pretty talented, huh?"

"A future Picasso," Josie said in all seriousness. Betsy had indeed captured her friend Julia's essence in a primary colored abstract extravaganza.

"Their mom was pretty talented."

Looking up at her dad, Betsy asked, "What'd Mommy make?"

A wistful look settled on his usually stoic features. It softened him. Gave him a vulnerability Josie hadn't before noticed. "She used to set up her easel and watercolors by the duck pond and paint for hours. I teased her that her long hair rode the breeze like weeping willow branches."

The warmth in his eyes for a woman long gone knotted Josie's throat.

"Sometimes she'd paint what she saw." He tweaked his daughter's nose. "Other times, especially when she was pregnant with you, she'd paint what she imagined. Like one day sharing a picnic with you and your sister."

"Sounds amazing," Josie said. "I've always wanted to be more artistic."

Upon hearing her voice, Dallas suffered a barely perceivable lurch—as if until she'd spoken, he'd forgotten anyone but he and Betsy were even in the room.

"Yeah, well…" He cleared his throat. Did he even know what she'd said?

"Stop, Bonnie!" Megan began crying. "I don't wanna get in trouble for you!"

Josie's stomach sank. So much for her peaceful afternoon.

"What happened?" she asked upon facing a horrible mess of what she presumed was Bonnie's making. Her entire paper was coated with paint, as well as the table and carpeting underneath.

"Well…" Bonnie planted her paint-covered fists on her shirt. "Since Megan is tall, I ran out of paper. I tried getting you, but you were talking to Daddy. I didn't have anywhere else to paint, so I painted the floor."

The girl stated her actions in such a matter-of-fact way that they nearly sounded plausible. Nearly.

Don't yell. Keep your composure.

"Bonnie," Josie said after forcing a few nice deep breaths, "just because you ran out of paper, that doesn't give you the right to complete your project wherever you'd like."

"You're not the boss of me," the girl sassed. "My daddy is, and he—"

Dallas stepped up behind her. "—would like you to follow him to the cleanup closet where you'll get a bucket and sponge to clean *your* mess."

Looking at her father as if he'd spouted bull horns, Bonnie's mouth gaped. "But—"

"Move it," Dallas said, not even trying to hide his angry tone.

An hour later, Josie had gotten everyone tidied and on their way home for the weekend. Back in the classroom, Betsy sat cross-legged on a dry patch of carpet. Dallas had found a roll of brown paper towels and sopped the areas where Bonnie had scrubbed.

On her way inside from putting her students on buses, Josie had stopped by the janitor's office and he'd assured her that his steam cleaner would tackle the job. By Monday morning, no one would ever guess the vandalism had taken place. Josie hated thinking of a small child's actions in such harsh terms, but Bonnie had known exactly what she'd been doing.

"Almost done?" Josie asked.

"Uh-huh." Bonnie looked exhausted, but that hardly excused her from the consequences of her actions. According to the classroom discipline chart, this was a major offense. Punishable by missing the next week's recesses.

"Miss Griffin?" Betsy asked. "If we buy you a present, can you stop hating us?"

"Why would you think I hate you?" Josie asked, hurt by the very notion.

"Because you always look at us with a frowning face."

The knot returned to Josie's throat, only this time for a different reason. The Buckhorn family packed quite the emotional punch. "I'm not making a mad expression, sweetie, but sad. When my students break rules on purpose, it makes me feel like I'm not a very good teacher or you would've known better."

"I guess." Tracing the carpet's blue checkered pattern, the girl didn't sound convinced.

Dallas took his wallet from his back pocket. "Clearly, Bonnie and I are not going to be able to make this right without a shop vacuum. If I give you a couple hundred, think that'll cover the cost of getting someone out here to clean?"

"This isn't about money," Josie said, saddened that he'd even asked. "The custodian will handle whatever you can't get up. But, Bonnie, what lesson have you learned?"

The little girl released a big sigh. "I learned if I paint the floor, I don't wanna get caught."

Chapter Four

"Wrong," Dallas snapped. Bonnie's bratty answer made him sick to his stomach. It reminded him of the epic battles his parents and younger sister, Daisy, had had when she was a kid. When she'd taken off right after her high school graduation, Georgina and Duke blamed themselves for not having used a stronger hand in dealing with her many antics. Now, with the benefit of hindsight, he understood his parents' pain over their own failings. Damn, he hated being wrong, and when it came to his daughters' poor behavior, not only had his mother been right, but their teacher had been, too. As a parent, he looked like a fool and had no one to blame but himself. "The lesson you were supposed to have learned was that if you'd followed Miss Griffin's directions, you wouldn't now be in trouble."

Bonnie put her hands over her ears and stomped her

feet. "You said I'm a princess and that means I only do what I want!"

"Clearly," he said to Josie, too embarrassed to meet her gaze, "Bonnie and I are failing to communicate."

"That's okay," Betsy said while her sister screamed. "Bonnie does this to me when I tell her to share Barbie's clothes."

"How do you get her to stop?" Josie asked.

"Tell her if she doesn't stop, I'm going to tell Nanny Stella."

Great plan, but the middle-aged woman who'd cared for the twins practically since the day they'd been born just happened to have quit.

Grimacing, he scooped up his little hellion, tossing her over his shoulder. "Miss Griffin," he managed over Bonnie's increased volume, "I'm not exactly sure how, but by Monday, I promise to have this situation under control."

Betsy rolled her eyes.

By the time Dallas turned his truck onto the dirt road leading home, Bonnie was asleep and Betsy huffed on her window with her breath, drawing stars and hearts in the fog.

He wouldn't have blamed Josie Griffin if she'd laughed him out of the school. Bonnie's behavior had been unacceptable. How had she managed to get so spoiled without him noticing?

At the memory of how many times his mother or one of his brothers or Josie had warned him of impending doom, heat crept up his neck and cheeks. How had Bonnie gotten to this point? He gave her everything she'd ever wanted. What was he missing?

Dallas knew his mother was the logical person to turn to for advice, but he also knew her sage counsel came at a price—admitting he'd been wrong. Only his shame wouldn't end there. She'd delight in telling his brothers and sister-in-law, neighbors and old family friends just what a disaster he was as a father. Give her twenty-four hours and she'd have blabbed his predicament to everyone between Weed Gulch and the Texas border.

Unacceptable.

Tightening his grip on the wheel, he turned onto the ranch's drive. His brother Wyatt didn't have kids, meaning he didn't know squat about rearing them. Cash and his wife, Wren, had one-year-old Robin, but that cutie could barely walk, let alone sass.

Which left only one option—Josie Griffin.

Not only was the woman highly trained on the inner workings of the kindergarten mind, but by not rubbing his face in his failings, she'd made him feel less of a fool. She could've laughed at him during Bonnie's fit. Instead, she'd quietly and efficiently gathered his girls' things and the cowboy hat he'd hung from the coat pegs at the back of the room, delivering them all the way out to his truck.

At the ranch, Dallas carried Sleeping Beauty into the house, laying her on the sofa. While Betsy tucked a pillow under her head, he took the throw blanket from his favorite chair, draping it over his girl.

"She all right?" his mother asked, wiping her hands on a dishrag on her way into the room. "That child *never* sleeps this early in the day."

Betsy was all too happy to volunteer, "Bonnie got in *big* trouble at school."

"Oh?" Dallas's mother sat on the sofa arm, smoothing Bonnie's blond hair. "What happened?"

"Well…" Hands on her hips, Betsy sported a huge smile. "First, she—"

"Can it, squirt." Dallas could feel a headache coming on. "Go clean your room."

"No." Arms folded, chin raised, Betsy retorted, "If Bonnie gets to sleep, I don't wanna work."

Teeth clenched, Dallas silently counted to five. What was going on around here? He'd never had the slightest problem with either of his girls—especially not Betsy—now, she was also giving him lip?

"Betsy," his mother warned. "Do as your father asked. Your dirty clothes need to be in the hamper."

"Yes, ma'am." Chin to her chest, Betsy pouted on her way toward the stairs.

"Honey," his mother said, her tone characteristic of a nice, long speech, "you know I don't usually interfere with your personal business, but—"

Dallas snorted. "With all due respect, save it. After the day I've had, I'm seriously not in the mood." Taking his keys and wallet from the entry-hall table, he asked, "Need anything from the store? I'm going to town."

"Why? You just came from the girls' school. I don't understand why you'd now be driving all the way back, when—"

"Dogs on a biscuit, Mama, could you just this once leave me alone?"

Shaking her head, she snapped, "I'll leave you alone when you agree to get your head out of your behind."

"Kitty, gimme a break. Thanks to the Trouble Twins, I'm only twenty minutes late." Judging by her cat's frantic meows, he'd had a long, hard day lounging on his window seat in the sun.

Josie set her purse, keys and mail on the kitchen table, abandoning her plan to glance through a Victoria's Secret sale catalog. After taking a can of Filet Mignon Surprise from the cabinet, she popped off the top and spooned it onto a saucer. Kitty not only liked fine food, but eating it on fine bone china.

"You do know you're spoiled rotten," Josie noted as she set the cat's dinner on the floor. Considering how she catered to her "baby," was it fair for her to think of Dallas as being such an awful parent?

Had Emma lived, would I be any better?

Sighing, she took an oatmeal scotchie from the cookie jar, then lost herself in making imaginary purchases.

Fifteen minutes later, her phone rang. One glance at the caller ID and her stomach lurched. "Hello?"

"Josie, this is Dallas. Hope you don't mind me calling after hours, but your number was in the book, so I figured—"

"It's fine," she assured him, kneeling to pick up the cat's empty dish. "Is something wrong with the girls?"

"Not exactly. More like me."

"Oh?" Dish in the sink, she wasn't sure what else to say. "I'm sorry. Is there anything I can do to help?"

"Yeah, well…" He cleared his throat. "What I was hoping is that if you aren't too busy, you could meet me at Lucky's for a quick coffee. I'd only need a few minutes of your time. This wouldn't be like a date—just me picking your brain for kid management ideas."

A smile played across her lips. How the great Dallas Buckhorn had fallen after considering himself World's Finest Father. "You're welcome to more than a few minutes. Maybe even sixty."

"Really?" His tone grew brighter. "That'd be great. How soon can you be here?"

"You mean you want me to meet you now?" Not that

she had anything special on tap for her Friday night other than a load of laundry.

"That was kind of my plan—that is, if you're amenable."

"Sure," she said, telling herself her pulse had become erratic from pacing rather than thoughts of sharing an intimate booth with the man with no distractions other than an occasional waitress refilling their drinks. It was tough enough keeping her cool around him in front of her class. On her own? Whew. "Um, I suppose I could fit you into my schedule."

"Oh, hell. I forgot it's the weekend. Do you already have plans?" He actually sounded as nervous as she felt.

"No," she said, reminding herself that, like the man had told her, this was hardly a date. More like an off-campus parent/teacher conference. As such, there was no logical explanation for why she'd taken the cordless phone into her walk-in closet, already searching for the right thing to wear. "Give me a few minutes to change out of my school clothes and I'll be right over."

Dallas stood when Josie approached.

She'd ditched her simple work dress in favor of jeans, a tight black T-shirt and those red boots of hers he'd already decided he liked. Her hair hung long and loose and wild. He liked that, too. He tried not to notice how her curls framed her full breasts.

"Sorry," she said, hustling between tables to get to his booth. "I'd have been here sooner, but got held up by a train."

"Hazard of small-town living."

Sliding onto her black vinyl seat, she laughed. "True."

"Hungry? The coconut cream pie is great."

She wrinkled her nose. "Thanks, but I'm not a big fan of coconut. Had an incident as a child. Long story."

"Fair enough." Had her smile always been so contagious? "Blueberry á la mode?"

"Now, *that,* I can do. With a hot tea, please."

He signaled to the waitress and gave her their order.

With pleasantries out of the way, Dallas was unsure of his next move. Issues with his girls that'd seemed pressing back at the ranch now felt embarrassing.

"It's okay, you know."

"What?" He looked up to find her staring. Smiling. Unwittingly making his chest tight with the kind of attraction he hadn't felt for a woman in God only knew how many years.

"For you to ask for help with Bonnie and Betsy. They'll turn out fine. You just need to set boundaries now as opposed to when they're sixteen and drag racing their matching Lamborghinis."

With a grimace, he said, "Guess I deserve that."

Reaching across the table, she covered his hands with hers. Not only was her gesture comforting, but joltingly erotic. As if her fingertips were supercharged with emotion and heat. "Promise, I was only teasing. And please, don't take this the wrong way, but in my professional opinion, you've equated loving your girls with letting them have or do whatever they want."

Nodding, he admitted, "My mom says the same thing. But for the life of me, I can't see why making my girls happy is wrong." More important, he'd promised Bobbie Jo that no matter what, their children would always be his top priority.

"It's not wrong. It's wonderful. But part of making them well-rounded people is teaching them self-discipline and to follow rules and routines. Right now, Bonnie and Betsy seem to struggle in those areas. All I'm suggesting is that you start with baby steps to establish a sort of baseline order."

"Okay, whoa…" Dallas whooshed his hand over his head. "You lost me back at routines."

"Take, for instance, their school routines. In order to get my students used to their new classroom setting as opposed to hanging out at home, where their days are less structured, we do the same things over and over until they become second nature. We make lines for hand washing and recess and lunch. We say the pledge and then first thing every morning review our previous days' letters and learn a new one. Because our schedule rarely varies—unless some parent shows up with cupcakes and ponies—" she winked "—by the end of the first quarter, most of my little munchkins could probably tell a substitute what they should be covering at any given time."

For the life of him, Dallas failed to see what all that had to do with him. "As far as routines—tooth brushing and bath and bedtimes and stuff—that's all Nanny Stella's domain."

"Who makes sure they do their homework?"

"Used to be Nanny Stella. Now…" He shrugged.

"And chores?"

Starting to get the picture, Dallas reddened.

"Enforcing table manners?"

"My mom, but if the girls are way out of line in playing with their food, I'll growl in their direction."

Josie frowned.

"What? Dad always ran a tight ship when it came to mealtimes."

"Uh-huh. So let's see, pretty much the only interaction you have with the girls is at mealtime?"

"Not at all. We fish and go toy shopping and watch movies. They're all the time out in the barn with me, and a few days each week we pack a picnic and take off on trail rides."

"All of that sounds amazing but, Dallas, during any of that fun, do you ever get to be a disciplinarian?"

Luckily, he was spared answering Josie's latest question by the arrival of the pie and her tea.

The bell over the door jingled as a family of five came in for early supper. With yellow walls, faded linoleum floors and mismatched booths, the diner might have been lacking in decor, but the food was stick-to-your-ribs good. A couple soon entered, followed by another family. Why, Dallas couldn't say, but it made him feel good to see the empty diner filling. There was safety in numbers, and even though he'd asked Josie for help, he felt under attack. Which was ridiculous. His girls loved him and for now, that was enough.

"That was delicious," Josie said, patting her napkin to her lips. "I can't remember the last time I had pie."

"Mom makes it at least once a month."

Pouring herself a second cup of tea, she asked, "Do you ever get tired of living with your mom?"

"Surprisingly not. We get on each other's nerves, but since she lost Dad and I lost Bobbie Jo, we've leaned on each other."

"Makes sense," she said, swirling honey into her mug.

"How about you? After your husband died, who'd you turn to for support?"

Turning introspective, she said, "Mostly friends. My parents retired to Maine."

He whistled. "That's a long haul."

"No kidding."

"What moved them up there?"

She looked away. "Long story."

"I have time." He finished the last of his meringue.

"Wish I did." She grimaced while pushing herself out of the booth. "I don't know what I was thinking. I have an appointment."

He checked his watch. "It's nearly seven."

She flashed a hesitant smile, and not that he was by any means an expert when it came to deciphering women, but damned if she didn't look ready to cry. "I really should go."

An apology rode the tip of his tongue, but seeing how she already had one foot out the diner's door, it wouldn't do him a hell of a lot of good. Which led him to the conclusion that he'd have had a more productive evening staying in the barn to oil his saddle.

Halfway home, Josie swiped tears from her cheeks, feeling weak and silly. It'd been four years. Why had such a casual question concerning her parents caused a meltdown?

Maybe because with all of Dallas's talk about family, she knew she was a fraud? Oh, sure, when it came to deciphering the mind of a kindergartener, she was a pro, but when it came to her own damaged psyche, all bets were off.

In the house, Kitty hopped down from his window seat to rub against Josie's calves. She set her purse and keys on the entry-hall bench before picking up the cat, burying her face in his fur. "Why am I such a mess?"

Kitty answered with a satisfied purr.

Sighing, she returned Kitty to his favorite spot. Though she knew better than to make her next move, she did it anyway. One of her favorite features of her home was the split levels. The sunken living room. The three steps at the end of the hall leading to Emma's room.

Pushing open the door, greeted by the soft haze of sun setting beyond western-facing windows, she saw three-year-old Emma jumping on her canopy bed. Giggling while building a block tower only to knock it down. Sleeping with lashes so long they'd brushed her cheeks.

Josie hugged herself, stepping farther into the room. Deeper into her daughter's spell. Her parents had begged her to change the sanctuary into a sewing or exercise room. To reclaim the space for herself. What they didn't understand was that touching Emma's bird nest collection, gathered from nature hikes and from the yard after storms, if only for a moment, returned Josie's daughter to her arms. Upon finding each treasure, she'd said a singsong prayer for the winged creatures who'd lost their home before reverently handing it to her mother to be placed upon her "special" shelf. Then, Emma held out her arms to be picked up, asking Josie to tell her a story about all of the songbirds living in their backyard.

Together, they'd squeezed into the comfy armchair in Emma's room where Josie would spin tales of a fanciful bird kingdom presided over by bossy King Jay.

Seated in the chair, Josie ran her hands along the floral chintz upholstery, hoping to release some of her daughter's precious smell, knowing the action was futile, yet going through the motions all the same.

She hadn't indulged in licking her emotional wounds in a long time. Months. Maybe even a year. Yes, she'd been in the room to dust picture books and dolls, but not to mourn. More to celebrate the miracle her precious little girl had been.

The fact that she'd now backslid into the wreck she'd once been told her she wasn't anywhere near ready to be with another man—even for an outing as seemingly innocuous as talking over pie. Conversations naturally led to questions. The answers to which, she was too mortified to tell.

Chapter Five

Monday morning, though typically Nanny Stella would take the twins to school, Dallas volunteered for the chore. He told himself he wanted to spend more time with his girls, but truth be told, he was still irked by the way Josie had ditched him.

Yes, he might be attracted to her physically, but that only meant he was a man and all that that implied. After stewing on the issue all weekend, Dallas was ready for answers.

What he wasn't prepared for was finding Josie surrounded by three other teachers, looking red-eyed and blotchy as if she'd recently cried.

"What's wrong with Miss Griffin?" Bonnie asked. "She looks bad."

"Be nice," Dallas snapped, not in the mood for a repeat of his daughter's Friday performance.

"She was being nice, Daddy." Betsy raised her chin while grabbing her sister's hand. "Miss Griffin *does* look bad."

He shook his head. "Less talk and more stowing your gear."

"You mean our backpacks?" Bonnie scrunched her face. "'Cause I'm pretty sure I don't have anything called *gear*."

Upon steering his daughters toward their cubbies, Dallas helped remove lunches and Hello Kitty crayon boxes. Next on the agenda was making sure Green Bean had stayed home in his jar. Satisfied no immediate shenanigans were planned, he got both girls settled at their respective tables with their chubby pencils and writing tablets.

Satisfied both of his daughters were working as opposed to faking it until he turned his back, he went out into the hall.

Josie was finally on her own, greeting students as they entered her room.

"About Friday night…"

"Good morning, Thomas. Have a nice weekend?"

"Uh-huh," the boy said with an exaggerated nod. "We went to the Tulsa state fair and saw a *gigantimous* pumpkin the size of my dad's truck!"

With plans to go Wednesday night, the monster pumpkin was at the top of Dallas's girls' to-do list.

"Whoa," Josie said to her student without missing a beat. "That must've been amazing. Did you bring me a fried Twinkie?"

"Nooo!" he said with a giggle. "Mom said those cost, like, a million trillion dollars and we're not rich."

"Me, neither." Loudly sighing, she shook her head and

smiled. "But when I win the lottery we'll go nuts. Buy all the fried food our stomachs can hold."

"Promise?"

Nodding, she rubbed the top of his head before pushing him into the room. "But before we start eating, you need to get to work on your review letters."

"Okay…" Head drooped, he marched off to put away his things.

Suddenly alone with Josie, Dallas found himself in the unfamiliar position of feeling like a five-year-old, vying for teacher's attention. "Where were we?"

Her smile pinched, she said, "Not sure, but regardless, I've got a long day ahead of me."

"I know—" he moved between her and the door "—and I'm sorry to barge in like this, but please, just tell me what I did to make you run off like that."

"Dallas…" The way she glanced at the ceiling and then back into her room, even the first grader skipping down the hall while playing with his zipper would've been smart enough to recognize Josie was trying to avoid him.

"I'm sorry. Whatever it was."

"No." Eyes pooling, she swallowed hard. "It's me who should be apologizing." Hand on his forearm, she managed, "I do need to get to my class, but—"

"If that's the case—you being in the wrong—make it up to me by going with Betsy, Bonnie and I to the state fair Wednesday night."

"I couldn't," she said. "I'm sure the girls have been looking forward to it and the last thing they'd want would be for their teacher tagging along."

Clearing his throat, Dallas reminded her, "Weren't you just telling me how I should be the grown-up? I want you to come. Plus, what better place for you to show me how to be the best possible dad."

"Dallas, thank you, but no." Edging around him, she'd almost made it through her door, only all of his work with calf wrangling had finally paid off in that he was a fraction of a second faster.

"Wrong answer. Agree to help me or when the girls show up for school on Thursday, they'll be so hopped up on cotton candy and caramel apples it may take you the rest of the week to get them off the ceiling."

She might've crossed her arms, but her frown showed signs of cracking.

"Worse yet," he persisted, "with me in charge, they might run wild, letting loose all of the livestock and pitching gum at all of the rides. It could damn well turn into an international incident."

Rolling her eyes, laughing but somehow not looking happy, she finally relented. "Okay, I'll go. But only because at this point, you sound as if you need more help than your girls."

"How are you?" Natalie asked the Wednesday afternoon before the fair, during their biweekly spa pedicures and manicures. The Korean family who ran the place spoke just enough English to do business, making it the perfect place for indulging in nice, long talks. "And I don't mean your polite version."

"Not going to lie…" Josie winced while her calluses were pumiced. "It was a rough weekend. Everything I did brought back painful memories of Emma."

"You should've called me." Natalie lightly rubbed Josie's forearm.

"I know, but I should be over it, you know? I don't

mean forgetting my daughter, but at least being able to cope."

"What do you think brought this on?"

"No thinking involved. I can pinpoint the exact second it started. You know the disaster Friday turned out to be with the Trouble Twins, right?"

"Yes..." Nat grimaced.

"Well, out of the blue Friday night, Dallas called. Wanted me to meet him at the diner for coffee."

"Dallas Buckhorn? As in the most gorgeous man on the planet?" her friend interjected.

Josie laughed. "He's not *that* good-looking. And, anyway, would you just let me finish my story?"

"For the record—yes, he *is* that gorgeous. Though his brother Cash inches him out for the world title by a fraction, but please, do continue."

Loving her friend for making her laugh, Josie hit the high points of what'd happened, closing with, "All of his parenting questions made me think about Emma's silly tantrums and then about Hugh, and when Dallas asked why my parents were so far away in Maine, I lost it." Hands over her face, Josie forced a few deep breaths. "I hardly know the man. The last thing I wanted to share with him was how devastating it is to me that my own parents—people I thought were in my corner—moved half a continent away to avoid me."

"That's so not true. Your mom's geographically closer to your brother and his wife and kids. They begged you to go."

Meeting her friend's gaze, Josie's mind flashed on her daughter's grave in the Weed Gulch cemetery. "You and I both know I'm not going anywhere."

"Josie..."

"Don't start on me."

"I'm not. Promise. I only wish you'd—"

"What *cullah?*" her nail technician asked.

Josie handed her a bottle of OPI's Candy Apple Red. To her friend, she said, "Did I mention Dallas asked me to go with him and his girls to the fair?"

"No, but I'm liking the sound of that. Getting right back on the dating horse. Good girl."

"It's hardly a date. The man needs my help and for my sanity, I need Bonnie and Betsy to chill."

"I want that gorilla NOW!" Betsy punctuated her demand with a scream loud enough to make several passersby cover their ears while still others looked on not sure whether to call police.

"She *really* wants that gorilla, Dad." Bonnie, looking like a pint-size forty-year-old, calmly met his gaze.

"I'll try again," Dallas mumbled in front of a carnie's milk bottle game. "But I'm pretty sure these things are weighted."

"Daddy, I want it!" Betsy screamed.

Josie cleared her throat. "Not to butt into your business, but this would be a perfect time to drag Betsy away from here, explaining why she can't always have her way."

"You think?" Eyebrows raised, the man honestly appeared stunned by her suggestion. "She *really* wants it."

"I'd love a new Lexus, but that doesn't mean I'm getting one any time soon." Kneeling in front of the child, Josie took hold of her flailing hands. "Betsy, hon, I know the gorilla is pretty cool, but we're going to go look at some real animals. I heard there's a baby giraffe in the petting zoo."

"Gorillas are waaay better." Bonnie shoved a wad of cotton candy into her mouth.

"I—" sniffle "—still—" sniffle "—want—" sniffle "—him."

"Listen up, princess." Dallas hefted the girl into his arms. "Miss Josie is right. Let's head over to the real animals. If you're good, we'll get snow cones."

"O-okay."

While Dallas's new promise at least provided temporary calm, throbbing rock from the midway combined with temperatures in the muggy high-eighties proved not a good combination when Josie was already worn out from a tough day at school.

The petting zoo was more quiet, but also more frenzied with dozens of little bodies darting in all directions.

"Want to find an out-of-the-way bench?" Dallas asked.

"Sounds perfect."

While Josie found a seat, Dallas purchased feed for the girls, instructing them to stay within the fenced area.

"Feels good to take a load off," he said, gazing toward his daughters who giggled while tiny goats nuzzled grain pellets from their palms. "Ready?"

"For what?" she asked with a sideways glance, trying to ignore tingly awareness on the side of her body where their thighs and shoulders brushed. She'd forgotten his size. How just being around him filled her with the sense that whatever happened—aside from kid disasters—he'd be in control.

"To tell me what was wrong Friday night?"

Her stomach sank. "Why do you care?"

"You're spending all of this time helping me with the twins, yet aside from buying you a half-dozen fried Twinkies, I've done nothing for you."

"First, I only had two Twinkies, thank you very much. Second, what's bugging me has nothing to do with you." Looking at her fresh manicure, she traced the outline of her cuticle. Maybe if she tried hard enough to avoid Dallas's probing gaze, he'd get the hint that she didn't want to share certain portions of her personal life.

"Sure? Because it wouldn't be the first time I ticked a woman off. The few times my mom's book club have tried fixing me up on blind dates they've ended in disaster."

Who wouldn't like you? was the first thing that entered her mind. Beyond his looks, Dallas was funny and hardworking and well-mannered. Had she been remotely interested in giving the whole relationship game another try, he would certainly be a prime candidate. But her last weeks with Hugh had been a nightmare. He'd single-handedly taken everything she thought she'd known about love and turned it upside down.

"Once, ten minutes into our date, I asked a woman if her hair hurt."

"Why would you do that?" The question provided the perfect opportunity to angle away from him, giving herself space to breathe. Even over the barn's perfume of straw and manure, Dallas smelled of leather and citrus and sun. Like the kinds of outdoor adventures she'd never take.

"Evelyn had it all stacked up high with a bird wing barrette sticking out of the side. Looked like it was stabbing her. I thought I was being polite. Judging by her sudden need to stay home to clean carpets, she thought different."

"You're terrible," she admonished. "Kind of like a certain pair of your offspring..." Pointing toward a llama, Josie was already on her feet to hopefully ward off trouble.

Bonnie had climbed halfway over the fence, with Betsy not far behind. They'd dumped their feed buckets and now wore them as hats.

"Let me handle this," Dallas said, passing Josie midway.

Already out of breath, she paused, hunched over, bracing her hands on her knees.

Wonder of wonders, Dallas snagged each girl around their waist, giving them stony looks before setting them to their feet. "What are you two thinking?"

"Betsy wanted to kiss the llama," Bonnie explained, "but he wouldn't come close enough, so I was gonna try picking him up, but then I got stuck so Betsy was gonna help."

Hands braced on his hips, Josie was pleased to see Dallas finally looking the part of an aggravated father. "Not only could you both have been hurt, but what if you'd landed on top of the poor llama? Why do you think the fence is even there?"

"Just to bug us?" Betsy suggested. "It would've been lots easier to kiss him if there wasn't any fence."

"Yeah," Bonnie said. "That's my answer, too."

"You two are a mess." Dallas looked to the sky. "No wonder Miss Josie's tired of trying to fix your impossible behavior."

"That's not nice." Betsy's big blue eyes looked near tears. Directing her pouty look toward her teacher, she asked, "Do you hate us?"

"Of course, I don't hate you," Josie assured. "But your dad's right. I am tired of always scolding you. You're big girls. Too big to even think about going someplace you know you're not supposed to be."

"But—"

"Stop," Dallas said to Bonnie. "You're not going to talk your way out of this." Taking each girl by their hands, he led them toward the exit.

"You're going too fast!" Betsy complained.

"Should've thought about that before you tried breaking *into* a cage."

"Are we going to ride the Ferris wheel now?" The closer they got to the midway, the more excited Bonnie looked. "I love riding rides. It's the best."

Much to Josie's surprise—and delight—Dallas marched right past the Tilt-A-Whirl with its pulsing rock music. He did the same with fifteen other rides.

"Daddy, we're missing all of the good stuff." Betsy looked longingly toward the fun house.

"Uh-huh." On and on Dallas walked until finally stopping at his truck.

"Are we going to the *auntie em* to get more money to buy us more stuff?" Assuming this must be the case, she jumped up and down with excitement.

Betsy joined in on the celebration.

As the girls scrambled into the backseat of the extended cab, fastening their safety belts, Josie asked Dallas under her breath, "Where are we really going?"

"Home."

Josie flashed him a surreptitious thumbs-up.

Considering the twins' numerous tantrums followed by the attempted llama raid, enough was enough. Punishments were in order.

"There's an *auntie em*, Daddy." Bonnie pointed at a

bank. "Get *lots* of money. I want a gorilla and more cotton candy and some of those purses."

"I want cheesecake on a stick!" Betsy bounced on her seat.

"Surprise," Dallas said, glancing in the rearview as he steered the truck off Yale Drive and onto westbound I44, "the only place you two are going is Choreville."

"Where's that, Daddy?" Bonnie had so much cotton candy in her mouth Josie was surprised she could even speak. "Is there lots of money?"

"Not likely." He passed a painfully slow minivan. "Since you'll be mucking out the horse stalls."

"What? Why?" Bonnie pitched her cotton candy bag into the front seat. "I thought we were going back to the fair?"

"Nope."

From the backseat, tears and wails erupted. Wails so loud Josie had to fight the urge to cover her ears.

"Sorry about this," Dallas said.

"Me, too. I was looking forward to riding the mini-coaster."

His sideways glance and smile made her heart flutter. He'd always been handsome, but in light of his stern reaction to the fence-climbing incident, her new respect for him was infinitely more appealing than his rugged cowboy face. "Rain check for tomorrow night—this time, without squawking kiddos?"

"I can't," she said with genuine regret above continued backseat sobs, "I have a dance class."

"Seriously?"

"You say that like you can't imagine me performing even the most simple pirouette." Did she really come off as that clumsy?

"I didn't intend it like that— Cut it out back there. I can't hear myself think."

"You're mean!" Bonnie informed her father.

"Like I was saying," Dallas continued without acknowledging his child's latest complaint, "that came out wrong. Actually, I meant *seriously*, as in I'm impressed."

"Oh." Oddly enough, she'd wanted to be upset with him. It would have made it easier to tell herself she wasn't disappointed about missing out on a private night together.

"How about Friday?"

"I can go to the fair *any* night, Daddy." Suddenly tear-free, Betsy was all smiles.

"You're not invited," he noted. To Josie, he asked, "So? Up for a do-over?" His easy smile not only stole her breath, but crept into her long frozen heart.

Though she knew better, Josie said, "Absolutely."

Chapter Six

"When I asked you to join me on this thing, I didn't plan on staying up here the whole night." Dallas peered over the edge of the Ferris wheel's car, more than a little queasy about how small all of the people looked below.

"I think it's kind of cool." Far from being spooked by the height, Josie gazed at the panoramic view with enough wide-eyed awe to suggest their predicament was a special treat. All of the midway's bawdy sights and sounds and smells were still there, but muted, as if she were watching them in a movie.

"Ugh." He edged closer to the seat's center, in the process, pressing even closer to her. "Sorry about this. I'd hoped tonight would be fun, but it's turning out to be a disaster."

"Why, Mr. Buckhorn," she teased, "are you afraid of heights?"

"Nope," he said with a vehement shake of his head.

"So if I made the cart swing, you wouldn't mind?" She bounced just enough to rock them with the magnitude of a 6.0 earthquake.

"Crap on a cupcake," he muttered with a white-knuckled grip on the safety bar, "please stop."

"You are scared." Arm around his shoulders, she gave him a supportive squeeze. "I'm sorry. I shouldn't have pulled that last stunt."

"Might've been nice if you'd skipped it." Teeth gritted, he willed his heart rate to slow. Damned embarrassing was what this was.

"What brought this on?" When Josie took hold of his hands, he focused on her. The sincere warmth behind her brown eyes. The way a light breeze played with her curls. She was country pretty, freckles providing the only makeup needed.

"Wh-when my brothers and I were kids, Wyatt—he's next oldest to me—dared me to jump off the barn roof and into a cattle tank. I'm thinking I must've been around eight or nine, but feeling immortal. I not only took him up on his dare, but broke my right leg in two places. Spent that whole summer cooped up in bed and the damned thing still hurts in the rain." Focusing on Josie's eyes, her soft lips, he forced a breath. "To this day, I can't stand being higher than I sit up on my favorite horse."

"Then why did you suggest riding the tallest ride on the fairgrounds?"

The simple logic behind her question brought on a smile. "Okay," he admitted. "Truth? I wanted to show you how manly I am. But I loused that up good, didn't I?"

"Men…" She laughed, but something about the gesture struck him as sad. "I was more impressed by your recent handling of twin shenanigans than I would ever be by a daredevil stunt—even one as impressive as sitting on an upright track, slowly circling round and round." Her sassy wink told him she was teasing, but her tone implied more.

"Taking a wild stab in the dark," he said, glad for the diversion, "why do I get the feeling you're not all that thrilled with men as a species? Been hurt?"

"More in the realm of pulverized, but let's not ruin our night." Logic would dictate that after such a statement, she'd free her hold on his hands, but instead, she tightened her grip.

"Want me to roughen him up?" Dallas suggested. One thing he never backed down from was a good fight.

"No use. He did the job for you."

Forehead furrowed, he said, "I don't get it."

"Never mind. I shouldn't have said anything."

"But you did." And he needed to know why those few words had her rummaging through her purse for tissue she used to wipe the corners of her eyes.

With a jolt, their car began the long journey down. All of the occupants around them clapped and cheered.

"What a relief, huh?" Josie's smile was forced. Her expression tight, as if the effort of making casual conversation was too much. "Bet you'll be glad to get your feet back on the ground."

A few minutes earlier, he would have, but now, all he wanted was to return light to her eyes.

"How adorable." Josie knelt in front of the 4-H craft display, wondering at all of the work nimble fingers had put into the dollhouse. The home had been outfitted with pint-size solar panels and was part of an exhibit designed to explore nontraditional forms of energy. "I never get tired of seeing what kids can do."

"You seem to have a real affinity for children."

"They're amazing." She studied the bios of the eight fourth-graders who'd worked on the project. "With them you always know where you stand. No mind games."

"Experienced much of that? People messing with your head?"

She shrugged. "Enough to know it sucks."

Moving on to a photo display, he said, "Considering how many times you've dealt with my girls and your recent Ferris wheel rescue of me, I owe you an ear if you ever need anyone to listen."

"Thanks." She angled toward him, fidgeting with her hands. The turn in conversation was awkward to say the least. In fact, the whole night had been forced. Oh—and she wouldn't even try denying that while they'd been crammed together three stories in the air, every time they touched sparked hot, achy awareness she'd rather forget. "Really. But when it comes to personal matters, I prefer keeping them to myself."

"Ouch. I would've liked to think we're friends. Especially since this is our first official date."

"Is that what tonight is?" Two boys ran between them, shooting at each other with wooden rifles. The distraction gave her time to think. "Because the idea of *dating* someone—even a guy as great as you—isn't at all appealing."

Alongside a terrarium loaded with lizards, he froze. "Talk about a ballbuster. That hurts."

"Please don't take it personally. It's not a rejection of you, so much as the principle. I have a hard enough time figuring out what to do with myself, let alone someone else."

"Fair enough. Truthfully, I feel the same. But then chemistry kicks in. Confuses the hell out of me."

Sharply looking away to hide her blush, Josie fought for air. He'd noticed? The way each time they touched the temperature rose by ten degrees? "You're making me uncomfortable."

"Good." They'd wandered into the vegetable area of the show barn. Judging had long since been completed and plates of carrots, zucchinis and green beans were no longer a big draw. Nearly alone in the mammoth space, Dallas stopped in front of her, bracing both of his hands on a display table. He hadn't even touched her, yet his proximity was unbearable. As usual when he was near, caged excitement coursed through her. As if whenever the man was around, *anything* could happen. "It's only fair you be as far from your comfort zone as I am from mine."

"Wh-what's that supposed to mean? Beyond our conversations about Betsy and Bonnie, I hardly even know you."

"Yes, but would you like to? That was kind of the idea behind tonight."

"No," she said, ducking under his arms to escape. "That's not what I want at all. I lead a wonderfully peaceful life—at least I did before your twins took over my classroom."

"Me, too—I mean, my days are all fairly predictable. And that works for me. Only thing not working lately, are my irrational urges to kiss you."

Josie was no medical expert, but didn't people die from racing hearts? Dallas stood miles into her personal space, smelling like every forbidden fruit. Cotton candy. Caramel apples. All things she craved, but as a responsible adult, steered clear of. His warm exhalations teased her upper lip. His blazing blue eyes held an open challenge.

"Please, Josie, tell me I don't want to kiss you."

She gulped. "You don't. For the twins, we should be friends, but nothing more."

"Agreed."

"Th-then why," she asked with hitched breath, "are you still so near?"

"God's honest truth?" He leaned in close enough for her to taste his sweet breath, but then sighed before backing away. "Don't have a clue. But trust me, won't happen again."

"*Oooh*, a boxed set of *Dawson's Creek*." Josie snatched her treasure before any of her fellow yard sale aficionados had the chance. For only eight on Saturday morning, the crowds were already thick.

"Avoid the topic all you want," Natalie said, having found her own treasure in the form of three wicker baskets. She used them for making care packages for sick coworkers or students whose families could use a little anonymous help. "But mark my words, you're falling for Dallas Buckhorn."

"That's the stupidest thing I've ever heard you say." Josie added a few lightly read picture books to her must-have pile. "I'm not sure how, but Dallas and I have forged a unique friendship."

Natalie snorted. "Based upon mutual hotness?"

Josie hit her over the head with a Thomas the Tank Engine pillow.

"No need for violence," Nat complained, "especially when you know I'm right. You're cute. He's approaching human god status. Whatever you want to label it, you two just might work."

The day was gorgeous. Cool and crisp without a cloud in the sky. So why did her friend seem intent on ruining it? Natalie, better than anyone, knew her past. She knew why Josie had dedicated her life to teaching and helping children while whenever possible avoiding men.

Though Natalie's lighthearted tone told Josie she was kidding, it was hardly a secret that as much as Josie didn't want a romantic entanglement, her friend did. "I've got an even better idea. What if you believe me that I'm not interested in Dallas and you go for him?"

"Nah." Nose wrinkled, Nat said, "Considering how hard he's tried to impress you, what with the ponies and cupcakes and donuts, I think he's all yours."

Monday morning, Josie found herself in the awful position of not only being called to substitute bus duty, but doing it in a relentless downpour. Cold to the point her teeth were chattering, she tried being cheerful about directing shrieking first, second and third graders off their buses and into the school gym. Only two of her students rode the bus and they were both already safely inside.

The few students who walked to school wore rain boots and carried umbrellas. The girls huddled together to stay dry, while the boys pretended they had swords, giving little thought to the fact that they'd be sitting in wet clothes for a good portion of the day.

Traffic for the children whose parents drove them to school was heavy. More than a few wrecks were narrowly avoided and typically well-mannered drivers had resorted to honking and rude gestures in futile attempts to escape the crowded lot.

When a familiar black truck pulled alongside the curb, Josie's stomach lurched.

"Hi, Miss Griffin!" Bonnie, decked out in sunny-yellow rain garb, hopped out. "Betsy lost a tooth."

"I wanted to tell her," Betsy complained, her raincoat, hat and boots pink. "You ruin everything!"

"At least I'm not ugly!" Bonnie hollered.

An ear-splitting whistle came from behind the driver's seat. "Ladies, remember what I told you about bickering? Especially at school. Now, get inside."

"Bye, Daddy," they said in unison, chins drooping.

"Call if they give you any more trouble." Warmth blasted from the truck's heater vents. Even better, was the heat radiating from his smile.

"I will." Why was she suddenly breathless?

"You look cold—but in a cute way."

"Thanks?" Cute was good. At least it had been back in high school. But she felt a million years from that girl.

"Need me to bring you anything? Coffee? Hot cocoa?"

"Sounds delicious, but I'm on duty. Ten more minutes before I can even think about getting warm and dry."

He nodded. "I understand. Well…hope the rest of your day goes better."

"Me, too."

As the crowd dwindled outside, the more Josie was left on her own with her thoughts. Lately, a place she didn't like to be. When she'd seen his truck, she'd dreaded meeting Dallas again. Then he'd wowed her with his smile and she'd been a goner. What was it about the man that left her off balance? Making her doubt her carefully placed emotional walls that thus far had served her so well?

The bell rang, and she no longer had time to think of anything other than squeaky sneakers on the hall floors and her squirming class complaining of being cold and wet. With everyone miserable, she abandoned the usual lesson in favor of story time in the nap corner.

Midway through the tale of a dachshund who hates his brothers and sisters, Natalie entered the room. She carried a steaming, extra-large paper cup from the town's only coffee shop. As surreptitiously as possible with so many eyes on her, she knelt to whisper, "A certain father of twins left this in the office for you. He said seeing you shiver made him sad."

Accepting the drink, sampling it to find hot chocolate so sinfully rich and yummy she felt guilty drinking it in front of her students, Josie tried drawing less attention by getting back to the story. No such luck.

Still in whisper-mode, Nat said, "Care to explain why a guy like Dallas Buckhorn would even care if you're shivering?"

"No."

"What about my dad?" Bonnie asked.

"Nothing, sweetie." Josie cast Nat her most stern Teacher Glare. It only broadened the size of her friend's smile.

"You finally warm?" Dallas asked when he saw his call was from the girls' school. He assumed it was Josie, because the girls were in music class at this time on a Monday.

"Yes. Anyone ever told you you're crazy sweet?"

"Not lately," he said, followed by a laugh loud enough to startle his horse. With a couple of cows ready to calve, despite the rain, he made the long ride out to the south pasture to check them. He could've driven, but he liked being out on days like this. Made him feel closer to all of the cowboys who'd worked the land before him. "How have my little deviants behaved this morning?"

"Surprisingly well. Ever since leaving the fair, I've expected to be blamed for them having to go home early, but they never said a word about it."

"Good." He pulled down his hat to protect his phone from the rain.

"Where are you? It sounds like you're standing under a waterfall."

"Pretty much sums it up," he said, guiding his horse beneath a stubby oak. With no lightning, it was as good a place as any to take shelter.

"You're outside?"

"It's my office. Where else would I be?"

"Duh." Her laughter brought out the sun. "Stupid question."

He couldn't resist teasing, "I've always heard there aren't any stupid questions, just stupid people."

After making a cute little growling sound, she sassed, "You're going to pay for that, mister."

"Sounds fun."

"On that note, I need to go make copies. But seriously, thank you for the cocoa."

"It was my pleasure."

Long after hanging up, a sense of well-being stayed with him. At least until his cell rang again an hour later.

"Mr. Buckhorn?" asked a woman whose voice he didn't recognize, though the number was the same as when Josie called.

"Yes."

"This is Marge Honeywell. I'm the school nurse. I have Bonnie in my office and we're afraid she may have a concussion."

Chapter Seven

"It hurts!" Bonnie wailed, breaking Josie's heart.

The tighter the girl clung to her, the more memories of Emma flooded her system. There'd been so much blood. E.R. doctors and nurses had done everything they could, but internal bleeding couldn't be stopped. Josie had known Emma was gone when her arms slipped from around her neck.

The mental image was so striking it stole her breath.

"Miss Griffin, are you okay?" Betsy asked, pressing herself against Josie's left side. "Your face is really white."

"I'm fine," she assured Bonnie's shaken twin.

"Y-you are white," Bonnie managed between hiccupping sobs. "Thank you for saving me." When the girl snuggled still closer, resting her head beneath Josie's chin, the sensation was mesmerizing. It reminded her of how motherhood had changed her in every conceivable way. It'd shown her the magical, healing power of hugs and kisses and tender words. She'd loved Emma to what'd sometimes seemed like an impossible degree. Now that her daughter was gone, Josie knew she never wanted to be a mother again. Suffering another loss would be the end of her.

"You're welcome," Josie said, "but you're going to be fine." The rain had stopped just long enough for the kids to have outside recess. Bonnie had taken the opportunity to once again climb the big tree. This time, however, the bark had been slippery and she'd fallen. In the process, scraping her knees, palms and forearms. She'd also gotten quite a bump to her forehead that was already bruising.

While Josie was busy with the nurse, Natalie was watching her class.

"Bonnie Buckhorn…" Doc Haven, the town's only physician, ambled into Nurse Honeywell's office. "Girl, I believe I've spent the better part of my career patching up your whole family—except for your grandma. She's the only sane one in the bunch."

"You gave us shots," Betsy said. "We don't like you."

The kindly old doctor chuckled. "If I had a nickel for every time I've heard that." Gesturing for the girl to move from Josie's lap to the nurse's exam table, Doc said, "Hop on up here and let me take a look at you."

"No." Bonnie refused to release Josie's neck. "I want Miss Griffin."

"Sweetheart," Josie said, "the doctor needs to check your eyes and head to make sure you aren't seriously hurt. Would it be all right if I carried you to the table?"

"Is he gonna shot me?"

"I don't think so." Looking to the man in question,

Josie asked, "Doc Haven? Any shots in this girl's immediate future?"

"I'm sure I could think of something she'd need one for." His wink told Josie and the nurse he was joking, but Bonnie wasn't so sure.

After a thorough exam, the little girl was found to be banged up, but in otherwise good condition. Relief shimmered through Josie, making her ache with wishes that her daughter's diagnosis could've gone so well.

"You okay?" Dallas burst through the door, gaze landing on Bonnie.

"Uh-huh." She raised her arms and he went to her, hugging her against him for all he was worth.

Doc Haven gave Dallas a quick rundown on Bonnie's condition, asked him to keep an eye out for dizziness or nausea, then excused himself to make a house call out to Oak Manor, the town's retirement home.

Josie hadn't thought much about it, but in many ways she and Dallas had similar pasts. Having lost his wife, he knew how tough it was coming back from the dark places a loved one's death can take you. He knew about Hugh—the basics. Like her former husband was dead. But he didn't know how he'd died, and she certainly wasn't ready to share Emma with him—if ever.

"Daddy," Bonnie said, "I was gonna see Mommy in Heaven, but Miss Griffin saved me."

"That was awfully nice of her," he noted with a grateful nod in Josie's direction.

"Yeah," Betsy said, "Bonnie was all upside down and broken, but Miss Griffin came and brought her to the nurse."

"I'm glad." The sight of Bonnie in Dallas's arms and Betsy hugging his legs, knotted Josie's throat. Here was this superrugged cowboy. Every inch manly man from the tip of his hat down to his boots, yet he also had an innate gentleness that appealed to children and apparently kindergarten teachers. Swallowing hard, she looked away. No matter how attractive or kind the man might be, she wasn't falling for him or his mischievous girls. "You know, since Miss Griffin saved Bonnie's life, it might be nice for us to have a party for her. What do you think?"

"Yay!" Betsy danced and Bonnie wriggled. "I love parties!"

"That's not necessary," Josie said. "I would do the same for any student here. All in a day's work."

"Yes," Dallas reasoned, "but on this day, you happened to save *my* student. We'll expect you at the ranch at six Saturday night."

After a full Saturday morning of yard sales in Tulsa, Natalie draped herself across the sofa while Josie grabbed them both Diet Cokes.

"What're you going to wear?" Nat shouted into the kitchen.

"Don't have a clue." Josie handed her friend a drink before collapsing on a lounge chair. "Hasn't the Buckhorn Ranch main house been featured in *Architectural Digest*?"

"Yes, ma'am." Nat sipped her cola. "Best as I can recall, it was back when Duke Buckhorn was still alive. When I was a kid, I remember limos driving in from all over the state, filled with bigwigs heading to their holiday parties. Fourth of July, Christmas, New Year's. Back then, practically any occasion was a good reason to whoop it up."

"Thanks for the intimidating history lesson, but that

doesn't help me with tonight. Are we talking ball gown? Jeans? Church dress?"

"Relax. You're overthinking the whole thing."

"And who made me so stressed? You! My supposed best friend." Natalie looked so innocent, Josie couldn't help but laugh, even though she knew her statement to be true.

"You said you aren't at all attracted to the man or even remotely interested in dating, so what's the big deal? Wear sweats."

"You're a lot of help—*not*. Come on…" Pushing herself upright, she aimed for her bedroom, intent on searching her closet.

Nat followed. "Given any more thought to cleaning out Em's room?"

"Nope." Opening the door to her walk-in closet, Josie pretended her so-called friend hadn't even broached the subject.

"Might be healthy for you."

"Drop it, okay?" Snatching a simple black dress from its hanger, she asked, "How about this? Too fancy? Not fancy enough?"

Lying crossways on the bed, Nat asked, "Have you told Dallas anything about your past?"

"No. Why would I? We're friends. Nothing more."

"Keep telling yourself that and maybe one of these days it'll be true." She rolled over, fluffing her bangs in the mirror.

"Why are you being so mean?" Returning her dress to the rack, Josie joined Nat on the bed.

"I'm sorry." Up on her elbows, she looked to the ceiling. "I worry about you. How you keep your past neatly compartmentalized. But that's not the way life works.

It's all interconnected and I wouldn't be a good friend if I encouraged you to keep this up."

"Keep what up? Dallas and I are friends. Nothing more."

"But don't you see that if you'd let go of the past, you two could be more? Josie, you could have a family again. Instead of just pretending to mother your students, you may—"

"Please, go." Bolting upright, Josie folded her arms.

"I'm sorry I hurt you. Really." Nat stood and didn't look the slightest bit apologetic. "But all of that has been on my mind for a while. I want the best for you, and if that means breaking you down in the short run, then so be it."

Once Josie heard Nat close the front door, she threw a pillow at the wall. Damn her. How had the day gone from fun to awful in such a short time? How long had Natalie thought hurtful things about her? Months? Years? Was there a statute of limitations on how long you could mourn your dead child and the man who'd accidentally caused her death before killing himself?

"I haven't seen you this pumped in forever," Wyatt said, standing alongside him at the poolside grill. Whereas Cash, Dallas and Daisy were blond like their mother had been before turning gray, Wyatt was dark like their dad. Short black hair and brown eyes that kept more secrets than they told.

Sweet scents of barbecued chicken, sausage and ribs rose from the flames while the girls, Cash's wife, Wren, and Josie splashed in the heated pool. With slow country playing on the stereo and fireflies lighting the dark sky, Dallas couldn't remember when he'd last felt so content.

Cash was inside, helping their mom bring out potato salad and condiments to the cloth-draped picnic table.

"Gotta say, I'm feeling pretty good." Dallas used tongs to flip the chicken, then brushed on more sauce.

"Josie Griffin have anything to do with that?"

"Maybe." Dallas cast his brother a sly smile. The more he was around Josie, the more he liked her. Trouble was, she reminded him of a skittish colt. He so much as hinted at maybe wanting to be more than friends and she'd bolt.

"She's pretty. Wholesome."

"Yeah, she is."

"Are you gonna go for her?"

"None of your business. Chicken's done. Get me a damned plate."

"Yessir," Wyatt said, tipping his straw cowboy hat's brim.

"Ladies!" Dallas shouted above the splashing in the pool. "We're about ready for dinner."

The twins grumbled, but Wren and Josie helped them dry off, wrapping them sarong-style in thick towels before sitting them at the table. With both women in Buckhorn logo robes, they joined the girls. Wren and Cash's baby, Robin, was sound asleep in her blanket-covered carrier.

"Here we go." Georgina set a bowl of pasta salad and napkin-wrapped silverware on the table. "Who's hungry?"

"Me!" Betsy cried.

"Me, too!" Bonnie was never one to be outdone.

"Thank you for putting on such a beautiful spread." Josie forked a chicken breast onto her plate. "This all looks delicious."

"Dallas does amazing things with his grill," his mom

said. "His kielbasa is always perfectly done. A little hard on the outside, but soft and juicy inside. Overall, a really lovely taste."

"That's enough about my sausage." A glance toward Josie showed her eyes to be smiling.

"I don't know..." Cash speared his meat, holding up the link for all to view. "My wife has always enjoyed a nice, long sausage over the more stubby varieties."

Wren elbowed his ribs. "You're horrible."

"Yeah, but I'm damned good-looking and all yours, my beauty." When Cash kissed his wife, Dallas fought a jealous twinge. All of a sudden, he missed what his brother had—not his striking good looks, self-confidence or playful attitude that drew folks in like moths to a flame, but the intimacy he and Wren shared. The turning over in the middle of the night and having someone he loved right there beside him. He wanted it with a keen, cutting edge that tore through him, but he'd already had his chance at love and had lost.

"Earmuffs," Josie said to the twins, laughing along with Wren.

"Huh?" Having been so engrossed in buttering her corn cob, Bonnie had missed the entire conversation.

Betsy raised her chin. "Uncle Cash was being bad and Aunt Wren had to yell at him."

"Oh." Used to this occurrence, Bonnie returned her attention to flavoring her corn.

With dinner finished, the girls grew bored with conversations centered on brood mares and how late in the season they were in baling the hay in the east pasture. With them scurrying off to their playhouse, Dallas's mom opened white wine for the ladies and Wyatt grabbed beers for the guys.

"Thought Henry was joining us?" Wyatt helped himself to the few potato chips left in the bowl.

Cash shrugged. "I told him. Don't know what he could've found more exciting than hanging with us."

"More exciting than you, hon?" Wren pushed up from the table's bench. Robin had started to fuss. "Dominoes? Reading the phone book?"

"Ha, ha." Cash stood to help her while together they cooed over their creation. "Somebody's sleepy."

"Me," Wren admitted with a yawn. She wore her long, red hair in a high ponytail. Throw in her freckles and she looked all of twelve. As an intern at Saint Francis Hospital in Tulsa, she worked long enough hours that she was sometimes forced to stay over. This was one of her rare free weekends.

"I guess since my glass is empty, I'll head off to bed, too." His mom hugged Josie. "It was so nice meeting you. Please come again soon."

"Thank you." Josie smiled.

With Cash and Wren making their goodbyes, that left Dallas alone with Josie and Wyatt.

Dallas's younger brother cleared his throat. "Now that I'm officially the third wheel, how about I track down your girls and put them to bed."

"Sounds great to me. Thanks, man."

"No problem."

"Should we clean up this mess?" Josie asked, surveying what little was left from dinner.

"Probably, but I'd rather take our drinks over to that lounger." He nodded toward the cushioned seat built for two. On his way to the girls' playhouse, Wyatt had lit the built-in gas torches. Combined with the glowing pool lights, though the evening had turned nippy, the patio flowers were still fragrant and lush. His brother had also put on one of Cash's Garth Brooks compilation CDs. Countless times, Cash bragged he'd never used it without sealing the deal.

"It's getting late. I probably should just head home."

After consulting his watch, Dallas said, "It's nine-thirty and not even a school night."

"True, but…" Standing, she reached for the empty potato salad dish.

He stood, too, promptly taking it from her, putting the bowl back on the table. "Play with me. It'll be fun."

"The word isn't in my vocabulary."

Shifting deeper into her personal space, he asked, "Play? Fun? Be?"

"Stop." Her breathless giggle told him he was on the right track.

"Why?" Taking her hands, he placed them around his neck. His hands low on her hips, he swayed her in time to the music.

"Dallas…"

"You look awfully cute in that robe." He especially liked her messy pile of crazy-corkscrew hair. How the deep V at her throat guided his eyes to naughty places.

"I'm thirty-three. Hardly in the right age bracket for cute."

"Says who?" Pulling her close enough that even air couldn't squeeze between them, he nuzzled her neck.

"Dallas, please…" She made a halfhearted effort to push him away, but then he slipped his hand beneath her chin, drawing her lips to his. Their kiss was awkward and tender and the most exciting thing to happen to him in years. "…I can't."

"Why?" Dallas kissed her again, this time around,

increasing the pressure, the heat. "Afraid the principal's hiding in the bushes and she'll jump out to give you detention?"

She laughed, but tears formed in her eyes and spilled down her cheeks.

"Hey…" Brushing them with the pads of his thumbs, he asked, "What's this about? There's no crying when I'm trying to get some action."

"I—I know," she said with a sniffle. "Sorry. This is embarrassing."

"No, no I get it. Sort of." He knew the right thing to do was to release her, but instead, he hugged her for all he was worth. He stroked her hair. Whispered that everything would be all right even though he didn't even know what was wrong.

"You're the first person I've kissed since…" Fisting his T-shirt, she admitted, "And I liked it. I mean really liked it. But that's awful. You're a parent to two of my students and—"

"Whoa." Cupping his hands to her tear-stained cheeks, he pressed his lips to hers. When she moaned, he took the opportunity to stroke her tongue with his. "You're too beautiful to cry."

"I'm not," she insisted while he danced her to the chaise.

"You so are…" Guiding her down, he stretched out alongside her, kissing her again, slipping his hand inside her robe, sweeping her collarbone and shoulder. Lowering the robe, he brushed his lips along the trail his fingers had just blazed. Her skin called to mind the softest satin. Cool and smooth and inviting.

"I—I should go," she murmured.

"Later. Now, you have to keep kissing me."

She nodded and then shook her head. "There's so much about me you don't know."

"But I want to. Tell me everything."

"Maybe…" She kissed him again. "I wish I could abandon all that I am. I want to let go of the past—keep the good, but the rest…" She sharply exhaled, leading him to believe her convictions weren't as strong as she claimed. "Do you ever wish you could just delete the past from your brain as easily as a corrupt file from your computer?"

"Sure," he admitted. "Doesn't everyone? But, Josie, your past made you who you are. And I like this woman."

"I—I like you, too. I only wish things could be different—I could be different." Gathering her robe at her throat, she scooted off the lounger, scurrying toward the changing room.

"Josie, wait!" Chasing after her, he stood outside.

When she emerged, fully clothed in her jeans and a sweater and the red boots that'd been one of the first things that had attracted him to her, he searched for the right thing to say, only it wouldn't come. Why?

No doubt because she was right. He'd been a fool to kiss her. She was his daughters' teacher. A friend. Nothing more.

Extending her hand for him to shake, she said, "I had fun. Thank you."

"You're welcome."

Gesturing toward the dinner remains still littering the table, she asked, "Want me to help clean before I go?"

"I'm good. Might even leave it till in the morning."

"Aren't you worried about bugs or possums?"

"Not so much." How in the hell had they gone from kissing to a topic so mundane as night creatures licking the crumbs off their plates? He wanted more from her, but what? Clearly, they shouldn't be physical. But as friends, he'd welcome emotional depth.

"What are you thinking?" she asked. He fought the urge to trace the furrow between her eyes.

He shook his head. "Nothing important. Come on, let me walk you to your car." *And tomorrow, with any luck, I'll wake having forgotten your taste.*

Chapter Eight

"I want details." While her students were in music late Monday morning, Shelby popped into Josie's classroom. "How was the ranch? Everything it's made out to be?"

"Better. Only the curious thing is that I'd expected his family to be snobby—you know, like the stereotypical rich TV ranch family. But in reality, they were all genuinely nice people." Especially Dallas. How long would it take for her to stop reliving their steamy kisses every time she closed her eyes?

"Mmm, sounds dreamy. And here I sat at home with a Lifetime movie and a Lean Cuisine."

Josie couldn't help but smile. "What a coincidence. That perfectly describes most of my weekends."

"Seeing him again?"

"No." Worrying her lower lip, Josie contemplated asking her friend if it was wrong that she wanted to see him again. But why ask when Josie already knew the answer? "Neither of us is looking for anything beyond friendship."

Shelby wrinkled her nose. "He's great-looking, seems nice, has two adorable kids and is probably one of the richest guys in the state. What's the problem with a little canoodling?"

Sighing, Josie admired the diligence of her hard-working kiddos. They were drawing the state of Oklahoma and then adding elements such as the state flower and bird. "When I'm at school, I feel energized. Excited about what I do. But in my personal life…" She frowned. "Nat and I got in a huge fight Saturday afternoon. She thinks I should clear out Emma's room."

"What do you think?"

"I can't even imagine such a thing. Hugh made it somewhat easy on me. I was so angry over him taking his own life that I wanted to get rid of most of his stuff just to put that rage behind me. With Em, it's different. I can't let go."

"Who says you have to?" Sipping at fragrant coffee from the mug she cradled, she added, "Do you honestly think that remodeling her room is going to erase her from your memory?"

"Of course not."

"There's your answer."

"Miss Gwiffin." Thomas waved his paper in the air. "I forgot the bird."

"That's why I put a hint on the Smart Board." She pointed to the front of the room where an oversize image of a scissor-tailed flycatcher standing on the side of a country road was meant for the kids to use as a visual aid.

"Oh!" His big grin lit her heart.

"He's crazy-cute. If only being a grown-up was as simple, huh?" Shelby finished off her coffee.

"True."

Though Josie was still hurt by Natalie's speech, she also found herself in need of educated advice. Which was why, instead of spending lunch in her room sorting papers, she stood outside of Nat's office, waving a Diet Coke still cold from the vending machine. "Truce?"

"No bribes necessary," Natalie declared from behind her desk, wagging her own can, "but I will take a hug."

"Sorry I snapped at you," Josie confessed.

"Sorry I lectured you." Natalie put extra oomph into her hug. "You didn't need that on top of everything else you're going through."

"But that's just it," she said, occupying the nearest of Nat's two guest chairs. "I love my life. Granted, there isn't a day that passes when I don't still miss my daughter, but overall, I have a lot to be thankful for. A great job and supportive friends. Plenty of food in my belly and a roof over my head. Before meeting Dallas, I felt satisfied, but now…"

Nat gasped. "You sly fox. You kissed him, didn't you?"

"Technically," Josie said with a misty smile, "he kissed me, but then the lines of who did what to whom got blurred."

"Do tell." Leaning forward with her elbows on a pile of manila folders, she asked, "How far are we talking? First, second, third base?"

"Second. Get your mind out of the gutter. But what would you think if I confessed to wanting more? Am I a horrible person?"

Snorting, Nat said, "That's the stupidest question I've

ever heard. Why—for even a second—would you think you're not entitled to each second of happiness you can catch?"

"Guilt, I suppose." Worrying the cuticle on her thumb, she admitted, "There's a part of me that feels traitorous for indulging in purely selfish pleasures. I mean, enjoying my work with students is one thing, but sampling Dallas Buckhorn's physical attributes felt like an all-out sin."

"Good." Straightening, Nat clapped her hands. "Love the sound of that. Now, all you have to do is call him."

Josie shook her head. "I told you—and him—I'm not interested. Outside of school, I'm not seeing him again."

"Daddy?" Saturday morning, Dallas woke to Betsy peering at him from the foot of his bed.

"Hey, peanut." His eyes barely working, he asked, "What's wrong? Why are you up so early?"

"I think I'm going to—" She threw up. Everywhere. On his comforter. The carpet. Herself.

"Oh, baby." Going to her, he scooped her into his arms, carrying her to the big soaking tub in his room that she loved. Once he turned on the faucets, adjusting the water just right and then dumping in half a bottle of grape-scented bubbles, he tugged off her smelly, wet clothes before lifting her into the tub. "Poor thing. Did you eat anything weird last night?"

She shook her head.

"Daddy?" Behind him, Bonnie strolled up, her cheeks feverish and pink. "My stomach really—" Quick reflexes got his eldest daughter to the toilet before he had another mess to clean.

With both girls lounging up to their necks in bubbles, he jogged down the hall for cleaning supplies.

"DAAADDY!"

Dallas jogged back to his bathroom to find Betsy wrapped in a towel and hunched over the toilet.

"Good grief, baby…" He rubbed her back. "Think I should sell you and get a new kid who's healthy?"

"You're mean."

"Oh, I was teasing, Miss Sensitivity. You know how much I love you."

She retched again.

Mind reeling, Dallas wasn't sure of his next step. This was the kind of thing Stella or his mom would handle. But with both women gone—his mother on a weekend garden tour in Eureka Springs, Arkansas—he was on his own. Not good, considering that beyond the basics, he didn't know diddly about the girls' medical issues.

That fact served as yet one more reminder of what a crappy father he was. Despite the fact, he knew he was in over his head, and when it came to the twins' well-being, he wasn't opposed to asking for help.

Stepping into the hall, he punched Josie's number into his cell. She answered on the third ring.

"Hey," he said, not wasting time on pleasantries. "I've got an emergency here at the ranch. Mind helping out?"

After hearing a recap of the morning's events, Josie said, "Hang tight. I'll be right there."

Indian summer had been overtaken by a cool drizzle that suited Josie's mood. It wasn't that she minded helping Dallas and his girls, but she did wonder why, when he was surrounded by family, he'd called her.

After dressing in a comfy jogging suit, the trip to the ranch took under twenty minutes.

Dallas opened the door for her, ushering her inside. "Thank goodness you're here."

"If the twins are this sick, why haven't you called a doctor?"

"I'm guessing they have a flu bug, but I don't know the first thing to do. Last night, Mom took off for the weekend and the girls have been tag-teaming me for an hour."

"If it is a virus, hopefully they'll soon have it out of their systems. Have you taken their temperatures?"

"Can't find a thermometer."

"You really are clueless." Slipping off her lightweight jacket, she hung it on a brass hook on the wall. Dallas's dirty-blond hair stuck out at crazy angles and his jaw sported a dark shadow. Dressed in navy flannel PJ bottoms and a white T-shirt that hugged his muscular chest, her mouth went dry from the mere sight of him. What would it be like to have touching privileges? To be able to run her hands along his hard ridges any time she caught the fancy? Forcing her mind back to the matter at hand, she asked, "Where are the patients?"

"Right this way." He shyly extended his hand, and she took it, feeling all of thirteen due to shivery excitement stemming from just his touch. What was happening to her? She was a sensible, grown woman never prone to flights of fancy. *Practical* might as well be her middle and last name. A fling with Dallas would only bring her pain.

True, her conscience conceded, but in the short run, it could also produce an insane amount of pleasure.

"Miss Griffin!" Betsy and Bonnie jumped to the foot of Dallas's bed for hugs.

Bonnie quickly turned green and kept on jumping right off the bed for a run into the bathroom.

Josie chased after her, holding her shoulders. "Sweetie, you're a mess."

"What about me?" Betsy asked. "Am I a mess, too?"

"Absolutely." Josie took a washcloth from a pile of them tucked into a linen nook. Wetting it with cold water, she held it to Bonnie's forehead. "There you go," she soothed. "I know it hurts, but the more you get out, the faster you'll feel better. All of the bugs have to go away."

"I have bugs?"

"Sort of." Easing onto the cool tile floor alongside the commode, Josie drew the girl onto her lap, gently rocking. How many times had she held Emma like this? Truth be told, being a mom again—even on a temporary basis—felt amazing. "Teeny tiny germs get into your body and cause all sorts of trouble. That's why it's important to wash your hands a lot—especially this time of year."

"Oh." Bonnie leaned back against her, obviously exhausted.

"I like washing my hands and playing with the soap," Betsy exclaimed. "I like to squirt out lots of soap so it looks like slimy boogers between my fingers."

"That's gross," Bonnie said.

"I agree." Josie hugged her tighter, relishing the sensation, however long it lasted. Her emotions battled, but for now at least, the pleasurable present won over her painful past. It broke her heart to see Bonnie so ill, but to be needed again on such a basic level was bliss. "But at least it gets your sister nice and squeaky clean."

Betsy made a face. "I *don't* squeak!"

It took a while but the twins finally stopped throwing up. Josie tucked them into bed, and with both girls sleeping, she dared leave their side.

Dallas entered his room, thermometer in hand. "Found it in Mom's room."

When he offered it to her, she waved it away. "I've felt enough feverish bodies to guess they're running a tad over a hundred. Besides, with the girls finally resting, I'd hate to wake them."

Nodding, he said, "Sounds reasonable." After a moment's awkward silence, he said, "Thanks for coming. I know I could've handled this on my own, but it seemed too overwhelming."

Gesturing for him to follow her into the hall, she whispered, "I understand the first few months of school can be daunting but, Dallas, helping your children when they're sick is a pretty basic parenting skill." One she'd learned early on with her own daughter.

Scowling, he said, "I'm a horrible father. I get it. You don't have to rub it in."

"I'm not." But was she? She'd move heaven and earth if given one more second with Emma. Here, Dallas had been given the gift of two precious children, yet he didn't seem to realize how lucky he was.

Heels of his hands on his forehead, eyes closed, he suggested, "Feel free to take off. I'll handle things from here."

"Don't be like that."

"What did you expect?" Arms now tightly folded, he refused to meet her stare.

"Not for you to pout like one of your girls over a little constructive criticism."

Still beyond miffed by Josie's lack of support, Dallas led her toward his mother's favorite room.

His mom loved to read, so his father had the library built just for her. Ten-foot shelves lined one wall, a half wall overlooked the living room and the third wall consisted of custom paned windows that towered toward the ceiling's peak. Lounge chairs and ottomans provided comfortable seating while side tables held his father's statuary bronze lamp collection which illuminated pages with just the right amount of light. A study table built from a massive redwood slab had served him and his brothers and sister through too many term papers to count.

"This is amazing," Josie noted, staring up in awe. Six skylights provided an abundance of natural light. "The more I see of this house, the more I understand why everyone in town talks about it."

"I've never really thought about it, but yeah. Guess I'm lucky to have grown up here." The chair he sat in had a Sharpie stain on the rolled arm. Wyatt had been grounded for a week once their mother found out he'd tattooed the dog with the same pen. "How about you?" he forced himself to ask if for no other reason than to prove that as a grown man, he certainly didn't pout. "Where are your roots?"

"Here and there. I was born in Michigan, but spent most of my life in Oklahoma City. My husband's first job out of college was for the First National Bank of Weed Gulch. When I landed a position with the school, we felt as if our every dream had come true."

"How did he die?" The second Dallas asked the question, he regretted it. Her complexion paled as she pressed her lips into a thin line. "Not that it's any of my business."

"He shot himself."

"Holy shit," he blurted without thinking. "You're that guy's wife? I remember when it happened." The man used his grandfather's shotgun to do the deed. If memory served him right, Josie had been the one to find him. For a town the size of Weed Gulch, such shocking news traveled like wildfire, though Dallas by no means knew everyone.

Sharply looking away, she said, "You were right. I should go." She stood, but with his hands to her shoulders, he urged her down.

"Sorry. My question was innocent enough. Last thing I intended was to dredge up an awful time."

"I appreciate your apology, but it's best I go." This time when she stood, he didn't stop her.

Hands in his pockets, he admitted, "I—I don't know what to say."

"No one does." Already on the stairs, she beat him to the bottom.

Chasing, he tried stopping her from taking her jacket from the wall peg, but was too late. "Please, stay. I'm a pig."

"Far from it. To the contrary, I'm a woman whose husband was so desperate to escape her he put a bullet in his head."

Chapter Nine

Josie escaped to her car with Dallas running barefoot after her. "Get back in the house," she barked. "Your girls are alone."

"Just this once, they'll survive." He braced his hands on her car door. "Right now, you're my main concern. You can't drop a bombshell like that and then run."

"Watch me." She started the engine.

"Knock it off. Why the hell are you pissed? I asked a legit question, you told me the answer. End of story. We never need speak of it again."

"Just because we're not talking about it," she snapped, gripping the steering wheel with all of her might, "doesn't mean what Hugh did isn't always going to be with me. His blood has become a stain on my soul." She wasn't upset with Dallas, she was grateful to him for jolting her back to reality. She'd enjoyed feeling needed. Too much.

Lounging in a big, comfy bed with an attractive man and his girls had been like fate waving a huge, red warning flag smack in front of her face.

Don't get too close.

"Josie, please… Sure, I'd like to talk this out, but beyond that, I still need help with the girls."

Exasperated with this man who was incapable of doing a task as simple as holding comforting cool cloths to his daughters' heads, Josie shot him a look of raw disgust before aiming her car away from his maddeningly handsome face.

"Henry," Dallas said as he entered the barn office later that afternoon. The twins had slept off whatever had been ailing them and, after having them checked out by Wren, he'd helped saddle their ponies. Though low clouds hugged brown earth, the air smelling of wet leaves and straw, Dallas figured fresh air never did a body harm. "That woman's maddening as they come."

"Which one?" Henry asked, not looking up from whittling the body of a toy car. By each Christmas, he'd made dozens of them for a local church. The guy loved kids, and it warmed Dallas's heart that the same man who'd been a friend and confidant to him while growing up was now doing the same for the next generation of Buckhorns. "Ask me, any female over the age of ten is more trouble than she's worth."

Glancing up from the feed order, Dallas chuckled. "That's just because you've yet to find a woman who'd have you."

The old coot shook his hat-covered head.

"Anyway, I was talking about the girls' teacher."

"Pretty thing." He chipped off the portion of the pine block he'd use as a fender. "Like that mess of red hair."

"Me, too." Alas, she also possessed a forked tongue with the venom to match.

"So what's your problem?" He set his work aside on a battered leather trunk filling in as a side table. Using a whisk broom, he made quick work of cleaning his mess. "It's fixin' to rain again and I figure I'd better wrangle down the twins."

"I'll get them," Dallas volunteered, still fuming from Josie's digs at his daddy skills. "And, anyway, all I was gonna say is that the woman makes me crazy. One minute, running hot. Next, biting like a January wind."

Shrugging, Henry tipped his hat. "Ask me, you're better off on your own." Alongside the desk, the grizzled cowboy patted Dallas's back. "Come on. We'll get the girls in together, then have that sister-in-law of yours watch them while we grab a couple beers."

"Bet you ten bucks you won't climb that sexy behind up on the pool table and give us a dance."

"Oh." Josie tipped back the remains of her rum and Coke, flashing the cowboy at the bar her brightest smile. "After I've had a few more of these, I'll take you up on that bet and raise you twenty." Remington's Bar and Motel out by the toll road had a reputation around Weed Gulch for being the kind of establishment ladies didn't frequent, but so far, Josie had found all of the men to be extraordinarily nice—unlike Dallas.

With honky-tonk country music blaring from the jukebox, she ordered another drink before hopping down from her barstool to dance. Her favorite red boots stood out in stark contrast against the wood floor, making her giggle. Dancing was fun!

Someone in the growing crowd wolf whistled, only spurring her on. Removing the ponytail holder that held her hair, she bent at her waist, flipping her curls down and back, giving them a good shake. If these boys wanted a show, she wouldn't disappoint. Hugh might not have wanted her, but there were plenty of other men who'd be proud to have her for their girl.

Music pumping, she unbuttoned the top of her plaid blouse, showing just enough cleavage to tease before undoing the bottom as well, tying the tails halter style.

"Take it all off!" a man in the crowd shouted.

"You wish," she teased with a flirty sashay of her prairie skirt. "But if one of you bring me another rum and Coke with extra cherries, you might just get an extra-warm thank-you in return."

"Woo-hoo!" several men shouted, pumping their fists.

"Someone get this girl more rum!" a T-shirt-wearing trucker shouted. "We've got us a stripper ready to go!"

Swaying her hips in smooth figure eights while her audience cheered, Josie had just bent low enough to give the men in the front row more to cheer about when the music abruptly stopped.

"What gives?" one guy who'd been especially into her show groused.

Parting the crowd was Dallas.

Standing a good six inches taller than any of the men around him, the stony set of his jaw told all assembled to steer clear.

"Josie." He grated his words from between clenched teeth. "You need to get the hell out of here."

"Make me," she taunted with a shake of her hips.

Growling, he stepped up, grasped her about the thighs and swung her over his shoulder with no more care than if she'd been a feed sack bound for the horse barn.

"Put me down!" she shrieked, pummeling and kicking as he swept her through the gaping crowd.

"Hey!" the trucker protested. "Bring her back! This was just getting good!"

Ignoring the many complaints, as well as her continued shrieking, Dallas marched right out the door. Once he'd crossed from the bar lot over to the motel's, he finally set Josie to her feet. "What the hell kind of stunt were you pulling? You're a freakin' kindergarten teacher. Aren't you right up there on the virgin meter next to nuns?"

"News flash," Josie said, hands on her hips, "but I'm a grown woman and if I want to dance in a honky-tonk or anywhere else, I damn well will."

He winced. "No cussing from you, either—and button your shirt."

Raising her chin, she sassed, "I will cuss and strip whenever and wherever I like, thank you very much."

"Look, I did you a favor. Do you really want some clown chronicling your striptease on his phone, then posting it on the Web for the world to see?"

"Like that would ever happen. I was just having fun."

"Taking off your clothes?" Growling in frustration, he tossed his head back. "You're a disaster. How much have you had to drink?"

Giggling, she admitted, "Two. The cherries were *really* yummy."

"Uh-huh…" Glancing about the empty parking lot, he said, "Let's get you home."

"No." After stomping her foot to show him she meant

business, she turned back to the bar. "I came here to find a man who won't hurt me, and I'm not leaving till I do."

Dragging her back by her shirtsleeve, he asked, "Of all places in Oklahoma to find a man, why here?"

Biting her lower lip to keep it from trembling, she shifted her weight from one foot to the other. "I already went the traditional route—marrying a guy from college. You know what happened there. I've dated around, but they were all duds. Then there's you—has there *ever* been a bigger walking disaster?"

"Me?" He coughed. "I must need a few more shots of whiskey, because I thought you just said I'm not date worthy."

"Oh—I did." Her exaggerated nod made her yawn. Who knew dancing could be such hard work? "You're a lousy parent, don't appreciate even half of the blessings you've been given—worst of all…" she made a drum beat on the battered Ford pickup alongside her "…you're a tease."

"E-excuse me?"

"Oh—don't go pretending you don't know what I'm talking about. The night I shared dinner with your family, and then we played Five Minutes in Heaven by the pool, you kissed me breathless. You kissed me until I was consumed with nothing but horrible thoughts of having you inside me, but—" Lowering her voice, she asked, "Wanna know a secret?"

Arms crossed, Dallas leaned on a Chevy and said, "Why not?"

"I'm a kindergarten teacher. I'm not supposed to even know naughty things, let alone think them! It's bad. Very, very bad. And, anyway, since you're a horrible tease,

I suspect you don't even know how to *truly* please a woman."

"That a challenge?" The bar door opened and three drunken rednecks spilled out, carrying with them laughter and the chorus of a country song about whiskey making you frisky. "'Cause if it is…" He crossed to her Ford, bracing his hands on the front fender, effectively, deliciously, caging her in. "I'm more than happy to grab us a room and show you just how wrong you are."

"Big words, cowboy, but I'm not seeing a lot of follow-through." What she was getting was an awful lot of quivery, hot sensations overriding the alcohol. Somewhere far in the back of her head, a voice reasoned to call Natalie for a ride home to sleep it off. But how could she possibly do that when a cowboy of epic proportions stood close enough for her to realize the bulge pressing against her midsection was in no way the proverbial flashlight.

Tugging her toward him, he asked, "You sure this isn't just booze talking?"

"Only thing I'm sure of is that even though you annoy and infuriate me, for some unfathomable reason you still turn me on—despite not being able to deliver."

"Oh—if that's what you want, sugar, that's exactly what you're gonna get." He kissed her hard, but then soft, dizzying her with the sweep of his tongue. Suddenly too warm clothes left little to the imagination. It was no secret he wanted her and Josie was hot for him, too. Abruptly sober, tired of being the perpetual good girl, Josie abandoned everything she knew to be right and so-called decent in favor of unbuckling Dallas's big, silver belt buckle. Still kissing, she unfastened the button on his jeans, lowering the zipper to set him free.

He felt like hot, silken steel and she wanted him inside

her with a ferocity that bordered on madness. Her rum buzz had been replaced by plain old lust. Breasts swelling and aching against his chest, she wanted to forget all worries and focus on the here and now. On the sensations flooding her limbs with devil-may-care pleasure.

Hefting her skirt, tearing her thong only to let it fall to the gravel lot, Dallas rasped, "Let's get this party started."

Cloaked in the shadows, he lifted her, urging her legs around him. Hands gripping her buns, he slid her onto his erection. She gasped from his initial size, but then opened, taking him in, making them one.

Her backside cold against the Ford, the front of her felt superheated, clinging to him, trusting him to make everything better.

Lowering his mouth to her chest and then breasts, he sucked, biting through her lacy bra. Nipples hard, raw with sensation, his actions only worsened the wondrous tension building within her.

In and out he thrust with her clinging, clawing his back with her hands beneath his shirt. When the pleasure-pain was nearly too much to bear, white-hot heat drowned her in its light.

He tensed and then shuddered, with the bulk of her weight still resting on the truck, he nuzzled her neck, moving his attentions upward, ultimately landing on swollen lips.

"Take it back," he said, voice still sex-raspy.

"What?" she teased, knowing full well what he meant. The man might be a lot of things, but in this particular area, he'd more than delivered.

His growl culminated in another kiss that rocketed to her toes. "We're going to regret this in the morning."

With him still inside her, she refused to think further than the next few seconds in his arms.

"I already do," she admitted, yanking her skirt back to a decent level once he'd landed her on her feet. "I don't know what came over me."

"Judging by your taste, rum," Dallas mumbled, zipping his fly. "In my case, beer."

While each fumbled with the business of straightening their clothes, Josie fought the niggling fear that not only had she made a fool of herself, but she was also on the verge of being sick. What had she done? Why? Was she really so hard up for validation?

"I'm sorry," Dallas finally said, kicking gravel with the toe of his boot. "I never meant for this to happen—"

"I feel the same. Trust me, we need never speak of it again."

An audible sigh told the story of his relief. "You're in no shape to drive. Can I give you a lift? My ranch foreman will handle getting your car home."

Wanting to refuse, Josie mumbled her thanks, knowing Dallas was just being practical.

What she couldn't say—would *never* say—was that no matter how ill-advised their actions had just been, she feared it would be a good long while before she forgot his feel and taste. A horrible fate, considering she never wanted to see or think of the man again!

Chapter Ten

"**Y**ou okay?" Monday morning, Nat stood behind Josie in the school cafeteria lunch line. "The look of death doesn't become you."

Josie shot her supposed friend a dirty look.

Nat took an apple from the fruit bar. "Don't suppose your gray complexion and bloodshot eyes have anything to do with dancing at Remington's?"

Beyond mortified, not to mention still hungover, Josie focused on the chicken stir-fry Paula had put on her plastic tray.

"Mike—that UPS guy I've been seeing—was there. Said you put on quite a show."

"Remind me at the end of this school year to move. I'm tired of my private life being everyone's business."

Nat thanked Paula for her loaded tray. "Then you probably don't want to hear that gossip also has it that you and Dallas disappeared for a good thirty minutes out in the parking lot. Or that his ranch foreman drove your car home."

"Shh…" Turning her attention to Paula, Josie said, "I'll have green beans, too, please."

"The rumors are true?" The cafeteria worker's grin was even cheesier than Nat's. "You and Dallas Buckhorn are, like, a couple?"

"Of course not." How upset would Josie's principal be if she up and quit midyear? Not only didn't she frequent Remington's, but she definitely had never indulged in a parking lot liaison. Worse yet, Josie's mind refused to stop replaying the mortifying public tryst. Memories brought with them the scorching brand of Dallas's fingertips on her behind.

"She'll deny it," Nat said, adding her apple to her filled tray, "but check out those red cheeks. I'm telling you— something's up."

Josie elbowed her friend's ribs. "Knock it off. I'm as single as they come and planning to stay that way."

"Boo."

In line at Weed Gulch's only combination gas and convenience store, Josie spun around to face Dallas in all of his glory. "It's you."

"Oh, come on," he leaned low to whisper in her ear, in the process sending a myriad of shivers through her, "play nice. We shared a moment. That's all. We still have the rest of the girls' school year to get through."

"With that in mind," she fairly hissed, praying no one either of them knew witnessed their scene as they moved up in line, "I think it best we only see each other in a school setting." A week had passed since she'd last seen him, yet as far as her body was concerned it might as well have been mere seconds. He hadn't so much as grazed her, yet her whole body hummed.

Outside, she'd filled her car's tank, paying at the pump. Her only item was a twelve-pack of Sprite.

"Let me carry that for you." Without asking, Dallas took it from her, setting his own supersize pack of beef jerky on top.

Irritable and feeling achy all of a sudden, Josie grumbled, "I managed just fine on my own, thank you very much."

"Of course, you did." He winked and her stomach fluttered in response. "But would it kill you to let a guy be a gentleman?"

"No." But at the rate her pulse raced from his mere proximity—yes, technically, she may die. But oh, what a way to go. She'd forgotten his sheer size. The breadth of his shoulders and slightly bowlegged walk, as if he'd spent so much time on a horse, that even while standing on solid ground he craved being in his saddle. Reminding herself further nonprofessional fraternization between them would be ill-advised, Josie was beyond thrilled to have made it to the front of the line. "Could I please have my pop?"

He set it on the counter, but insisted on paying.

Though she thanked him, back at the pumps, she asked, "Was that necessary? What if someone had seen? What don't you get about the fact that I don't want to be associated with you."

He set the case atop her car. "Hell, woman, it's just soda. Nothing to get your panties in a wad about, because trust me, last thing I need—or want—is one more female messing with my life."

"No." Bonnie stomped her feet and clamped her mouth shut.

"Daddy," Betsy announced from in front of the twins' double bathroom vanity, "that means she's not going to brush her teeth tonight because the toothpaste is poison."

"That's stupid." Dallas flipped open the lid to the bubble gum sparkle flavor he'd bought specifically because Bonnie had wanted it. Taking a whiff, he noted, "Smells good to me—like a wad of that stuff you chew every day."

"It tastes icky and I won't stick it in my mouth." And to prove it, she ripped it from Dallas's hand only to toss it in the toilet.

"Oooh," Becky said. "You're in trouble."

Dallas's first instinct was to call for his mother. Then he was wishing for Stella to return.

Bonnie propped her little fists on her hips and raised her chin, challenging him with a ghostly blue-eyed stare he hadn't seen for five agonizing years. If for only an instant, Bobbie Jo returned in the little girl their love had created. And it physically, emotionally, drove him to his knees.

"Daddy?" Betsy wrapped her arms around him in a hug. "Are you crying?"

Swiping tears he'd never wanted his girls to see, he said, "Nope. I'm just fine, and Bonnie's going to stick her hand in the toilet and get the toothpaste. She's then going to muck stalls until she's earned enough money to pay for it."

"Am not! Am not! Am not!" After screaming her declaration at him, she ran for her room.

"Oooh." Betsy shook her head. "Now she's *really* gonna get it."

"Go to bed," Dallas said wearily.

Betsy scampered off, and he completed Bonnie's task, washed his hands then pondered heading to her room to lecture her, but on what? He had never missed his wife more. When it came to raising their girls, he suddenly felt as if he was failing miserably. When had they changed from adorable munchkins to monsters?

Before their wild night, Dallas would've asked Josie for help, but now that he recognized just how little self-control he had in keeping his hands off her, he felt powerless in that arena, as well.

Maybe someday he'd be ready for a second shot at love, but for now, becoming the father Bobbie Jo had trusted him to be was his number-one goal.

Of all the rotten luck...

Dallas stood in the candy aisle of Mefford's—the town's only pharmacy. Surveying the antacids in the next section was Josie. Outside, the wind was fiendish and her red corkscrew curls formed a sexy-as-hell mane. The cold had pinkened her cheeks and the lips that still haunted his every daydream.

Hoping to avoid the woman, Dallas took the long way to the checkout, down the bandage and corn pad aisle. Too bad for him, Josie must've used the same tactic. Her furrowed brows told him she was just as annoyed by another chance meeting as him.

"Fancy meeting you here," he said with what he hoped came off as a casual laugh.

"Getting ready early for trick-or-treaters?" she asked, eyeing his cart brimming with sweets.

"Nah. I've had trouble getting the girls to do their chores, so I figured positive reinforcement might work.

You know, get them to brush their teeth, hand them a candy bar—that sort of thing." He cringed. "Not that they'd get to eat it right then, but later."

Josie crossed her arms and pressed her lips.

"What? You think it'd be better if I spanked them?"

"Dallas, most kids want their parents' attention. Have you ever tried something as simple as talking to them—especially Bonnie—and hearing from her why she's developed a penchant for trouble?"

Rolling his eyes, he noted, "I'm a grown man, and if I can't figure out how to fix her, how is she supposed to tell me?"

Hands to her temples, she closed her eyes. "You're an impossible man. Just once, when you ask for advice, and I take time from my schedule to give it, would you at least grant me the courtesy of pretending to listen?"

"I did, but I seriously doubt something as simple as asking Bonnie why she's so sassy is going to produce radical change." Shaking his head and sighing, he muttered, "I'm starting to think maybe you're not such a great teacher."

"Funny," she snipped, "because I'm now certain you're an awful father."

In the drugstore parking lot, Josie was so upset by the nasty exchange that she retched in the grass alongside her car.

Life wasn't just unfair, but downright cruel.

In her heart, she knew she'd been an amazing mother. Emma had been the center of her existence. Josie had been firm when needed, gentle and loving and fun when not. She'd taught her basic numbers in fun ways like lying on the grass, counting clouds.

How dare Dallas accuse her of being anything less

than an excellent teacher? Because in doing so, he'd also touched a raw nerve. How many times had she blamed herself for not having been more in tune with her husband? If she'd recognized his drug problem in time to find him help, would her happy life have never changed? Would Emma still be here, a lovely little girl with her whole life ahead of her?

That line of thought sent Josie retching into the bushes.

"Hey…" Tone considerably softer than the last time they'd talked, Dallas stepped up behind her. "You all right?"

"Does it look like it?" she snapped.

"Whoa." Holding up his hands, he said, "I was just asking a simple question. No need to bite my head off."

"Oh—there's every need." She hadn't thought it possible to feel worse, but being near Dallas caused a headache in addition to her nausea. "You and I made a mistake. A horrible, *horrible* mistake. We're not friends. I don't need you coming over here to check on me, when I'm obviously fine."

"Whatever." Turning his back on her, he walked away. "But I'd do the same for a stranger."

Josie should have been pleased, but was instead oddly sad. Which made no sense. But then neither did this wretched flu refusing her a moment's peace.

"No," Bonnie said that night when Dallas presented her with a new brand of toothpaste.

Betsy announced, "She doesn't like that one, either."

Dallas was on the verge of brushing Bonnie's teeth himself whether she liked it or not, when he thought back to the brief conversation he and Josie had shared before things had gone bad. She'd urged him to talk to his daughters. Genuinely talk to them—as if they were old enough to understand.

"Tell me something," he asked his oldest girl on a whim, "why are you always giving me so much trouble about brushing your teeth? You didn't used to. What's changed?"

Opening her mouth, she put her finger inside, proudly wiggling her right front tooth. "What if when I stick the brush in there it knocks my tooth out and then I choke half to death?"

"Okay, wait—when you threw your last paste in the toilet, you said it was because it tasted bad."

"It did," she said with a cock of her head. "'Cause if it knocked out my tooth and I choked half to death it would've been poison."

Dallas supposed that was logical enough thinking— if you were five. "So let me get this straight, you refuse to brush until that tooth falls out?"

She nodded.

Betsy suggested, "What if she just brushes all around that one? Would that work, Bonnie?"

"I s'pose." And just like that, the battle and war had been won.

While Dallas was certain this small victory by no means marked the end of his parenting trials, at least he'd managed to do one thing right—and he hadn't even resorted to candy bar bribes.

Though he knew he had Josie to thank, his mouth went dry at the mere thought of admitting her victory. The woman made him crazy. Meaning the less he thought about her, the better off he'd be.

"I'm worried about you." A week later, Josie had just put the last of her kids on the bus when Nat approached, blowing on her hands to ward off the cold. "You're even more pale than usual."

"In case you hadn't noticed," Josie said, hustling into the warm school, "the sun hasn't been out in days."

"Still…" Nat held open the door.

Cheeks stinging from the sudden warmth, Josie asked, "Have I mentioned lately how great you are for my ego?"

"Don't blame me. Shelby and the office crew noticed, too. When was your last physical?"

"Oh, for heaven's sake." Ignoring her friend, Josie headed for her room to work on assembling student portfolios. "When you have something fun to talk about come see me."

Josie had barely been at her desk twenty minutes when her eyelids grew heavy. Exhaustion clung to her, weighing down on her shoulders like a warm velvet cape. Figuring a catnap wouldn't hurt, she rested her head on her desk…

Waking three hours later to find her classroom dark, Josie conceded it was time to give her doctor a call.

By Monday of the next week, Josie sat in Doc Haven's office, having her blood pressure taken by his nurse. She still hadn't shaken her bug and it was getting ridiculous how many times she'd had to ask Shelby to watch her class. It couldn't be normal that she spent more time in the bathroom than with her students.

"Perfect," the nurse said. "One-twenty over seventy-five."

"Good to know I'm not having a heart attack," Josie grumbled.

"Oh, now, can't be all that bad. Open up and let me take your temperature." When that turned out to be normal as well, she said, "Run on down to the bathroom and tinkle in a cup for me, and then the doctor will be in."

Josie thanked the woman before completing her task.

Back in the exam room, she sat on the crinkly paper, hating the way it felt beneath her. Adding cranky to her list of symptoms, she slid off the table to fish through a magazine basket. Settling on *People*, she was midway through an article on stars with their own Vegas shows when a knock sounded on the door.

"Everyone decent?" Doc asked, slowly opening the door while reading her chart. Looking up, he seemed surprised. "Well, hello. Don't I usually see you on your turf?"

"Nothing personal," Josie said with a wry smile, "but afraid so. We all appreciated you showing up so fast last week when Lyle Jenkins fell off the monkey bars. From the backward angle of his arm, even I could tell it wasn't a simple strain."

"No kidding," Doc said with a whistle. "Poor kid's gonna be in a cast for a while." Taking a seat on a rolling black stool, he asked, "Back to you, what seems to be the problem?"

Josie described her now-impressive list of symptoms, convinced she must've picked up some rare flu. "I love my job, but it's gotten to the point that I literally have to force myself out of bed in the morning."

"Hmph." Standing, bushy gray eyebrows furrowed, the doctor checked her eyes, nose and throat. He felt the lymph nodes at the base of her head. Had her lie down while he palpated her abdomen and stomach. "All of the usual suspects seem fine. When was your last period?"

"Few weeks ago. It was lighter than usual, but nothing too out of the ordinary."

"Is there a chance you might be pregnant?"

"Absolutely not." While carrying Emma, she'd never felt better. Now, she resembled the walking dead. Whereas she'd been upset with her friends for noticing how awful she looked, now it'd gotten to the point where it wasn't anything she could hide.

Nodding, he jotted the information in her chart. "Sit tight while I get my nurse back in here to draw blood."

Joy. Nothing made her already agitated stomach more uneasy than the sight of her own blood.

Another knock sounded at the door, but instead of the nurse like she'd expected, it was Doc. "Ran into the lab tech in the hall. Looks like we caught a lucky break in figuring out what's wrong."

Pregnant.

The whole ride home, Josie couldn't decide whether to laugh or cry. Spotting is normal for some women the doctor said when she'd told him about her period. As for her feeling great when carrying Emma, he'd explained that away, too. Apparently each pregnancy plays by its own rules.

In her cozy little house she fed Kitty before making a beeline for Emma's room. While some people went to the cemetery to talk with their deceased loved ones, she'd always felt closer to her daughter here.

"Sweetie, I never saw this coming, did you?"

When she'd heard she was carrying her daughter, she'd cried from happiness. Now, hands covering her still-flat stomach, she wasn't sure what to feel. Of course, she was excited, but in a cautious way. As she would be if it was rumored Santa was bringing her a new laptop for Christmas. No use in celebrating until she had the box—or baby, in this case—in her hands.

On her feet, Josie moved about the room, touching photos of Emma when she'd been a baby and then a toddler and then a little girl at her first teddy bear tea party.

The phone rang.

Josie jogged to her bedroom to answer and said with forced cheer, "Nat, great news. Doc Haven says I'm anemic." True. She wasn't ready to tell anyone the rest.

"That's it? Did you tell him how queasy you've been?"

"He gave me a head-to-toe exam and aside from the iron, I'm the perfect picture of health."

"Whew. That means you'll be able to come Christmas shopping in Tulsa this weekend with me and Shelby."

Laughing, she perched on the side of the bed. "I'm touched by the depth of your concern."

"You know how worried I've been."

"Yes, I do," she said, plucking a brown leaf from the ivy on her nightstand. "I also know how much you've been dreading hitting the malls."

"Got me there," she admitted, "but back to your health, so all you have to do is pop a few vitamins and you'll be fine?"

"Uh-huh." Especially in about seven and a half more months.

When Josie returned the cordless phone to its charger, she was trembling. Not so much from fear of once again becoming a mother, but from telling Dallas he was going to be a father.

Forcing a breath, she dug her cell from the bottom of

her purse and flipped it open to find Dallas's number. Once he answered, she said, "Are you available for dinner tomorrow night? We need to talk."

Chapter Eleven

Dallas was more than a little perplexed by Josie's invitation. Their last conversation wasn't even civil. When he'd questioned her as to why she felt the sudden need to play nice, she'd seemed evasive. Significant? Probably not, but as he parallel parked his truck in front of her vine-covered cottage home, he couldn't help but wonder if there would be more to the night than a simple meal.

Three weeks into October, though it was only six, darkness had fallen on an overcast day. The air was cool and crisp and laced with the scent of burning leaves. Somewhere on the block an old hound bayed. With no leaves on the trees, the lonesome sound echoed down the street.

He liked this season.

Crunching through fallen oak and maple leaves in

her yard, he mounted the few steps to the front porch, ringing the bell.

She opened the door, holding out her arm to gesture him inside. "Hurry. It's chilly."

On his way past, he handed her a bottle of merlot and a flower bouquet. "Thanks for the invite."

"You're welcome." She shut the door.

"What smells so good?"

"Roast. It's been in the Crock-Pot all day." He trailed her into a homey kitchen that was too frilly for his taste, but he could see where a woman would find it appealing. While she put the bouquet of fall blooms in an antique Mason jar, he started rummaging through drawers.

"What are you looking for?" she asked.

"Corkscrew." Why, he couldn't say, but his runaway pulse sent signals to his brain that this was a date, when nothing could be farther from the truth. He needed a drink. Preferably bourbon, but in a pinch, vino would do.

From down the hall, a cat came running only to hit a full stop, sitting back on his or her haunches.

"Who is this furry creature joining us for dinner?" Dallas asked, kneeling to stroke Josie's pet behind its ears.

"Kitty is the man of the house, and has highly discriminating tastes. I doubt he would lower himself to sample my fare."

Chuckling, Dallas scratched under the cat's chin. "Sorry, fella. I have a feeling you don't know what you're missing."

"Speaking of missing," she said, nodding behind him. "You might check over there for the corkscrew." Josie placed the flowers on an antique, hardwood table. "Second drawer down, to the right of the stove."

"Thanks."

While he popped the cork, she got glasses, holding them out for him to pour. "You're trembling."

"Hungry," she said, hastily setting them on the counter. "Thomas lost a tooth, then misplaced it. Took a couple hours to find it. My whole afternoon was shot. With what little time was left over, we played number bingo."

"Sounds good to me." He grinned. "Especially since my girls weren't involved in the tooth incident—I hope."

Pushing aside her wine, she said, "You're safe. They actually helped with the search."

"Whew." He feigned wiping sweat from his brow.

"We've got about twenty minutes till the potatoes are ready. What would you like to do? Cards? TV?"

Finishing his wine, pouring a fresh glass, he asked, "How about we use that time to get to the heart of the matter—why you called."

"Yes, um, about that…" Her complexion blazed, much to his dismay, making her all the more attractive. Making the night in general all the more strange.

A timer dinged—saving her from giving him a straight answer.

While Josie took homemade yeast rolls from the oven, she delegated jobs for him like retrieving milk and butter and sour cream that Josie used to create decadent mashed potatoes. Fresh asparagus and gravy rounded out the meal.

Kitty slept through it all, lightly snoring on a thickly padded window seat.

"My mother would be jealous of your skills," he admitted after dishing out thirds of roast. Creamy horseradish dipping sauce made his taste buds sing. "At the ranch, she's the only one allowed to prepare meals."

"What did your wife have to say about that?"

"Actually, she enjoyed it. She was a cowgirl through and through. Loved working cattle with me. Hated being indoors." Aside from their love of children, the two women couldn't have been more different.

"Oh." She lowered her gaze to her plate.

"Why would you care? It's not like you and I would ever have a connection that would place you out on the range."

Paling, she excused herself before making a mad dash toward a hall bathroom.

By the time she returned, some of her color was back, but not all. He'd cleared the table and managed to put most of the food away in the Rubbermaid tubs he'd found in a bottom drawer.

"Thanks," she said with an awkward wave toward the nearly clean kitchen.

"Sure. No problem."

She took a Sprite from the fridge, rolling the cool can across her forehead before popping the top.

"You're scaring me," he admitted, alarmed by the way she clung to the counter edge for support.

Waving away his concern, she said, "I'm fine."

At least, Josie's doctor had assured her that physically she and the baby were in tip-top condition. During the first trimester, nausea and exhaustion often came with the territory. But it hadn't with Emma. Which made Josie's predicament all the more confusing. On the one hand, she felt beyond blessed to have been given a second chance at motherhood. On the other, she felt terrified and guilty and shocked. Worse yet, Dallas was an incompetent father.

At least he'd helped with the dishes.

By the time the kitchen was clean, Josie was a nervous wreck. She'd invited Dallas to her home for a very specific reason. One she'd gotten nowhere near broaching.

Mouth dry, she forced breaths, willing her pulse to slow.

No such luck.

Dallas handed her a plate, which, because it was still wet and she was still shaky with nerves, she promptly dropped.

"I'll get it," Dallas said, already on his knees, plucking five clean-cut pieces from the floor and tossing them in the trash. From an undercabinet dispenser, he took a paper towel, dampening it before running it across the floor. "There you go. Safe for your bare feet and Kitty's."

"Thanks. I don't know what's wrong with me. I'm usually not so clumsy."

Back at the sink, washing the gravy pan, he asked, "You ever going to get around to why you're talking to me again?"

"Okay…" Sitting hard on the nearest chair, she sharply exhaled. "You're here for a couple of reasons."

He turned off the faucet.

Seated beside her, he took her hands in his. "Does this have to do with your husband?"

She shook her head.

"Then what? Out with it, already."

Standing, she summoned her every shred of courage to say, "Come on. There's something I want to show you."

Following Josie down the dimly lit hall, the heavy meal Dallas just inhaled threatened to bolt. What the hell had she been hiding?

She stopped before a closed door.

Tears shone in her brown eyes.

One hand to her chest, she used her other to turn a crystal doorknob. The night was moonless. The room black. She fumbled for the overhead light switch. With the room immersed in a soft, golden glow, Dallas lost all words. The scene was reminiscent of the twins' room. Pretty and pink with piles of stuffed animals and a pint-size table set for young ladies and dolls. A canopy bed, dripping in lace, took center stage along with custom-built shelves filled with books and toys and whimsically framed photos. The only thing missing from the enchanted space was the little girl it'd obviously been meant for.

Josie backed into an overstuffed lounge chair, cradling her face in her hands. "Even after four years, the pain feels crushing—like a heart attack no medicine can heal. I wasn't sure if you remembered hearing about the car crash before Hugh's suicide."

Sighing, he perched beside her. "Vaguely, but again, I never connected it with you. Why, Josie, did you feel you needed to hide something like losing a child from me? I mean, I know lately, we haven't exactly been close, but…" Her private pain was none of his business, so why did he feel betrayed? As if her having lost her daughter was a fact he should've known?

"It wasn't that simple." Her expression morphed from grief to all-out rage. "Hugh—he hid an addiction from me. Playing flag football of all things, he tore his rotator cuff. After his surgery, he was supposed to have gotten better, but he was in constant pain. I—I didn't know, but after his prescription pain meds expired, he started buying online. God only knows how many he was taking a day. The night it happened—the accident that took my Emma's life—I had to stay late at school for parent/ teacher conferences. I asked Hugh to pick her up from my parents'. On the way home, it started to sleet, and—"

"That's enough," Dallas said, connecting the awful dots. "Bastard. Not that it excuses his actions, but I can see why your husband did what he did." What he couldn't understand was Josie keeping all of this from him. She always seemed as if she had everything together, when obviously, her world hadn't been all sunshine and roses.

Sniffling through tears, Josie nodded, then shook her head. "If I'd kept a closer eye on Hugh… If we'd spent more time as a couple. We had such trouble conceiving. Back then, teaching was a job. Emma was my world. We did everything together. I let Hugh become an afterthought. If only I'd—"

"Stop." He needed time to process all she'd confessed.

Could she have missed warning signs? Though he was hardly in a position to judge, part of him had to wonder how she could have not seen something so horribly broken in a man she'd supposedly loved.

He had to ask, "Is this why the rest of your family moved away? To get a fresh start?"

She nodded. "M-my mother blamed me for what happened to Em and then blamed me again for Hugh. She said horrible things. Called me a pathetic excuse of a mom and wife. As if I hadn't been through enough, her rejection was…unspeakably cruel."

Dallas's heart would've been made of stone if he hadn't felt for her. The woman had been through hell— twice. But why was she sharing all of this now? What was the point? As far as he was concerned, whatever attraction they might've shared was long gone. Their differences were just too great.

He should've gone to her, wrapped his arms around her or kneaded her shoulders, but his feet felt frozen to the floor.

"All of this must seem out of left field," she said, wiping her eyes with a tissue she'd taken from a side table, "but in light of what else I have to tell you, I needed you to understand—everything—that makes me who I am today." Wringing her hands on her lap, she asked, "Remember our night at the bar?"

He damn near choked. "Kinda hard to forget."

"Yes, well, now it will be doubly so. I'm pregnant."

"What?" He knew if he hadn't already been sitting, he would have fallen. This couldn't be happening. Not in light of everything else going on with his girls. Dammit, but he hated himself for being stupid enough to have unprotected sex. For degrading his wife's memory by bringing dishonor on the entire family. Worse still, for putting Josie in an unfathomable position. What the hell was wrong with him? He wasn't eighteen anymore and he sure as hell wasn't in any position to take on a second wife.

"S-say something," she pleaded, looking on the verge of again being sick.

"I want to, but I'm not sure what." He stood and paced, but the room was too cramped for the movement to work off much frustration. "Whereas I presume you've had at least a few days to get used to this idea, you might as well have just hit me over the head with a two-by-four."

Rising, Josie said, "Now that you know, feel free to leave."

He held out his arms only to slap them against his sides. "What do you want from me? An on-the-spot proposal?"

"No, Dallas. You can relax. I don't expect to marry you—ever." Marching to the front door, she opened it for him. "But in the same respect, don't you expect to play a role in my baby's life."

"That's it, sweetie," Natalie soothed, rocking Josie on the foot of her bed while she sobbed, "let it out. I'm sorry I ever pushed that creep on you. I had him all wrong."

"Y-you didn't do anything. I was the one s-stupid enough to sleep with him."

"Yeah, but I did go on about how good-looking he was."

Nodding, Josie mumbled, "But he's not. I hope the baby looks just like me."

"Of course, it will." Nat combed her fingers through her friend's hair.

"A-and I never want to see Dallas again."

"I agree," Nat said with more rocking. "Whatever it takes."

"A-and I need ice cream. Chocolate. Lots and lots."

"Right away." Gathering her purse from where she'd tossed it on the floor, Natalie was instantly on her feet. "You sit tight and I'll be right back with enough sinful calories to keep you and baby happy for weeks to come."

"Not that this is something you wanna hear," Cash said after Dallas had told Wyatt and him his news over beers in the ranch's barn office. "But it wasn't too long ago that you were lecturing me about how I owed it to the Buckhorn name to make an honest woman of Wren."

"True," Wyatt said after a swig from his longneck bottle.

"Back off," Dallas warned. "You both know diddly about this situation."

"What's to know?" Wyatt asked. He'd rested his feet on the desk, but drew them down, resting his elbows on his knees. "You got Josie pregnant. She seems nice. *Really* nice. Like a small-town kindergarten teacher should. Now how's it going to look when a few months from now, she starts showing and naming her baby's deadbeat father?"

Slamming the last of his beer, Dallas argued, "Not my concern. I have the girls to consider. They're my top priority."

"This isn't like you." Wyatt's direct stare made Dallas uncomfortable as hell. "What's really the problem? Bobbie Jo?"

"Leave her out of this." Taking another beer from the minifridge, Dallas used the desk's edge to pop the top. "You of all people, have nothing to say on the topic of love."

"He's got you there," Cash chimed in. To Wyatt he noted, "When it comes to the ladies, your track record isn't so hot."

Sighing, Wyatt was out of the chair. "That's it. I've had my daily allotment of you both. I'm out of here." After slapping on his hat, he was gone.

"Feel free to follow," Dallas barked to his little brother.

"Oh—I will. First, you need to ask yourself if Josie's child will mean any less to you than Bonnie or Betsy. If Josie has a son, are you going to give him your name?"

Leaning his head back with a groan, Dallas urged, "Please, leave."

Thankfully, for once in his life Cash did as he was told.

Alone save for racing thoughts and more guilt than

a sober man could handle, Dallas reached for a pen and yellow legal pad. He'd always prided himself on his logic. Business sense. What this situation called for was a sound plan.

First, he'd list pros and cons of marrying Josie.

On the pro side, when fire wasn't flashing from her eyes, Dallas liked Josie a lot, as did the girls. Their one time together had been sheer, X-rated fantasy.

In the con column, Josie currently hated him. Thought him an unfit father, which seriously irked the hell out of him. Then there was the not-so-little matter of what went down with her past. Her loss had been tragic, but for Josie's mother to have virtually disowned her, was there truth to the matter of Josie having being negligent by not keeping closer tabs on her husband's drug dependency? If so, what did that say about *her* parenting skills? Was she fit to raise the child they'd created, let alone become a stepmother to Betsy and Bonnie?

A matter Dallas could hardly bear to dwell on were his own unresolved issues with grief. He was apparently well enough for casual sex, but more? A real, lasting marriage took not just love, but a lot of work from both sides. Was he in any way emotionally prepared to offer those things to a woman he hardly knew?

Negatives clearly outweighed positives, but Cash's question wouldn't stop ringing through Dallas's head. Dallas had been man enough to make a child. Was he really prepared to turn his back on the child just because the baby's mother happened to be so wrong for him?

Chapter Twelve

"Come on, guys," Josie urged her students two days later. It was time for them to gather their things to go home. Considering it was Halloween, the day hadn't gone as badly as it could have, but the entire school had seemed especially rambunctious. "Let's hustle."

Watching the Buckhorn twins efficiently fill their backpacks with the day's papers, it occurred to Josie how much they'd grown—at least at school. For the most part, they did their work and conformed to school and classroom rules. As warmly as she felt toward them, she was that perturbed by their horrible father.

Shelby had bus duty, so she stopped by to gather Josie's crew. Next, the children who walked were dismissed, followed by those whose parents picked them up.

Typically, the twins met their father outside, but on this day, they held back, scuffing their sneakers on the hall's tile floors.

"What's up?" Josie asked. "Do we need to call your grandma for a ride?"

"Daddy!" Both girls raced toward Dallas who strode tall and impossibly handsome toward her.

He knelt to scoop them into his arms. "I missed you."

"We missed you, too, Daddy." Betsy squirmed to be let down. "I wanna show you my scary black cat."

"No, me first," Bonnie demanded. "My ghost is *waaay* scarier."

"Tell you what," Dallas said, "while you get them out for me to see, let me talk to Miss Griffin."

"Okay." With both girls momentarily occupied with pilfering through their backpacks, Dallas crammed his hands into his pockets. "Have a second?" he asked Josie.

"Not really." Entering her classroom, she sat behind her desk, moving her mouse to disengage a spook house screen saver.

"Josie," he said in an urgent whisper, "for the other night, I'm sorry. You caught me off guard in more ways than one and—"

"Look, Daddy!" Bonnie held up her ghost. "Isn't he, like, the scariest thing you've ever seen?"

"He sure is."

Betsy pouted. "You don't like my cat?"

"Honey," Dallas assured, "your cat is awfully scary, too."

"Tell you what," Josie suggested, "how about you two take some paper from the special art drawer and make spooky pumpkins, to match?"

"But we're not allowed to *ever* go in that drawer," Betsy reminded.

"True," Josie said, "and I'm proud of you for remembering. But just this once, go ahead."

"Cool!" Bonnie ran in that direction.

"Thanks," Dallas said. "I'd planned a big speech, but…"

"Why are you even here?" she asked, her pain growing exponentially for each minute he was near. "The other night, you pretty much said everything that needed to be said."

"I didn't come close," he admitted. "But like you once told me, we need to talk. Come with the girls and me to the Halloween Festival tonight. We'll make it a no-conflict zone. Maybe we'll figure some things out, maybe we won't, but we owe it to the little guy or gal inside of you to try."

In the worst way, Josie wanted to stick to her guns and deny him, but having always prided herself on putting Emma's needs before her own, Josie knew she'd do the same with this child. Though she had no intention of growing any closer to Dallas than necessary, for the sake of their baby she'd at least be civil.

"Aren't they adorable! Are they twins?" The white-haired woman manning the Weed Gulch Chamber of Commerce's basket-toss booth patted both girls' heads. "I love nothing better on Halloween than Cinderella."

"We're not stupid princesses," Bonnie said, whipping a plastic microphone from her purse. "We're Hannah Montana."

"Oooh…"

Dallas apologized to the woman, confessing, "I didn't know who that was, either."

Josie straightened Betsy's blond wig. "You look cute. Just like Hannah."

"Thanks." The girl added lip gloss. "I don't know why nobody knows us."

"They're dumb," Bonnie said.

"That's enough out of you two." Dallas cupped his girls' shoulders, guiding them through the crowd. After stops at more carnival game booths than he cared count, Dallas finally found himself alone with Josie when the girls ran off to a giant, spider-shaped Jupiter Jump.

"Want a Polish sausage?" she asked, nodding toward a stand.

"Sure." He reached for his wallet, but she shook her head. "I don't need your money, Dallas. I'm more than capable of caring for myself and my baby."

"Our baby."

Lips pressed, she graced him with a hard stare before going for their food. With so many issues between them, where did he even start? They'd kept their conversation pleasant around the girls, but now that they were on their own, what would develop?

While she stood in line, Dallas grabbed an empty picnic table.

The Kiwanis sponsored a haunted house, complete with creaking door and cackling witch sound effects and fog rolling out from under the foundation. The home was manufactured and on loan from a Tulsa company that'd set up an adjacent advertising booth.

"Here." Josie set their food in front of Dallas before straddling the bench across from him. With the girls in view, she said, "I didn't know what you wanted to drink, so I grabbed you a Coke. That okay?"

"Yeah." He bit into his kraut- and onion-covered dog. "Good call. This is delicious."

She nodded. "So? Where do we start?"

"You mean on repairing us?"

"News flash," she said after her latest bite, "but there never was an *us*. We shared a few kisses, secrets and one hot night I'd rather forget."

"Meaning," he asked, "if you had it to do over again, you'd wish you weren't having my baby?" Just asking the question had been surprisingly hard. He wouldn't have expected to even care what she thought on the matter, but inexplicably, he did.

Setting her meal to her paper plate, she molded her hands to her stomach. Was he imagining things, or did the motion produce a wistful smile? She looked beautiful, yet fragile. Her complexion was like porcelain specked with just enough freckles to give her a mischievous smile. At least, what he remembered of her laughing. How long had it been? "No matter how rocky things are between us, I view this child as a blessing."

"On that we agree." If only there wasn't so much more on which they disagreed.

At her ballet class Thursday night, Josie felt heavy and awkward and cranky.

Typically, everything from the classical music to camaraderie with her friends boosted her spirits, but tonight, she just wanted to finish already so she could curl up with a good book and a spoon constantly loaded with ice cream.

"This baby kicking your butt?" Shelby asked when class was over. "Last week you looked ready for *Swan Lake* auditions. This week, more like an off-off-Broadway version of *Duck Lake*."

"Ha-ha." Josie knew her friend was teasing, but the words stung all the same. Daubing her sweating chest and forehead with a towel, she admitted, "Last night, I went with Dallas and the twins to the Halloween Festival. On the surface, with the girls, we kept things civil, but an underlying tension ruined the whole night. It's no secret I think he's a horrible father, but what he doesn't get is that beyond that, I deeply resented him for still having his girls, yet botching his duties toward them. Now that I'm pregnant, I feel almost traitorous to Em's memory, like I'm trying to replace her. And along with my second chance, I find myself wondering if Dallas deserves the same. Only we've said such ugly things to each other, I'm not sure if we'll ever be able to take them back. Let alone regain trust."

"Slow down," her friend advised while Josie took off her toe shoes and tucked them into her dance bag. "Everyone at school views you as the most levelheaded, sane one of our bunch. With a baby on the way, the last thing you need is stress. Obviously, if you and Dallas were once hot enough for each other to make this baby, there has to be at least part of a foundation left for you to start building a new friendship."

"I know." Josie slipped on her coat over her leotard and crammed swollen feet into fleece-lined Crocs. "And for the baby's sake, I'm willing to see if I might've judged Dallas too harshly. But what if he doesn't feel the same?"

"Josie," Dallas's mother said Sunday afternoon, greeting her at the ranch house's front door with a warm smile. "It's so nice to see you again. The girls talk of you all the time."

"In a good way I hope," Josie asked with a cautious smile.

"The best." Taking her coat, the older woman then led

her toward a big country kitchen fragrant with lasagna. "I can't tell you how pleased I was when Dallas asked if it would be all right for you to join us for Sunday supper."

"Yes, well…" Josie's stomach lurched. "I was flattered by the invitation."

Friday, when picking the girls up from school, Dallas had confessed his brothers knew she was pregnant, but not his mom. He'd asked her to join him in presenting a united front that they were firm in their decision not to marry, but to jointly raise their son or daughter.

Funny thing is, she had never really agreed to any of that—just took it all in while Dallas outlined his plan as if raising their child meant no more than any ordinary business transaction.

"My son has been acting strangely." Chopping tomatoes for a salad, she asked, "Any chance you know why?"

The back door burst open and in dashed two pink-cheeked energy balls, running to her for hugs. "Miss Griffin!"

While returning their embraces, Josie looked up to see Dallas in all his cowboy glory. No matter their differences, her instinctual, physical attraction to the man was undeniable. Over faded jeans and dusty boots, he wore a long duster, leather work gloves and his hat. His whisker-stubbled cheeks were ruddy from the cold, and when he flashed a cautious smile, his blue eyes shone like the promise of spring. Granted, it might be a long time coming, but in the real sense and metaphorically, she indulged in cautious hope.

"Dinner smells delicious," he said to his mom. To Josie, he said, "Glad you could make it."

"Grandma," Bonnie said, hopping onto a counter bar stool, "I'm hungry. Can I have cookies?"

"No. Dinner's almost ready."

"But I'm hungry now," the girl whined.

"Bonnie…" Dallas warned with a sternness to his tone Josie had never before heard. "How about you and your sister go get Uncle Cash, Robin and Aunt Wren."

"Okay…" Chin drooping, Bonnie held out her hand to Betsy. "Come on, let's go."

Wearing oven mitts, Mrs. Buckhorn noted, "Josie, ever think you'd see the day when Bonnie actually did what she was told with only a minimum of fuss?"

"When it comes to my students, I confess to being an eternal optimist. Both girls are performing much better in class."

Dallas cleared his throat. "While we're on the subject of kids, Mom, Josie and I find ourselves in a bit of a jam, and—"

"Save it," the eldest Buckhorn snapped to her son, taking the lasagna from the over. "It's no secret Josie's carrying your child. The news is all over town. It's my hope that on the afternoon agenda is damage control? I'll spare you both the lecture on birth control and go straight into asking about the wedding. Because as I've already proven with Cash, there will be a wedding. No grandson or granddaughter of mine will be born without legally taking our name."

More than anything, Josie longed to run off to the nearest bathroom and hide, but that wouldn't solve anything. "Mrs. Buckhorn, this isn't my first time to the so-called rodeo and I don't have the stomach for weathering a second failed relationship."

"Weed Gulch isn't exactly the best place for keeping secrets," Georgina said while buttering French bread, "and I'm also well aware of your past. Trust me, my heart goes out to you for your loss, but that doesn't in any way give you the right to bring my grandchild into the world on a hotbed of scandal. You're a kindergarten teacher, for heaven's sake. What sort of example does it set for our young people when supposed role models are running around town unwed and pregnant?"

"Mom," Dallas said, "that's enough. Josie and I are adults, well aware of the ramifications of our actions."

"Ramify *this,* Mr. Fancy Words, if I have to drag you two down to the courthouse with my own bare hands, you will be married by the time this baby is born."

Chapter Thirteen

"Sorry about all of that," Dallas said to Josie after the longest afternoon on record. In waning sunlight, they stood next to her car. "My mom can be a bit overbearing."

"A bit?" Josie laughed. The light breeze caught her curls, floating them over her face. In that moment, whatever spark had first physically attracted him to her returned tenfold. But no matter how much he wouldn't mind tucking her crazy hair behind her ears, then kissing her until the sun set, he couldn't ignore the bad blood also still simmering between them. "I'm actually a little scared. She does understand that just because the town gossipmongers feel marriage is in our future, it's us who will ultimately decide, right?"

Hands in his pockets both to ward off the chill and to keep from drawing Josie into a reassuring hug, he said, "We'll wait her out. Eventually, she'll get the hint that we control our lives—not her. Trust me, by the time the baby's born, she'll love him or her all the same."

Josie didn't look so sure. "I won't be pressured into anything I'm not ready for."

"You think I would? And lest you've forgotten, before you accused me of being the worst father ever, we used to actually get along. You're the one who started all of our troubles. And for the record, you were also the one spurring us into..." he moved his hands at his hips "...you know."

"That's ridiculous." She raised her chin. "That night was a mutual mistake. You're certifiable," she declared, climbing into her car.

"Ditto."

Watching her drive off until the dust cloud out on the main road faded into rolling hills of winter wheat, Dallas couldn't hide a smile. The woman was infuriating, insulting and downright aggravating. At the same time, she raised his blood pressure to a degree he should've found alarming, but was actually more in the realm of invigorating.

"Bonnie," Dallas said to his daughter after Thanksgiving dinner had been put away. "No matter how many times you ask, my answer's still the same. You're not riding Cookie in this weather."

"But why?"

"Because sleet isn't good for either of you."

Bonnie added hopping to her whines. "I wanna ride my pony."

"She really does," Betsy pointed out.

Josie remained on the fringe of the conversation, drying the turkey roasting pan.

Though Natalie had invited Josie to share the holiday with her family, Josie had thought it best she try making amends with Dallas's mother. Stress was unhealthy for the baby, and no matter how much she wished for the anonymity of living in a giant city where no one gave a flip what she did, the reality of her life was that people were already talking and their whispers hurt.

"You seem awfully quiet." Dallas's sister-in-law Wren nudged Josie's shoulder. "Let me guess, either you have indigestion from too much giblet gravy or you're letting Georgina under your skin."

Wincing, Josie confessed, "I suffer from a little of both."

Forcing a deep breath, Wren said, "Feel free to tell me to butt out, but if you'd like to talk, it wasn't too long ago Cash and I faced the same kind of heat."

"How did you manage?" Josie asked, glad for any advice. "Aside from, well, you know—" she reddened "—Dallas and I are practically strangers. I can't even imagine getting married again. Then there's Dallas himself. Look at him fighting with Bonnie like he's no more mature than her."

"You might want to look again. Since meeting you, he will never admit it, but he's worked hard to get on the right course with his girls."

Dallas had slipped on his duster and now helped Bonnie with her puffy down coat. After tugging on her pink hat, he said, "We'll be right back."

"Where are you going?" Josie asked.

His stare locked with hers. Almost as if he wanted this moment to be about just them, but didn't know how to make it happen. "Bonnie and I had a talk. She's worried Cookie feels bad that she didn't want to ride him on Thanksgiving."

"Yeah," Bonnie chimed in, "but Daddy said if we go visit him and bring him a carrot or apple, he'll still be happy even though he didn't get to ride."

"We compromised," Dallas said with an intensity that left Josie wondering if he'd eavesdropped on her and Wren's conversation.

"I'm glad." When he took both girls by their hands, Josie flashed Dallas a genuine smile. When he returned one of his own, her traitorous stomach flip-flopped. Had she misjudged him? Maybe he wasn't such an awful father, after all?

With Betsy on her lap and Bonnie pressed against her with wide-eyed concern, Dallas watched on from just outside the otherwise deserted classroom as Josie said, "Sweetie, I'm sure Thomas didn't mean it. Maybe he's even jealous that you lost a better tooth than him?"

"You think?" Betsy asked.

"He was real mad when my front tooth fell out," Bonnie assured. "Now that yours is out, too, you're gonna be so rich when the Tooth Fairy comes."

Sniffling, Betsy said, "He still didn't have to call me donkey girl."

"I know," Josie assured, smoothing his daughter's long, brown hair. "And if you think about it, he's a silly boy, anyway, because everyone knows donkeys have two gorgeous front teeth."

Eyes wide and looking stricken, Betsy asked, "Does that mean I'm not gorgeous?"

Laughing, giving his daughter an extra squeeze, Josie promised, "You and your sister are the most gorgeous princesses ever. Once Thomas gets a little older, he'd be lucky to have you for a girlfriend."

"Eeuw!" both girls shouted with shrieking giggles.

"I hate boys," Bonnie said.

"Me, too." Betsy nodded.

"What about me?" Dallas asked past the knot in his throat.

"You're not a boy," Betsy giggled. "You're a daddy!"

"Oh, well in that case—" he snatched her from Josie's lap to tickle "—does that mean you'll go on a date with me to get cheeseburgers?"

"Yeah!" Bonnie did her happy dance.

Betsy kissed his cheek. "Can Miss Griffin come?"

"Depends," he said, working to ignore the quickening of his pulse, "did you ask if she wants to go?"

"Do you?" Betsy asked.

Josie's teary-eyed smile rocked him to his core. "I'd love to have cheeseburgers with you—but only if we have onion rings, too."

"Eeeuw," Bonnie said, accompanying Josie to her desk while she grabbed her purse and coat, "I hate those, but Daddy and Uncle Wyatt eat them all the time and then Grandma says they have smelly unjun breath."

Two weeks before Christmas, Natalie sat on Josie's floor in front of a crackling fire. In the winter, they replaced Saturday morning yard sales with scrapbooking and while Nat worked on documenting her summer Grand Canyon rafting trip, Josie put the final touches on matching minibooks for Dallas's girls.

While Josie changed the TV channel to a home makeover show, Natalie said, "You're getting awfully cozy with the Buckhorn clan. Thought you despised Dallas."

"I do—*did*. Guess he's growing on me. No doubt because his son or daughter's growing in me."

"Rethinking your antimarriage stance?"

"Nope." Back at the card table holding her masterpieces, Josie added snapshots she'd taken of the girls at the Halloween festival, tacking mini foam candy corns to each corner. "For the moment, Dallas and I are back to being friends. That's enough. And the twins are finally settling in. What's it going to do to them if all of a sudden they find out their teacher is carrying their little brother or sister? Talk about freaking them out."

"True." Nat pressed twinkling star stickers over a nighttime campfire shot. "But you're a smart cookie, Josie. So are Dallas's girls. Once you start showing, there are going to be questions you can no longer avoid. Now you're only dealing with the fallout from old biddy gossips. What happens when our school principal and the PTA find out? Dallas's mom was right in that for all of Weed Gulch's so-called advances like the new grocery store and coffeehouse, we still live in a societal vacuum where folks like their pregnant women married."

"Way to ruin an otherwise perfect morning." Josie abandoned her friend in favor of making a run to the kitchen for cocoa with plenty of marshmallows. While waiting for the milk to warm, she stared out the window at the gray day. The only spot of color in the otherwise brown yard was a cardinal looking for food in the empty feeder.

Fear and self-doubt suddenly consumed her.

She couldn't even manage caring for her backyard songbirds; how was she supposed to care for this new baby all on her own? Worse yet, old doubts taunted her with deep-seated fears at the possibility of what had hap-

pened with Emma happening all over again. What if that
night Josie had been able to prevent Hugh from driving?
What if instead of being the good mother she'd thought,
in reality, she'd been an accessory to her beautiful daughter's death?

"Daddy, puh-leaze can we sit on Santa's lap?" Though
Bonnie was the one begging, each girl had a deathgrip on
his arms. The Saturday before Christmas, Tulsa's Wood-
land Hills Mall was a mob scene. Santa was apparently a
popular guy as the line to visit his workshop wound all
the way from JC Penney to Macy's.

"Quit," Dallas barked. "With all the shopping we still
have to do, the wait is too long. Besides, if you two pull
on me much harder, my arms are going to fall off."

Betsy wasn't buying it. "Miss Griffin, is that true?"

"'Fraid so," she said with a deadpan expression he'd
have to thank her for later. "When you're in second grade,
you'll learn all about how you have to be careful not to
pull fingers, toes or arms too hard. It can be a real problem."

"Whoa…" Wide-eyed, Betsy cupped her hands to
Bonnie's ear.

Bonnie whispered back before asking, "If we can't
visit Santa, can we have ice cream for lunch?"

Sounded good to him, but lately, whenever he was
around Josie, Dallas found himself hyperaware of making the right parental decisions. Her doubting his abili-
ties still irked him and if it was the last thing he did, he'd
make her eat her words. He was a good father. Getting
better every day. Did he feel one hundred percent con-
fident he was doing the sort of job that would've made

Bobbie Jo proud? Not even close. But for the moment, he craved Josie's approval.

"Tell you what," Dallas offered, "how about we have some nice salads. Then maybe fruit for dessert?"

Both girls hung their heads in pouts.

"You know," Josie said, "since it is almost Christmas, it might be a fun tradition to start something silly like rewarding ourselves for being good shoppers by eating an equally silly lunch like nothing but cookies or ice cream."

Dallas argued, "What about the girls getting proper nutritional value?"

Kneeling to give Bonnie and Betsy winks, she said, "That's why God made vitamins, right?"

With both twins smiling, they trekked off to Dillard's to find a gift for Dallas's mother. The jury was still out on what he thought of Josie overriding his healthy lunch plan, but considering he was also in the mood for junk, he'd let it slide.

"Thanks for doing this with me," he said to Josie, wishing he wasn't loaded like a pack mule with packages. "As you can tell, I need help. Especially with Mom. I always end up getting her a gadget she secretly donates to the annual church yard sale."

The housewares section was not only overwhelming, but dull. China, sheets and pillows. None of which—as much as Dallas loved his mother—he gave a flip about.

"If you check the oil on my car," Josie offered with a playful wink, "I'll tell you what your mom told me she wants."

Grinning, he said, "Done." After trailing her toward sparkling crystal, feeling like the proverbial bull in a china shop, he asked, "Where are the girls?"

Josie nodded toward a bed display where Betsy and Bonnie were pretending to sleep.

"Perfect. With any luck, they'll stay right there until we're done."

She laughed. "No kidding. Maybe you should make a side barter with them?"

Emboldened by her smile, he teased, "A good cowboy's always ready to deal."

"Oh, really?" Her flirty banter reminded him of the days when they'd first met. Seemed like a million years ago. Back then, neither had had doubts about each other, only blazing hot curiosity. "There was once a time when I only liked *bad* cowboys." Her wink stole his breath. Made him crave things he had no business wanting. "Thankfully, I've since learned better."

"Pardon." A sales clerk cleared her throat. "Are those your two little girls?"

Glancing over the woman's left shoulder, Dallas spied his daughters jumping on an expensive-looking bed.

With a mischievous sparkle in her eyes, Josie said to the clerk, "Nope. Those aren't my kids."

"New wineglasses," Dallas's mother exclaimed Christmas morning. "Swarovski crystal even. Dallas, how did you know?"

"I'm that good."

An elbow to his ribs from Josie left him coughing. "They're from me, too."

"Thank you, honey." Georgina waded through the sea of wrappings to give Josie a hug. "I should've known the man who gave me a Halloween-themed scarf last year didn't select a gift this nice on his own."

"Hey," Dallas complained while Wyatt, Cash and

Wren laughed at his expense. Robin and Prissy—Wren's Yorkie/Chihuahua mix—slept through the festivities, and the twins were temporarily outside playing with their new bow and arrows. "That scarf was originally a hundred bucks. When I got it for ten, I figured you'd appreciate my finding a bargain."

She grimaced. "Son, you might be my eldest, but when it comes to finesse, you've got a lot to learn."

"Amen," Wren said, seated on the hearth, warming herself by the crackling fire. "He gave me a fruitcake that was harder than any brick. FEMA could use a bunch of them for rebuilding storm-damaged homes."

"Ha, ha, ha." While Dallas pouted, Josie took Wren's gift from under the tree.

Handing it to her, Josie said, "For the record, the only role Dallas played in this item was surrendering his credit card at the checkout counter."

"I'm intrigued." Wren gave the small box a slight shake, but it made no sound. The wrapping was especially pretty—gold foil with a black velvet bow. "Oh!" Upon opening the even smaller black leather box inside to find a pair of perfectly matched diamond studs, she said, "Dallas, this is too much."

"Considering I never bought you two a wedding gift, and I missed your birthday back in May," Dallas admitted, "I'm hoping those get me back in your good graces."

"Done." Wren hugged her brother-in-law and then approached Josie, but when Josie stood, she touched her forehead and fell back to the sofa.

"Whew."

"Okay?" Wren asked, her voice laced with concern.

Josie nodded. "Just dizzy."

"Did you take your iron tabs?" Dallas asked.

"Yes," she snapped. "Sorry. All of a sudden I'm not feeling so hot." She made a mad dash for the guest bathroom, but unfortunately, Wren, Dallas and his mother were hot on her heels. Once her heavy breakfast came up, her stomach felt better, but her embarrassment level was through the roof.

"Oh, dear," Georgina crooned. Wetting a washcloth, she offered it to Josie. "Should we put off opening the rest of the gifts until after lunch?"

"No," Josie said, relishing the cool fabric against her superheated skin. "Please don't let me ruin your day. Dallas can run me home and then all of you can finish out the holiday without interruption."

"Nonsense." Georgina turned to her son. "Get Josie a blanket and pillow, then shove your brothers off the long couch and help Josie onto it. A *single* woman in her condition shouldn't spend Christmas alone."

While Dallas did his mother's bidding, Josie remained in the bathroom, rinsing her mouth and trying to get her stomach feeling stable.

With Georgina hollering out the front door for the twins to put coats on or come inside, Wren whispered, "It's okay, you know?"

"For what?"

"To lean on us. Georgina, me—especially Dallas." Hand on Josie's forearm, she continued, "I used to be like you, convinced I could single-handedly take on the world, but ever since figuring out it's more fun to share, I've never been happier."

"Truthfully," Josie said with a slow exhale, "it's not that I'm eager to raise this baby alone, or spend the rest of my days talking to just my cat, but so much more, I'm afraid of everything—loving this child too much. Falling for Dallas only to realize we've made a mistake. In turn, hurting the twins." Hands to her still-spinning head, she fought tears. She'd never been more confused. In the same respect, she had never needed a friend more desperately. Was it possible she could rely on Dallas to help her through not only her pregnancy, but negotiating the treacherous water of being a small-town, unwed mom? "Everything's a mess. My whole life feels upside down."

"I get that. Initially, the only reason Cash and I were together was for our baby. But with time, our relationship grew into more. Now, I can't imagine my life without him."

"I'm happy for you," Josie said, mind swirling with doubts. "But what if Dallas and I never get to that place? What if we were to get together, only he grows to resent me and our baby, instead of loving us? Can't you understand how it would be much simpler leaving well enough alone?"

"Simpler, yes." Wren tidied Josie's hair. "But I guarantee Dallas would be a lot more fun to snuggle with on a cold winter night than your cat."

Chapter Fourteen

"Aside from you getting sick," Dallas said late Christmas night, walking Josie to her front door, "this was a nice day. Good food. Good company—" he gave her a friendly hug "—doesn't get better than this."

"True." Inserting her key in the front door, she said, "I usually spend Christmas with Natalie and her family. They're always welcoming, but then Nat's mother starts lecturing her about how much she'd like grandkids before she turns eighty and next, her dad starts yelling at her mom. Typically, before we've finished breakfast mimosas, Nat's fuming and I'm wishing I could hide in a closet."

Laughing, Dallas knelt to pet Kitty. While he couldn't say they were best buds, at least the cat now tolerated him. "Sounds like you made the right choice in hanging with us. Although we've had our fair share of holiday turmoil. Last year, a little before Christmas, Cash and Wren got married and had Robin all on the same day."

Josie whistled. "I can't top that."

"Wouldn't want you to." Now that Kitty had been properly greeted, Dallas wasn't sure what to do with his hands. He'd liked hugging Josie. Enjoyed the feel of her in his arms, but did she feel the same? How big a dufus would he be if he went in for a smooth move only to have Josie dodge his advances? "On a more serious note, are you feeling better?"

"Much." Was it normal that she seemed fidgety, too? Did she want him to make a move? Even if he did, how far did he go? They might've already gone for a home run, but lately, he felt as if they'd grown to know each other all over again. This time, at a much slower pace.

Deciding to ignore his fears and just go for it, he tenderly drew her against him. When she showed no signs of struggle, he rested his head atop of hers. "Ever notice how we fit? Like puzzle pieces that've been waiting to be put together."

"Read that on a greeting card, cowboy?" The light in her eyes told Dallas she was giving him an old-fashioned ribbing, but in that moment, he wasn't kidding. Yes, he hated the fact that she possibly still didn't think him the most qualified of fathers, but he was getting better every day. By the time his new son or daughter arrived, he'd be the expert all of their kids deserved.

"I'm serious." When she stared up at him, he kissed her. Long and leisurely. Like they had all the time in the world. They'd both learned the hard way that love could be fleeting, but with a little luck and whole lot of prayer, things just might turn out different this time around. "Josie, I'm falling for you."

"I'm not sure how—or even, when—but me, too."
After returning his kiss and then some, she admitted,
"Since our falling out and then coming back together,
I'm still scared what I'm feeling isn't real. But in the
same regard, I can't deny that lately, when we're together, everything's better. Fall colors were more brilliant. Thanksgiving turkey more tender. Christmas lights
twinkle brighter."

"Talk about sounding like a greeting card..." Sweeping her jawline with his thumb, he said in an emotion-
filled whisper, "That was beautiful. I feel the same."

After more kissing and caressing and sharing feelings with words, they naturally gravitated toward her
dark bedroom.

"Sure this is what you want?" she asked, her voice a
husky fraction of her normal self.

"Can't you tell?" he asked, pressing her against his
swollen need.

"I'm just so unsure—about everything. But most especially, you." As he drew off her blouse and then bra,
she shivered.

Stroking the chills from her upper arms, he pulled her
into another kiss.

Drawing back only long enough to turn on the bedside
lamp, he sat on the edge of the bed, settling his hands low
on her hips, pulling her in. With their eyes at the same
level, he said, "You're starting to mean the world to me.
Sometimes, when I'm alone out on the range, I fantasize
about you, me and the girls being a real family."

"I do, too," she said, albeit dropping her gaze. "But..."
Her melancholy expression told him she didn't believe
him.

Cupping his face, she kissed his forehead and closed

eyes and nose. "I'm scared. All of this has happened so fast. We went from flirting to pregnant to hating each other and now this all in the blink of an eye. It's confusing and exhilarating, yet I don't trust it to be real."

"Me, neither," he confessed, skimming his hands over her full breasts, cupping them, teasing her nipples until she sharply inhaled, burying her hands in his hair. "But at the moment, I'm thinking this is about as real as I can stand without tossing you back on the bed."

"Are cowboys generally this touchy-feely with words?" she teased. "Because as hot as you've made me, I'd prefer less talk and more action."

Shaking his head, Dallas gave the lady what she wanted.

New Year's Eve, Josie could scarcely contain her excitement. With Nat at her house, dressing for the Buckhorns' fancy party, she felt more like they were headed for prom than a ranch.

"I love that," Natalie said, smiling in approval of Josie's silver-sequined cocktail dress.

"Thanks. You're not looking too shabby yourself in that hot little number." Josie's friend rocked a black gown she'd found on a half-off rack at the Tulsa Saks Fifth Avenue.

"Think tonight Dallas will pop the question?" She sat at Josie's vanity table, applying eyeliner.

"Maybe." Josie was on the hunt for the chandelier earrings she rarely had a chance to wear, but loved. "I'm not even sure I want him to. Christmas night, our conversation got pretty heavy. Clearly, neither of us has a clue what we're getting into, but oh, what a delicious way to go."

"You look so happy I'm scared for you. And praying that this time, your fairy tale lasts."

"Don't go there," Josie begged of her friend. "This time around, I'm taking life day by day. No expectations. Just stealing joy where I can. Now, where are they?" It took dumping her jewelry basket on the bed to finally find her earrings. Could Nat be right? Should she be looking for more? Like a lasting relationship with a man whose company she enjoyed?

"Organize your jewelry much?" Glancing over her shoulder at the mess, Nat said, "Relax. No matter what, let's promise to have fun."

Extending her hand for her friend to shake, Josie said, "I'll make that deal under one condition."

After brushing on mascara, Natalie asked, "What's that?"

"I promise to party till dawn if you ask Dallas's brother Wyatt to dance."

"Why would I do that?" she asked with a frown.

"Because he happens to be single and a great guy?"

"I went to elementary, middle and high school with him. Trust me, there's a lot about him you don't know. Plus, he has women falling all over him." After adding bold red lipstick, Nat turned her attention to her nails, adding a clear topcoat. "Besides, I've eaten so many teachers' lounge Christmas cookies that I'm starting to resemble Mrs. Claus."

Josie rolled her eyes. "Who hasn't packed on a few holiday and/or pregnancy pounds? And as for Wyatt, you going to rely on his past discretions or me? The few times I've met him, not only has he been charming, but there hasn't been a vixen in sight."

"No doubt he hides them in the pool house, fearing his mother's disapproval."

At that, Josie had to laugh. "Trust me, if there's one thing I've learned since Dallas and I have been together, as much as the Buckhorn men love their mother, no matter what she may think, if they see something they want, they'll go for it." Hugging herself to ward off a sudden chill, Josie prayed tonight brought both her and Natalie the happiness they deserved.

Josie had never seen the ranch look more beautiful— or crowded. The Buckhorns were known for hosting a good party and tonight was no exception.

The living-room furniture had been put in storage and in the roomy corner that typically housed Mrs. Buckhorn's rolltop desk, was a five-man swing band. Hundreds of twinkling white lights had been strung from the open rafters and an equal amount of fragrant red roses in silver and crystal vases adorned tables hugging the dance floor's edge. In the dining room was a sumptuous buffet. Waiters roamed, offering champagne and decadent treats from silver trays.

"Whoa," Nat said for only her to hear. "I'm feeling a smidge out of my league."

"Relax," Josie urged. "The whole family is just as gracious as can be."

"Easy for you to say. You're an actual guest. I'm a lowly guest of a guest."

Laughing, Josie took her friend by her hand, leading her to the bar.

Along the way, they encountered Dallas who looked beyond handsome in his tux.

While Nat asked the bartender for champagne, Dallas

whispered in Josie's ear, "You look gorgeous and I want to do naughty things with you."

"Sounds good to me." Easing her arm around him, she felt as if they'd known each other years rather than mere months. How they'd gotten so close so fast was a mystery about which she wasn't complaining. "Where are the girls?"

"At Cash's with Mrs. Cahwood. You haven't met her, but she's their housekeeper and sitter." After kissing his date, he added, "Is it wrong that I want tonight to be just about us?"

"Hear me complaining?"

He laughed, then turned to Natalie. "So Josie says I should fix you up with my last single brother."

Choking on a sip of bubbly, Natalie cast Josie an evil glare. "We've, ah, already met and—"

"Come on," he said, guiding her through the still-growing crowd. "Last I saw he was in the den smoking cigars and playing poker, but once he catches sight of you in that dress, I'm sure he won't mind the diversion."

Josie was thrilled that for once her interfering friend was getting a taste of her own medicine.

Nat complained, "I don't even have anything to say."

"You'll figure it out," Dallas assured.

When Natalie glanced back at Josie for help, she just grinned.

"Need me for something?" Wyatt asked upon finding the trio standing beside him.

"No," Dallas said, "but Josie's friend Natalie, here, needs a dance partner."

"Ah, sure." Glancing down at his cards, he said to the six men sharing the table, "Gentlemen, I'm out."

"Come on." Dallas took Josie's arm and practically sprinted out of the den.

"Aren't we going to wait and see what happens?" Josie complained. "I want to know if they hit it off."

"Not to be mean," he said, leading her toward the dance floor, "but I really don't care. My only focus is you. Wanna dance?"

Josie nearly swooned from the intensity of his stare. His white smile. The way his breath smelled of whiskey and that special, indescribable something that her soul recognized as uniquely his.

After slow dancing and fast dancing and laughing more than she could ever remember, Josie was parched. "Whew, I need a break and a drink."

"Both items easily remedied." At the bar, he grabbed two bottled waters.

Striving for a breezy tone, she said, "Next year, I want gallons of champagne."

Kissing her forehead, he said, "Done." Once she'd finished her beverage, he asked, "Want to get out of here for a while?"

"And go where? Last I heard it's eighteen degrees outside."

"Which is why you'll be wearing my coat." Sneaking out the back door, holding Dallas's hand, dressed in the long duster he wore when working cattle, Josie felt as if he were leading her on a grand adventure.

"Where are we going?"

"You'll see…"

Teeth chattering as they struck out down a winding stone trail, she asked, "Is it far? My shoes and swollen feet aren't exactly ideal for late-night hiking."

"Need me to carry you?"

"If you don't mind," she said with a giggle.

Over the crest of a hill was a small log cabin. Candlelight shone through paned windows and sweet wood smoke rose from the stone chimney.

"Here we are." He set her to her feet on the rustic front porch. "This was my great-great-grandparents' home back in the day. It's been updated with luxuries such as plumbing, electric and running water, but otherwise it's pretty much the same."

When he opened the door, Josie couldn't quite believe her eyes. "It's fantastic…"

On the main level was a stone fireplace with flames merrily crackling and stone floor covered in thick throw rugs. A galley kitchen outfitted with a mini-stainless-steel stove, fridge and wine cooler. All of the furniture was buttery leather strewn with throw pillows. On an upper level stood a wrought iron bed beside a sunken, glowing hot tub. Through a partially open door she caught a glimpse of a bathroom featuring an oversize, claw-foot tub. Lighting it all were at least a hundred ivory candles.

"My ancestors knew how to live it up."

"I'll say." Warming her hands by the fire, she asked, "Who stays here?"

"Some of Mom's out of town friends. A few East Coast aunts and uncles. Occasionally, folks we've hired to bring out studs or bulls."

"Who lit the fire and candles?"

"I bribed Henry. Wasn't too hard, considering he hates big parties and this gave him an excuse to stay away." On a love seat across from her, he cleared his throat. "Sweetheart, there's a reason I brought you out here." His gaze dropped to his hands. He'd clamped them tight.

Was he nervous? If so, why? Her pulse took off on a runaway gallop.

"I-if you're calling it—*us*—quits," she barely managed to get out without crying, "please just go ahead and do it."

"What are you talking about?" he asked with a laugh. "If I were breaking up, would I honestly have bought out all of Dollar General's candles?"

She quivered with relief. With Natalie, she'd put on a brave front, but the more time passed, the more her resolve crumpled. She didn't want to have her baby alone, but with him.

On one knee in front of her, he said, "Enough suspense." From the chest pocket of his tuxedo jacket, he withdrew a gasp-worthy diamond set in platinum. "Josie Griffin, I know this has been kind of a whirlwind thing, but will you marry me?"

Tears started and showed no sign of letting up. Tossing her arms around his dear neck, she hugged him for all she was worth.

"Baby, what's wrong?" Now, he looked even more stressed. "Is this a yes or no?"

"Yes, you silly man. Yes, yes, yes."

"You mean Miss Griffin is gonna be our mom?" Over her chicken finger kid meal at McGillicutty's steak house in the neighboring town of Lakeside, Bonnie grinned. "Does that mean you have to give me a perfect report card?"

"Bonnie Buckhorn," Dallas snapped, "that's a terrible thing for you to ask."

"Yeah, but, Daddy, you never said if it was true." Betsy had chosen spaghetti and currently wore more than she'd eaten. Josie wiped the girl's face with a napkin.

"For the record," Josie said, cutting into her medium-well filet mignon, "since we're planning a Valentine's Day wedding, we both think it would be best if you two transferred to Mrs. Conklin's room."

"But why?" Bonnie whined. "I *really* love you lots and if you're not around to rescue me, who's gonna save me if I fall?"

"I *really* love you lots, too," Josie said, "but have you ever heard of the big word *unethical*?"

Bonnie shook her head. She wore her long hair in braids and they whacked her ears.

Raising her hand, Betsy wriggled in her chair. "I know what it is. Uncle Cash drinks *lots* every Friday night."

"That's *alcohol*," Dallas said. "And I'd hardly say one or two beers are overindulging."

"Good guess, sweetie." Josie took another bite of steak. "But in this case, the word means that if I had you and your sister in my class, some of the other moms and dads might say I was treating you better than the other kids."

"But if you love us more," Betsy reasoned, "why is that a bad thing?"

Josie turned to Dallas for help. "Look, ladies, let's say I had one cow I loved more than all of the others."

"You do, Daddy. You named her Lola and she has superlong eyelashes and likes to lick us when we feed her."

"Her tongue is super scratchy," Betsy said with a giggle.

Tossing up his hands, Dallas admitted defeat. "I know—*we* know—switching classes isn't going to be fun, but this is a grown-up thing and you're going to have to trust we know what we're doing."

"You don't." Bonnie sat with her arms crossed and

chin hanging low. "I used to really love you, but now I'm mad at both of you."

"That's too bad," Josie said, "because we have more news for you, and this time, it's good."

"Are we going to Disneyworld?" Betsy asked. "I hope so, because more than anything in the whole, wide planet, that's where I want to go."

"Duly noted—" Dallas chewed a bite of his porterhouse "—but tone it down a notch. And, anyway, this is way more exciting than a vacation." Reaching across the table for Josie's hands, he said, "Remember how much fun you two have with Robin? How you think of her like a real-life doll?"

Bonnie dredged a chicken strip in ranch dressing. "Her poop is stinky."

"Yeah," Betsy said, "and she does it a lot."

Josie laughed. "You two are a hoot. You should have your own sideshow."

"What's that?" Betsy nabbed a French fry from her sister's plate.

"Give it back!" Bonnie demanded, snatching it by the portion still dangling from her twin's mouth.

"I hate you!" Betsy declared.

Bonnie stuck out her tongue.

"Break it up." Dallas gave both of them a stern look. Once they'd stopped huffing at each other, he said, "I'd hoped this would be delivered with a lighter mood, but here goes…" Flashing Josie a reassuring smile, he announced, "Surprise! We're having our own baby."

The twins were not amused.

Chapter Fifteen

"Good grief," Josie said across the table, giving Dallas her meanest teacher glare. Under her breath, she scolded, "We talked about your delivery and it was supposed to be sensitive."

"Miss Griffin?" Bonnie asked. "Is there really a baby inside you?"

"Yes, honey, there is. But you know what?"

She shook her head.

"This is scary for your dad and me, too."

Betsy's eyes were huge. "Our mommy died having us. Are you gonna die, too?"

"No," she assured, wishing Dallas would feel free to jump in. "What happened with your mom was a very sad thing, but not everyone who has a baby gets sick."

"Aunt Wren did," Bonnie said. "She had to stay in bed all the time and then we went to see her in the hospital. She looked dead. Like when my frog died."

"That's enough." Dallas signaled to the waiter pushing the dessert trolley. "For the last time, no one's dying."

Betsy started to cry.

"Oh, honey…" Josie welcomed the little girl onto her lap. "You'll see, once we're a family, and the baby is born all pink and pretty and healthy, we're going to be so happy."

Bonnie crossed her arms. "I don't know if I like this baby."

"Now, you're just being silly," Dallas said. When the waiter finally arrived, he told his daughters, "Pick out some cake or pie. Sugar makes everything better."

"So much for my sugar hypothesis," Dallas said after leaving the girls with his mom and then driving Josie home. They sat at her kitchen table eating the chocolate cake they'd had their waiter box to go. "Guess I could've handled that better."

"You think? Your girls are five and everything in their whole world has been turned upside down. Considering how their mom died, they're no doubt shaken by the implications of pregnancy itself, but also losing you to me or the new baby. On top of all of that, they have to change classrooms. They must feel lost."

"Sorry. I promise to from here on out be more sensitive." Dallas helped himself to a glass of milk. He poured her one, too, setting it in front of her. "Drink."

"Way to go on that pledge of sensitivity." She shot a scowl his way, but did follow his suggestion. Finished, she put their cups in the sink and their take-out containers in the trash.

"I could've done that for you."

"Why? I'm perfectly capable."

"That's not the point." Rising to rinse the glasses and put them in the dishwasher, he said, "In fact, I've been thinking, how about moving out to the ranch before the wedding? That way, you'd have Mom to help cook for you and I can make sure you're taking your vitamins and getting enough rest."

"No." Up from her seat, she went to the living room to see what was on TV.

"Why?" He followed. "It's a perfectly reasonable idea."

"Absolutely not. I have lots to do here before the wedding. And then there's the not-so-small issue of letting the girls slowly adjust to us being a couple. I also need to deal with Em's room." Flipping through channels, she settled on *Iron Chef*. "I want to take my time. Keeping some things out for our baby, storing other items for me to pull out and reminisce over when I'm ninety."

"You're going to be a sexy senior," he crooned, sidling alongside her on the sofa. He never tired of touching her, sharing her warmth. "I totally dig blue hair."

She kissed him. "I'll keep that in mind."

"Want help with Emma's room? Even if I'm just in the house for moral support?"

"Thanks, but I don't think so. You didn't know her."

He wished he had. Didn't that count?

"Please don't take that as a dig. I just mean that it wouldn't have the same impact on you as it's going to on me. It's a task I've already put off for far too long. And if I want to cry or scream at the universe, I don't want you getting concerned."

He sighed. "But as your future husband, isn't it kind of my job to worry about you? Comfort you?" It killed him that on this issue, no matter how hard he might try, there was nothing he could do to help. As a take-charge man, it was inconceivable that there was a problem or pain he couldn't fix.

"Yes," she said, cupping his cheek, "and I love you all the more for feeling that way. Please just try remembering that I had a life before meeting you. Emma... She isn't a loose end to tie, but part of me."

He nodded and understood. And loved Josie all the more for holding strong to her convictions.

"Who did this?" Hands on her hips, Josie surveyed her students, noting that all but a certain two weren't afraid to meet her gaze. Her gorgeous new Coach purse—the one her future mother-in-law had given her for Christmas—had been scribbled on with red, black and green permanent markers. As a teacher, she'd been trained to keep her cool, but this was one time when her patience was sorely tested. "Betsy? Bonnie? Would you please come here."

"We didn't do it, Miss Griffin." Bonnie gave Josie her best wide-eyed innocent look, batting her Buckhorn blues.

"Yeah." Betsy stared at her feet.

"I'm writing both of you passes to go to the office, where I'd like you to tell Principal Moody what you've done."

An hour later, while her students were at lunch, Josie sat at her desk with a peanut butter and strawberry jam sandwich and milk.

Her classroom door creaked open and in walked Dallas. His scowl told her he was as upset with the girls as she was. "I'll get you a new purse."

Rising, she stepped into his outstretched arms. "I'm

not upset about the purse, but how the girls have suddenly regressed. I thought they'd be excited by our wedding and the baby."

"I know." He left her to sit on a pint-size table. "What are we going to do?"

"Nothing we can do other than be patient. I do think it would be best if you officially request to transfer them to Mrs. Conklin's room sooner rather than later, though. It'll give them time to adjust."

"Agreed." Sighing, he swiped his fingers through his hair. "I suppose you think I should be the one to tell them?"

"Until the wedding," she teased with a kiss to his firm lips, "you *are* their primary caregiver."

Groaning, kissing her back, he said, "After that, I'll gladly pass you the disciplinary reins."

"No such luck, stud. I'm afraid that with your new and improved parenting skills, you're in this for life."

"Have I mentioned how excited I am about you officially becoming my daughter?" Georgina Buckhorn had joined her son and Josie and the girls for a Sunday trip to the Tulsa zoo. The day might have been sunny, but blustery wind made it a relief to hide out in the balmy rain forest building.

"Thank you." Josie gave the once-imposing woman a quick hug. "I'm pretty excited to have you for a mother."

While Dallas and the girls ran ahead, looking at exotic fish, monkeys and birds, Josie and Georgina took a more leisurely pace. "It's also an honor you've chosen to marry in the main house. Call me a silly old woman, but to have all of my children's weddings there would be…" As her words trailed off, Josie wondered if she was thinking of Dallas's runaway sister, Daisy.

"It won't hurt my feelings if you'd rather not talk about it, but have you tried looking for your daughter?"

"Gracious, yes," she said in front of the anaconda. "When she first left, we had a P.I. searching full-time. He explained that if a person wants to vanish, it's really not that hard—especially if they're off the so-called grid. Once she turned eighteen, with the entirety of her trust fund at her disposal, there's no telling what she did. The man's still on retainer and every so often calls to tell me he's checked out another dead-end lead."

"I'm sorry."

"Me, too," she said with a resolute nod. "It kills me, knowing she's out there, but wants nothing to do with us. I can't fathom what drove her to such an extreme."

From farther down the trail came a familiar voice issuing a Tarzan jungle call.

"Oh, dear…" Georgina gritted her teeth. "Looks like one of my darlings is in trouble again."

After hustling in that direction, Josie was appalled to find Bonnie swinging from a vine hanging at least ten feet over where they stood.

"Look, everybody! I'm Jungle Girl!"

"You're Grounded Girl," Dallas scolded. "Get your behind down from there."

A zookeeper came running. "Sir, we have strict rules about that sort of thing."

"I know." Turning to Josie, he asked, "What do I do?"

"Knock her down with a spear," Betsy suggested. "I told her not to be climbing."

Hands on her hips, Josie said, "Bonnie Buckhorn,

scoot right back the way you came. That vine is for monkeys—not you."

Bonnie stuck out her tongue. "You're not my mom or my teacher. You can't tell me what to do."

The zookeeper momentarily vanished only to return with a ladder. As if he'd had prior experience at this sort of thing, the man calmly scaled to Bonnie's height and plucked her down.

"Thank you," Georgina said, reaching into her oversize leather purse. "Are you allowed to accept tips?"

"No." He folded the ladder. "But I'm afraid per zoo rules I'm required to ask you to leave."

Betsy crushed Bonnie's toes with the heel of her sneaker. "Thanks a lot, monkey brain."

"You're a monkey brain!"

Dallas sighed. "So much for our big day of family fun." Just when he'd thought he had everything together, why did he now again feel as if he was letting his girls and Josie down? Where were the manuals covering what to do when your kid goes nuts at the zoo? Had he been premature in proposing? If he couldn't handle his kids, how would he cope with yet another child and wife?

"It's perfect," Josie said, gazing at the dreamy white wedding gown in Special Day Bridal Shop's octagonal mirror. "Think it'll still fit in another three weeks?"

Natalie cocked her head sideways. "From this angle, it looks like there's room to spare in the waist. And surely to goodness you're not going to put on that much weight before the wedding."

"It's ugly." Bonnie stopped twirling in her purple bridesmaid dress just long enough to cast Josie a mean look.

"I think so, too," Betsy chimed in.

With a knot in her throat, Josie made it to a count of five in her head, but Nat beat her to the punch.

"Why did you say that?" Natalie asked the girls.

Bonnie pressed her lips tight and crossed her arms.

Betsy resumed twirling.

"Conference time," Josie said to her future stepdaughters. Hands on their respective shoulders, she marched them to the nearest chair. "Bonnie, we're going to talk first. Remember when you used to sit on my lap and give me your best hugs? I thought we were friends?"

The girl didn't say a word.

"And, Betsy," Josie continued, "you once told me I was not only the teacher, but the best movie friend ever. What's happened for you two to suddenly be so mean?"

"Are you upset about the wedding or the baby?" the school counselor in Natalie asked.

"I hate that baby," Bonnie said. "It's not gonna be cute like Robin. We're gonna have a ugly baby."

Tears sprang to Josie's eyes and she was dubious as to whether she'd be able to hold them at bay. She knew the girls—Bonnie especially—were just acting out over hurt feelings. They were not only upset about having to change classrooms, but no doubt about how much time Josie had spent with Dallas and their grandmother in planning the wedding.

"Bonnie Buckhorn," Nat scolded, "you should have your mouth washed out with soap."

"If you did that," the girl said, raising her chin, "I'll tell Daddy and he'll ride his horse over you."

Hands covering the tears on her cheeks, Josie asked her friend, "Please help me get out of this dress. I think it's best we go."

* * *

Friday night, with the girls at a sleepover, Dallas lounged with his future bride in the ranch's guest cabin. They'd just finished practicing for their honeymoon and if practice made perfect, they'd have an awesome time. "Sure you can't get in the hot tub? It looks inviting."

"I know…" She rested her cheek against his chest. "I can take regular baths, but all of my pregnancy books say spas aren't a good idea."

"Fine," he said with a slow, sexy grin. "Be a party pooper."

"Listen here, cowboy, if we *partied* much harder, this antique bed would break."

"Excuses, excuses." Gliding his hand up and down her back, he said, "I keep forgetting to mention it, but Mom's been nagging me to ask you what's going on with the girls' dresses. She said you'd know what that means."

Groaning, holding the sheet to her chest, Josie sat up in the bed. "I didn't want to bother you with this, but the girls, Nat and I had an incident at the bridal store."

"Oh?" Eyebrows raised, he asked, "Bonnie didn't knock over any racks or climb a rentable trellis, did she?"

With a halfhearted laugh, she said, "I wish that was all she did." Relaying the hurtful things the girl had said, Dallas watched helplessly as Josie's eyes welled with tears.

Trying to be practical, he edged closer to her. "Sure those were her exact words? Maybe you heard wrong? I can't imagine my Bonnie being that deliberately cruel."

She snorted. "You also couldn't imagine her smashing cake in a boy's hair, either."

"That was ancient history. Bonnie's matured a lot since then."

"I agree." Josie scooted away from him and off the bed, in the process, treating him to a magnificent view. Her belly was just starting to curve outward and the sight never failed to stir him both on an emotional level and a little farther down. "But lately, she's backsliding."

"Agreed. I promise, I'll talk to her. But you need to give her time. She's a kid. Don't rug rats need extra space to adjust to big life changes?"

In the bathroom, she turned on the shower.

"Want me to get in with you?"

When she didn't answer, Dallas took it as a bad sign.

Resting his hands behind his head, it dawned on him that if kid angst was the toughest hurdle they'd have to face, they'd be lucky. Five minutes passed. With the water turned off and Josie standing on the bath mat, wearing nothing but water drops, he asked, "How's the house packing going?"

"So-so." Was it wrong of him that he loved watching her pull on silky panties almost as much as watching her take them off? "I went ahead and called the Realtor you recommended. The asking price she suggested was more than I'd expected in this market."

"That's good." Holding out his arms, he said, "Come here so I can kiss the baby."

She indulged him, but didn't look happy about it. "I think the baby's had enough attention. Remember how we're supposed to be planning a menu and looking through bridal magazines for floral ideas?"

Wearing nothing but a hopeful smile, Dallas patted the

empty space on the bed next to him. "By now you should know I do my best work between the sheets."

Tuesday afternoon, Josie waited in front of the school with the twins for their father. They were all going to taste wedding cake samples and then make their final selection. She and Dallas hoped that by including the girls in every aspect of the festivities that they might be more accepting of the change still to come. Alas, so far, their plan hadn't worked.

"I'm hungry," Betsy complained.

"I'm cold." Bonnie wriggled in an attempt to look as if she were shivering.

"Your dad will be here soon," Josie said to Bonnie, hugging her for added warmth.

As if Josie had the dreaded cooties, Bonnie lurched away.

To Betsy, Josie said, "You'll be eating lots of cake in only a few minutes."

"That's too long. I'm going to starve half to death."

"Yeah," Bonnie said, "Betsy's gonna starve and it's gonna be all you and your baby's big, fat fault."

The force of the girl's anger struck Josie like a punch. How long were the twins going to keep this up?

Thankfully, Josie's parental back-up finally arrived.

"Daddy!" All smiles, Betsy and Bonnie ran to the truck.

At a more sedate pace that would hopefully allow her to sneak in a few deep, calming breaths, Josie followed.

"Hi," she said, climbing onto the front seat next to Dallas. Before fastening her seat belt, she leaned over for a kiss.

"Hey, girls," he said to the backseat crew. "Have a fun day?"

"No," Bonnie snapped. "I'm hungry and Miss Griffin said I don't get to eat."

"Daddy," Betsy said in her best woe-is-me tone, "why does Miss Griffin hate us?"

"Oh, for heaven's sake," Josie couldn't keep from exclaiming. "You two know how much I love you, but that doesn't mean I'm not going to do everything in my power to help you grow into responsible and respectful young ladies. Dallas, pull over. We all need to talk."

"Something going on I'm not aware of?"

"Plenty." As she filled him in, Dallas's expression grew ever darker.

Parking on the shoulder of the cake lady's dirt road, he turned off the truck, unbuckled his seat belt, then turned around to face the girls. "Out with it. What's the problem? I know you both love Josie. Why are you treating her this way?"

Neither of them said a word.

Josie sucked in a deep breath. "You two don't know this, but I used to have a little girl. Her name was Emma and I loved her so much it hurt."

"Where is she?" Betsy whispered.

"In heaven," Josie managed. "I'm not telling you this to make you sad, but to let you know I understand about hurting and being confused and sad and angry all at the same time. I know how much you love your dad, and I promise—" she crossed her heart "—I will never, ever take him from you. All I want is for you two to give me and this new baby a place in your family. It's been a long time since I've had a family and more than anything, I could really use one."

Bonnie said, "But I'm scared if we give you and that baby our daddy, we won't have one."

"Yeah." Betsy nodded.

Dallas sighed. "What do I have to do to prove to you guys that just because Josie and the baby are now going to be part of our lives, that nothing's really going to change? We'll live in the same house. Go to the same places. Watch the same TV shows. Not only will you still have me and Grandma and Henry and Uncle Cash and Aunt Wren and Robin and Uncle Wyatt to love, but Josie and a new baby brother or sister. No one's taking love away from you, only giving you more."

"Oh." Now Bonnie began to cry. Unbuckling her seat belt, she scrambled over the seat to sit on Dallas's lap.

Betsy did the same, only clinging to Josie.

"How great is this?" Dallas asked, rubbing his daughter's back. "Now, you all don't even have to share laps."

As much as Josie appreciated the current calm, she couldn't help but wonder if this was but their first family storm.

Chapter Sixteen

"What a relief that for the moment, anyway, everything's worked out." Standing on one of the kitchen-table chairs, Natalie took a vase from an upper cabinet. Josie had offered to spring for pizza if Nat helped organize for the big garage sale she was holding that weekend. "Do you think from here on out, the girls will behave?"

"I hope so. I don't blame them for being jarred by all of this. I'm a grown woman and it's still taking me a while to adjust."

"After the wedding," Nat said while washing dust from a waffle iron Josie hadn't used in years, "things will get better."

"From your lips to God's ears."

After Natalie left, the remaining mess was overwhelming. Knowing the only sane portion of the house was Emma's room, Josie shuffled past boxes and packing wrap and tape to the one place she'd always felt surprisingly strong. As if her daughter watched over her, assuring her, *Everything's going to be all right, Mommy.*

For the longest time, Josie sat in her favorite chair, eyes closed, imagining the feel of Emma on her lap while reading a bedtime story. She'd smelled so good. Like sweet baby curls infused with her favorite strawberry shampoo.

They'd played the little piggy game with her chubby toes. Sang silly songs and tickled and giggled and talked of handsome princes and princesses and happy kingdoms where everyone smiled all the time.

Without realizing it, Josie had begun to cry.

Rather than drying her tears, she wore them as badges of honor. She carefully gathered tissue paper and special-bought plastic bins. One by one, she took tiny dresses from tiny hangers. She smelled them, caressed them, held them to her nose for just one imaginary trace of her little girl's essence. And then she neatly folded them. Wrapped them in pink tissue. Kissing each one before putting it away.

Part of her very much wanted another girl.

Another part feared she couldn't bear it.

Saturday morning, though the temperature was a chilly fifty, with no wind and plenty of sun, the day promised to be perfect for the liquidation of Josie's former life.

"Where do you want your tables set up?" Dallas asked with forced cheer. Though he had ranch duties to perform, he'd volunteered to come by early to help.

She pointed to either side of her driveway, while across

the garage opening, she strung a line from which to hang clothes.

It was only seven in the morning, but already a few folks with big trucks and, she suspected, flea market booths had stopped by to rummage through items she had yet to set out. With the pending move, she'd taken to parking on the street, using her garage for box storage. She'd finished the painful process of sorting Emma's things and had donated a box of clothes to a nearby town's women and children's shelter. For treasured items such as stuffed animals that held special meaning and Emma's cherished sterling silver tea seat, she'd wrapped them in tissue and placed them in extra-sturdy plastic bins.

Betsy and Bonnie were inside on her sofa, groggily watching cartoons and eating donuts.

With her sweet house nearly empty and the yard sale assembled, Josie sat in a lawn chair and finally allowed the finality of what she was doing to sink in.

"We okay?" Dallas set up a chair next to her.

Swallowing the lump in her throat, she admitted, "I'm scared. Most everything I own is out here on the lawn."

"I can see where it must be upsetting, but—" he took her hands, eased his fingers between hers and raised them to his mouth to kiss "—once you get past this, you'll never look back. We're going to lead a great life."

Promise?

As the day wore on, so did Josie's exhaustion.

The girls grew bored in the house and they were now pretending to be storekeepers with the crowd.

"This clock thingee's dirt cheap," Bonnie said to a woman wearing Coke-bottle glasses and a crooked red wig.

"Thank you, doll," the woman said, "but I don't need one of those."

"What do you need?" Betsy asked. "Betcha we got it."

The shopper patted each girl's head before fishing through a ragged coin purse. "Here you go," she said, giving them each a penny. "Buy yourself some nice candy."

The girls looked unsure as to where they'd buy candy that cheap, but thanked the woman anyway. Watching, Josie and Dallas shared a laugh.

The day wore on.

Dallas brought them all sub sandwiches and chips for lunch.

Georgina stopped by and purchased a well-read copy of *Wuthering Heights*. "I loaned mine out years ago and never got it back," she explained, giving Josie a quarter.

"I wanna quarter," Bonnie demanded, holding out her hand. "We're making deals."

"If you want money," Georgina explained, "you have to sell me something. What do you have that I might be interested in?"

Betsy tugged her grandmother by her hand toward a pile of movies and CDs. "I think you'd looove this." She held one of Hugh's old slasher movies.

"Do you have anything more scary?"

Considering the bloody cover, Betsy was again looking confused.

By day's end, most everything was gone. Josie's furniture and dishes and small appliances. Collectibles that didn't mean all that much and movies she never watched. Electronic gadgets she rarely used.

After the wedding, she'd move into Dallas's room at the ranch. He had promised, however, to clear out more than half of the walk-in closet. He'd also assured her there would be plenty of well-ventilated attic space for Emma's things or anything else she wanted to store. As for her framed pictures and favorite mementos, Josie was given free rein from Georgina to scatter them amongst the rest of the family photos. After all, the ranch was to be her and the baby's home, too.

"Want me to start boxing the rest of this for donation?" Dallas asked after a big yawn.

"Sure." She gathered the last of the clothes from the line, placing them in a pile. The knot that had held the rope in place was tight, but by standing on a paint can, she managed to work it free.

Stepping behind her, Dallas barked, "Get down from there. What if you fell?"

"See…" Once down, she performed an elegant pirouette. "I'm still in perfect working order."

Hands on her hips, he knelt to talk to her tummy. "Baby, are you hearing the amount of sass your father has to put up with?"

"Yeah," she retorted, "and if you don't help me finish so the baby and I can eat, you're really going to feel my wrath."

"Remind me next time you see Doc that he needs to give you anticranky pills."

With all of the leftover items boxed and in the back of Dallas's truck, they went inside for the girls, who lounged in front of the TV.

"Ready to eat?" Dallas asked.

"Only if we get ice cream," Betsy said.

"News flash," her father announced, "you're going to get what you get and not pitch a fit."

Bonnie rolled her eyes.

"Go ahead." With everyone else on the porch, Josie held back. "I'll lock up and close the garage door on my way out."

Dallas waved acknowledgment.

Kitty sat in the middle of the kitchen floor looking mighty perturbed at the change in scenery. At least his window seat cushion hadn't been sold. He, too, would be making the move to the ranch, but Josie worried he'd spend half of his life under beds and the other half under sofas.

With the space empty, the garage had taken on a lonely feel. Josie told herself she wouldn't get melancholy about selling her home, but that was easier said than done. After pressing the door's button, she made a mad dash to get out, feeling like Indiana Jones easing under just in time.

Only outside did it dawn on her that the garage was too empty. She'd had two plastic tubs filled with Emma's favorite toys, and two more with clothes to be worn by the baby. Had Dallas carried them inside for safekeeping?

She punched in the code for the door to open.

Sure enough, the items weren't where she'd put them. Trying not to panic, she performed a room-by-room search, but still came up empty-handed.

Running out to the truck, she asked Dallas, "What happened to Emma's things?"

"I never touched them. As far as I know, they're still where you set them."

"Oh, God." Hands over her mouth, nausea struck with a vengeance. Racing to the evergreen bushes ringing the porch, up came lunch. The contents of those boxes were all that remained of her precious daughter.

"Relax," Dallas said, rubbing Josie's shoulders, "they've got to be here somewhere. Stay out here with the girls and I'll look."

He returned, shaking his head. "Let me call Mom. Maybe she remembers something."

Throughout the brief conversation, Josie fought for air.

Dallas finally ended the call, only to pull her into a hug. "Honey, I'm so sorry."

"For what?" she practically shrieked. "What did your mom say?"

Lips pressed into a tight line, he glanced across the yard to his truck, to the two girls chatting up a storm in the backseat. "When you and I were helping that couple who bought your entertainment center, Mom saw Betsy and Bonnie tell a man he could have all four boxes for five dollars. Mom remembers because she made a point of asking the girls if the items were supposed to have even been in the sale."

"No..." Josie whispered with sorrow stemming from deep in her soul. "Please, no."

"I'm sorry." Dallas held her through her tears. "Is there anything I can do to help? Name it. Hell, we'll book a private jet to Paris if that would in any way make up for what the girls have done."

Chilled and angry and hurting, she snapped, "What I want are my child's belongings to have not been carted away in a yard sale. What I want is for you to ground those two for the rest of their little lives."

"Josie, I know you're hurting, but the girls didn't mean it. They assumed anything in the garage was fair game to sell. They were trying to help."

Dallas might have been saying one thing, but all she heard was: *no matter how badly my daughters hurt you, they will always come first.*

"How do I forgive them?" Josie asked Nat during a commercial break from their favorite reality show. With only two weeks until the wedding, Josie's friend had invited her to live in her guest room now that her house no longer felt like home.

Kitty, still full from his dinner, had curled into a ball in Natalie's scrapbooking box.

Muting the TV, her friend said, "Wish I had an answer for you. For years, I've prayed you'd stop putting so much emotional stock in Em's things. Now, I get the feeling you're mourning her all over again."

Unable to speak past the knot in her throat, Josie nodded.

"I was so sure marrying Dallas was right. Now, I've never been more uncertain. Even worse, the Realtor came by school this afternoon with a full-price offer on my house."

"Why didn't you tell me?" Nat asked. "We should've gone out to celebrate."

"How can I be happy about a transaction I'm no longer sure I want?" Playing with a throw pillow's fringe, Josie knew Dallas was the one she should be talking to, but how could she when she was having such doubts?

"Worst-case scenario, you move in with me until we find you a new place. But please don't do anything drastic. There's no way Bonnie and Betsy could've known how much the contents of those boxes meant."

"I know." Cupping her newly rounded belly, Josie prayed for answers. Why did her dream now feel like a nightmare? As if her life's foundation had been ripped out from under her. "But that does nothing to ease my pain. I feel raw inside."

"When's the last time you talked to Dallas?"

The teapot whistled on the stove.

"He called while the kids were at morning recess."

Josie headed for Nat's efficiency kitchen to make a cup of orange spice.

"Did you have a good conversation?" Natalie asked beside her, reaching in a cabinet for graham crackers.

"Not really. We ran over a few items for the wedding. That's it." The tea scalded Josie's tongue. Wasn't it just her luck that while she'd been aiming for something nice and soothing, she'd only wound up more annoyed?

"Want my advice, you—"

"Not really." Josie forced a grin.

"Ha-ha. Call him. Now. Even if you all just hit the Waffle Hut out by the toll road for a late-night snack, it'll be good for you to talk."

"I'm glad you called," Dallas said, taking Josie's hands across the Waffle Hut's booth table. "I hated how we left things Saturday."

"Me, too." She looked as beautiful as ever, but fragile, with dark circles under her eyes.

"Getting adequate sleep?"

She shook her head. "Too much on my mind. Plus, Nat's guest mattress has more lumps than her disgusting mashed potatoes."

He winced. "You're welcome to stay in our guest cabin. It's impossible to not get a good night's rest out there."

"Thank you. I would, but I don't want the girls getting any more confused. I thought our marriage would help them, but I'm afraid it's only going to hurt."

"Help them with what?" he asked after a waitress took their order. "They've got everything kids could ever want or need. You and I both have been spending more time with them than ever."

"True." Her usually bright complexion was sallow. Her tone dull, as if she'd rather be anywhere on earth than out to eat with him. Though her stomach had swelled, the rest of her appeared gaunt.

Leaning forward, he said, "Be straight with me, Josie. Do you still want to get married?"

After a pause, she said, "Of course." Giving his hands an extra-strong squeeze, she added, "But everything's changing too fast. First, my body. Now, my house. Emma's things being sold off for practically nothing to a flea-market dealer. I know what happened was an accident, but I can't get past how badly I want my daughter back." She'd choked on her last words and tears streamed her cheeks. "I'm swimming with nowhere to get out of the water."

"Sweetheart..." He left his side of the booth to join Josie, pulling her into a hug. "That's just it. Emma will always be with you. In your heart. You don't need dresses or books or a tea set to remind you. All you need is to close your eyes and remember." Stroking the tops of her fingers with his thumbs, he said, "If that doesn't work, lean on me. When are you going to learn that no matter what, I'm here for you. But I'm not psychic. You have to ask. Tell me exactly what you need whether it's a late-night cheeseburger or strong shoulder to cry on."

Nodding, her teary-eyed expression struck him as alarmingly hollow.

"What does Natalie say about all of this? She's the school counselor, right?"

"I'm pretty sure she thinks I'm going off the deep end."

"Nah." He smiled. "You're just understandably tired from lugging around my big, strapping son."

Ignoring his stab at humor, she asked, "Please take me home with you. Maybe I could sleep if you'd hold me."

"Done. How about we get our food to go, and you can eat in a nice, warm bath. Sound good?"

"Like heaven."

Thirty minutes later, Dallas had helped Josie off with her clothes and settled her in the water. He assembled her meal on a plate, nuked it for a minute and then set it on the stainless steel toiletry rack suspended across the tub.

"Need anything else?"

Upon taking her first bite, ketchup dribbled on her left breast. "Napkin, please."

Grinning, he leaned close, lapping up the mess.

"Mmm." Closing her eyes, she finally gave him the satisfied smile he'd been craving.

He took the burger from her, stealing a bite for himself. When more ketchup fell, he licked that, too.

"You did that on purpose, didn't you?"

"I'll never tell."

Holding out her arms, she commanded, "Leave the food alone and get in with me."

"Thought you'd never ask."

After making awkward, splashing, laughing love, Dallas added more hot water and then took the fancy spa shampoo his mom had placed in a basket and poured some into his palm. He warmed it, then with Josie leaning against his chest, massaged it into her scalp. Her hair was one of his favorite things about her. It was long and vibrant and unpredictable—just like her.

"Feel good?" he asked when she groaned.

"Indescribably so. You might want to ration this spoiling or I'll be expecting first-class service every night."

"I'm sure we can work out a deal," he said in a suggestive tone.

"You look pretty," Shelby mentioned as they moved through Wednesday's lunch line. It was pizza day and both craved junk food.

"Thanks. I feel pretty—and hungry." When it was her turn in line, she asked Paula for two slices.

"How's the wedding planning business?" her friend asked on the way to the teachers' table. "You're down to what? Only a week and a few days?"

"Don't remind me." Seeing Shelby struggle with her milk carton, she opened it for her.

"You have ninja skills when it comes to opening these things."

Josie teased, "That's why I make the big bucks."

As more friends joined their table, conversation ebbed and flowed. Josie glanced across the cafeteria to see Bonnie and Betsy bathed in midday sun. They were laughing with the girls in their new class and looking adorable with the braids she'd made for them that morning. They didn't know she and their father had spent the night together in the guest house, just that she'd decided to join them for breakfast. Their actions still stung. Josie wanted to forgive them for selling Emma's belongings. It had been an accident. Her brain understood, but her heart hadn't gotten the memo.

She and Dallas had made love that morning. Slow and sweet and tender, Dallas had shown her in fifty little ways how much he cared. Her worries about marrying him should have vanished. Instead, the knot in her throat felt like a grapefruit.

Chapter Seventeen

"Surprise!"

When Josie walked into the dark school gym hand-in-hand with Dallas, the shock of encountering at least a hundred friends all assembled for what was supposed to have been a low-key bridal shower was enough to send her pulse racing.

"Did you know about this?" she asked.

"Nope." Wearing a big grin, he indeed looked as stunned—and flattered—as she was.

A DJ played a rock-and-roll version of the wedding march while friends and coworkers crushed them with well wishes. The normally utilitarian space had been transformed into a Valentine wonderland. Round tables dotted the room and the wood floor had been covered in rose petals. It took three tables to hold all of the gifts and another long table bowed from the weight of appetizers, punch, candy and cake. Foil red and pink hearts hung from the ceiling along with plenty of red streamers.

The cake was a work of art shaped like an old-fashioned red schoolhouse complete with a candy playground, students, a teacher and of course, a cowboy.

Bonnie and Betsy ran up to their father. Their grandmother grabbed hold of their hands, trying to slow them down.

"Are all of those presents for me?" Bonnie asked, gaping at the colorful pile.

"They're for Josie," Dallas said. "This is her bridal shower. One day when you and Betsy get married, you'll have a party like this, too."

"Do I have to marry a boy?" Betsy asked. "I want the presents, but no kissing."

Laughing, Dallas seized the moment to lay one on his glowing bride-to-be.

Shelby handed Josie a glass filled with red punch. "Considering the theme, we should have warned you not to wear white."

"I'll be careful," Josie assured. Though her white, cashmere sweater was a favorite of her few new maternity clothes, she was also parched. The ginger ale-cherry blend hit the spot.

"We've got great friends," Dallas noted, nodding across the dance floor at Henry and their neighbor Dorothy boogying with the twins.

Snuggling against him, Josie couldn't have agreed more.

After everyone had worn themselves out from doing the Chicken Dance, eating and getting their entries ready for the toilet paper wedding dress contest, it was time for gifts.

Bonnie and Betsy didn't even try hiding their displeasure at not receiving a single thing. While most guests oohed and clapped for everything from an exquisite vase to sumptuous lingerie, the twins sat in a corner with crossed arms and scowls.

Finally, Dallas headed over to talk to them.

Josie wasn't sure what he'd said, but a few minutes later, the girls were running and laughing with the few other kids and politely asking for seconds on cake.

Wonder of wonders, Dallas was turning into a surprisingly good father.

The rehearsal dinner was being held poolside, and through the magic of lots of money and Georgina's considerable party-planning skills, she'd rigged a heated tent over the pool deck, completing the scene with floating candles and fake floating swans. She'd fought for real birds, but Dallas had convinced her that if they paddled into flames it could result in adding them charbroiled to the menu.

"Georgina," Wren said, "you've outdone yourself. I've never seen the house look more beautiful."

"Thank you." Dallas's mother beamed. "I can't claim all the credit, though. My new daughter-in-law is no slouch when it comes to planning."

"You're being overly gracious," Josie said. "All I remember saying is I love a good filet mignon and you took it from there."

Adjusting an off-center floral arrangement, she said, "Every party has to start somewhere."

A jazz singer crooned Dean Martin favorites while a chef created flaming shrimp kebab appetizers. Everywhere Josie turned was laughter and the tinkling of fine crystal and silver.

The event was like a featured magazine article, dreamed up by set and costume designers. Her silk ivory dress was so exquisitely tailored that it managed to hug her body in all of the right places, making her feel sexy instead of pregnant.

"Have I mentioned how gorgeous you look?" Dallas asked while his mom and Wren kept chatting.

"Not lately, but I'm always amenable to compliments."

The evening wound along without a hitch through dinner and Dallas's favorite key lime pie for dessert. After heartfelt toasts from Josie's maid of honor, Natalie, and Dallas's best man, Wyatt, came more dancing. Josie abandoned her agonizing heels on the seat of her chair in favor of going barefoot.

Midway through their dance, Bonnie came over, announcing that she'd like to dance with her father.

Exhausted, Josie was pleased to bow out.

She was also in need of a restroom, but since both downstairs powder rooms were in use, she headed upstairs to Dallas's room. It seemed surreal that the big, beautiful home would be hers, as well.

Eager to return to the party, she washed her hands, then surveyed her hair in the mirror.

Back in the bedroom, she paused to see if Dallas had cleared the dresser he'd promised she could use. Opening the top drawer, she found it brimming with socks and boxers. She'd changed her entire life, and he couldn't even bother cleaning a few drawers?

Suddenly the gravity of what she was on the verge of doing hit hard. She sat down on the bed, her mind and emotions whirling. Thinking that if Emma was looking down at her she might feel abandoned, Josie was consumed with grief. The crushing pain stemmed from so deep inside it was hard to breathe.

"Hey, gorgeous." She looked up to see Dallas enter the room. He looked every bit as handsome as ever—if not, more. Only now she realized how little she really knew him. "I've been looking for you. Apparently Mom has fireworks and she understandably doesn't want them to start without the bride."

"We need to talk."

"Sure," he said, taking her hands, urging her to her feet, "but let's make my mother happy first. You know how she gets, especially when it concerns a wedding."

"No, Dallas." Yanking her hands free, she scooted away from him. "You don't understand. There isn't going to be a wedding."

"What are you saying?"

"I can't let go. Emma needs me—if only to keep her memory alive."

"Honey," Dallas said, voice laced with concern, "are you even listening to yourself? You're not making sense."

"Seeing as how you couldn't even empty a sock drawer, neither does this marriage."

"Want to help me with a few hundred calls?" Georgina asked Dallas Saturday morning. "While you were still puking whiskey, Josie called bright and early, apologizing and telling me that she'd call all of her guests, informing them that there isn't going to be a wedding. Well, you know what I say to that?"

"Can't imagine," he said, head feeling as if one of Cash's bulls had stomped it.

"Horse manure. I've got a lot of time and money invested in this wedding, and by God, if I have to drag you two to the altar kicking and screaming, that's what I'll do."

"I had enough dramatics last night." Fishing aspirin from the medicine drawer, he chewed four and swallowed.

"Not enough to get your head out of your behind. Josie's understandably terrified. You should've reassured her. Held her through the night."

"Please stop." Sitting at the counter, he willed her to vanish from his life and prosper elsewhere.

"I'm just getting started. For years, I've watched you spoil those girls rotten and focus anything left on this ranch. When you met Josie, for the first time since Bobbie Jo passed, you've seemed truly alive. You've even done the impossible and wrangled in your kids. Josie was the answer to our prayers. She wasn't afraid to not only tell you how it is with your girls, but show you. And after that, she even worked her magic on you. Now you're going to let her get away when what she needs is reassurance and your loving support?"

"Dammit all, Mom, I'd appreciate you staying the hell out of my business." He held his aching head in his hands.

His mother glared at him and left the room.

Only when she took off up the back staircase did he finally dare relax. Lord, but she was a hot thorn in his side.

"Oh," she shouted down the stairs, "lest you think I'm canceling this Hollywood-worthy event, you've got another thing coming. Get up off of your derriere and get your bride back here by seven o'clock sharp."

Just when Josie thought she didn't have enough liquid in her to cry anymore, tears started up again.

"Please, eat," Nat urged Saturday morning. "You need your energy. We have a long day ahead of us, calling all of your guests and returning presents."

"I know," Josie said.

"While you were in the shower," Natalie said, hovering like a mother hen, "I called Georgina and she was not only understanding, but concerned."

"That's because she knows I'm right. This wedding came about way too fast."

Natalie set a glass of orange juice alongside Josie's scrambled cheesy eggs and toast.

The doorbell rang.

Josie groaned.

"I'll get it." Natalie headed for the front door.

When Josie heard a commotion in the foyer, her stomach fell. How was she supposed to forget she'd ever met Dallas Buckhorn when he was at that very moment, striding his way down the hall?

"I've, um, got errands," Nat said, taking her purse and keys before bolting outside.

"Hey." With a night's stubble and sleep-tousled hair, Dallas looked heartbreakingly handsome. With every breath in Josie's body, she now knew she loved him. She just didn't trust herself to know if in marrying him, she'd be doing the right thing. He held a pitifully wrapped package out to her. "I planned on saving this for tonight, but figure it might do me more good now."

"Thank you." She took the box from him only to set it on the entry-hall table. "But the wedding's still off. I can't just ride into the sunset with so much pain remaining in my past."

Hands fisted, he made a guttural growl. "Ham on a cupcake, woman, you frustrate the hell out of me. You don't think I have a few issues of my own? That's what marriage is—the two of us coming together to heal each other."

"I get that," she snapped, arms tightly folded, "but none of that changes how I feel. Don't you understand that once your husband betrays you to the tune of killing your child—even if it was an accident, it still tends to sting? Now I'm supposed to happily skip down Bridal Lane all over again? I can't even begin to describe how Hugh's suicide destroyed me. Then, when my own mother declared I was the cause for every tragedy that's happened…" Josie broke down, releasing years of grief in great, racking sobs.

Dallas didn't care that she tried pushing him away, he held her through the worst of it, until she was too exhausted to do anything but cling to his arms.

"I brought you something else that was supposed to have been a surprise." He kissed the top of her head. "You'll no doubt be mad at me for this, too, but before *we* can be whole, you need to be whole."

"There isn't going to be a *we,*" she insisted through more sniffles.

"I know, but just sit tight for a few minutes. I have a feeling someone else is at the door." He went outside, a few minutes later returning, pulling someone behind him.

Josie's mother.

"I'm so sorry," her mom cried in a rush, running into her daughter's arms. "I said awful, unforgivable things to you. I was out of my mind. Losing little Em was unnatural. Grandparents don't bury their grandchildren."

"I know." Josie crushed her mother to her. In mere moments, years vanished, as did the pain. Yes, her mother had hurt her, but just as Josie had opened her heart to love again, she'd also learned to forgive.

"You've got a good man, here," her mom said with a nod to Dallas. "He flew every last one of us all the way out here from Maine. He had some harsh, much-deserved words for me, but nothing but love for you. Don't let him get away."

Holding out her hand to him, drawing Dallas into their circle, Josie simply said, "I won't."

After saying their vows and dancing and eating more cake than her barely fitting wedding dress could comfortably hold, Josie finally found herself cozy and warm in the guest cabin, nestled next to her husband of approximately five hours. In lieu of sexy lingerie, she wore roomy sweats and thick white socks.

In the morning, Henry was driving them to the Tulsa airport for a plane bound for a surprise exotic location Dallas had promised would be warm. The girls were staying with his mom.

Her parents, brother and his wife and kids had already planned a return visit when Josie's baby was due.

"You're beautiful," Dallas said, cupping the side of her face. "Thank you for taking a chance on me—us." He kissed her. Softly. Sweetly. The way a husband tenderly kissed his beloved wife.

"Thank you for being strong enough to see me through…" Grasping his wrist, she kissed the palm of his hand. "Emma will always be in my heart. I just needed reminding that there's also plenty of room for you, the twins and our baby."

"Speaking of your daughter…" He reached beside the bed, drawing out the ragged gift he'd tried giving her that morning. "As you can see, gift wrapping's hardly my forte, but hopefully what's inside will more than make up for my lackluster presentation."

Intrigued, she scooted up in the bed, sitting cross-legged with his package on her lap.

With the paper gone, she lifted the flaps of an equally ugly box. Upon looking inside, she gasped. Looked at Dallas. Back to the box. "No…" Hands over trembling lips, eyes stinging with happy tears, she dared ask, "Is it really hers?"

Swallowing back his own tears, he nodded. "Henry ran this place for days while I searched every flea market and antiques store between here and Oklahoma City."

Nestled on a bed of pale pink satin was Emma's silver tea set. Lifting the delicately filigreed pot, she read the inscription, *For our precious Emma on her third birthday. We'll love you forever and always, Mommy and Daddy.*

"Even though your daughter will always be in your heart," Dallas said, "I thought it important that a part of her also shares a prominent place in our home."

There were no words to describe the love swelling Josie's heart. In Dallas, she'd found a friend, confidant, champion and love. A gentleman cowboy through and through. Together, she now knew they'd weather any storm. Emerging from the darkest clouds to walk in endless sun.

* * * * *

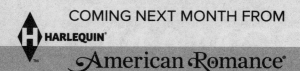

SPECIAL EXCERPT FROM

HARLEQUIN®

American Romance®

Read on for a sneak peek of
New York Times *bestselling author Cathy McDavid's*
HER RODEO MAN,
the second book of her
RECKLESS, ARIZONA *miniseries.*

Ryder stood at the pasture fence, his leather dress shoes sinking into the soft dirt. He'd have a chore cleaning them later. At the moment, he didn't care.

When, he absently wondered, was the last time he'd worn a pair of boots? Or ridden a horse, for that matter? The answer came quickly. Five years ago. He'd sworn then and there he'd never set sight on Reckless again.

Recent events had altered the circumstance of his enduring disagreement with his family. Liberty, the one most hurt by their mother's lies, had managed to make peace with both their parents. Not so Ryder. His anger had not dimmed one bit.

Was coming home a mistake? Only time would tell. In any case, he wasn't staying long.

In the pasture, a woman haltered a large black pony and led it slowly toward the gate. Ryder leaned his forearms on the top fence railing. Even at this distance, he could tell two things: the pony was severely lame, and the woman was spectacularly attractive.

The pair was a study in contrast. While the pony hobbled painfully, favoring its front left foot, the woman moved with elegance and grace, her long black hair misbehaving in the

HAREXP0315

mild breeze. She stopped frequently to check on the pony, and when she did, rested her hand affectionately on its sleek neck.

Something about her struck a familiar, but elusive, chord with him. A memory teased at the fringes of his mind, just out of reach.

As he watched, the knots of tension residing in his shoulders relaxed. That was, until she changed direction and headed toward him. Then he immediately perked up, and his senses went on high alert.

"Hi," she said as she approached. "Can I help you?"

She was even prettier up close. Large, dark eyes analyzed him with unapologetic interest from a model-perfect oval face. Her full mouth stretched into a warm smile impossible not to return. The red T-shirt tucked into a pair of well-worn jeans emphasized her long legs and slim waist.

"I'm meeting someone." He didn't add that he was now ten minutes late or that the someone was, in fact, his father.

"Can I show you the way?"

"Thanks. I already know it."

"You've been here before?"

"You…could say that. But it's been a while."

Look for HER RODEO MAN by New York Times *bestselling author Cathy McDavid, available March 2015 wherever Harlequin American Romance books and ebooks are sold!*

www.Harlequin.com

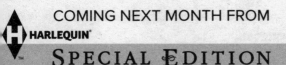

COMING NEXT MONTH FROM

HARLEQUIN®

SPECIAL EDITION

Available February 17, 2015

#2389 MENDOZA'S SECRET FORTUNE
The Fortunes of Texas: Cowboy Country • by Marie Ferrarella

Rachel Robinson never counted herself among the beauties of Horseback Hollow, Texas...until handsome brothers Matteo and Cisco Mendoza began competing for her attention! But it's Matteo who catches her eye and proves to be the most ardent suitor. He might just convince Rachel to leave her past behind her and start life anew—with him!

#2390 A CONARD COUNTY BABY
Conard County: The Next Generation • by Rachel Lee

Pregnant Hope Conroy is fleeing a dark past when she lands in Conard County, Wyoming, where Jim "Cash" Cashford, a single dad with a feisty teenager on his hands, resides. When Cash stumbles across Hope, he's desperate for help, so he hires the Texan beauty to help rein in his daughter. As the bond between Cash and Hope flourishes, there might just be another Conard County family in the making...

#2391 A SECOND CHANCE AT CRIMSON RANCH • by Michelle Major

Olivia Wilder isn't eager for love after her husband ran off with his secretary, leaving her lost and lonely. So when she scores a dance with handsome Logan Travers at his brother's wedding, her thoughts aren't on romance or falling for the rancher. A former Colorado wild boy, Logan is drawn to Olivia, but fears he's not good enough for her. Can two individuals who have been burned by love in the past find their own happily-ever-after on the range?

#2392 THE BACHELOR'S BABY DILEMMA
Family Renewal • by Sheri WhiteFeather

The last thing Tanner Quinn wants is a baby. Ever since his infant sister died, the handsome horseman has avoided little ones like the plague—but now he's the guardian of his newborn niece! What's a man to do? Tanner calls in his ex-girlfriend Candy McCall to help. The nurturing nanny is wonderful with the baby—and with Tanner, too. Although this avowed bachelor has sworn off marriage, Candy might just be sweet enough to convince him otherwise.

#2393 FROM CITY GIRL TO RANCHER'S WIFE • by Ami Weaver

When chef Josie Callahan loses everything to her devious ex-fiancé, she leaves town, hightailing it to Montana. There, Josie takes refuge in a temporary job...on the ranch of a sexy former country star. Luke Ryder doesn't need a beautiful woman tantalizing him—especially one who won't last a New York minute on a ranch. He's also a private man who doesn't want a stranger poking around...even if she gets him to open his heart to love!

#2394 HER PERFECT PROPOSAL • by Lynne Marshall

Journalist Lilly Matsuda is eager to get her hands dirty as a reporter in Heartlandia, Oregon. The locals aren't crazy about her, though—Lilly even gets pulled over by hunky cop Gunnar Norling! But the two bond. As Gunnar quickly becomes more than just a source to Lilly, conflicts of interest soon arise. Can the policeman and his lady love find their own happy ending in Heartlandia?

YOU CAN FIND MORE INFORMATION ON UPCOMING HARLEQUIN® TITLES, FREE EXCERPTS AND MORE AT WWW.HARLEQUIN.COM.

HSECNM0215

*Matteo Mendoza is used to playing second fiddle
to his brother Cisco…but not this time. Beautiful
Rachel Robinson intrigues both siblings, but Matteo
is determined to win her heart. Rachel can't resist the
handsome pilot, but she's afraid her family secrets might
haunt her chances at love. Can this Texan twosome find
their very own happily-ever-after on the range?*

Read on for a sneak preview of
MENDOZA'S SECRET FORTUNE by USA TODAY
bestselling author Marie Ferrarella, the third book in
THE FORTUNES OF TEXAS: COWBOY COUNTRY
continuity!

***

Matteo knew he should be leaving—and had most likely already overstayed—but he found himself wanting to linger just a few more seconds in her company.

"I just wanted to tell you one more time that I had a very nice time tonight," he told Rachel.

She surprised him—and herself when she came right down to it—by saying, "Show me."

Matteo looked at her, confusion in his eyes. Had he heard wrong? And what did she mean by that, anyway?

"What?"

"Show me," Rachel repeated.

"How?" he asked, not exactly sure he understood what she was getting at.

Her mouth curved, underscoring the amusement that was already evident in her eyes.

"Oh, I think you can figure it out, Mendoza," she told him. Then, since he appeared somewhat hesitant to put an actual meaning to her words, she sighed loudly, took hold of his button-down shirt and abruptly pulled him to her.

Matteo looked more than a little surprised at this display of proactive behavior on her part. She really was a firecracker, he thought.

The next moment, there was no room for looks of surprise or any other kind of expressions for that matter. It was hard to make out a person's features if their face was flush against another's, the way Rachel's was against his.

If the first kiss between them during the picnic was sweet, this kiss was nothing if not flaming hot. So much so that Matteo was almost certain that he was going to go up in smoke any second now.

The thing of it was he didn't care. As long as it happened while he was kissing Rachel, nothing else mattered.

**

Don't miss MENDOZA'S SECRET FORTUNE
by USA TODAY bestselling
author Marie Ferrarella,
the third book in
THE FORTUNES OF TEXAS: COWBOY COUNTRY
continuity!

Available March 2015, wherever
Harlequin® Special Edition books and ebooks are sold.

JUST CAN'T GET ENOUGH?

Join our social communities
and talk to us online.

You will have access to the latest
news on upcoming titles and special
promotions, but most importantly,
you can talk to other fans about your
favorite Harlequin reads.

Harlequin.com/Community

Facebook.com/HarlequinBooks

Twitter.com/HarlequinBooks

Pinterest.com/HarlequinBooks